TRUMPET

A Novel of the Regency Era

BY

BILL HAYES

&

SUSAN SEAFORTH HAYES

Decadent Publishing Company

www.decadentpublishing.com

Trumpet
Copyright © 2012 by Bill Hayes and Susan Seaforth Hayes
ISBN: 978-1-61333-257-3
Cover design by Patricia Schmitt and Cribley Designs

Published by Decadent Publishing Company
www.decadentpublishing.com

Printed in the United States of America

"The purest treasure mortal times afford
Is spotless reputation: that away,
Men are but gilded loam or painted clay."

King Richard the Second, William Shakespeare

Dear Reader,

Working as professional actors over two lifetimes gave Hayes and Hayes the experiences and emotional insights to tell Elizabeth Trumpet's story, but the distance in time from 1803 required more. So your writers took a high dive into the bottomless waters of historical research. We've been swimming in the Regency Age ever since.

In London, we spent hours at the Theatre Museum Reading Room, perusing two-hundred-year-old playbills from Charles Dibdin's shows at Sadler's Wells, and original programs from Drury Lane and Covent Garden. We investigated Islington, ate at Rule's and the Grenadier, toured the underground heart of Covent Garden, strolled Duncan Terrace and the New River, Smithfield Market, Savile Row. In Sir John Soane's house, we gazed at the Seti sarcophagus; we ticked off every object in the British Museum that Belzoni had discovered. Bath, Chester, Plymouth, even Budleigh Salterton had to be given their due.

We went to Alexandria, Cairo, and points beyond, entering the Great Pyramids, Abu Simbel, numberless tombs and the Khan El Khalili Bazaar. Georgie's experiences took us to Spain. In Belgium, we walked the battlefield of Waterloo. In Charleston, we prayed at St. Michael's. On Gibraltar, we met the Barbary apes. In Albania, we met a professor whose wife was a descendent of Mohammed Ali, the "Father of Modern Egypt." As you can imagine, that made for a great day.

When the idea for this book began to take shape, a *Smithsonian Magazine* story on the Great Belzoni came to mind. It had been squirreled away in 1985, and remarkably surfaced in our papers twenty years later. That's when we began to write *Trumpet*. His saga was so vivid, we decided our characters must have known him. Our first book, the double memoir, *Like Sands Through the Hourglass*, was a pleasure to write, but creating this fiction has been a cornucopia of joys.

From Aunt Peg's salt pig to Belzoni's pornographic terra cotta figurines, the objects we describe we have seen in museums all over the world. Snapping away, we kept a digital record of arresting portraits from the era. These faces inspired Georgie, Emily, Dampere and all our characters. The Trumpets and the Sloanes are entwined with people who really lived: Irby and Mangles, the Kembles and da Ponte, Mrs. Siddons, even Junius Brutus Booth.

Lizzie Trumpet's vulnerable heart—is us. The theatricals she meets we've known and loved. We hope you have as fine an adventure in her company as we have. And here's a happy secret: Carlo really lives and coaches singers to this day.

~Susan Seaforth Hayes and Bill Hayes

~DEDICATION~

To Theatricals, living and dead, God bless 'em!

Chapter One

March 1803

THE DAY was warm with a fragrance of young grass and the coming spring. A few big-bottomed clouds floated over Islington, shading the poplar trees and the Sadler's Wells Theatre. Travelers to nearby London arrived and departed from the old coaching inn at The Sign of the Angel. Smoke wafted from the chimney-pots of fine houses that faced the new garden squares. Yellow coltsfoot flowers bloomed in the open pastures, and a coach-horn saluted the world as the Royal Mail sped up the Great North Road, away and away.

Afternoon sun shone on a home named Longsatin House. Outside this tidy two-story dwelling, on the unpaved street of Duncan Terrace, three young persons were disporting themselves. Two, dressed in masks and padded white jackets, were engaged in fencing combat, while the third sprawled on the home's front steps, shouting out comments and encouragements.

"No quarter, Lizzie! Show him no quarter!"

The smaller duelist advanced against the taller one, weapons whipping the air and striking sparks when they touched. The slender fencer was a girl, as full of promise as the day. Yet Elizabeth Trumpet, just turned sixteen and lovely, was promised to no one.

Lizzie had been practicing her moves, dressing in her brother's old clothes and slashing about the backyard when her disapproving mother wasn't in sight and her father was performing at the Theatre Royal Covent Garden. William Trumpet was an established actor in the king's company. His daughter dreamed of acting, too.

"She has not triumphed yet!" George Trumpet, a well-muscled nineteen year old, called out breathlessly, pleased to be so energetically tested in mock battle by his little sister. Cool, blond, and stolid in disposition, he was the very opposite of the volatile, warm-hearted Lizzie. With a strong riposte, he drove her back towards the tall oak growing on the corner of the family property.

Months ago, he had needed a combatant to fight against as he prepared to enter the Royal Military College. When Lizzie had volunteered for this duty in her customary helpful way, Georgie was not surprised. He knew she loved him dearly and was fearless to a fault. Now, caught up in his cadet duties, he had barely noticed the recent rounding of her silhouette. To Georgie, she was still a child; while to Lizzie, her brother was already a hero, sure to drop Bonaparte in the dust.

"She's your equal, Georgie. Admit it," Roger, a stoutish lad with floppy hair, shouted from his perch on the front steps. He was the dutiful son of Sidrack Sloane, proprietor of the notable gentlemen's clothing shop, Adam & James of Savile Row. Roger's future was assumed to be in trade, surrounded by wooly bolts and hairy buttocks—a safe, middling future—but at seventeen it rankled him. Roger was entranced with the glamour of the Trumpet family he had known since babyhood, when Lizzie used to tyrannize their play and order him around.

Georgie lunged for his sister, but missed. "I'm wearing her down, Roger. Can't you see?"

She was not worn down at all. The girl's weapon sang as she initiated feints and slashes from all sides at once. The challenge of combat made handling the foil her delight, so much more thrilling than gliding to a minuet at Madam Bonnet's Academy for Young Ladies.

"*Touché*, brother!"

Instantly retaliating, Georgie nicked her side. "Keep your guard up, infant!"

Lizzie came at him in a lightning ballestra. The two fairly danced up the side garden, avoiding the vegetable patch and into the waste ground behind the house with its boiling cauldron in front of the gated chicken yard.

Great Aunt Peg called out piercingly in her Irish brogue, "Stay clear of my hens, you two, and for Jesus' sake, don't rile Banty."

The siblings fought on around the well-water pump, enjoying the contest and mad for victory. Excluded from the match, Roger had followed them through the garden. He smiled at the old lady watching from the open kitchen window. The stringy little woman did the thousand tasks it took to run Longsatin, tirelessly keeping house for a family whose minds were often elsewhere.

"May I be of help to you, Miss Pegeen?" Roger took off his hat to bow grandly.

"Take this, me boyo." Aunt Peg handed him an axe through the window. "And stand by to hold the victims." Leaving the house, she limped into the chicken yard that was a chaos of poultry. Peg spread her apron wide to herd several hens into a corner of the back fence, built bull-strong, horse-high and pig-tight. She snatched up two speckled beauties. "Carry that one by the feet, boy, and not too close to your coat."

Roger held the gate for her and quickly latched it closed. Peg laid a hen face up on a flat oak stump, then glided her index finger between the chicken's eyes. The fascinated bird stayed still while Peg grabbed the axe from Roger and lopped off its head.

"It's the French Revolution all over again." Lizzie laughed, still parrying and thrusting, as she leaped over the stump and the decapitated bird body running in circles underfoot.

"This sword sport is unnatural in a girl," Aunt Peg muttered. "Useless. Brutish." *Whack!* Another neck severed. Blood flowed. Roger gawked.

"Enough punishment." Georgie saluted his panting sister and pulled up his mask. "Well done, infant!" Both of them were in a muck sweat and thoroughly pleased with themselves.

"That was a hit, Georgie, a palpable hit." Lizzie lifted the mask from her face, pink with excitement and exercise. Her classic features were large, the expressive hazel eyes shining with health and lips laughing with pleasure.

"Your attack is formidable, sister, but you leave yourself too open." Georgie's bright blue eyes were serious, his tone lecturing. "You must keep that guard up ever and ever."

"Yes, whatever. But, don't you see I'm stronger now? I've worked with Papa's heavy rehearsal sword every day to improve my arm muscle and wind."

"Excellent wind." Roger applauded, joining them.

"Thank you for the bout, brother." Then, quite overcome with joy at having Georgie home for a mid-term holiday, she threw her arms around the cadet and playfully pulled his ears.

Roger tried to help remove Lizzie's fencing jacket and got entangled in unexpected buttons and her long, dark locks of hair.

"Don't bother, Roger. Oh, have a care!" Lately, she found her old playmate mysteriously addled and tongue-tied when they were together.

"Children!"

Lizzie turned round to see her mother hurrying towards them, a portrait of upset. "Mama? Do you need me?"

"Your father is going to grace us with his presence at supper before tonight's performance." She did not sound pleased. Jessie Trumpet was a fair-haired beauty whose looks were fading fast. She had once performed herself, in a small way, before William set her down in Islington to raise their children. "There is supposed to be some sort of surprise. He sent a messenger to warn us at this late hour. Oh, Roger, your father is expected, too."

At the disturbed tone of Jessie's voice, the atmosphere lost its gaiety and even the chickens grew circumspect.

"Put on something more suitable, Lizzie. Look at the state of you all. You must have a wash. Straight away." She pushed her strawberry blonde curls under a cotton head-cloth and, joining Aunt Peg, began resentfully plucking a wet hen by the boiling cauldron. "Put those weapons out of my sight, Lizzie." The feathers began to fly. "One day you're going to hurt someone."

Lizzie, accustomed to her mother's anxious behavior, despaired for her. Her father spent precious little time at home. When William was there, Jessie's normal soft manner became sharp, as though presenting a petition that had no chance of being heard. Lizzie's father's presence filled a room so completely there was little space left for the rest of them.

As for her own hopes of attention, the Trumpet parents were too preoccupied with their private dramas to give a young girl much of a speaking part. Her dream of going on the stage to share a scrap of her father's fascinating world remained a wish she kept to herself. When she had the chance to help William learn his lines, he never remarked on the fervor with which she read his cues or her devotion to his theatrical appearances. Surely, he realized she wanted to act, to become a leading lady of the first rank on the London stage—but there was never a word of encouragement from the father she adored. His reticence was hurtful. She saw him infrequently, forgave his neglect, and kept her dreams to herself. Loving both her parents, she tried to ease their discomfort with each other by being thoughtfully obedient, quick to smile, and ready to make the best of things.

To distract the boys from Jessie's unease, Lizzie grabbed a towel from the clothesline and gestured towards the lane. "I know where to have a wash. Come on."

She led them across Duncan Terrace to her favorite swimming spot in the New River, a man-made ditch that supplied much of London's drinking water. They scanned the round brick guard-house with a roof shaped like a witch's hat, to see if the watchman was near.

"All clear. *Viens, Roger!*" Lizzie commanded in her schoolgirl French, pulling off trousers and shoes and tossing her short jacket over a clump of meadowsweet. "*Plonge!*" She made a wonderful splash in the water, scattering a small flock of swimming white-faced coot.

Georgie's second-best shirt and drawers dropped to the bank. "Judas Priest, it's cold!" he screamed, dragging Roger up from the stony bottom where he had tripped falling in..

Lizzie floated face up, cloud-watching, and enjoying the

refreshing waters that shocked the boys. Her nipples were hard as cherries in the wet, her chemise quite transparent.

Washing his face and shaking out his hair, Roger tried to look away with decency...but couldn't.

"Preach not me your musty rules,
Ye drones that mould in idle cell."
Lizzie tripped down the stairs singing and spun off the egg-shaped newel post in the modest vestibule. The song was Dr. Arne's "Air From *Comus*," a favorite her father had taught her.
"The heart is wiser than the schools,
The senses always reason well."
She had tied a length of yellow silk with Corinthian trim over the bodice of her good white muslin frock, then covered the splendor with an apron, preparing to help in the kitchen.

Georgie, laying coals in the drawing room fireplace and blowing up the chimney, joined her soprano with his tenor in ringing tones.
"If short my span I less can spare
To pass a single pleasure by.
An hour is long if lost in care,
They only live who life enjoy!"
Still not dressed for dinner, their mother slammed shut the lid of the Italian wedding chest. "Oh, be still a moment while I think." Her children hushed themselves. Jessie handed a white linen tablecloth and napkins to her daughter. "We're that rushed to get ready."

"Mama, I'll lay the table while you put on something elegant," Lizzie said. "Perhaps your lilac gown? Papa loves you in that."

Jessie came close to saying her husband loved nothing of hers at all, but instead dropped the knife-box on the mahogany table. She was filled with feelings for William, who was always in her mind, the very front of her mind, but so rarely in sight. Her mirror assured her youth and its charms were slipping away, and her active imagination put Lizzie's father in bed with every actress she'd heard him mention. She could not bear to be forgotten and feared she was.

"No, Lizzie, it's too late for me to change. This frock will do. Your father won't notice anyway."

The rich scent of roast chicken hung in the air, sprigs of rosemary and bay leaves filled the prized silver bowl, and candles waited to be lit on the mahogany table. Aunt Peg was dusting the crisp brown potatoes from the kitchen salt-pig, when Jessie called the boys to decant the wine.

Roger held the etched glass decanter while Georgie filled it with a flourish.

"I'll drink to my son's future this very moment." Jessie ran a hand lovingly through Georgie's pale hair then, without pouring for anyone but herself, she downed a full glass.

"Soon to be a proud officer of the king," Roger offered wistfully.

Georgie's eyes were troubled as he gently took the empty glass from his mother's hand.

"What ho, the house—Longsatin House!" The over-door window vibrated as they all turned towards the sound of William's baritone vibrato.

"Papa! Dear Papa!" Lizzie flung open the front door for her father and eagerly kissed his cheek. William Trumpet was the very figure of a beau ideal, a tall, well-proportioned man of forty, whose curling black hair was shot with silver and cut as perfectly as his fashionable new coat. Lizzie was unfailingly proud of her father's good looks. She believed his straight brows, chiseled cheeks, and Roman nose had more majesty than any prince. Indeed, William behaved like the king of Longsatin House.

"My dear Elizabeth. Jessie. Welcome home from school, George-lad." He gave embraces to his family, a pat on the shoulder to Roger, then, in an aside to Lizzie, "Go outside to greet our guest."

In the afternoon's lengthening shadows, Sidrack Sloane, trim and elegant at sixty-three, was struggling to untie a parcel from his horse's saddle.

"Uncle Sidrack!" Lizzie bounded down the front steps to hug him.

"A very good day to you, Elizabeth, my dear. I come bearing gifts from America, sent by your grandparents with many kisses."

"What delight. We've made a grand dinner, Uncle." She used the honorary title, for their families were long entwined. The elder Sloane had always given Lizzie his complete attention, and she loved him for it. "Papa's new black coat is very beautiful, Uncle. You must have cut it yourself!"

He smiled at her warmly. Lizzie missed nothing.

"My grandparents are well?"

"Thriving, it pleases me to say. They always ask, 'How stands Longsatin House?'" The Trumpet home had been a gift from William's parents. Its name announced that once it'd been the domicile of a humble tailor.

Years before, Lizzie's grandfather had come to England from Naples with the daring hope of making a career in opera. In his native city, his voice was known, but not extraordinary enough to rise above a veritable sea of singers. Arriving in London with his wife, Ricardo Trombetta had promptly succumbed to the cold climate and colder reception of the hiring managers. Dismayed, he had lost both his courage and his voice, never to be found again. Too ashamed to return home, he took up his old country trade of sewing. His talent with a needle, combined with his wife's talent for thrift, enabled him to become Sidrack's most valuable employee and eventually a full partner in Adam & James. When Sloane traveled from the Baltic to Istanbul, gathering the cleverest workers and finest fabrics for his business, Ricardo ran the shop.

He fathered a beautiful son named Guglielmo, indulged by his mother and the star of the Trombetta firmament. Once grown, this son announced he did not wish to be a tailor but an actor. He took the name William Trumpet and even changed his faith in God to the Anglican version. In English society, including the free-wheeling community of the stage, there were limits to how high a Catholic could rise. Though devout, Ricardo supported his son's transformation, lived vicariously through his early struggles, and was justified by William's success.

This family saga was well known to Lizzie. It gave her hope that someday, despite her mother's disparaging and her father's indifference, she, too, could step upon the stage.

"Noddy! Noddy! Take the gentlemen's horses to the livery stable right now and give them a cooling down," Lizzie yelled to the family's boy-of-all-work, a frequently fuddled twelve-year-old with jug-like ears, who was never assumed to understand his duties without repeated instructions. The boy took the horses' reins and shuffled off. She turned back to her uncle with excitement. "Is the shop in Charleston doing well? Is there a letter for me from my grandparents?"

Sidrack put his hand on her arm to say in a low tone, "Calm yourself, dear."

"I'm just so happy Papa is home today, and we're all together."

The wrinkles around Sidrack's eyes deepened with understanding. "I know, child, and wish it were always so."

The candles flickered golden light on the rose-red walls of the dining room as the company tucked into their meal. The silver bowl reflected Jessie rubbing salt into the wine she had spilled on the tablecloth. Roger had happily, though thoughtlessly, devoured all four drumsticks and was sucking chicken gravy off his fingers.

Sidrack gave him a reproachful eye and laid his knife and fork to rest upon the blue flowers of his patterned plate. "Sir Henry Wentworth was by this forenoon for a fitting. No more potatoes for me, Noddy, thank you. His son is attending the Military College with you, George, I believe?" The cadet, who never refused potatoes, had a mouth full of them and could only nod. "When I was taking his measure and mentioned being invited here for this lovely occasion, Sir Henry regaled us with the story of your father's great wager at the Thalia Club."

Worrying a morsel caught in a back tooth, Peg asked, "Does the old tosspot recollect he lost?"

"Yes, Miss Pegeen, and he said he was happier to lose at an actors' club where the company is witty than win at White's where the aristocratic gamblers are so confounded dull."

In the general laughter, Jessie turned over her memory of the wager. Three years before, Sir Henry and William had been playing an evening of piquet at the club in St. James's Street. Risking far too heavily for prudence, William had won the high stake of a thousand pounds off Wentworth. Sir Henry was used to very deep play and suggested double or nothing. William, well in wine, said, "Cut the cards," and won. Then won again, and again, five times in all.

Jessie's dreams were often terrorized by this memory and the potential folly of her husband's recklessness. But, for once, fortune had blessed the actor with foresight. When Wentworth took out his money to pay immediately, in cash, as gentlemen at private clubs were required to do, William requested instead a military education for his boy and the purchase of a commission in a good regiment. Wentworth had graciously and cheerfully complied. Only the social influence of Sir Henry could make such a rise in station possible for an actor's son.

Georgie, like most boys, longed to be a soldier on a horse, so when William turned over the great windfall to make the boy's military dream come true, his mother cried for joy. Her son would become a person of consequence in the world. With one stroke, he had been set up for life, barring ineptitude, wounds, cowardice, and not unlikely, death, for this was the age of Napoleon and England's mortal conflict with France.

As for her daughter's future, the stage was never considered. To Jessie, theatrical life was vain, insecure, and a constant trial. She pronounced the very word "actress" as though it were a detestable species of reptile. She eyed her girl, basking in William's vibrant presence; their lightness of being always made Jessie wary. Her husband's buoyant optimism and self-confidence were traits she had grown to believe were unsupportable. Often she warned Lizzie never to believe in the theatre's make-believe, lest it enchant her with fantasies of poetry and love, impossible of attainment. Jessie did not wish to see her daughter as she saw herself, broken-hearted and sadly forgotten.

"Who made this so savory?" William asked, complimenting the

onion stuffing.

"We all cook in this house, husband," Jessie could not stop herself from saying. "You should try breakfast here sometime."

"When the season's on, I'm more a visitor here than I would wish," he responded in a conciliatory tone. "It's the price of popularity."

Jessie shot him a doubting look. Her long list of grievances with William was based on his frequent presence at the theatre and absence from home.

Family life always conflicted with an actor's working schedule. Rehearsals began at ten every morning on the theatre stage, moving to the greenroom in the afternoon while scenery was mounted for the evening performance. Plays rotated in repertory, with new ones scattered among the old chestnuts every week. Actors had many parts floating in their minds at once. Alertness was vital, for they were fined for missing a line, rehearsal or performance. The plays themselves began at six o'clock and lasted till midnight. Following the final curtain, principal actors were required to mix with the audience in coffee houses, clubs, and assembly rooms. By contract, players at the royal patent theatres, Covent Garden and Drury Lane, were expected to be beautifully dressed while socializing with the best people far into the night. Then the whole round began again in the unheated theatre the next morning.

William kept a tiny room at Grillon's Hotel, a bachelor-accommodation in town. Keeping up the appearance of prosperity devoured his salary. Meals, clubs, and bespoke tailoring, including a treasure of personal costumes, cost a fortune. Maintaining *la bella figura* was as important to him as to a woman.

Compared to the actresses and society belles of his acquaintance, whose lives were devoted to being looked at, the actor's wife and daughter wore homemade clothes and went unpainted, but were beautiful nonetheless.

William loved Jessie's heart-shaped face, the pointed chin a little softened by years. Despite the wearying, wounding words, her sensitive heart and fragile delicacy still cast a spell on him. The actor took a moment to admire his graceful daughter who so resembled him: olive skinned, square-shouldered, with lively black-browed eyes exactly like his own. This evening Lizzie looked more womanly than her father could recall. She was tossing French phrases at Roger as if she spoke them every day. Perhaps she did?

How I would have loved to put her on the stage with me, William mused, with the usual stab of regret. *What a hurricano of opposition Jessie threw when I suggested it years ago. That caused the first tear in our marriage. Can it never be mended?* William saw the girl was lovely and good-natured, with enough plain sense to make a more compliant wife than her mother. *She's too old to be taught the acting arts, and now I haven't the time, but I should make some plan for her future.*

Aunt Peg carried in her treacle pudding to shouts of appreciation from the three young persons.

William declined a portion and insisted Roger take seconds, then cast an eye over the unremarkable boy with the spoon in his hand and hair in his eyes. Perhaps Roger would do for Lizzie? *Does the boy have imagination? Like all women, Lizzie has too much. She will need a steadying hand when she leaves this house.*

William took a sip of wine. Roger was listening to Lizzie's French without a trace of comprehension, but plainly smitten. *Should take the boys out and show them what a man's life can be. Get to know Roger, then discuss this with Sidrack. Not tonight, of course. The performance. Lizzie and...Roger? Perhaps.*

When the treacle dishes had been scraped clean, the cloth drawn, and the port gone round with toasts to the muses and the ladies of Longsatin House, Georgie raised his glass with zealous dignity. "To His Majesty, King George the Third, God bless him."

All chorused devoutly, "The king!"

William turned to eye the case-clock. "We'd best get to it. I have my performance tonight."

"Ah, your performance," echoed Jessie from behind her empty glass.

William smiled without and winced within, saddened as usual by his wife's resentment of all he had achieved. Yet, hoping the evening's surprise would lighten her spirit, he bent to kiss her brow.

The parcels from America were resting on the pianoforte, awaiting a ceremonious opening in the salmon-grey drawing room. Georgie's fire cast a welcome glow as the family settled themselves on the comfortable, mismatched furniture. A framed costume-sketch of William as Hamlet's Father peered down reproachfully on the gold medallion woven into the Turkey carpet.

"These arrived today from your grandparents with some correspondence for Sidrack. Luckily, George, you are home to receive your gift." William passed the little bundle to his son, who unwrapped it at once. "I see my father has written a message to you in Italian. Can you translate it?"

"*For our grandson, George Mario, who makes us proud.*" The boy read slowly from a small card. "*May this remind him of Nana and Papi, who love him and pray for his safety every day.*" Georgie put the card next to his heart, then opened the velvet-lined box, to find a petit point watch pocket. "Nana embroidered this herself, I know." He drew out a round gold watch, gasping in surprise. "It's inscribed! *G. M. Trumpet, 1803. Serve with honor.* Oh, how very, very splendid." Georgie could not stop looking at it.

"Now yours, Elizabeth." William passed another card, written in lacy script, which Lizzie read with more ease than her brother.

"For Lisa-*cara*, the finest granddaughter we can imagine. In honor of your confirmation, we pray you will live in the sacred heart of Jesus, and may you be adored by all."

Seven years before, Lizzie's Italian grandparents had left England to establish the Adam & James tailoring business in Charleston, South Carolina. The girl sorely missed their love and shouted with pleasure to see Nana had sent her own golden filigree earrings, set with little sparkling diamonds. In a velvet wrapping were the twin miniatures of William and Jessie, painted on the occasion of Lizzie's birth.

"Look how beautiful you are, Mama," Lizzie cooed, placing the frames on the white marble mantel then immediately put the earrings in her ears. "Nana would never take off her diamonds and now she has given them to me!"

"Diamonds are just carbon, you know," Georgie offered brightly.

"Carbon!" Lizzie made a face.

"Yes, it's very elemental," Georgie went on, quoting his favorite professor. "When the earth was being formed, it was a great ball of fire, inconceivably hot; wherever that heat encountered the element carbon, it cooked up crystals of diamond, the strongest substance on earth."

"That's natural philosophy," agreed Roger, who didn't have a clue, but was always first in line to support Georgie.

William leaned back in his chair and linked his fingers over his cream-colored waistcoat. "Well, you know, children? That is an apt metaphor for life. Just think. It is adversity that creates character in a person. Struggle. Drama. Conflict."

"Ah, listen to himself," Jessie said sideways to Aunt Peg.

"I mean it, Jessie," William went on. "Easy times don't give you insight or wisdom; they leave you soft. Fighting for what you want makes you strong and shining. It is the hard times that turn ordinary people into...diamonds."

"Such a thinker you've become. What turns a common man into a philosopher?"

"Continuous conflict, my dear. As you doubtless know." He gave his wife a look, both sad and loving, as he rose from his chair. "Well, I must make my way to the theatre, and cannot be late."

"Oh, Papa, no, not yet," Lizzie cried. "Georgie tuned your mandolin. Let's make music together, like old times. "William smiled at his daughter, touched that she cared so much. Indeed, such spontaneous family concerts had always made William happiest as a father. "Well, if you wish. It will warm up *la voce*."

Georgie produced his violin, and Lizzie drew from the tall walnut chest-on-chest a wreath of fresh bay leaves. "You shall be our Queen of the Muses, Mama," she said, placing the green crown she had woven on her mother's hair. Jessie gave her daughter a tender kiss. Lizzie took the mandolin to her father, opened the pianoforte, and struck a chord. "A love song, Papa, *per favore*."

The actor gazed at his wife for a long moment then touched the strings softly. Unwanted tears formed in Jessie's eyes as she recognized the melody. The look that passed between them told Lizzie her complicated parents were recalling the memory of love.

"Have you seen but a white lily grow
Before rude hands had touch'd it?
Have you mark'd but the fall of the snow
Before the earth hath smucht it?"

Lizzie held her breath, thrilled to see this spark of tender feeling passing between the always-warring pair. Her father sang, beseechingly, to her mother.

"O so white, o so soft,
O so sweet, so sweet is she."

The plea for love was clear, and Jessie seemed ready to reach for her husband. Lizzie watched them with cautious hope; still neither moved a muscle.

"*'Scacciapensieri!'*" Georgie cried out suddenly, wildly bowing his violin and lighting into the tarantella William had composed for Jessie years ago. The tall actor handed his mandolin to Lizzie, while the others began to clap and stamp. The song was a family heirloom everyone knew and loved. Dispel thoughts, it said. Forget care. Enjoy life's dance!

Singing, William lifted his wife from her chair. In her day, Jessie had danced in William's provincial tours, a seductive magnet on stage.

"Scacciapensieri!
Laugh and be merry!
Dance till the break of day
Scacciapensieri!
Bright as a berry!
Throw all your cares away!"

Jessie was always more at home with Terpsichore than dialogue; her body yielded to the music and the joyful moment.

"Hike up your skirting and kick off your shoes,
Wake up your flirting, you have naught to lose!
Take my left hand with your right,

And Scacciapensieri tonight!"

William sang like a courting lover. Eyes locked, arms embracing, Lizzie's parents breathed and spun as one. Aunt Peg beat on a ribboned tambourine; a pan began banging in Noddy's kitchen corner while Georgie made his strings fairly smoke.

"*Now's the time for us to dance*
Now's the time for sweet romance
Whirling, twirling in and out
First you sing and then you shout!"

Lizzie, now playing the mandolin, was hard-pressed to keep up with her brother's tempo as the music pulsed faster and faster.

"*Smack the tambourine-o,*
Dance the serpentine-o,
Curtsey to your master,
Clap and then go faster!
Sugar candy,
Hot as wine;
You're a dandy,
And your mine!
Scacciapensieri!
Tonight! Ya!"

When the tarantella ended, William kissed Jessie's parted lips and lifted her over his head, crown and all. Both were gasping and laughing. Applause broke out by the pianoforte where Georgie and Lizzie were beaming at this unusual display of intimacy.

"Tonight the Royal Family is coming to the theatre, and my family is attending as well. That is my surprise, everyone." It was unheard of for a company actor to get tickets the night of a command performance, and here was William pulling out of his pocket a handful of "bones," the ivory chips engraved with his name and Covent Garden's insignia. "Roger, you shall come, too," William proclaimed. "Since Sidrack chooses to work everyday like a donkey, he's declined, but sets you free for tomorrow."

Lizzie's face lit up with happiness. She had helped her father learn the role. "This is a wonderful part, Mama." Her mother did not seem to hear. "You will be thrilled to see Papa in it."

Jessie stood panting before her husband, looking up into his eyes, knowing this night he wanted her, as much as she wanted to be taken. What about the hundreds of nights she had never been wanted? *He'll not work his power over me. I'll deny him his pleasure as he's cheated me of mine.* "I'm not going," she announced, still short of breath. "I cannot bear the crowds. Another time."

"But it's the last performance of this play for the season, Jessie." William fanned the ivory chips enticingly before her eyes. "There will be no other chance to see it."

"I've seen you on stage for years."

"Don't spoil this, Jessie, please."

"How could I spoil anything? Your life is perfect."

Sidrack and Roger pretended an interest in the Turkish carpet. Georgie snapped the violin case closed.

Jessie removed her crown of leaves. "You don't need me there tonight, William. You'll have the king." She straightened her long sleeves and left the room.

Lizzie saw her charming papa was not wounded in the ego, but, more deeply, in the heart.

Chapter Two

March 1803

BACKING UP the steps that led into the royal box was Covent Garden's large proprietor, Thomas Jupiter Harris. He carried a lighted candelabrum and deferred to the great personages following him: King George the Third, old, bewigged, and dressed in the style of the last age, Queen Charlotte, equally musty, and the Dukes of Clarence and York, smart as paint, who proceeded a mob of courtiers that overflowed the royal boxes, swagged in patriotic bunting for the command performance.

A guard of Beefeaters in their stiff white ruffs and red tunics pressed at attention against the green damask-covered walls. Four tiers of theatre boxes spilled over with silk-and-satin-clad audience. The candles in every chandelier and sconce of the house blazed as the king entered. There was much cheering and craning of necks in the galleries, too, for many attended just to see him.

Once the royals positioned themselves, the orchestra struck up the new wartime anthem, "God Save the King." All joined in singing lustily, including the monarch himself.

Lizzie was quite squeezed into her seat in the pit: a backless wooden bench with no room for legs, hats, coats, canes, or one more playgoer. She carefully rolled and stuffed in her reticule the long playbill of *The Doom of Troy*, with her father's name near the top of the cast. Roger and Georgie had forsaken her for the rowdy fun of "the gods," the top gallery seats. Lizzie had waited over two hours to secure a place near enough the stage to see her father working close up. She was tasting a moment of heaven, ignoring the oppressive presence of strangers' bodies, noises, and smells. For her, the playhouse was the center of the universe—the temple of all art, where triumph and tragedies unfolded in elegant language spoken by the most gifted actors in God's creation. *How could Mama have missed this?*

The moment the king's bottom touched his chair, the curtain rose to a fanfare of horns. Then the two thousand excited ladies and gentlemen of the audience returned to their conversations, flirtations, milling about, ordering apples and oranges, requests for directions to their seats, and complaints about the noise. The actors onstage were also milling about, dressed in an assortment of armor and drapery, reciting dialogue that set the scene, and nodding and waving to supporters in the audience.

Two wags behind Lizzie conjectured if the king was mad at this moment. A flutey voice said, "The Hanoverians usually avoid dramatic plays."

"Perhaps he thinks the Trojan War was a comedy." A bray of laughter.

"Wales is absent, of course." Since that unhappy night when the king had encountered the Prince of Wales drunk in the lobby of Drury Lane and slapped him across the face for it, father and son attended on different nights and maintained different boxes.

The Doom of Troy, written in iambic pentameter, was a new play in the repertoire that season. The scenery drop had been in many productions that featured old Greeks, and the incidental music was truly incidental, but John Philip Kemble, co-proprietor of the theatre, had a weighty style and favored weighty material.

Another fanfare and Lizzie's spine straightened as William Trumpet, playing Tyndarcus, strode onstage in armor, cloaked in purple, with brass greaves and a helmet sporting plum plumes.

"*Ah, vanity! Nay, rude and abject folly,*
For this Paris to a suitor be!"

William Trumpet's aura of authority quieted the audience enough to listen to his first speech. He pointed a helpful finger at Miss Claudia Clitroe, the willowy blonde portraying Helen.

"The blackguard dares to broach our Princess Helen!
Zeus's offspring! Thus immortal she!"

He directed this line to Jonathan Faversham, a promising newcomer playing Paris downstage left.

"His actions boggle all imagination,
Off'ring neither gold nor pedigree."

William crossed to the center float lights, where hot candles flamed against reflectors, then raised his eyes to the royal box.

"But, baiting traps with lust and wicked lies,
He fain would drag her to his destiny."

The audience murmured approvingly, and Lizzie dared to exhale. The actor plainly saw his daughter in the crowd and their eyes met momentarily.

"What catastrophic thought that one so crass
Might win this innocent, yea, lovely lass.
'Od's blood! The thought offends the fearful mind
And causes heart and humour to unwind."

"That one knows his business," said the talkative man behind Lizzie. She proudly concurred, but shushed the man anyway.

William spun his cloak, crossed to Faversham's level, and thundered,

"But, fie, I say to thee and say again,
Thou shallst not have her for thine own to be!
For tragedy would overcome this world;
'Twere better she were dead than under thee!"

He grasped his sword-hilt menacingly towards Paris, collected Miss Clitroe, and exited.

The audience rattled the air with applause and shouts of "Well done! Bravo! Bravo, Trumpet!" As was customary, the play stopped while the patrons voiced their enthusiasm. Queen Charlotte took a dip of her beloved snuff and sneezed generously.

Lizzie simmered with jealousy. *That Clitroe girl is so fortunate to work with Papa. What does she have to recommend her except all that blonde hair and a pleasing face? I could please in a costume that stunning—play Helen just as well. Better!* Her envious flow was interrupted, as the actor portraying Paris advanced downstage.

Faversham was an extraordinarily handsome young man, with eyes of unsettling blue, tall, lean, and looking as though he could use a good dinner. His hungry aura fascinated the lavishly dressed ladies in the boxes. And Lizzie, too. He raised his fist to his lips and began a soliloquy.

"Should Paris be affrighted by this boor,
This oldish man who trembles in his wrath?
If Helen be the fairest in the land,
Then none could force me to another path."

Opening his hand, he stroked himself from lips to inner thigh with haughty menace. Lizzie had never seen such a gesture onstage before. Unconsciously, she reached into her neckline and adjusted her bodice.

"Let every village villain, churl and squire
Know hence my mind on Helen be so led
That I with god and goddess shall conspire
To capture her and lure her to my bed."

From the king's seat in the royal box came the unmistakable sound of a snore.

"Meg, tell me about that new actor playing Paris, the one with the shoulders and naughty eyes," said Lizzie, furtively peeking at herself in the pier glass.

"Jonathan Faversham? He's just a vain puppy who thinks he's another David Garrick. Which he is not. He's too peculiar to be popular." Judgment given, square-jawed, capable Meg Wilson stuck a pin into the bib of her shop apron where scissors and threaded needles were kept for the emergency repairs required during performance. She glanced at Lizzie. "Take off Pomona's headdress, darling, and mind the gilding on the apples. You know not to touch my properties." Meg took the papier-mache fantasy of fruit and twigs out of Lizzie's hand to plop it on her waist-high work table piled beside a rainbow of hats in need of refurbishment.

During the interval, her young guest had come backstage to visit with the company seamstress. Meg's realm was a dark, commodious cavern in the theatre basement where long racks were hung with precious costumes, some over a hundred years old. Resting under white muslin covers to keep out the dust and damp, the garments waited to be called up from one production to another, belonging to no single actor but smelling of a multitude.

Meg and her husband, the droll comic, Dick Wilson, had toured with William and Jessie before Lizzie was born. Those were the happy times the Trumpets rarely spoke of anymore. Both Wilson and Trumpet had matured to become popular actors of stature with contracts at Covent Garden, always working, sometimes featured, sometimes in supporting roles.

"Where's your husband, Meg?"

"He's up in the stage machinery, playing Zeus with all the goddesses in their next-to-nothings. I'll have his one-eyed monster to deal with later, that's where Mr. Dick is. Is your mother enjoying *The Doom?*"

"Mama's blue devils were upon her tonight, and she felt too tired to come, though Papa importuned her. Aunt Peg stayed home, too." Lizzie couldn't bear to describe her mother's dark moods.

"I see." Meg didn't need to be told much to guess Jessie was denying William her presence to gain his attention. *What a foolish wife. To turn a husband out of her bed to make him love her more; and here's this bright sweet girl loving them both—forever trying to make things right.*

"Georgie is on holiday from Military College, and I nearly bested him at fencing today," Lizzie offered by way of a happier topic.

"Playing soldier again? Well, you look quite harmlessly feminine in that white dress, and blooming like a lily."

"Thank you. I found the yellow silk in Papa's costume trunk at home and twisted it round to emphasize the bodice. Isn't it fine?"

"Very fine. But aren't you cold, dear? It's icy here beneath the stage." A pokey mouse behind a hamper was indeed frozen to his spot.

"Where's your wrap?"

"I forgot one, Meg. No matter."

Meg adjusted her glasses. *Are Jessie and William so occupied with themselves they don't see their girl needs a warm spencer on a March evening? Do they even notice her?*

William rushed in, full of crisis, waving his purple cloak, nearly ripped in two. "Stitch me up, Meg! That idiot Faversham stepped on this." Then he saw his smiling daughter perched on the work table. "Oh! It's my Elizabeth. I spied you there in the second row."

"Oh, you had them, Papa. I didn't think the audience was going to let you off the stage."

"Yes, it did go well," he answered, fired with performance energy. "Wait till they hear my oration over Iphigenia. They'll be in tears."

"You are so full of life in this role, Papa."

"I wish your mother had been here." His voice dropped. "She didn't come after all, did she?"

Lizzie shook her head. "No, Papa."

From the stage came a distant fanfare.

William gasped, "Egad, I'm on," and, trailing his ripped cloak, flew out the door.

❧

"It was a wonderful evening, Mama, a triumph for the play." Lizzie spun around the dimly-lit grey salon to warm her cold toes. "The royal party stayed for nearly two acts! And I had a splendid visit backstage with Meg Wilson. She sends you her love."

"I'm much obliged," Jessie murmured from the depths of the scroll-armed sofa where she had brooded over the intervening hours.

"Everyone was perfect in their roles," Lizzie rattled on. "Except for the lady playing Helen, who seemed rather colorless to me." She dropped to the sofa and nestled against Jessie. "Roger was quite transported to be meeting all the actresses after the play. Then Papa thought the boys should see the Royal Saloon in Piccadilly."

"Your father has certainly seen enough of it," Jessie responded, her breath stale with wine, and her undone hair hanging in strings.

"So, they put you in a hackney coach in the middle of Covent Garden piazza and sent you home like a package? Unescorted?"

"Oh, that was all right with me, Mama." Lizzie was used to her mother finding insult in everything and as always, she ignored the bitter sentiments to share her more generous ones. "You really should have seen Papa tonight. Tyndarcus is one of his best parts. He was so powerful and moving; the audience applauded his every speech in Act Five. Oh, and there is a new young actor in the company, he played Paris, with the most fascinating way of...."

"Don't be such a fool as I was, lambie."

"What do you mean, Mama?"

Jessie sighed. "Nothing. It's very late. Go to bed now."

"I will, but I know it will be hard to sleep." The girl kissed her mother tenderly and started upstairs.

Lizzie believed she understood Jessie and William's domestic struggles. Her father's notable theatrical reputation brought no reflected glory to her mother. Jessie wanted a true marriage and William had married the stage. The pity of it made Lizzie's heart ache.

The yellow silk from her father's costume trunk was thoroughly crushed and damp. She hung it over the banister to dry. At her chamber door, she heard her mother sing, "*Have you seen but a white lily grow*," then laugh in a sorry way, and finally start to cry.

Chapter Three

April 1803

LIKE A snake striking for its dinner, a biting wind off the Thames blew against the figure pounding on the door of 15 Buckingham Street.

Pulling a wrapper over her warm breasts, Octavia Onslow, one of the "fashionably impure," hesitated behind the deadbolt. If this was another lover, drunk on the threshold at three in the morning, the redheaded woman would be inconvenienced, but not surprised. "Stop that noise! Who is it?"

"It's Elizabeth Trumpet. I'm looking for my father. Is he there? Please, I must talk to him, please." The female voice was pitched high with panic.

Octavia took a moment to light a candle from the fireplace coals, then walked to the mussy bed. "William, it's your Lizzie outside. Get up, dear. Something is wrong."

Such an invasion of a man's privacy was unprecedented, and the astonished William had a strong reproof forming in his mind. But when he opened the door, he saw his daughter was hysterical, hair streaming in the wind, her eyes wide with fright.

"Mother is dying, Papa. She is dying," Lizzie sobbed.

"What?" The meaning of his daughter's words struck William like a blow in the belly. Roughly, he pulled her off the threshold and inside. "Your mother dying? That can't be."

"She's had fever for two days, and she's been choking the whole night. Aunt Peg said to find you before she's gone. She is so low, Papa. Please come home. Please."

"Stop crying, Elizabeth," William said sharply. "I shall hurry." He moved behind a tapestry screen to dress, urgency making him clumsy. Could Jessie be ill enough to die tonight and her own husband not know? How many days since he had seen her? How many months since he told her he loved her?

"Fool," he whispered, tearing at sleeves and buttons, dread rising in waves from his stomach to his heart.

Wringing her hands by the doorway, Lizzie noticed the gleam of her father's polished boots lying beside the large unmade bed. Quickly she looked in another direction, but in the close, perfumed room, Octavia's presence was everywhere. So, all her mother's suspicions were true. Her father was faithless. Shock and anger began to stir in her already anguished heart.

"The call-boy at the theatre told me where to find you," she blurted out at the tapestry screen. "We can both ride Old Ember, the big grey I took from the livery stable." How she wanted to shout, "Who is this woman, Papa? Why are you with her when Mama needs you so?" She could not believe what she had just discovered.

Saying not a word to Octavia, William rushed past her, grabbed Lizzie's arm, and dashed down the steps. He untied the mount from the wrought-iron railing, jumped on and pulled his daughter up behind him. The horse's shoes struck sparks off the Strand cobblestones as they ran him through the darkness, William cursing and whipping the poor grey.

Arms wrapped tight around her frantic father's waist, Lizzie chanted over and over her grandmother's prayer, "*Ave Maria, gratia plena, Dominus tecum, benedicta tu....*"

When their ride ended, father and daughter found Jessie in a feverish dream. She would see her beloved come to her bed at last, hear him crying her name and begging her to live. She would feel Lizzie kissing and rubbing her icy hands. Aunt Peg's voice harshly imploring God to spare her. But, when Jessie tried to answer William's desperate words of love, there was no breath, no strength, no last chance to say goodbye. He had come too late. Death would wait no longer.

The showers had stopped for a moment and a pale sun touched the purple irises blooming around St. Mary's. Meg Wilson stood waiting outside the parish church door while her husband paid the hackney coachman. They had come to support the Trumpet family on this unhappy day. Other theatricals were there as well, suitably dressed for tragedy. Few of them had known Jessie; all knew William. Breathing in incense, the gathered friends took seats around Thomas Jupiter Harris, manager of Covent Garden and a kind of patriarch to the community of actors.

The Trumpet family filled the first pew, all bathed in silvery light coming through the clear-glass, rain-laced windows. The simple, rectangular sanctuary was decorated for Easter; a long purple cloth draped the great cross, towering over Jessie's little coffin.

Vicar Strahan, well along in years, mounted the pulpit and began the service. "'I am the resurrection and the life,' saith the Lord." His flat voice hardly did justice to the majesty of the words.

Diphtheria, a swift and common killer of children, had taken Lizzie's mother. She had breathed it in nursing Marco Mantino, the neighbor child whose parents owned the livery stable. Marco was recovering, but the thick grey mucus in Jessie's throat had hardened to a murderous, strangling knot.

Lizzie began to weep again, though her eyes were running out of tears. She had cried almost continuously since her mother stopped breathing. *The things I should have done—the words I should have said.* She was angry at God for the first time in her life. Angry at her father more. Some part of this was Papa's fault. Some great part. Georgie, deep in his own grief, leaned against her shoulder, which shook with stifled sobs.

The verses rolled from the pulpit. "'Whosoever liveth and

believeth in me shall never die.'"

⚬

The mourners filed out, holding their hats against the April breeze. Noddy was waiting under a dripping tree in the churchyard with a last gift in his hand.

"We therefore commit her body to the ground, earth to earth, ashes to ashes, dust to dust, in the sure and certain hope of eternal life."

At the grave, Vicar Strahan dropped a handful of earth on the coffin. Then Georgie and Lizzie did the same and returned to their father's side. The death knell began to toll from St. Mary's steeple. Noddy crept toward the family to hand William a bouquet of white lilies he had picked from the rain-washed garden.

William, always so rehearsed, so ready to perform, was living a tragedy that would not end in applause. He stared at the coffin, confounded. He could scarcely see, for conscience made his mind stand still, frozen with agonizing regret. Jessie had grown impatient with his way of life, and he had punished her for that. *I could have made her happy. Christ knows how much I loved her.* Now the chance to prove his feelings was gone forever.

With a cry that pierced the air, William stepped toward the open grave, sobbing and falling to the ground, shaking in a fit, his body stretched rigid and inhuman.

Not a person there had ever seen William helpless before. Georgie leaped to lift his father up from the dirt where he lay like a suffering beast. Lizzie heard a voice screaming and realized it was her own. The mourners watched, still and gaping. When the seizure passed, Roger helped Georgie ease William upright where he swayed against the boys, looking vacantly at the little crowd, a stranger to them and himself.

Lizzie realized William didn't know what had happened. The shocked girl wiped a smear of mud from his cheek and whispered against his ear, "You've had a fall, Papa, just a little fall. We're going to take you home now." William's dark eyes returned her gaze,

38

uncomprehending.

The boys half carried him out of the churchyard while people crowded around Lizzie to assure her and themselves that William would be himself again soon. Meg and Dick Wilson kissed her and said they would come by. Then every one of the shaken mourners left for the theatre. The evening performance would go on.

Noddy and Sidrack filled in the grave. Aunt Peg stood silent and straight beside her niece as the rain began again. Lizzie opened the old shawl of Jessie's she was wearing to spread over Peg's boney shoulders. They stayed in the churchyard until the white lilies were covered with earth.

The Islington apothecary mixed Ward's Drop and Godfrey's Cordial for William "to rekindle his life force, to calm his confusion, induce sleep and re-awaken his identity." The costly medications did little harm but no good. Meg and Dick sent a surgeon who declared it was apoplexy, ventured no suggestions for recovery and bled the patient. It was all useless.

In their grief, Lizzie, Georgie, and Aunt Peg spoke to each other in hushed tones, and only when they had to. Lizzie hovered by William, feeding him meals, asking Georgie to stoke the fire when their father grew cold. She busied herself, milking Boozel the cow and tending to the chickens. She answered the door to neighbors come to express condolences, baked bread in the cast iron oven, washed clothes, and thought up errands for Noddy. But, all the work in the world could not keep her mind from death. In her misery, she returned to the salon many times a day to kiss and cherish Jessie's miniature.

The world went heartlessly on. The sun rose in a high heaven over London's murky air. Coaches came and went at the Sign of the Angel. The speckled hens laid down their eggs. When the daffodils her mother had planted appeared in the garden, Lizzie wept afresh. To the Trumpet children such common events seemed impossible. Hadn't the whole world changed? The future, that great question mark, had arrived like an unexpected guest, all unprepared for.

⁶ℱ

Lizzie drew the bright razor down her father's cheek while Georgie held the porcelain-shaving basin under William's chin. The actor had not spoken or seemed to hear his children speak to him. Brother and sister whispered together as William, still wearing the dressing gown and slippers Georgie had put on him three days before, stared into the drawing room fire.

"Have we lost both our parents, Lizzie?"

"Don't say such things, Georgie. He'll be better soon."

"I've been thinking, infant. I must leave Military College and find a position straight away, so there will be money coming in. Uncle Sidrack will surely put me on at his shop. Whatever it is Roger does there I can do, too. I must take care of you and Aunt Peg until Papa's mind is more...clear."

Lizzie looked hard at her brother's earnest face. Of all the things that were happening to them, this suggestion seemed the saddest yet. *No, that mustn't be.* "An excellent idea, but unnecessary, surely. Stay in school, Georgie. Aunt Peg and I shall nurse Papa. Just because there's no money in the house doesn't mean we aren't well off." She passed a towel over her father's soapy cheek. The blame she had placed on him for her mother's death had disappeared when this shocking change took hold of him. Fleetingly, she had wanted William punished for ignoring Jessie, but not like this. *Absent in his mind? Speechless with regret? No, not like this.*

"There's no reason to throw over your military career," Lizzie said aloud. "It's time to look up the Trumpet investments Papa always spoke of. They must be in some bank. Mr. Harris at the theatre will tell us where. We've but to ask him."

"Harris should give a benefit for Papa, too. Think of all the performances Papa's done for every retiring actor in the company." Georgie wiped the razor back and forth on the towel draped over his arm.

"But he won't be retiring, Georgie. He needs to recover from the terrible blow of losing our mother. Papa will act again." Lizzie spoke so her father could hear her and believe. She touched the white hairs that had appeared overnight on his curly head. "He's taking a little tour in his mind, perhaps thinking of Mama right now." William had always strutted through his daughter's life with strength and optimism to spare. She willed herself to copy that optimism for her brother's sake.

"I'll explain to Mr. Harris how Papa can't perform just yet, and he will arrange a benefit at once. That will raise money to keep Aunt Peg and me snug here for months. You must return to school." Lizzie watched her fair-haired brother hesitate between a sacrifice that might not be necessary and what he really wanted to do. "Some day we may all have to live off your service pay, brother. If you quit now, there won't be any of that," she added reasonably.

Georgie snapped the razor shut, struggling against such reasonableness and his own sense of what was right. He was applying himself with might and main at college; to throw it all over for clerking in a shop would be more than awful. "Very well, for now I will stay on at Wycombe. That's what mother wanted, and it is my best chance. But if things do not change, you must send for me, sister."

She picked up the basin of cold shaving water and said, with an acting talent she had never used before, "Things will change. Papa could be himself again tomorrow."

Chapter Four

April 1803

"WELCOME, MISS Trumpet. You bring good news of William, I trust?" Thomas Jupiter Harris lifted his bulk from behind the large untidy desk in his backstage office at Covent Garden to greet her with a small bow.

Lizzie had prepared carefully for this meeting, so important to her Papa and all their futures. In her black bonnet, mouth dry and hands wet in her mourning gloves, she explained her father was still recovering from the fall he'd suffered the day of her mother's funeral and was not quite himself.

"When will he be himself, Miss Trumpet?" Harris was used to mendacious actors. "You see, I have him scheduled in May for—" he raised his bushy brown eyebrows to consult a large chart tacked to the wall, "five *Pizarros*, three *Tempests*, a *Way of the World*, and a week of new comedies by various playwrights. If Trumpet isn't able to perform, I must recast immediately."

Sitting tense on the chair's cushion, Lizzie forced up the hard truth. "He's not well enough to act at present, Mr. Harris. He does not speak."

"That is unfortunate." Harris made a note on the performance chart. "Might his condition be permanent?"

"I pray not." The probability of her father's silence being eternal filled Lizzie's eyes with tears. "I don't know, sir, how to answer."

Harris regarded the girl, whose composure was collapsing before him. "Then how can I help you, Elizabeth?"

"You have truly been a friend to Papa. More than an employer, he always said. So, if you could inform me of...." There was no way around revealing her ignorance. "Papa always spoke of the family fortune and how he was investing in it, but in his own charming way he never gave us any details. Do you happen to know which bank it might be in? Money is a bit short at the moment." Having gotten the agony out, Lizzie looked expectantly across the desk.

The girl's naivete caught the theatre manager up short. He was indeed familiar with William's foibles. Idly twisting the wiry hairs of his eyebrow, he said, "I believe he must have meant his talent, my dear. That was his fortune entire. As to the bank...." He withdrew a dark green account book from a low drawer, thumbed to a page, and showed it to Lizzie. *Advanced to William Trumpet against Future Salaries*, the heading read. Below it was a full page of sums owed with very few crossed out. "As you see, one hundred sixteen pounds is outstanding."

"My father owes you that?" This history of borrowing was a sad surprise to Lizzie.

"Now if William returns next season, he will work the debt off. But—" he took up a pen, dipped it in the square inkwell, and crossed out the total, "if he does not recover, I relieve you of the responsibility."

"Oh, thank you, Mr. Harris," Lizzie said, very subdued. She had not wanted to bring up Georgie's suggestion, but what else was there to do? "Would there be a chance of putting on a benefit for Papa?"

Actors' small salaries were augmented every season by individual benefit performances. They were allowed to keep the full profit of the tickets. Stars, minor actors, playwrights and theatre personnel all had benefit nights.

Harris brightened. "I could schedule a benefit for William directly after the night for pit-musicians. There are several details and expenses involved, you know."

Lizzie did not know; her father had kept his family ignorant of his business. Harris enumerated the details, gulping air in his asthmatic way, for the list of requirements was long: The engraving of special tickets to avoid counterfeits, the selling of those tickets directly from the actor's home, the buying of newspaper adverts, securing his fellow actors' consent to appear for their usual salary, paying those salaries, engaging someone to write new material or paying for old material, providing musical arrangements, costumes, lights, props, a cold collation for all involved and, finally, the fee for the use of the theatre. The fee for the use of Covent Garden was two hundred pounds.

Long before the meticulous Harris reached the non-negotiable two hundred pound figure, Lizzie had dismissed the idea. Nothing was going as she had imagined. Feeling anything but bold, she was ready to make a more humble suggestion.

"There are no funds in the house for such an enterprise right now, Mr. Harris, but could you use me in some small capacity backstage? I could be a dresser. Or I could sew costumes with Meg Wilson. She's known me all my life."

Harris sighed. "Our backstage folk have been here for years, some of them for generations. You know Fluff Tidbett's story, don't you? She used to dance in the ballets, had a terrible fall one night and her leg never healed properly. For more than twenty years, she's been a ladies dresser. I couldn't let her go to make room for you now, could I?"

Lizzie was past caring about old Fluff, but answered, "No, sir."

Harris seemed to take this for acceptance and pushed himself back from his desk. "Well, then...."

"I could perform," Lizzie ventured, knowing she sounded desperate. "Papa was one of your best, and though he didn't train me, I've helped him learn speeches, and songs, too. I'll work harder than anyone. Could I have something in the chorus?" She smiled weakly. "Anything, really."

At that moment, the connecting door to the next office opened. "Pardon, old bean," John Philip Kemble said, addressing Harris. Much at home, the new co-manager of Covent Garden wandered to the mantel and picked up a pipe.

Harris gestured to make an introduction. "This is William Trumpet's daughter, Elizabeth."

The great man in his own estimation offered no greeting in reply.

"Elizabeth was just asking if we could put her on in some small parts before the season ends."

The wide-browed tragedian lit his pipe from the fire with a paper spill. Striking a pose, the forty-five-year-old star exhaled a rich balloon of smoke and appraised the girl. He found her nervous, unusually tall, exotically featured, and exuding upset. "Miss Trumpet," he said in mellifluous tones that were his specialty, "one does not begin one's acting career at the Theatre Royal Covent Garden. I'm sorry." He smiled superciliously. "My sister, the greatest actress on the stage...."

"Oh, I adore Mrs. Siddons," Lizzie rushed to say.

But Kemble was only listening to himself. "My sister failed in London when she was your age, with a wealth of stage experience, too. She returned to the provinces and toiled for seven years to perfect her art."

"I know," Lizzie got out.

"You know nothing at all, Miss Trumpet, and a know-nothing may not step on my stage. The London audience does not tolerate amateurs. Jupiter here was doubtless telling you to go and learn. Somewhere. But," he paused to blow another balloon of smoke, "not here." Kemble strode out and smartly shut the door.

"I'm sorry for that, Elizabeth, but, alas, he is right." Harris coughed from the departing actor's pipe fumes. "Now that Kemble has met you, I'm afraid there's no chance of my using you, even in crowd scenes." Reaching into his striped waistcoat, he pulled out a five-pound bank note. "Take this and good luck to you. My sympathies to your father."

In Savile Row, Roger Sloane was nailing a set of sporting prints to the fitting-room wall of Adam & James. He had persuaded his father that gentlemen of his clientele would recognize the bruisers pictured in manly attitudes. Roger admired the fashionable fighters greatly. Setting the hammer aside, he raised his fists and began to box towards the tall mirror, bouncing and jabbing. Thrice-weekly boxing classes at Sergeant Mento's Parlor of Self Defense had begun to firm his pudgy center and straighten his posture.

"Roger!" Sidrack's voice cut through the fitting room door. "When you've finished playing fisticuffs with yourself, come out and greet Elizabeth."

Heat rose noticeably to Roger's face, swelling the pimple on his chin. Hurriedly, he put his jacket back on and adjusted his tight neck cloth. He opened the fitting-room door to find Lizzie in a mourning dress, responding to Sidrack's questions about her family. She looked like a painting, seated amongst the tobacco brown furnishings of the shop salon, and more lovely than all his daydreams of her.

Turkolu, the new apprentice tailor with the thick sidewhiskers, was offering Lizzie a cup of tea off a silver tray. Forgetting his English, he muttered, *"Chai alivimisin?"*

Accepting the refreshment, she told Sidrack that Georgie had returned to Military College, then quietly took a sip. "I've just learned Papa has some unpaid loans at Covent Garden, which will be set aside until he can return there." Her voice was small and serious. "Papa purchased a frock coat here a few weeks ago, and I want to know if he paid or put it on account." She took a breath. "If Papa owes you money, Uncle Sidrack, I have five pounds in hand for you today. You may have to wait for the rest, but I promise to pay every penny."

Sidrack excused himself, to say he would check William's account. Lizzie drank deeply from the teacup. The shop was momentarily empty of customers.

Seizing the chance to enjoy Lizzie's company in private, Roger eased himself onto a chair at her side. "If you'd been here an hour earlier, you would have met Mr. George Brummell, the taste-maker of the ton."

Preoccupied, Lizzie's gaze drifted towards the sound of a desk drawer opening in the rear of the shop.

Roger took no notice, hoping to display his *savoir faire* by sharing a commercial confidence. "Brummell's custom is wonderfully good for business. He wanted a morning ensemble of bath-coating. That's a weave of superfine broadcloth and keysermere. Very difficult to work with. When father said we'd been cutting bath-coating for two seasons, Brummell demanded a fitting on the spot." *Her lips are like rose satin.* "I assisted father, of course. That Beau gentleman is the cleanest one we've ever served, positively reeks of soap and water. Perhaps the Prince of Wales will turn up next. They are thick as thiev—"

"Whatever you are running on about, Roger," Lizzie interrupted, "my thoughts are elsewhere."

Hurt, Roger slid a biscuit off the silver tray and chewed in crushed silence.

Sidrack emerged saying, "Have no concerns about a bill at our establishment, my dear. Your father's account is paid in full."

William, like so many customers, lived on the tick of credit and actually had a large balance owing. Roger knew his father lied through his smiling teeth, and was glad of it. Once Lizzie was gone, he reproached himself all afternoon. *Why did I babble on about Brummell's bath-coating? I must have sounded like an idiot child.*

Chapter Five

April 1803

LIZZIE DROPPED her black shawl on the kitchen table. For the sake of economy, she had just given up attending Madame Bonnet's Academy. Why devote hours to costly study now that she spoke French, played music, and wasted time in watercolor painting? Or so her Aunt Peg had declared. The Irishwoman's own education was so thin she could barely read a signpost.

The French Revolution had driven Madame Bonnet to refugee into England, hidden at the bottom of a fishing boat, under a catch of cod. She scrambled to make a living, teaching deportment and the French language to girls whose families could afford to spend a small amount on their daughter's education. Madame taught her young charges charming manners, to walk, talk, and get in and out of a carriage with grace. William Trumpet's sprightly daughter was brighter and more naturally graceful than the other girls. Madame took pleasure in discussions with her clever student, lending Lizzie books and music to enjoy.

"How did the old aristocrat take your news?" Peg wanted to know.

"Sadly. Madame gave me a copy of her Rules for Young Ladies."

"That and a shilling will keep us in salt all summer."

"Longer." Lizzie shook her cloth purse to make the coins clink.

"She also returned half my tuition."

"She charged too much in the first place," Peg chided, washing dirt off a bunch of carrots from the garden. Lizzie didn't want to hear Peg's opinions of the mercenary French just then. *My beloved Auntie is like a splinter sometimes, little, brittle and sharp.*

She stole into the drawing room to sit on the loveseat next to her dozing father, and opened Madame's paper-bound book to translate the French inscription. *For Elizabeth Trumpet, my best student. Affectionaely, Françoise Bonnet.* There would be no more talks with the intrepid Madame about the world and its beauties. Lizzie already missed her teacher, and longed for the sweet hours she treasured with her mother. How merrily they'd danced together the old Irish steps. With a rush of grief, she wrapped her arms around William.

Aunt Peg's crow-like voice called out from the kitchen. "Toby Carey, the old character actor, came to call. Do you remember him? Left a bottle of wine and three shillings wrapped up with a little cheese."

"Did you accept the money, Aunt?" Lizzie was about to lecture her relative for taking charity, a token of defeat, when someone knocked at the front door.

She opened it to see a blaze of tangerine plumes framing a pretty and confident face.

Standing outside was a woman, resplendent in a military-cut pelisse of naccarat velvet and sporting a helmet-shaped hat feathered like a Roman soldier's. "We have not been formally introduced, Miss Trumpet." Her smiling lips were full as ripe peaches. "My name is Octavia Onslow."

Lizzie was thunderstruck. *This woman—cause of my mother's misery—my father's whore!*

Onslow was fashionably called a Cyprian, an allusion to the natives of Cyprus, that delightful Isle of Venus. Her personal delights included a sensuous body, humor, and masses of coppery hair. For some years the large-spirited demi-rep had been supported by William Trumpet, but only partially. She had contracts with several men who made appointed visits—Wednesday mornings for a prominent brewer,

Saturday afternoons with a Whig scrivener—and, as infatuation waxed and waned, the catalogue of admirers changed. During her most triumphant season, she'd kept a box at the opera costing two hundred guineas. This spring, she had the rent of a shiny green cabriolet for driving through London's Hyde Park, where feminine splendor could be shown off and fresh acquaintances enticed. She was past being a new face, but men could talk to Octavia and she was canny enough to never look bored. William Trumpet was the least boring man she'd known, so talented and filled with pent-up sexual energy. Octavia favored him with special rates and a singular place in her heart.

"I sincerely ask your pardon for not finding a proper person to present me. Pray accept my condolences upon the death of your beloved mother." She proffered a large ivory calling-card, the size suitable for ladies, with her name and address engraved in rose ink. She waited, gloved hand outstretched, looking directly into Lizzie's eyes, so like William's, knowing her presence was inappropriate, knowing the girl must be remembering William in her bed. A distant meadowlark warbled while Octavia's feathers danced against the black crepe still darkening the door. Finally, Lizzie took the card.

"Miss Onslow."

"When I saw that Mr. Trumpet had been replaced in two plays at Covent Garden, I inquired after him at the theatre. I was informed that your father had experienced a debilitating fall." Lizzie said nothing. "Miss Trumpet, William means a great deal to me. Please, what is his condition?"

"His condition is serious." Lizzie was tight-lipped.

"I am grieved to hear it. May I see him, if just for a moment?"

"Papa is not dressed, Miss Onslow. I think he would not wish to be seen."

"Of course. Well, please tell him he is not forgotten." Octavia turned to go.

"Wait." Lizzie wished to do the right thing. Onslow engaged in "criminal conversation" for a living. Jessie and Aunt Peg would have directed her straight to hell. *But she seems truly concerned for my father. How many are?* Ignoring her own discomfort, Lizzie opened the door. "Please, come this way, Miss Onslow." A perfume of flowers and musk enriched the air as the beauty entered the room where William now spent his days.

The handsome actor's face expressed some inner conflict, his posture slumped and hopeless, like a character he might be playing, instead of the straight-backed vigorous man he had always been.

Octavia moved to the loveseat and sat down. "Dear William," she said tenderly, taking his hand and smoothing the long fingers. She spoke about missing his performances at the theatre and longing to see him on stage again.

A little hiss in the hallway turned Lizzie round to find Aunt Peg gesturing in pantomime that their visitor must be thrown out or perhaps murdered. Just as vigorously, Lizzie waved her aunt back to the kitchen. Her father raised his face to the dazzlingly-dressed woman at his side. His spine straightened. *He must see her*, Lizzie thought, *how will he respond?*

William's hand pulled out of Octavia's grasp. "My dear," he whispered in the rough sound of someone who had not spoken in days. Lizzie gasped with relief. *His enunciation is perfect, the words not even slurred.*

Octavia opened her arms to embrace William, but he tightened the wrapping of his dressing gown and rose to his feet. "Hold just there, as you are," he ordered and walked unsteadily to the center of the room, paused, then pointed grandly towards Octavia saying,

"'It is the east and Juliet is the sun.
Arise, fair sun, and kill the envious moon
Who is already sick and pale with grief
That thou her maid art far more fair than she.'"

He moved to Octavia, touched the coppery curls on her neck, and looked deep into her eyes. "This is not my Juliet." He glanced around uncertainly. "Wrong play. I am in the wrong play. So sorry." He shook his head in confusion and sat down.

"Papa!" Lizzie rushed to her father. "Papa, nothing is wrong. You are better and Miss Onslow has come to pay a call." She knelt at his knees. "This isn't a play. Talk to us, Papa, please." But William took no notice.

52

Lizzie was both jealous that he had spoken to this stranger and immensely relieved that he had spoken at all. "Miss Onslow, those were the first words out of my father's mouth since his seizure," she said in a low intense voice. "I was afraid he had lost the power of speech; this means his intellectuals are still intact. I'm grateful to you, more than grateful." Then, speaking more loudly, "Papa, is it not kind of this lady to visit you?"

He looked away from the women. Octavia went to the fireplace and beckoned Lizzie to join her. "Miss Trumpet, may I seek a doctor in London who could treat your father? Or do you have a physician?"

"We do not," Lizzie said, feeling inept and exposed. "The high fees of a physician are temporarily beyond our means."

"I'm sure your care is most comforting to William, but there may be medicinals you know nothing of that might speed his recovery. I would be honored to pay all doctors' fees for whatever treatment and physic is necessary."

"I thank you for the offer, Miss Onslow, but...."

"I wish to help. Your father has been a great friend to me."

The true meaning of that speech stabbed at Lizzie's heart. Deciding she must stand up to this intimidating stranger, she replied very civilly, "The words he spoke just now I take for a good sign. I am optimistic he will improve. I shall ask my father himself what he wants done."

After a moment, Octavia smiled. "You were very kind to receive me, Miss Trumpet. I shall be going." She wiped under her eye. "Thank you for the Shakespeare, William. It was beautiful." With the propriety of a sister, she kissed his forehead in farewell.

The two women walked outside to Duncan Terrace where Noddy and some stable boys from Mantino's Livery were gazing enviously at the large yellow wheels of the Cyprian's expensive cabriolet.

"You know where I live, Miss Trumpet. Again I say, I am ready to help."

Noddy and the stable hands fell over themselves helping Octavia into her rig. Watching her drive away, Lizzie was in a perfect stew. Her father had momentarily awakened from his silent melancholy. *Does he love this creature? Is Miss Onslow and her fine feathers what he needs? But she is....*

To stop her mind from charging on, Lizzie slammed the front door shut and announced to the face of the tall case clock, "Whatever she is...Papa spoke. Good for him." She looked at her father, so diminished and changed in his big chair. So unable to care for her. "For the rest of it, we must somehow help ourselves."

Knotting up her hair in a black ribbon, Lizzie began her third rummage through the house, praying for something valuable to turn up, not neglecting William's prop box, her mother's apron pockets in the clothes press, and the pages of every book on every shelf. From a bound copy of Garrick's version of Hamlet, a grand-looking document had fallen out. It proved to be William's large investment in a failed road-building scheme.

"Your da is the only man in England to lose money on roads," Aunt Peg hooted. This came after a long tirade against "that brazen Babylon whore coming here in her jaunty cart" and many recollections of how William had always been "a vain, improvident, adulterous fool altogether."

"Enough! Enough, Aunt!" Lizzie yelled out from the piles of books and play manuscripts, strewn around her in the salon. "Please speak no more unless you have something helpful to say."

"Here! Here's something." The old woman limped to her niece, a leather saddlebag in hand. "It was on a peg in the kitchen all this time, under his greatcoat."

Lizzie opened the flaps in a rush.

"A pound note. There's the beginning of fortune." Peg sniffed.

Lizzie dumped out the rest: a razor wrapped in a handkerchief, tooth powder, a folded review from *The Times*, riding gloves, and a dark blue canvas-bound ledger, tucked full of loose papers. All bills of accounts owed. To Grillon's Hotel for the keeping of rooms, twenty pounds. To a Bond Street silversmith for the bowl William had given Jessie as a birthday gift, fifteen pounds, and overdue for a twelve-month. Dues to the Thalia Club, thirty pounds, unpaid. To Berry

Brothers for a case of claret they had drunk long ago, ten pounds. On and on, each item haphazardly entered in William's distinctive hand. There was even a notation for Dick Wilson: owed, one crown, or the price of a dinner.

"So much debt." Lizzie began to shake with dread. All together it came to more than three hundred pounds—a hopeless burden. She felt the weight of it dropping on her shoulders. The blue ledger was proof of poverty. *How could Papa—so masterful, so mighty in his confidence—have let this happen?* "Harris might forgive what was owed, but these strangers and merchants will not, once they know Papa is off the roster at Covent Garden. Couldn't these people make 'common cause' and take Longsatin House? Take away our home?"

"Or lock William up in debtor's prison. An example to his kind for flying too high," Peg had to say.

The thought of her helpless father in Fleet Prison or the Marshalsea drove Lizzie to her feet in fear, crossing and re-crossing the Turkish carpet. All she could imagine was catastrophe. Back and forth, back and forth.

Peg sat down at the mahogany table, uncorked the wine from Toby Carey, and poured out two glasses. "I see you're on fire to do something, Lizzie. It's your nature to take action."

"I shall use my tuition money from Madame Bonnet to make everyone a token payment."

"Piddling."

The letter to America, telling Mr. and Mrs. Trombetta of Jessie's passing was in the post. Hoping not to frighten her grandparents, Lizzie had written that her father was resting from theatre work. Any reply would take three months to reach England, so no immediate help could be expected from Charleston.

"I just don't know how we are going to get on, Auntie."

"I can sell eggs from the chickens, greens from the garden in summer. If Boozel doesn't go dry, we still share her milk with the Mantinos. Not a chance of starving," Peg said in her most positive way. "And you could take those ear-bobs from your grandma to the pawn."

"Never! Bite your tongue." Lizzie considered, then cocked her head. "Could we let a room?"

"A lodger? Yes, with your mother gone to Jesus, I suppose we can shift a space upstairs." The old woman rubbed her knuckles. "We could put out a dressmaker sign."

Lizzie cast her mind over the work a female could do that paid wages. There were factories all over London. *A ropewalk? A brickyard?* Most laborers began at a tender age, the poorest of the poor. An untrained young woman going into such a hell would earn pennies, no more. *Find a position in a Dame's School, teaching small children? Or tutor for a family?* Decent enough, but unproven girls, such as she, lived with their employers, working for room and board, making a pittance in wages. *And what if next week Papa became himself again, as King George did so long ago?* She left the wine untouched.

Aunt Peg tapped a fingernail to her glass, remembering her working days. On the road between Belfast and Londonderry stood a traveler's inn run by Peg's flint-hearted brother-in-law, Hugh McGinty. He made his way by cheating his customers and grinding his wife and children into slave-like servitude. Of his fourteen offspring, pretty little Jessie was the only child with some spark in her soul. Peg was already a widow then, earning dribs and drabs of money sewing clothes. To give her favorite niece some joy in life, Peg had introduced her to the magic of theatre, dragging Jessie off to see the performances of every traveling troupe. One night, *The Tempest* was presented in the McGinty Inn courtyard. Jessie lost her heart to the handsome actor playing Ferdinand, nineteen-year-old William Trumpet. When Jessie ran away with him, Peg believed she had started it all. Years later she, too, escaped the McGinty Inn, and came to live with her married niece in England.

As though Saint Bridget were whispering in her ear, an idea sparked. "Listen child, I know what to do. Dress to look adorable and present yourself at the Sadler's Wells Theatre. They'll be putting together the summer spectacle now."

Lizzie looked dumbfounded. "Sadler's Wells? Auntie, that place is for acrobats and dancing dogs."

She had never been allowed near the Wells, because of its rowdy reputation. Secretly, Georgie had once crept into a show and enthralled his sister with what he had seen: bawdy singers, a knife-thrower, dancing girls and, most wonderful, the brave-hearted collie *Moustache* leading a troupe of performing dogs.

Drury Lane and Covent Garden audiences, though noisy, were completely out-shouted by the unbridled behavior of Sadler's Wells crowds. In the rural suburb of Islington, spectators were gleefully raucous and sexually uninhibited. The ambience was so casually iniquitous the Wells management offered escorts after dark, to conduct patrons in safety to the center of London.

"Besides, Aunt, if Covent Garden refused me, where they know me for William Trumpet's daughter, what would I do at the Wells? Be a barmaid?"

"I'm certain you're superior to all those acrobats and dogs you mention, but the fact is you've never walked across any stage except in your imagination. Your mother was so set against your being an actress she stopped you playing a fairy in a Christmas panto when you were but three. I remember well. What a lot of screaming that led to!"

Lizzie could just recall the screaming, getting slapped by Jessie and slapping her mother back. She quickly dismissed the recollection. "Papa said Sadler's is infamous, no better than a raree-show with music."

"And just down the road, too. As good a place as any to learn performing, and isn't that what you want?"

Lizzie had hidden her dreams of the stage from her mother, but Peg was not so easily misled. "I have no stage training."

"They'll train you! You are young and pretty as a petunia!" Peg slapped the table. "Ye'll keep a smile on your face and your big yap shut. Look sharp and be willing. Not too willing, mind. The Wells is not quite a brothel, despite what happens in the bushes every night. But that's life, darlin'. Men will take their cocks out in a lively atmosphere."

Lizzie had heard such salty talk from her aunt before, but never in regards to herself. It was sobering. But exciting. "And if I fail to be chosen, no one will ever know?"

"You'll be chosen, darlin', if ye but try." Peg put her nose close to Lizzie's. "Or shall I tell Noddy to make a dressmaker sign right now and spare you an encounter with those clowns and dancin' dogs?"

"Subtlety, Auntie. There's no word for it in Irish, I imagine?" Lizzie considered what Georgie, stiff in his uniform, and Jessie, cold in her grave, would say. Then she cast a glance at William, all silent in his chair. He had played the King of the Fairies in that panto when she was three. *Papa's debts must be paid, God help us. And if God doesn't help? This may be fortune's way of making me an actress.*

The atmosphere had changed from desperation to celebration. Performance was in the air. William felt it. He watched his daughter, now in lilac, balancing on a footstool while Peg let down the hem of Jessie's frock, the one he loved.

Peg struggled up from her knees, gasping, "The bodice needs to be lower, with a stay in the center to show off each boosy. I'll do the sewing and the pressing at first light, so it will be ready for you to wear tomorrow morning. Be there early to introduce yourself." With a worn hand, the older woman toasted her niece. In the last half hour, they had shared the whole bottle of Toby Carey's wine.

Lizzie twirled around her father. "Do you like me in Mother's lilac, Papa?"

William gave her a loving look and wondered if he would have a part in tomorrow's play.

Chapter Six

April 1803

"'ERE COMES Lizzie! In a tizzy!" shouted little Simon, a "sweeper," whose trade was helping pedestrians cross the street. At the confluence of rutty roads that comprised the Angel, he carried customers on his ten-year-old back in all weathers for tips. The boy lifted his crushed-in round hat and waited for a nod. "I volunteer...to help, my dear."

On this sunny, momentous morning, Lizzie had planned to walk the path alongside the New River from her home to the theatre, but the drainage ditch at Goswell Street was full of running muck and too wide to jump in her fine, narrow frock. "I only have a farthing, Simon."

"A farthing it shall be. Dry feet I guarantee," he responded, with a winning smile, only a shade spoiled by the green decay of his teeth. Simon plodded his pretty customer through the mud and horse-debris to the drier side of Islington High Street.

Lizzie turned into tree-lined Myddleton Place and approached the Sadler's Wells Theatre, retying the bow of her bonnet strings, then touching her grandmother's earrings. The tall stone building was quite plain, more like a country house than a temple of entertainment. In the morning light, dappled and golden under the budding poplars, the old place looked tranquil, and the unattended front door was ajar.

The springs of water Richard Sadler had discovered beneath his vegetable garden in 1683 were said to have medicinal properties. At least Sadler said so, attempting to take monetary advantage of a soggy bottom. He testified the waters would treat every malady he could think of: dropsy, jaundice, scurvy, green sickness, and distempers to which females are liable—ulcers, fits of the mother, virgin's fever and hypochondriacal distemper. As added inducement to those not troubled by virgin's fever, the enterprising farmer opened the Sadler's Wells Musick House for concertizing. London's lower classes had been crowding in for generations, every spring when the weather turned warm.

Lizzie slipped into the theatre and, in the gloom, noticed dilapidation everywhere. The plain wooden boxes were kicked in places, the worn chair-cushions sadly ripped and filthy. With no one around to direct her, Lizzie sat on a bench at the rear where the smell of spilt wine was strongest. A pear-shaped man of thirty-and-a-bit stood on the edge of the fore-stage, greeting a motley assemblage of types gathered in the pit.

"Top of the day to you all. Awfully glad you're here. The dear old Wells is under new management, which is myself, Charles Dibdin. I have purchased this venerable theatre, which shall be shortly tarted up with fresh paint and new upholstery, for a glorious premiere on the eleventh of May. The title of my first extravaganza is *New Brooms* and today, I will begin hiring my cast. Show me what you can do, ladies and gentlemen; I shall create around your talents. Should you require musical accompaniment, Maestro Carlo Tomassi plays everything in all keys." He gestured to a rotund, prematurely white-haired man of sanguine complexion seated at the pianoforte stage right. The maestro played a little trill on the higher keys. "Right, then." Dibdin stepped down into the pit, taking his seat at a candlelit table.

"We shall see everyone, starting with you, sir." He nodded to a bow-legged man who bounded to the stage, handing a sheet of music to Tomassi. The eager fellow pulled numerous beets and rutabagas from his capacious pockets, juggling them while singing a song about smoke and oakum, which Lizzie took to be a ballad of Navy life. He closed with a somersault, vaulting into Mr. Tomassi at the piano with such velocity, the maestro was knocked off his stool, giving a cry of high-pitched alarm.

Charles Dibdin's manner was not at all like the men Lizzie had known from the royal patent theatres. He lacked their grandeur and pomp. Instead, she was reminded of a workman, a well-prepared master mason, say, building a wall. He showed courtesy to the amateurs, which gave her hope. She was awed by his ability to decide in seconds whether those auditioning were usable or not.

"Strongest lungs in England, I dare say," this, to a barrel-chested street singer, "but if you can't stay on pitch, you're no use to me. Next!"

The dancing twin brothers, Messrs. Horace and Morris, were told, "Delicious shoe music. I adore that toe and heel. Ten shillings a week. Each. See Mr. Grudgely. Next!"

An ample woman, enormously wigged, heaved herself to the very lip of the stage to perform a naughty lyric a capella.

"There was a young chap from Dundee
Who wedded an ape for a fee.
The result was most horrid,
All bum and no forehead...."

"Stop, stop! My little flower, you shall have a featured role!" The wig was pulled off and kisses were exchanged. Lizzie learned this was the manager's wife, Mary Dibdin, a formidable lady, tellingly pregnant.

A compact young man with a comical rolling walk introduced himself as "Just Joe."

Dibdin shouted, "Sir! You do not audition. Ladies and gentlemen, this is the inimitable Joseph Grimaldi, England's most famous clown, so daring and spontaneous. We are proud to have an artist of Mr. Grimaldi's expertise in our company." Dibdin applauded respectfully and all the hopefuls joined in. Lizzie had seen Grimaldi's caricature on playbills where he looked quite lunatic. In person, he struck Lizzie as modestly shy.

By one o'clock, the roster included Jack Bologna, a rubbery-legged fellow known for his Harlequins, Mr. Bradbury and His Precocious Piglets, Signor Cipriani, who could climb up the proscenium arch, run across the boxes and down the other side while singing in Italian, and a score of rather forward ladies, many of whom had already experienced long hard years in the chorus.

A boy, whom Lizzie judged to be around eight years old, had been sitting near her. Scooting closer on the bench, the freckled child doffed his cap. His spiky red hair popped up like a brush. "Say, miss, you'd do well to get your arse up there. All the places'll be taken."

"Well, you're cheeky."

"I'm Master Menage, and I'll be playing all the skin parts."

"Skin?"

"You know, animals."

"I didn't know."

"Oh, well, most actors and whatnots get their starts dressed as monkeys. This yer first time?"

Lizzie nodded. "I'm not even sure how I'm going to audition."

"Oh, just strut a bit. Old Dibs likes young ladies." The redheaded boy leered precociously up at her breasts. "Go on now," he whispered.

Feeling cold as ice, Lizzie removed her bonnet, shook up her curls, and pulled down her neckline. *If this child—this imp—can do it, what am I cowering in the back for?* She walked to the stage steps, and Dibdin waved her on. The chorus ladies had flirted and preened. Too terrified for that, Lizzie attempted dignity and, speaking in a voice as stentorian as her father's in *Macbeth*, announced, "I am Elizabeth Trumpet and I can do anything you ask." Someone in the darkness snorted a laugh.

Dibdin sat back in his hard rush chair, studying the girl in lilac, her athletic figure slender in the hips with a high budding bosom, her face a girlish oval with round brows and truly beautiful eyes. Innocent, gently bred, this young lady was bright as a lamp up there. "I ask your age."

"Rising sixteen."

"Can you sing, Trumpet?"

"I can."

"Do so."

She cast a panicked look to Maestro Tomassi who was obviously enjoying her audacity.

"John Dowland, my dear?" A nod. "Come Again Sweet Love"? A quicker nod. "Soprano?"

"I think."

The maestro tinkled a brief romantic introduction, and she began to sing.

"Come again: Sweet love doth now invite
Thy graces that refrain to do me due delight,
To see, to hear, to touch, to kiss, to die
With thee again in sweetest sympathy."

Her pitch was true and the voice had a shimmering lovely timbre.

Dibdin made a note. "Thank you. Not nearly loud enough, though, for this theatre. Do you know what it means, 'To touch, to kiss, to die with thee again'? It is passion! Men and women together!"

"I understand the words, sir." Lizzie shifted her weight like a pony waiting to perform its trick.

Do you now? "Keep them in mind. Dance, do you?"

"I've never lacked for partners."

"Not the ballroom. The ballet."

"No ballet, sir."

"A disadvantage. Do you have any talent? A particular skill you've perfected?"

"Skill? I, uh...I fence quite well."

"Fence...did you say?"

"Yes, sir. My brother, from the Royal Military College, has been my personal instructor."

"Well now. Let us see the results of this tutoring." Dibdin clapped his hands sharply. "Mrs. Bloore! Put this girl in fleshings and something to make all visible."

"Right, your nibs," a Cockney voice answered from backstage.

Ten minutes later, Lizzie was glad of the protective mask and tipped weapon in her hand, for she never had been so naked in public before. Mrs. Bloore had put her in tights and a pink transparent skirt. A tiny red bodice was tied below her bosom instead of a protective pad. Called to center stage, she raised the rusty foil to salute the manager and a muscular acrobat Dibdin had matched against her.

"*En garde!*"

Combat commenced and when she bested the acrobat, a second man sprang out of the wings. Neither could get near the red bodice for a touch as a crowd of the curious looked on. Grimaldi appeared with a borrowed blade, but Lizzie continued advancing and dominating, thrusting and parrying against them all. Soon the whole assembly was shouting and applauding her.

Clapping loudly himself, Dibdin cried out, "Trumpet! Cease! Don't kill my actors!"

Lizzie froze. "Sir, I never...."

"Compose yourself, Trumpet. Carlo says he can train that voice. You're in the chorus. Eight shillings a week. See Mr. Grudgely. Next!"

Lizzie's heart, already beating like a drum, now thundered in her ears. She bobbed a curtsy. Leaving the stage, she realized again she was dressed almost exclusively in joy.

Mr. Grudgely put a cap on her elation. Lizzie discovered Dibdin's money manager shaking with chilblain under a long woolen coat, deep in the dark stage wings. It was not his style to enthuse over gross amateurs, however eager and curly-haired. The underbred, owl-eyed fellow regarded her from behind a small cash box on his desk.

"Good day, sir. My name is Trumpet," she said, with a try at self-assurance.

"I heard. Having a lark, are we? First job, is it?"

"Well, yes. I was enrolled...."

"Six shillings a week." Grudgely rubbed his cold, red nose.

"Excuse me, sir, but Mr. Dibdin said eight."

"Mmh." Grudgely put pen to ledger with ink-stained fingers. "Have you any questions of a business nature?"

"Shall I be paid for the weeks of rehearsal?"

"Of course not. What would the theatre be if every ignorant

novice was paid to rehearse? You will receive wages at the end of your first performance week, Saturday morning, along with the rest of them."

"Thank you, sir." Chastened, Lizzie asked, "Shall I be needed any more today?"

"Certainly! Immediately! Be off with you."

Dismissed, she scurried to put her clothes back on.

Lizzie redressed in the closet Mrs. Bloore had provided, rank with the smell of male sweat permeating the old costumes hanging around her. She tried not to inhale. And hurried.

Reticule in hand, she emerged from the stench and was searching backstage for someone to tell her what to do next, when a great crash and horrible shriek came from the front of the theatre. All in sight rushed towards the main entrance. Lizzie tentatively followed them out into the sun-flooded street.

A huge delivery wagon, top-heavy with wine bottles in hampers, had fallen over on its side, trapping a white-faced man beneath. The wagon's mules had been pulled to the ground where they were scrabbling to get up, braying and kicking wildly. A yellow dog barked ceaselessly. Dibdin yelled for a piece of lumber to help lift the wagon off the man. The panicked theatre personnel pushed and pulled and got in each other's way.

"Lockwood's dead, crushed like a bloomin grape," Jack Bologna was saying.

"Not dead, sir," Grimaldi told Dibdin, cradling the pinned man's head.

"He jumped up on my load and tipped it over, stupid bugger," the driver put in, trying to raise the vehicle and slipping in the spilt wine puddling around the victim.

Amid all the yelling bystanders, Lizzie was praying for the unlucky Lockwood's life when she noticed a tall man running towards the toppled wagon. As he approached, the man grew taller and taller. He was young and brunette. Before she could tell more, he had reached the melee and put his shoulder against the wagon planks. Spreading his arms and planting his feet like Atlas, the man heaved and the wagon rose a few inches.

Dibdin screamed, "Everyone together!" All nearby took hold and lifted as one. Grimaldi pulled Lockwood out through the broken bottles, and cried, "He lives!" A cheer went up.

The manager caught Master Menage by the arm. "Fetch Dr. LaSalles. Run, boy."

Attention turned to the very tall, dark stranger, smiling then as Dibdin shook his hand. "God was good in sending you today, sir. You saved a life. What is your name, sir, and may we offer you...some wine?"

The tall man began speaking in a passionate manner, gesturing to his heart, the wagon, and the semi-conscious Lockwood.

"I don't understand him. It's Italian, I believe. Who can translate?" the manager asked.

Grimaldi admitted to no skill with Italian, despite his name. Signor Cipriani, the human fly, had buzzed off for the moment. The yellow dog had parched his throat with barking; he slipped between Dibdin and the stranger to lap the wasted wine at their feet.

In all the hurly-burly, Lizzie had remained quiet, but hearing her grandparents' language, she dared to touch the sleeve of this giant Good Samaritan and say in Italian, "*Signore*, we are so grateful." Then, smiling up into the shining eyes of the robust hero of the hour, she continued, "How are you called, *signore*?"

"Belzoni, *signorina*," he answered. "Giovanni Battista Belzoni."

"And you are from Italy?"

"*Sì, sì*. Padua. I am just arrived in London. I look for work."

Lizzie turned to Dibdin and spoke confidentially. "This man seeks employment, sir."

"For a new-hired chorus-girl, Trumpet, you are unusually helpful," the empresario responded. "Tell Signor Belzoni he has a job at my theatre, if he wants it."

While Lizzie and Belzoni spoke, Dr. LaSalles arrived to bind up Lockwood's broken ribs. Dibdin was assured his employee had merely been knocked senseless.

"His most general condition," Grimaldi remarked.

Dibdin ordered the victim carried inside and everyone back to their duties.

Lizzie caught the manager's eye again. "Signor Belzoni is eternally grateful, sir. He wants the job. He says you are *molto gentile*."

"Can he sing?"

Lizzie didn't bother to confer. "He is Italian, sir. What do you want Signor Belzoni to do?"

"I'm thinking."

"While you are thinking, sir, I suspect this man has not eaten in a long while."

"Ah." The producer fumbled in a deep pocket to pull out a coin. "Take him up to the Old Queen's Head and buy him a sustaining meal and a bite for yourself. Food is never provided by the management, but you both have done me a service." Dibdin waved them off, adding, "Return with my change."

Belzoni was a tall man indeed, standing six-foot-eight with no boots on. As they entered the Old Queen's Head, his ear grazed the weathered pub-sign. Lizzie explained the flaking face of the woman who looked like a man, was supposed to be Elizabeth Tudor, Queen of England.

"Ah! You are named after her?"

"No, I am named after my grandmother Trombetta, *la mia nonna*. She taught me your language."

The dirty old pot-house had never charmed Lizzie before, but following the transforming events of the morning, and in the company of her talkative companion, it seemed nearly cosmopolitan. She explained Dibdin was paying for their meal in gratitude for rescuing the theatre barkeep. Belzoni devoured three pies of spring pork and downed two mugs of porter. One pie sufficed for Lizzie, who was mindful of returning with that expected change and too excited to eat much.

"First, *signore*, how may I address you?"

"Giovanni," he said, collecting a crumb from his plate. "*bella*, how is it that a well-bred young lady like you is engaged by a theatre?"

"The circumstances of life. I confess the eventful hours just past had almost driven them from my mind. You see, a few weeks ago, my dear mother died and my father, one of England's foremost actors, became ill. Until he is well, I must work."

"Ah," he responded gently. "You have had sorrows, Lisabetta."

"But it is marvelous for me to be engaged at the Wells today. I shall follow in my father's footsteps. This was always my dream."

"I also help my family, but my father is only a simple barber with many children. My mamma gets great pains in the head worrying about all of us. How I love her."

"And you can still tell her you love her." She swallowed the lump in her throat. "How fortunate you are."

Speaking her grandmother's language to this enormous fellow was testing Lizzie's concentration, for Belzoni was a beauty of a man. His glowing olive skin, touched with the sun's umber, covered round muscles that stretched his buff shirt and grey breeches to bursting. A worn coat was thrown across one huge masculine shoulder with a careless air. Sadly, for the son of a barber, his curly hair wanted trimming, but his frequent smile was full of sweetness.

"Are you a barber, too?" she asked.

"My father taught me, but I want more from life than clipping beards, so I model myself on the great men of history. To improve my prospects, my mamma sent me off to Rome." Belzoni gestured for a fourth pie. "I lived at a monastery in Trastevere, where the brothers taught me the beautiful science of waters—hydraulics. I labored repairing fountains all over the Holy City. When the *Grande Armée* of Napoleon invaded and took over our monastery for a barracks, I fled. To escape serving in the French army, I walked across the Alps. Now, at twenty-five years, I am ready to begin my English life."

Lizzie was charmed by his story and his optimism. "You have begun. Magnificently." She wanted to hear more of Rome, but feared being late for her new career. "We must go, Giovanni. Mr. Dibdin is expecting us. 'Promptness is the first rule of the theatre,' Papa always says." Lizzie called for the bill and paid. "*signore*, you are now part of a theatre company. *Bravo!*"

He shrugged. "I do not seek to be an actor."

"Be encouraged, *signore*. There is no better calling in the wide world."

"And what will Signor *Deebdeen* make of me?"

"Something big."

They roared together in happy innocence.

When they rose to leave, Belzoni's physique drew whistles from arriving customers, but he seemed used to such things and walked out proudly. A carriage splattered past. The giant easily lofted Lizzie across a puddle without a by-your-leave.

She caught her breath, surprised by such effortless strength and gave a giddy wave to little Simon, who was plainly envious.

Lizzie and Belzoni entered cobblestoned Myddleton Place, where boys were fishing in the New River. Atop the theatre steps, the yellow dog, besotted with wine and afternoon sun, lay on his back, paws splayed in the air.

"*Ubriaco!*" they both shouted gleefully as they stepped around the dog. "He is drunk!"

They found Charles Dibdin at his candlelit table, writing and humming to himself. Lizzie dared to interrupt only after the manager paused to sneeze prodigiously three times.

"Dust from the curtains," he muttered, taking his five shillings of change from Lizzie's hand. "Tell the Italian Hercules to find Mr. Snap, the under-carpenter. He can help him uncover some old flats and prepare them for painting. The Walls of Jericho will do nicely for a Humpty Dumpty song I have in mind."

"*Grazie, signorina. Arrivederci.*" Belzoni bowed to his benefactors and took his leave.

"Did I call him the Italian Hercules? Oh, I like that." Dibdin scribbled a note amongst his tatty papers. He drew out a red handkerchief and prepared to sneeze again, but first passed his watering eyes tenderly over Lizzie's figure. "Miss Trumpet, you will be here long hours in rough conditions. In future, wear old clothes for rehearsals. Now take a lesson in stage-singing with Maestro Carlo before the chorus sitz-spiel."

Thrilled that her real duties were beginning and filled with trepidation, Lizzie sought out Tomassi at the corner of the stage.

The dirty theatre fairly buzzed, a hive of activity. Men were cleaning the house-chandeliers that had been lowered to the floor, while others struggled to hang the venerable velvet curtains. The smell of casein paint permeated the air. The "shoe music" twins, cinnamon-skinned and identical, were high stepping on the apron to get the feel of the stage. Behind them, the platinum-haired maestro composed orchestra parts with a large quill at furious speed, swiveling back and forth on a stool between the pianoforte keyboard and a table covered with music paper. Somewhere, out-of-sight hammers were pounding a ragged tattoo.

"Welcome to 'Bedlam on the Boards,'" Carlo said in a basso profundo like the voice of God. Then, in another voice entirely, a kind and confiding one, "Your first lesson is to concentrate, my darling. Ignore the noise and the smells. Just listen to me."

Eager to do well, Lizzie was all attention, standing straight as her brother Georgie on parade. She learned she had a diaphragm just below her lungs that was there to support her breath. The maestro demonstrated, moving his vast belly in and out like a bellows. Lizzie sucked in so much air and dust in the first five minutes, she felt quite faint. After the deep breathing came simple scales.

"Keep those lovely shoulders down, and no floppin-titzin," Carlo barked, but Lizzie distinctly heard a man call out, "*Brava, Lisabetta!*" It was Belzoni, single-handedly carting one of Mr. Snap's twenty-foot flats across the stage to the paint shop.

Maestro Carlo was bubbly as a bee when the company assembled for the chorus rehearsal. Everybody sang to boost volume: acrobats, clowns, actors of no renown, Young Master Menage, rough backstage men who would fill in during crowd scenes, and dancing girls Lizzie classified as mutton dressed as lamb.

The music was all new-composed, but old in style: jolly little point-songs and choruses about how brave the English nation was, and to hell with Old Boney. Carlo had warned Lizzie not to push too hard, but excitement overtook caution, and she wailed herself hoarse by the last song.

In the front window of Longsatin House, Miss Pegeen stood holding a lighted taper and peering out into the falling darkness, watching for the niece she loved. *She's been gone all the day; surely they must have taken her on.*

The old lady was glowing brighter than her candle, more animated by the dream of glory than the pay. She imagined herself telling Mrs. Mantino the news. "Our Lizzie is going to sing and dance onstage at the Sadler's Wells. Won't that be the finest thing?"

During the long afternoon, Peg had baked a dish of custard to reward the girl for taking life in her two hands and dealing with it— whatever the outcome.

At last Lizzie appeared, rushing towards home, calling out, "I've done it! I'm in the company at the Wells!"

Lizzie spun her aunt about, dropped bonnet and reticule onto a chair, and ran to her Papa, seated behind a bowl of soup at the dining table. She kissed him and told the highlights of her day with such passion that nothing was comprehensible, but the gist was clear.

Flopping into a chair at the mahogany table, Lizzie trilled her thanks, plunged a spoon into Peg's golden pudding, eating and talking at *agitato* tempo. She proudly displayed her new music sheets. The wagon accident was reenacted and Belzoni impersonated, Charles Dibdin was a genius, and Carlo Tomassi the finest musician in all England.

Peg took in every word, interrupting once to question the theatrical genius of the Wells manager, but it was useless; Lizzie's experiences were too fresh and wonderful to be wilted by dry wit.

William had awaited his daughter's return, too. He followed her every move with his far-away composure and a pleased expression. When Lizzie bent to kiss him goodnight, she didn't notice the little tear in his loving eye.

Undressing before the mirror in her room, Lizzie appraised her new self, striking attitudes and brushing out her long, dark hair. The death and debts that had been so overwhelming yesterday were far from her mind. Then she spied Jessie's gown thrown across her chair. The hem was pulled out at the back and stained with wine. She rubbed furiously on the sullied dress. The shadow of loss engulfed the bright colors of her day. How could she have forgotten her mother, even for a moment?

When she stretched out on her narrow bed, guilt and triumph lay down beside her in a stream of tears that kept dropping in the dark. "Can you hear me, dearest Mama? Everything is changing. Papa is quite broken without you, so I have to be strong. I'm going to be in the theatre now. Don't be angry. Whatever I have to do, I'm still your daughter. I know you are watching. Pray for me."

Chapter Seven

M ay 11, 1803

"TIME TO tie on my talent," shrieked Pansy. "No secrets in the dressing room."

Lizzie watched the experienced dancer search through a cloth bag and pull out two pointy hollow mounds of *papier-mache* covered in flesh-toned linen.

"How they love me in these."

Good heavens, they're breasts, Lizzie realized, *and generous, too, if a bit rigid.*

"Give us a hand there, girlie, will ya?"

She helped as Pansy adjusted fabric ties and admired her long, enhanced torso in the little table mirror.

"You don't need extra help with your boosies, Trumpet. Be glad and learn to shake a bit o' tit."

She was trying to ignore the chatter in the crowded room and stay calm on her very first opening night.

At her first dance rehearsal, she had been vexed at herself for being slow to learn, feeling clumsy as Noddy and nearly as dim. The ladies of the chorus Lizzie had dismissed as mutton on the hoof were accomplished, tireless performers. Mr. Jimmy, who staged the endless dances across the sixty-foot-wide proscenium, placed the amateur Miss Trumpet well to the rear of any complicated maneuvers.

Her second day, Pansy had taken Lizzie aside, marking the steps and counting slowly. "It's one-and-two-and-three-four, one-two-three." The dancer's eyes were set close together and looked comic when she was most sincere. "Now say something in that rhythm to help you remember."

By afternoon, Lizzie was in step for the first time, chanting to herself, "Pansy wants a plum cake? Oh, yes please!" Her thighs twitched with exhaustion as she rubbed them and drank cup after cup of Sadler's well water, the only bonus she'd received from management so far. Never forgetting Dibdin had given her the job, Lizzie obeyed his commands with smiling grace.

"I see you admire the manager," Pansy whispered in her ear, as they tried on the pink-dyed tights called "fleshings" in Mrs. Bloore's fitting room. "Well, never get behind a locked door with old Charlie. Not unless you're ready for an 'impromptu,' as he calls it. Charlie's as fast at copulation as composition."

"Surely not," Lizzie whispered back, round-eyed. "Doesn't he have enough to do without playing favorites?"

"There's always time for sex, Trumpet. Ask any man."

"At his age, too. Does Mary Dibdin know about the impromptus?"

"After all their years together? She can't be blind." Pansy shook her head and shrugged. "But he keeps her onstage, though her best soprano years are far behind her. And another thing," she babbled on. "If Charlie writes you a good tune, when you learn to sing it bright and bold, expect Mary will take the song for herself. He always goes along. Old Charlie has to keep things smooth at home."

"Oh my. And she's increasing mightily, poor woman."

"Mary's no saint. See how she looks at Belzoni? She's as curious as the rest of us."

Dibdin made no favorite of Lizzie, but kept her doubly busy translating at Belzoni's rehearsals. She cheerfully explained stage business in Italian while the company waited. The strong man had been given so much to do that had he been less humble and pleasant, his fellow performers would have loathed him. The ways of these show folk confused him.

Escorting her home after a day of rehearsals, he inquired innocently, "Lisabetta, why have they dressed me in a yellow catskin and no breeches?"

"It's supposed to look like a lion's skin. One assumes cats are easier to catch."

"I look like a savage."

"The costume shows your muscles, Giovanni. It becomes you, like a classical hero." In his "wee nappy," Lizzie thought the robust man a memorable sight.

"Am I too poor to wear clothes? Mamma would be so ashamed."

"She will be proud that everyone in London admires your strength and soon you can send her money."

"Well, yes, she will like that."

Receiving so much advice from Pansy put Lizzie in a mood to give some herself, by way of a cautious suggestion. "Perhaps with your salary, you can buy new clothes that fit."

"Will you help me choose new clothes, Lisabetta?"

"I promise. And I know just the place to get them." The twilight chilled as they walked up Duncan Terrace. "Giovanni, three times today Mr. Dibdin asked that you smile. It's important that you look glad to be onstage."

"Smile like the clowns? Then I will have no dignity. I am a person of gravity, Lisabetta. I think thoughts and know the things in books."

"Well, smile because of the things you know. Smile like a king."

"Lisabetta, *mi capisce!* You understand me!"

"I understand we must do as they tell us to survive at the Wells."

"Sì, sì. I endure it, but you love every moment at that place. I don't need to know the English to understand that."

"Ah, *é vero!* Thank you for bringing me home." They had reached Longsatin House and she turned to say farewell.

"Lisabetta, your family, they are happy you are performing, too?"

"My aunt is. Papa is not well enough to tell, and my brother...."

Well, I haven't had the time to write him." Unwittingly, Belzoni had brought up a problem the girl had yet to face.

Tentatively, Lizzie dusted on some rouge with a hare's-foot brush from her father's stage kit. A dab of crimson to the lips completed her *maquillage*. Her hands were shaking too much to draw black around her eyes as Pansy had done. The doors had opened and the house wine was selling briskly. At six-thirty, the curtain would rise. The great buzzing sound of an excited audience taking their seats carried backstage to the half-dressed girls.

The evening would transform Miss Trumpet. Once on the stage, for even a single appearance, a woman was forever an actress, and no more a lady. Lizzie blithely dismissed this received wisdom. She had grown up hungering for the theatre, convinced that acting was wonderful and her father's profession exalted. Sadler's Wells was no playhouse. She understood full well her contribution to the show was less important than Lockwood's at the wine bar; still this was a stage, and in moments she would be on it.

"Beginners, please!" The chorus girls ran out of the dressing room to answer the call-boy's command.

Lizzie stopped breathing, frozen with nervous dread.

Pansy circled back and grabbed her hand. "Come on, Trumpet. Don't miss your own debut!"

Roger Sloane and his lively gang of tailors from the shop had purchased quantities of Lockwood's vintage. In the boxes, many an enthusiastic toast had already christened the new upholstery. As the insignificant house pianist concluded the tunes nobody in the jabbering crowd listened to, they pushed their way down front, onto a bench sagging with customers. Then Maestro Carlo paraded into the pit in a silver-sequined frock coat, leading the musicians of the orchestra carrying their instruments. Roger and the tailors whooped and cheered.

High up in the very front row of the one-shilling gallery seats sat Aunt Peg. William was securely tucked into his Longsatin bedchamber. Mrs. Mantino had been engaged to guard the staircase, should he decide to roam. Peg clutched her crucifix, praying to Saint Bridget to hold Lizzie in her holy hands this night.

The Sadler's Wells orchestra struck up a brassy tune and the curtains parted on a backdrop of Piccadilly. Jack Bologna, colorfully dressed as a broom vendor, opened the show singing,

"My brooms are new and, sirs, I ween
You'll all allow new brooms sweep clean."

The ladies of the chorus jigged onstage, literally sweeping their prop brooms, Lizzie the last in line.

"Fat 'frogs' in air balloons do rise,
But let them sweep what e'er they please,
'Tis Britain only sweeps the seas."

Lizzie could see the audience, swaying to the music, leaning towards the stage, two thousand of them crammed into four tiers of boxes and balconies. The human aroma was strong: old boots, unlaundered shirts, and beef gravy. They certainly smelt different from the Covent Garden customers, but their animal energy came pouring over the "float lights" at her feet. It was thrilling. Life, ah life indeed, and she a part of it, doing her steps as if born to them until on the exit she took one too wide and her face smashed into Pansy's broom. *Aiii! The pain!* But she jigged off in perfect step, smiling broadly, blinking her watering eye.

To a ruffle of drums, Sir John Bull pranced on. This symbol of British pluck was played by Grimaldi in a fat-suit. The war with France had been halted for months by the Peace of Amiens. Of course, it was no real peace, but rather a pause in conflict. Napoleon's shipyards were hammering together thousands of vessels for an invasion of England. Militia regiments were patrolling coastal towns, and the British people expected a great fight any day. Patriots in the house rose to their feet as Grimaldi bristled with bravado.

"John Bull is my name;
None my spirit can tame!

I'm upright and downright withal;
I laugh and grow fat,
Crack jokes and all that,
And live at old 'Liberty Hall.'"

"Liberty Hall!" shouted Roger. "That's us tonight, boys." The excited tailors, released from long hours of toil, were ready for anything. Roger was hosting his friends, who had been told by some wag that the girls in the show were available to do more than sing and dance to entertain a fellow. Young Sloane was as much an amateur as Lizzie at such spectacles. In his stimulated haze, he hadn't recognized her and had no notion her life had taken such a startling turn.

By the time John Bull was bowing off, a pretty whore joined the rowdy shop boys' party. The "dasher of the pave" spread herself invitingly across Turkolu's lap.

"This one is *vih stick g'bi*, built like a peanut." Turkolu chuckled, his sly hands taking the girl's measure from the ankles up.

Bradbury's Learned Pigs waddled onstage in strap-on spectacles. They rang musical chimes, tossed a ball to Carlo in the pit, counted to three by tapping their trotters, and exited to wild applause in a red wheel-barrow pushed by an Irish setter.

In the gallery, high above the performing pork, Aunt Peg asked a sober patron to read the playbill to her. Jack the Giant Killer was next, featuring, "for the first time on an English stage," Signori Belzoni. It was the first time on any stage for Lizzie, too, but her role was too lowly for the name Trumpet to appear in even the tiny print. The sight of Belzoni in a wild-man wig set the audience to screaming with pleasure. When he sang "Fee faw fum," his accent wasn't noticeable.

At the interval, Lockwood boomed from the bar, "Ladies, direct your minds to drinking." Those who had already slaked their thirst made for the famous bushes outside to answer the call of nature. Turkolu emerged from a shrubbery with the pretty whore, the back of her gown stained a grassy green.

"Ah, Liberty Hall," Turkolu sighed. "Nothing like this in Kushadasi."

Peering into her mirror backstage, Lizzie saw her eye looked thoroughly squashed. "My eye is awful," she moaned.

Pansy did not commiserate as they made a fast costume change. "Is your leg broken? Can you stand? Then, girl, your show must go on."

After nine o'clock, the rowdier half-price crowd squeezed in amongst the customers who had been in the house since five-thirty and were happily dazed by so much entertainment. The second half started at ten with Mary Dibdin's soprano solo. It did not go well. The mother of several little Dibdins was close to delivery. Like most theatrical-warhorse ladies of the age, she planned to perform right up to the first labor pain. One of Roger's tailors made an audible remark about "whales in harness," which raised a huge laugh.

"Drunken sots," Mrs. Dibdin hissed on her exit, colliding with Lizzie who was sidestepping a hot pig turd, mistakenly let loose in the wings by one of Bradbury's porcine performers. "Watch where you're going, miss!" Mary slapped at the half-sighted girl as she pushed past.

In the audience, Roger looked for the brunette who reminded him of Lizzie Trumpet to reappear onstage. Enough wine had flowed through his body to make identification difficult. To top off the evening, he hoped to introduce himself and perhaps escort her into some shrubbery. If he had the courage and the actress proved amiable.

Up in the gallery above the tailors, Aunt Peg was having a fine time, too. Lizzie had popped up throughout the show; now Belzoni, whom her niece talked about constantly, was coming on.

Charles Dibdin had titled his discovery "The Patagonian Samson." Geography aside, Belzoni looked like Samson, in a lion-skin tunic with chest exposed and a tawny plume topping his still-unbarbered locks. Though the Italian was a novice at entertaining, he had invented an inspired prop: a large yoke, built to rest across his shoulders with steps tapering down on each side. Two male assistants in tights strapped the contraption to Belzoni and jumped onto the lowest step. Doing handsprings out of the wings to furious music, more and more men mounted Belzoni. Finally, the most nimble of the Dibdin babes was lifted to the very top of the human pyramid, whereupon the strong man circled the stage carrying this burden: eleven men, one charming child and, for good measure, a six-foot flag in each hand.

As the theatre shook with applause, Aunt Peg felt her stomach twist. She knew Lizzie, in *Harlequin's Holiday*, was up next. The traditional harlequinade featured a chase. Jack Bologna, as Harlequin, and his pursuer Grimaldi, as Clown, dueled comically while painted drops of famous English sights rolled up and down. The audience cheered the scenery.

"Look, it's London Bridge!"

"Vauxhall Gardens!"

A large bed fashioned of *papier-mache* in Tudor style rolled onstage.

"Eh, that must be the Great Bed of Ware!"

Harlequin entered and jumped under the covers of this famous sleeper. Then Lizzie popped up from between the sheets, clad in a fairly diaphanous night-dress. Laugh. Harlequin pulled her back under, their forms bouncing vigorously. Bigger laugh. Clown entered, poked the covers, leered and dived in, too. Biggest laugh of the night. Rakes in the crowd offered to join them. The comics emerged to fence with each other while a deliciously tousled Lizzie, in high dudgeon, drew her own foil from beneath the counterpane and joined in the knockabout comedy. Seeing a beautiful girl thrusting and parrying with true skill excited the audience, which behaved as though at a cockfight, shouting, clapping and putting bets on Lizzie. Thrilled by the applause, she leaped off the four-poster to attempt every move she had ever mastered and many she hadn't. The mayhem ended when Grimaldi grabbed Lizzie from behind and ran off with her.

Turkolu shouted to Roger, "That brunette is a *lokum ghibi*, a Turkish delight!"

"Who's that girl?" everybody asked everybody else.

Roger Sloane sat straight and still as the boisterous crowd rose to leave. His brain had sobered enough to focus on what his eyes had seen. "That was our Lizzie up there, by God." Paying no attention, his comrades disappeared in all directions like a herd of tomcats, except for Turkolu, who announced, "*Sahr hoshum*, I'm drunk!" Singing of Liberty Hall, he wrapped himself affectionately all over Roger.

"Ya bastard, Turk," Roger gasped. His chum had "shot the cat"—vomited—across his best coat. Sloane wanted to find Lizzie before another moment passed, but the plight of his companion, the state of his coat and the general chaos made it impossible.

At finale's end, Lizzie learned to her dismay she had caused a ruction in the company. After the curtain call Jack Bologna and Grimaldi, hot in their costumes with face-paint running, stayed on stage to shout at her. It seemed she was a reckless, dangerous fool for abandoning the choreographed fencing.

"Are you stupid, girl?" Bologna thundered at her. "We don't wear masks, ya know. Never strike an actor in the face! Are you daft?"

"You don't change the moves in a staged fight. For safety's sake, girl!" Grimaldi explained at the top of his lungs. "Use your wits."

Lizzie gasped, reddening with shame at the dressing down. "I'm so sorry. But, the audience seemed to like it. They clapped and cheered—"

"Don't you know they'd cheer to see one of us killed? You wicked, brainless...." Bologna sputtered to find a word low enough to describe her. "Amateur!"

"You will be fined," Grimaldi spat out.

"Dismissed!" Bologna promised with satisfaction.

When her humiliation was at its peak, Charles Dibdin stepped into the circle of ill will. "That's enough, gentlemen. The girl is a beginner, if you remember." He glared at her. "My clowns are right. Trumpet, you will never improvise in my theatre again."

"No, sir, never. I do apologize to everyone, sir. I do." Breathing hard, Lizzie tried to stay composed, expecting the empresario's death blow of dismissal with downcast eyes.

"However, you did show spirit, Trumpet, and enlivened the sketch with your daring." He looked around to include the whole company. "I shall have notes for everyone tomorrow morning. Thank you, ladies and gentlemen. Jolly good show. As for Miss Trumpet here, you'll have to make do with her."

Quick as ever she could, Lizzie sped off to leave the theatre before Dibdin changed his mind.

Aunt Peg was holding a lantern that glowed orange under the popular trees where she waited to walk her elated niece home.

Lizzie catapulted out the stage door into her embrace. "I nearly put my eye out in the broom dance. Did you see? The manager's wife slapped me when I ran into her in the dark, and, after the harlequinade, the clowns told Mr. Dibdin I should be dismissed! But he's keeping me! He praised my daring, too. Anyway, I'm still in the show!"

"I saw everything, darlin'. Sure it was a wonderful debut."

As the moon rose overhead, Roger Sloane watched Miss Pegeen tottering towards Islington High Street with Lizzie at her side. In an agony of mind, he was still mopping up Turkolu and himself by the New River. Lizzie's romping on the boards had thrilled him, but men everywhere knew actresses were drenched in sin; it was their greatest charm. If she stayed on at the Wells, where sin loomed so large, she would have an actress's tainted reputation. There would be no turning back.

Roger scratched at his messy neck-cloth and wondered who had allowed this? *William is out of his wits, so it couldn't have been him. Miss Pegeen's sense of propriety is questionable. Georgie probably knows nothing of his sister's appearance. Once he finds out, he'll pull her off that stage. My old friend must be told at once.* Roger's brow tightened with imaginings if he failed to act. Georgie could be disgraced before his military career even began. The Trumpet family would be made sport of if Lizzie's name appeared in the program. It was all very dire.

"Oh, hell and death, I'll write Georgie tomorrow," Roger vowed. "Get up, Turkolu, you swine."

Chapter Eight

May 1803

"So, WE are at war with France again. The frog fleet may appear on the next wind, but we Londoners make a bold face of it, eh? What do you think of war, Miss Trumpet?"

"It seems the natural state to me, Mr. Dibdin. You know I'm too young to remember how it was in the old days before Napoleon."

During a break in morning rehearsals, Lizzie watched her employer unfold a Gillray print to hang on the Wells Theatre callboard. In the crisp, hand-colored caricature, Bonaparte, looking long-haired and fierce, was mounting a globe of the world. Down in one corner, John Bull held up a cautioning fist, to say, "Not so fast, sir."

"War is good for business, Trumpet. When British blood is up, spirits rise." The manager dispensed this theatrical wisdom with his usual charged-up energy. "Soldiers leaving to fight want a good time to remember. Coming home, they want to celebrate being back. Civilians need shows to help forget how afraid they are. These days, every family in England has someone fighting on land or sea, sad to say."

Lizzie sopped up each word like a sponge. "Yes, that's true, sir. My brother's at High Wycombe, learning to be an Army officer. I'm very proud of Georgie. He'll be in the battles one day."

"He's the one who taught you how to fence? I'll give him a free ticket to the show when he gets to London. He'll be euphoric to see what good use you make of his lessons."

Lizzie smiled wanly, remembering Georgie's painful last letter to her. *Euphoria? Highly doubtful. He threatened to "drag me off the by God stage." Pray heaven he won't be granted leave soon.* "Thank you, sir. I'm sure my brother will be just agog."

"My pleasure." Taking out a pocketed nail, Dibdin inclined over the shoulder of his young employee. "Ah, that hammer there. Hand it to me, girl." He drew in a great lungful of dead backstage air.

Lizzie picked up the tool from the prop table, feeling the manager's breath on her neck. *Am I being sniffed? He looks at me as if I were a delicious lamb chop. Take care, Lizzie.* She produced the hammer and hopped back a step. *I'm not on the menu today, sir.*

Dibdin turned his attention to Bonaparte, giving the figure on the callboard a few good whacks. "That new bit of business for you in the *Beanstalk* sketch is one of my true inspirations. If I do say so myself." *Whack, whack.* "Where did our giant disappear to?"

"Signor Belzoni tore his garment rehearsing the new crossover with me, sir." *Ripped out the bottom, and no smallclothes either.* Lizzie suppressed her smile with laudable decorum. "He's searching for a needle from Mrs. Bloore, in wardrobe, to close the breach in his breeches."

"Very good, Trumpet. I collect you're nearly punning. Don't forget to look passionate when the big fellow carries you across the stage, not like a sack of potatoes."

"I'll be rapturous, Mr. Dibdin."

"Splendid, Trumpet. Remember, in this house, rapture is always good for a laugh."

Miss Trumpet noticed everything at the Wells centered on the sports of love. The chorus sang about the news of the day, or the glory of the British fighting man, but they always did it half-dressed. Changing costumes without any sort of privacy had shown her some memorable sights. Cipriani, the human fly, was ever to be found in sweaty fleshings, ungirded by a dance belt, scratching his crotch long and ardently. Jokes about anatomy and assignations were constant fare in the dressing rooms. Belzoni's proportions excited the ladies of the chorus. They let out squeals of lust whenever he chanced by in his lion-skin, knowledgably using slang to fantasize about the giant's organ of gender. Sex was in the air. It was the nature of the place.

Lizzie stayed quiet around the more boisterous girls' confessions, hoping not to betray her ignorance and fascination with the subject of mating. Seeing all the pain love had caused in her own home, not to mention the frightful warnings from Aunt Peg, she was determined to avoid romantic encounters. But occasionally, she experienced a moist tingle between her legs. She'd learned these feelings were the overture to rapture—a rapture still mysterious and remote.

An immense shadow loomed over the callboard. "*Scusi*, Lisabetta, please thank *Meestair Deebdeen* for my wages, and do you remember your promise about the clothes? My pantaloons are a sadness."

Lizzie looked up at Belzoni, the one man at the Wells who never made unseemly jokes or forward advances in her company. Despite what the girls might say, Lizzie thought him a natural gentleman she was training in the English language and English ways.

"You just need a good tailor, Giovanni. I'll acquaint you with a fine one if you have the time to go into London."

Walking towards the city with a handsome giant to protect her and coins in her reticule that she had earned, Lizzie felt new-made. Truly in the days she had been at the Wells, everything about her life had changed. Elizabeth Trumpet's name was now printed on a playbill. She performed nightly in a show, a show with acrobats and pigs, of course, but her dream of becoming an actress, part of the marvelous theatre fraternity, was coming true. Sometimes the pleasure of it all was so strong, Lizzie thought she was touched by magic, her body sparkling all over. She executed the harlequinade moves perfectly now. Grimaldi had said, "Spot on, Trumpet!" Praise indeed. Confidence lightened her step.

The sun came and went, threatening showers as they pressed on. All the city sights that once were common enough, in her new circumstances seemed dusted with charm. In St. John Street, the pair gave two farthings to a strolling muffin-man for pastries off his tray and consumed the treats without pausing. Giovanni headed into Smithfield Market where the scent of cattle-slaughter and butcher's meat was pervasive.

"This stinks to heaven when summer comes," Lizzie observed, passing between a display of sausages and a table of tripe. "I always take another way."

"The smell does not distress this nose." Belzoni tapped his proud proboscis. "My small rent is excellent compensation for the odor of the corrals."

"You live here?"

Belzoni pointed to a dilapidated wooden structure overlooking the meat-market shambles. "I share a garret with three Sicilian plasterers, but I will not be there forever."

Though the Trumpets kept Boozel the cow and had lived downwind of a livery stable for years, Lizzie could not imagine sleeping above an abattoir.

"Mind your frock." He jerked her by the wrist. Lizzie's white muslin swayed perilously close to a puddle of fresh blood.

When they entered Giltspur Street, an old-clothes man, wearing a tower of used hats on his head and a dozen layers of waistcoats buttoned across his chest, pushed his cart along the cobblestones. "Nothing there will fit you, Giovanni. Just pass those dirty linens by. We have a way to go yet."

Lizzie directed them into Cock Lane.

"Gardiloo!" yelled a voice on high. From a window overhead, a red-elbowed arm emptied a chamber pot into the street. The shower of piss missed them by inches and they laughed aloud.

At Blackmoor Street, a sidewalk chiropodist worked in shirtsleeves. "Corns to pick," he hollered to the neighborhood. Belzoni hurried Lizzie past the gathering line of ingrown-toenail sufferers. They were both too young and nimble to imagine the curse of bad feet. He stopped to look at a silhouette-maker camped under a lamp post, his black and white wares spread on the cobblestones. The artist was a veteran of the army, still dressed in his old red uniform coat, now gone to rags.

"How much to make one of those, Lisabetta?"

"Too much. Sixpence for a profile."

"I want one of you." He pointed and the old soldier went to work, staring at Lizzie and twirling his scissors through some black paper. In two minutes, the silhouette was perfect.

Impulsively, Belzoni put the image in his coat pocket. "I will send this home to Mamma with some money. She needs to see the girl who has helped me so much."

"Oh, not that much, Giovanni. You flatter me, I think. May I stop in to see an old friend at Covent Garden? It's on the way to the tailor."

"*Certo*, Lisabetta."

The big man took Lizzie's arm protectively. They had reached the theatre district where thriving brothels also provided entertainment. Whores and rough characters loitered in the streets. "Shall I go in with you, or perhaps wait under these arches?"

"Come along with me." She darted through the stage door, skirting the offices of Harris and Kemble, down to the wardrobe rooms in the cold basement.

Meg Wilson, wearing her spectacles, was seated at a secretary clutching a handful of cloth swatches, engrossed in conversation with a small man in his middle years, elegantly dressed in a garnet tailcoat. Belzoni and Lizzie interrupted their business meeting.

"Upon my honor, it's the giant!" the small man exclaimed as Belzoni entered. "Mrs. Wilson, this is the new attraction at Sadler's Wells. 'The Patagonian Samson,' he's called. And you, miss, are also appearing, doing some swordplay in a sketch with Grimaldi. Am I right?" Lizzie's face lit up at the pleasure of being recognized for the first time. "You both are memorable, not to say unforgettable."

Phillip Eggleston, a lifelong theatrical, a writer, manager, producer of spectacles and entertainments, sought new talent everywhere, with an eye to sending companies out on the road for his own enrichment. Lizzie thought him an elfin fashion plate. His pomaded hair was combed fashionably forward like Julius Caesar. His feet in patent-leather boots were noticeably dainty, small as a girl's.

Lizzie found him working out the costume plots of a tour he was putting together for the Midlands. Eggleston was famous for his thrifty budgets, and Meg supported his projects by employing half a dozen poor women willing to sew for low wages. Once pleasantries were exchanged, he made his way to the door, telling Meg he would meet with her in a fortnight.

"Oh, Miss Trumpet, when your summer season with Dibdin is over, stop by my rooms. A superbly athletic girl should never lack employment." He passed her his card. "I might find something for you." Belzoni had inconspicuously pressed his backside against the wall. Eggleston batted his eyelashes at him. "Bring along your Italian friend, by all means."

"Thank you, Mr. Eggleston." Proud to have been invited to call on the entrepreneur, she slid his card into her reticule.

Belzoni watched the straight-backed older woman and Lizzie fondly embrace. Lizzie drew a penny-post letter from her bosom, her face growing sad when she said the names Roger and Georgie. She read from the letter in an angry manner and then began to cry. The Italian knew Georgie was her beloved brother, but who was Roger? He could not follow the ladies' rapid English. But if this Roger had hurt Lizzie, this gently bred girl who had made his good luck in London possible, then he, Belzoni, would personally throttle him.

To give the ladies privacy, he faced away to the racks of costumes hung high and low, and waited with his thoughts. *What a precious girl Lisabetta is...untouched...pure...trying to make her way in a life far beneath her. Such a charming girl deserves a good marriage. But not to me, of course.*

There could be no entanglement till fortune granted him a share of greatness. His future greatness Belzoni was sure of, yet in what manner it would arrive was unclear. Meanwhile, the stimulating company of Lizzie and her trust in his honor kept him in a state of perpetual temptation. *A glorious misery.* As the theatre mice skittered through the walls, his gaze returned to the hazel-eyed object of his desire.

"If I last at the Wells, Meg, there will be money for Papa's debts and doctors." Lizzie folded up the letter. "I don't understand Georgie; he writes as though he dislikes the theatre as much as Mama did."

"I sympathize with your distress, but remember, your brother has always taken life seriously." Meg handed the girl a handkerchief. "To my mind, that's a virtue, not a failing, Lizzie. And, God rest Jessie, she loved your father, not his profession."

"If Mama hadn't opposed it, do you suppose Papa would have trained me to be an actress?"

"Who can say? Surely your papa wanted you to be happy."

"I was born to be an actress, Meg, no matter what Georgie thinks."

Meg repressed a smile. In her wide experience, every pretty girl who had been applauded thought she was touched by destiny. "Unquestionably, you're getting all kinds of experience at the Wells." She looked at the enormous Italian, waiting so patiently. "Where does this lumpkin fit in?"

"I'm his translator for Mr. Dibdin. Giovanni's not a real performer at all, just penniless and new to England." She sniffed into the handkerchief. "He wants to do something with waterworks, I gather." Lizzie shrugged. "I'm not playing the game of hearts with him, Meg. How could I be? He's embarrassed on the stage, but I'm much at home there."

Meg laughed. "After two weeks, you've found you're born to it. Well, bless you for your courage and may it be true."

"Meg, you know Mr. Eggleston. Is he an honorable man?"

"Yes, and someone you *should* know." Meg nodded emphatically. "More important, don't forget your brother loves you and feels responsible for your safety. My husband and I shall both write Georgie and set his mind at rest."

"Thank you, Meg." She hugged the wardrobe mistress. "That means the world to me."

"I can spare you no more time." She rose and kissed Lizzie goodbye on the cheek. "Just don't be tripped up by those clowns at the Wells. Or Charles Dibdin!"

Chapter Nine

May 1803

AFTERNOON SUN burnished the panes of arching windows that crowned the front door of Adam & James of Savile Row.

"Signor Belzoni of Sadler's Wells, may I present *mio amico Signor* Sloane, owner of this establishment," Lizzie said with charming dignity. "Here you will find the best of gentlemen's tailoring."

The tall Italian bowed so deeply, the stitches in his weary old breeches opened audibly. Giovanni's face turned scarlet.

"Uncle Sidrack," Lizzie said quickly on her friend's behalf, "this man needs breeches or trousers immediately. Whichever you think suitable. Nothing lavish, but of a strong cloth that will wear well. Would it be too bold to ask for the family rate on the labor? He has coin in hand, so no credit need be advanced."

"Trousers, by all means. You bring me a stupendous client, Elizabeth," the silver-haired man chortled. "Roger and the shop-boys enjoyed Signor Belzoni on the stage some nights ago."

"Yes, I've been made aware of Roger's attendance," Lizzie replied tensely.

"*Scusi*, Lisabetta, would that be Adam or James?" Belzoni gestured towards Turkolu, who was hovering at his elbow.

"Neither. That is the gentleman who will assist you, Giovanni. This business is named after Mr. Sloane's father and grandfather. We English honor our families that way."

Hearing of this tradition so delighted the sentimental Italian, he engulfed Turkolu in a smothering embrace. The embarrassed young tailor hastily gathered up bolts of "wears-like-iron" wool and herded Belzoni into a fitting room.

"Uncle Sidrack," Lizzie began when they were alone, "perhaps you don't know, your Roger has written to Georgie telling him of my debut at Sadler's Wells. I would have preferred my brother learning the news from me, rather than in a tattling letter." She frowned. "I'm dismayed at Roger."

"Will you sit a moment, Elizabeth?" he asked seriously. "Tell me first, is William better?"

"No better. Papa walks the house in silence, and only speaks lines from plays." She searched for something good to say, fidgeting against the sofa cushions. "He gives me loving looks and is handsome as ever, though his hair's turning white." Sidrack patted Lizzie's gloved hand. "It was because of the uncertainty of Papa's health that I presented myself at the Wells for employment. My small salary will allow me to pay something towards Papa's debts and medicinals. It was not an ill-considered step, Uncle. I regret Roger interfered between Georgie and me, giving my brother an altogether wrong impression. I am working very hard at the theatre, and it was the right thing to do."

"I dare say you are offended at Roger, but my son acted correctly," Sidrack said calmly. "You have done a rash thing, Elizabeth, and it was wrong not to inform your brother before the deed was done. I'm surprised you did not consider coming to me for advice."

"I've done nothing to be ashamed of." Lizzie raised her head to a defensive angle.

"You have appeared on a stage of low reputation. Fencing in a nightdress is not the same as playing Ophelia at Drury Lane. Your Aunt Peg may not see the difference, but your father could tell you. I speak to you as a loving parent. If you continue dancing at the Wells, it will ruin your prospects of making a good marriage, or any marriage at all." Voice heavy with embarrassment, he added, "In such sordid, common company you may lose what a girl can only lose once."

"Please stop, Uncle." The justifying words came tumbling out. "I see you are of the same opinion as Roger and Georgie. I wonder at all of you! I did this for Georgie's good, too; we must have money while he finishes his schooling. If you are speaking as a parent, Uncle, then know I am not a child." She waved a deprecating hand. "Besides, Papa loves his profession, and I want to be just like him. Men think all actresses are prostitutes, and that is a brutal, unjust assumption. I am capable of being both an actress and a respectable woman."

Shamed by her own anger, Lizzie turned from the man who had shown her only love and support all her life. She stood up in misery, searching for words to explain herself. "Instead of believing whatever it was Roger said, come to the Wells and see me yourself. I have been a good girl," she finished with a sob.

Sloane shook his head. He knew enough of the young not to be surprised, and believed that being female, she was no wiser than a child. *She has slipped the net of guidance, poor little minnow. She is swimming into a sea of flesh-eating sharks.* He opened his mouth to soothe her hurt, when a commotion outside ended their privacy.

Roger, blotchy faced with exertion, burst through the front door, yelling, "The king is coming! His Majesty and all the princes are riding out of the palace to rally the people!"

At this urgent announcement, Belzoni, Turkolu and the tailors rushed into the salon, but Roger saw only Lizzie, looking daggers at him.

"Which street?" she snapped.

"They are marching towards Piccadilly. I'll show you." Roger started for the door.

"Don't bother. I'll make my own way." Lizzie turned to Sidrack. "Thank you for helping my friend, Uncle." She took Belzoni's arm. "Giovanni, we are going to see the king!" Lizzie shot the younger Sloane a punishing glance that said he was nothing to her. Nothing but a fat and foolish boy. "Good bye, Roger."

Joining the throng pushing into Piccadilly, Lizzie and Belzoni hurried down Sackville Street. In the uproar of the crowd she tried to put thoughts of her own hurt feelings out of her mind. Truly she had rushed into the life she wanted, but it was too late to take back her sharp words to her Uncle Sidrack. *I shall prove them wrong about me. Georgie and the Sloanes...they will be heartily sorry one day.*

They stopped under the new-leafed trees in front of Burlington House, where the big man lifted Lizzie onto his wide shoulder, giving her a perilously fine view of the parade. The pressure of Belzoni's head against her thigh gave her a sudden thrill.

At the Haymarket, shiny black horses of the Life Guards wheeled round the corner, eight abreast, prancing and dancing. The mounted guardsmen wore feathered cocked hats and red tunics, some clutching flags in their white-gloved hands. A military band followed, tooting brassily in a flow of high spirits. The day was coming to a golden close, the sky above purpling with evening clouds.

"I can see them, Giovanni. Can you make them out?" Lizzie was fighting to keep her balance.

Two royal equerries on matched greys escorted a chalk-white stallion walking with measured dignity. On the stallion's back sat George the Third, a very frail king now, big-bellied and round-jawed, the hairs of his wig disturbed by the breeze. He had removed his general's hat and was looking gravely into the faces of his people as if to say, "Now, my dear subjects, we have work to do." He turned his head from side to side, squinting his blue eyes that had lived too long to see clearly.

Men doffed their hats. Women curtsied and held their babies up to see the monarch of England. Impassioned voices shouted, "Long live the king!"

He looked at me...looked into my eyes.... The love she felt for her country shot like an arrow towards His Majesty. *Dear bluff old king, dear as home itself!*

"Huzzah!" Lizzie yelled. Then she saw all the Princes of the Realm, bedecked with swords and decorations, riding in silent echelon behind their father, to the ominous pounding of deep brass kettledrums.

First came the Prince of Wales, heavy and handsome in an extraordinary uniform dazzling with diamonds. Then Fredrick, Duke of York, the king's favorite son, and beside him the ugly Duke of Clarence who had had so many children by the famous comic actress, Mrs. Jordan. Amongst the reverent thousands in the crowd, a few street urchins dared to run up and touch a horse or a booted leg. The Duke of Kent followed Earnest Augustus, Prince of Hanover, a place that Lizzie could never locate on the map. The Dukes of Sussex and Cambridge brought up the rear. Their presence assured London, though war had returned, "Fear not! Your Royal Family is unshakable and steadfast as God."

"The king's family is as large as mine." Belzoni laughed.

"Oh, there are many more," Lizzie informed him with enthusiasm. "Younger sons and princesses a-plenty home at Windsor."

As mounted officers rode by, she imagined the scenes of tragedy if the French landed. She pictured herself defending England in hand-to-hand combat with the *Grande Armée* in front of Longsatin House.

"England will never be conquered, Giovanni!" Lizzie said when he eased her off his shoulder.

"War is murder," he answered levelly. "All are losers when so many die. There can be no glory in war." Lizzie's eyes widened at this most un-English sentiment. "Let us speak of other things, *cara*. Some day in times of peace, you must travel as I have. See the world, see Rome. Such fountains!"

They proceeded slowly, impeded by the many people rushing in all directions. At the corner of Haymarket and St. James's Street, Belzoni's flowing descriptions of Roman fountains stopped.

"*Attenzione!* A sign in Italian. 'Antiquarian Books!' We must go in," he said with delighted urgency.

Within 28 Haymarket, fine old volumes in many languages were stacked on a threadbare French carpet, piled high on the dusty tables, and threatening to burst the wooden shelves. The careless abundance surrounded one slender gentleman in his sixty-fifth year, writing at a table. He was not a customer. There had been no customers all day, despite the crowds in the street. His colorless hair was combed in swirls above his collar of exhausted velvet. When Giovanni opened the door to say, *"É permesso?"* he jumped to his feet, pointed a long pale chin at the handsome couple, and his toothless face brightened with animation.

"Buon giorno, dottore." Belzoni's booming bass-baritone caressed his native language.

"Benvenuto, amici." The gentleman spread his hands in welcome, and his thin black brows rose happily. "I am Lorenzo da Ponte, theatre poet of the Royal Opera. I can supply your needs from my personal library of the greatest writers, collected over a lifetime of serving the muses." Da Ponte offered his wide-backed chair to Lizzie. "Would *la bella* care to seat herself?"

"Grazie, signore. I should like it of all things." She sank gratefully into the chair's soft comfort, catching her breath. Belzoni introduced himself with more reticence than the poet, but Lizzie proudly added their most notable accomplishment, "And we are currently appearing in our debut engagement at the Sadler's Wells Theatre."

"Per Bacco, you are embarking on careers in the highest art—the performance of music!" He drew a brown bottle of fragrant sherry from beneath the counter. "Let us drink a toast to your success."

All quaffed a thimbleful.

"How delicious," Lizzie sighed.

"Life is short," da Ponte observed. "Drink the good wine first. Friends, you found me polishing a new work to premiere at the Royal Opera this month. It is called *The Grotto of Calipso.*" The poet's lively sharp-nosed face turned to Lizzie. "You know who Calipso was, *signorina?*"

"The enchantress?"

"Sì! Sì!" Da Ponte raised his wine glass with delight. "Her little grotto is the place of seduction. You know my other operas, I suppose?" He sang a few bars, flirtatiously fingering Lizzie's wrist.

"La ci darem la mano,
La mi dirai di sì...."

Lizzie recognized the tune. "It is the seduction duet from *Don Giovanni*," she answered, charmed by his piping voice. "Ooh, I do love Mozart."

"Ah, yes. Wolfie was one of my collaborators, gifted but disorganized, you must believe."

Belzoni admired the colorful leather books, embossed with gold and the dust of London's air. He peered at a volume on mathematics from the seventeenth century. "Your books are precious, signore, marvelous, but beyond my ability to buy."

"But you appreciate them." Da Ponte shrugged. "I am introducing the language of Dante to the English gentry a little at a time. Here, engage your mind a while." He passed the mathematics book into Belzoni's hands. "Now, *bella*, regale me with the story of your life. The giant's, too. I have plenty of time."

With innocent candor, Lizzie described their poverty of funds and richness of expectation.

"Such struggles are typical in an artist's life," the poet assured her and turned to the studious Giovanni, poring over his book. "Attend, signore." Belzoni looked up. "Your appearance is striking, magnificent, but if you remain only a giant in burletta, do not expect to be taken seriously." Da Ponte raised his index finger. "Work to be your own master, signore. That is the great thing."

"*Buon' signore*, you gratify me beyond words."

"Now, Miss Trumpet, I've written for the greatest voices in Europe, but I confess at this moment I recall no soprano who would surpass your beauty of face." Lizzie dipped her head under this unexpected avalanche of flattery. "Such freshness. How long have you been singing professionally, my dear?"

She broke into a grin. "Two weeks."

"Fresh indeed, unspoiled by bad habits." Da Ponte's gimlet eyes sparkled. "As you study *la voce*, look for the soul of the music in the text. Believe in the librettist's words. He is telling you how to sing them."

The man must think I'm a soloist. "I'm just in the chorus, sir, and the songs are only Mr. Dibdin's ditties about roast beef and British tars," Lizzie confessed.

"Listen. Be it roast beef and sailors or Mozart and Handel, devote yourself. Take every role seriously. I give you jewels, *bella*. Youthful beauty is ephemeral. Fleeting, *che peccato*! You must learn all aspects of the art." Fiddling with the neck-cloth at his throat, da Ponte deftly led the conversation back to himself. "Even I, who have been kissed by the very mouth of fame, never cease to search. My poetry and libretti—especially the libretti—were always written against fearsome obstacles." His long chin shook, his eyes closed. "Everywhere my ability was met with jealousy, my career thwarted by lesser men. It is the nature of small men to attack great ones. Oh, I could tell you stories."

And he did. Da Ponte's charm had ensnared them. Lizzie had never met a man so anxious to be appreciated as the lonely librettist, while Belzoni was clearly moved and sympathetic to the artist's rambling soliloquy.

"*Dottore*, you have given us treasures indeed," Belzoni said, rising to go and bowing to the poet. "When fortune blesses me, I shall return and buy a whole shelf of your books."

"Keep the mathematical treatise, *amico*. I expect to hear great things of you and this lady." The little gentleman led them grandly to the door. "Always remember," he said, again raising one finger. "He who believes in his dreams is mad; and he who does not believe in them—what is he?"

Soldiers passed as Lizzie turned into the Strand. Inspired by the encounter, she vowed to never forget the poet's words. Keeping up with Giovanni's long stride, she imagined her future: command performances at Covent Garden, triumphant seasons at Drury Lane. *To believe in dreams is everything.* Her own enchanted her.

Chapter Ten

September 1803

"THE GENTLEMEN are ready for you now."

"And the ladies will be ready in five minutes," Pansy answered saucily to the footman on the other side of the locked door.

Lizzie shivered in the cold, cramped servant's closet. The strange surroundings of the great house and the aloof attitude of Lord Landsdown's staff was unsettling, despite the assurances of her trusted friend.

On closing night at the Wells, Pansy had suggested they work together at a *fete du plaisirs*, hosted by Viscount Landsdown. Only posing was required. The viscount's personal coachman would fetch and return them, and the evening paid two pounds to each "artist," plus a few more trifles of monies if the guests were pleased.

"This can be a real opportunity for you, Trumpet," Pansy had promised. "It's how Emma Hamilton got started and look what happened to her."

Inexperienced Lizzie had become Pansy's *protégée*, progressing from the back of the line to the "superior girl" position at the front where the nimble and fair were featured. The older dancer was flattered to have her advice followed to the letter by a cheerful fellow female. She thought enough of Lizzie to introduce her to a new type of performance—a performance where an amiable disposition, fresh looks and poverty were the chief requirements. Pansy was well known at such entertainments.

The dancer handed Lizzie a scant length of hyacinth gauze with three gold clips. "Just drape this on fetchingly. We'll be working barefoot on the tables, once we're in there."

Heart sinking, Lizzie accepted the practically transparent cloth. She had lost some of her physical modesty in the theatre dressing room by this time, but it was obvious Pansy expected her to be "striking attitudes" in a near state of nature. A private salon would be less protected than a conventional stage, but Lizzie realized there was nothing for it now but to soldier on. Her lavish fee, paid in advance, was already tucked into her reticule.

"Leave your hair pinned up, goddess style with that gold cord. Ya let it tumble down later if one of the nobs requests it. Hold your poses statue-like; that's most dignified. Remember, Trumpet, this is art."

The girls hurried up a back staircase behind the maroon-liveried footman, along a lavishly mirrored hallway to a pair of ornate doors enameled in black and cream. Within, many male voices were raised in cacophonous song.

Lord Landsdown's three-storied mansion in Hanover Square, built of palatial Portland stone, was the grandest house Lizzie had ever entered. If she had felt less stupefied with nerves over this "posture girl" debut, she would have looked about to relish her beautiful surroundings. Pausing to preen before their entrance, she did notice the footman's leer as he caressed Pansy's buttocks with his eyes before he opened the elegant black doors with white-gloved hands.

Men of the upper class, in attitudes of the lower class, were drinking and conversing in an unbuttoned atmosphere, attended by expensively dressed and bejeweled females. The air was tobaccoey and dense. The wall-sconces had already burned down to a dripping mess.

"The nymphs have arrived!" A giddy young buck whistled and clapped. "Who's feeling like Pan tonight?"

A bottle of brandy crashed to the floor as one smirking fellow dressed in a dandy's dozen fobs and tight pants unceremoniously hoisted Lizzie onto the long gleaming table in the center of the room. A huge silver wine-cooler decorated with goaty satyrs was in the way. The dandy knocked aside empty wine bottles and glasses with his sleeve, to make space for a confused Lizzie. Farther down the same table, Pansy climbed a chair to take her place as a living centerpiece.

"Make room for the maidens!" An aged spark, in an old-fashioned bag-wig and no teeth to speak of, laughed and pressed against the table's edge with dozens of others who looked drunkenly up into Lizzie's frightened face.

Pansy had settled into her first "posture," a demure pose with eyes cast down and a hand cupping her own breast. Lizzie kept her knees together and stood like an acolyte of Venus, arms raised to heaven, or in this case the chandelier. One of the "birds of paradise" had begun to play rollicking chords and runs on a pianoforte, while the gentlemen made comments and continued drinking beneath the high painted ceiling.

Lizzie tried next for an arabesque without lifting a leg, since the toothless old man had positioned himself for a better look up her drapery. A footman opened a lead-lined door in the sideboard, exquisitely inlaid with tortoise shell, to remove a porcelain bowl into which a guest aimed to relieve himself. She winced to hear the urine hit its mark then splash onto the carpet.

Pansy's end of the room was boisterously appraising her. "Now that's a perfect bum for Doser; he's still a boy at heart. Wake him up. Let's see a bit of rear door, girl. Arse in the air." Lizzie watched Pansy comply artfully and with a smile.

Someone was too late for the sideboard convenience and vomited from his comfortable place under the piano. Lizzie changed position carefully, trying to block out the rough language, as she had learned to do onstage at the Wells. The pianist had stopped playing runs when a guest raised her skirts to mount her, pushing the musician into the ivories. Lizzie had never witnessed copulation before, nor imagined it as a group endeavor. She was appalled.

"Lord Dampere and...friend," the footman bawled out. A gorgeously dressed couple joined the party.

"Ah, Dampie, have a look at the new talent; that dark one has the tits of Juno," a happy voice called across the room.

Jesus and Mary, that's me, Lizzie realized, blinking up into the smoking candles while the ancient admirer pawed her naked leg, demanding attention. More than frightened now, she desperately wanted to get off the table.

"I'm a connoisseur of beauty," the old man whined. "Drop down here and show me your splendid little gem, all black and curly." Lizzie crouched to cover herself. Gleefully, the man opened his breeches to take his half-flaccid organ in hand. Sprawling across a gilt chair, he snickered and pulled on himself supportively. "Mmm, cunt...I'm a cunnyseur...um...yes...put it in...stuff it in...um...yes." He was grunting and squirming.

Revolted at the sight, Lizzie shut her eyes.

"Miss Trumpet, will you come this way?" A woman's voice cut through the laughter and animal sounds around her. "This way." Someone helped her off the table, then to the door. "Whatever they paid you, you have earned your wage. Do you want to stay or go, Elizabeth?"

"Go," Lizzie answered. She opened her eyes to see Octavia Onslow. "Oh God, Miss Onslow! What are you doing here?" she blurted out, then remembered exactly what her father's friend was usually hired for. A portly young dandy with sweating cheeks was at her side.

"I am the guest of Lord Dampere," Octavia answered, with perfect tact, indicating the dandy. Her companion nodded and even seemed to sympathize with Lizzie's distress.

"Will they take my money back if I leave now?"

"They will not, and it looks to me as if no one will miss you," Octavia said smoothly. "This is hardly the venue for you, Elizabeth." She summoned another man in livery and put coins into his hand. "This lady is to be treated with respect, do you follow? Her father is a well-known actor of the king's theatre. Get her into Landsdown's carriage and safely home."

Hurrying away, Lizzie looked back for Pansy. Still on the long table, drapery pulled open, the dancer was scissoring her legs with abandon to wild applause.

⤙

In her bedroom at Longsatin House, Lizzie washed herself with hard soap and cold water. She scrubbed violently in the china bowl, pouring from the matching pitcher to rinse and rinse again. Her curiosity about sex had betrayed her, like an adorable dog that returned a pat with a nasty bite. Now she knew what the teasing moves she'd learned from Pansy's tutoring were meant for. *All for that mysterious male eruption. Is that romance...love? Is that what drives the world?* She wanted to know nothing more about it.

Around her, the little bedchamber looked untidy and neglected. All her attentions and energies had been directed to performances at the Wells for many weeks. *What a pig I've become.* Dawn was still hours away as the miserable girl began folding and dusting. On the spindly writing table lay Georgie's last letter, written two months ago. She reread it by the light of a candle while an awakened linnet bird sang in the lane.

> *July 15, 1803*
> *Dearest Sister,*
> *I hope you find it in your kind and generous heart to forgive me for the manner in which I dismissed your going on the stage. My visit home proved to me that Papa may never recover. To provide for his comfort and my continued training here, you have chosen a difficult path. When Ted Wentworth and I saw you in the show, dancing, singing and fencing (very deftly, I must say), I was amazed. You have talent. I was proud of you, infant, truly proud. When I'm an officer I will look after you as a brother should, and never forget these times when Papa, Aunt Peg, and I depended on you for material support. We Trumpets are made of strong stuff, are we not? At High Wycombe, I am known as "that son of an actor," but I persevere.*
> *So kiss Papa for me, and don't let Aunt Peg get the upper*

*hand. Thank her for the cakes. I can slice through an onion
with my saber from a galloping horse. Please, don't try it.*
   In haste,
   George M. Trumpet

Lizzie had felt justified when she first read those words. They had
set her free to think all was going to be well, as indeed it had
been...until Charles Dibdin had pulled her into a tiny changing booth
in the wings before the finale of the season's last performance.

Her affection for "Old Charlie" had been sincere. Every two
weeks, when the bill changed, she had been given more to do, and her
salary had increased by three shillings. Dibdin had just made the
customary farewell speech to the audience, promising great surprises
next season, but Lizzie was the one surprised.

He'd embraced her in the musty booth, saying her dedication was
a pleasure to behold and in future he planned to feature her talents.
Then, as she began to say a tremulous "thank you," the man she owed
so much to began unbuttoning his trousers.

"Now, Trumpet," he had whispered, "a quick impromptu to seal
the bargain!"

Mary Dibdin, freshly delivered of another little thespian, was
singing piercingly on stage, just a few feet away. It was the very scene
Pansy had warned her about. The manager pulled open her bodice
and began groping between her legs. Gratitude did not trump Lizzie's
dismay. She slugged the energetic composer in the jaw just as his wet
mouth opened to take her breast.

Master Menage was poised on tiptoe by a fire bucket as she broke
out of the booth. He was rewarded with a devouring look at her
bosom and eagerly asked, "Did Old Charlie get the fuck he's been
wanting all summer?"

It appeared the whole company had wagered on their leader's
chances. What a blow that had been. Choking with shame, Lizzie had
not appeared in the curtain call that night, nor confided her
experience to Pansy. Perhaps Pansy herself had done the deed with
Dibdin just to keep her job. After the Hanover Square exhibition,
Lizzie assumed as much. She was sad and sorry over it.

Was the famous notion true? Acting is nothing more than whoring? Lizzie had never believed it. Yet, she could not even call herself an actress. She had spoken no lines, merely fenced with clowns, danced in a chorus and writhed on a table. "I'm no closer to being an actress at all," she said aloud, wrestling with her blue devils.

Nana Trombetta's letter from Charleston lay under Georgie's envelope. Her grandmother had written she could only send her love, not carry it to London in person, because Grandpa Trombetta had hurt his back severely and needed her at home. "Lisa-cara, you are a woman now and will understand a wife's duties supersede everything." Then she asked what roles her son was playing at Covent Garden this season, "since he must be completely rested by this time and returned to the stage."

The sleepless girl looked out the window for the bird that sang so sweetly, but could not see him. Painfully, Lizzie faced the fact she had told her family she was capable, and they believed her. *Everyone expects me to "get on."*

But at that moment, in the night's deep darkness, she had no notion how to do it.

When Peg shuffled to the kettle to brew William's morning tea, she found her niece had already collected her chickens' lay in the egg basket. She heard the girl mucking out the hen house as the sun rose. Peg stepped outside. "Leave that for Noddy, darlin'."

"Noddy has left it undone for weeks," Lizzie snapped. Banty, the rooster, pecked at her shovel, his displaced fowls scolding and scratching around her.

"Well, good morning to you, too." Concerned, the old woman guessed what might be wrong. "Did the dancing at Hanover Square go well yesternight?"

"My pay is on the table, Aunt, beside your eggs."

"Was the Landsdown crowd more genteel than at the Wells?"

"The same."

"Did the gentlemen...?"

"Get their cocks out in the lively atmosphere? Yes, Aunt, they did. Out, but not into me." Peg waited to hear more as Lizzie shoveled fowl-muck under a rose bush. "I was spared that by Papa's old friend Miss Onslow—a person I'd misjudged entirely."

Before Peg could make further inquiries, she turned to the sound of heavy footsteps in the kitchen. Her charge, who never showed improvement, was awake. "What now?" she sighed under her breath.

William walked out into the crisp morning air, wearing his dressing gown. As usual these days, he was deep in some fantasy of a past production. Sporting a long Charles the Second wig, he addressed the chickens as the Merry Monarch. "If you lot put money in my show, I can deliver Nell Gwyn playing Lust in *The Masque of Folly*. She's even agreed to sing two songs in the afterpiece. What say you?"

Despite feeling dirty, disappointed, and robbed of her innocence, Lizzie had to laugh.

Chapter Eleven

September 1803

THE CASE-CLOCK struck four while Miss Pegeen and William both snored the afternoon away. Lizzie had exhausted herself scrubbing the kitchen floor and was more than ready for a bath when she heard footsteps approach the house. Something thumped against the front door and a muffled voice barked, "Trumpet delivery!" She hurried to the vestibule, opened the door and picked up a package marked *Elizabeth*. Inside, she found a set of scenes and a scribbled note from her father's old acting partner Dick Wilson.

> *Lizzie dear,*
> *Meg tells me you have been appearing in the chorus of Dibdin's menagerie and have plans to become an actress. Tonight, I'm appearing in* Love Laughs at Locksmiths *at the Peerless Theatre in Hammersmith. The ingénue has broken something irreparable and cannot go on. We are up the spout: house sold out, must play. You have an opportunity because every young actress we know seems to be working out of London. Just learn this part. From my own salary, I will pay you five shillings. Our cast will collect you at five o'clock in a hackney coach and tell you what you need to*

know on the way to the theatre. I've assured the management you will be delightful, and look forward to meeting you again onstage.

Courage,
Dick Wilson

Lizzie clutched the scenes like a relic of the true cross and burrowed into the mountain of lines. *Acting...acting...acting at last!*

When Wilson announced to the Hammersmith audience that Mrs. Overshot was discommoded and would not be performing tonight, a moan rose up from the crowd as if the Muse of Comedy herself had dropped dead in the lobby.

"Who is Overshot?" Lizzie nervously whispered to *Locksmith's* sharp-featured leading lady.

"Local favorite. Very skilled."

"I've never heard of her."

"And we've never heard of you," the older actress said graciously.

Thus encouraged, Lizzie stepped out in front of the curtain to present the endless prologue that set the scene and, miraculously, she spoke the lines as written. However, hearing the sound of her own voice delivering a speech for the first time caused the tempo of her tongue to match her rapid pulse, fast, then faster, then faster than human comprehension. Lizzie heard the playgoers rustle and remark negatively. Inwardly, she cringed.

Well into Act One, Wilson came on and, over his entrance-applause, hissed, "Christ, slow down."

Earlier, during the rollicking hackney-coach ride to the Peerless, the cast of strangers had said how grateful and how fortunate they were to have her, then returned to talking spiritedly amongst themselves *about* themselves. No one actually explained the plot of the piece or who was who. Which actor was playing Lizzie's husband and which her lover remained unclear, and once onstage in fops' costumes, she could not tell them apart. This proved to be an essential failing.

By Act Two, Lizzie overheard the leading lady say to Wilson, "Where did you get her?"

Shod in Miss Overshot's too-tight costume and smelly, too-large shoes, Lizzie stumbled making an exit. The crowd whistled. Never having read the whole play, she clutched her rumpled pages backstage, tried to suppress her panic and not miss an entrance. She stepped on other actors' laughs. Coldly, the cast ignored her.

In the closing scene, Wilson had a wonderful bit of comic business with a pistol center stage. Far upstage, amongst the actors she had wronged, Lizzie, eager to learn, crept downstage to get a clearer view of Wilson. She stayed in character, but walked during the most comedic moment.

Wilson cried out, "Damn the fellow. I'll shoot him at the crossing of his eyes!" *Boom!* Flash of harmless powder. A small chuckle from the audience. Exeunt all. As the curtains brushed closed, the master of comedy grabbed Lizzie by the shoulders and shook her. Heat was radiating off his shovel-shaped nose. "Trumpet! What were you doing? How dare you take attention off my comedy? Why in hell were you maneuvering downstage? To what end?"

"Mr. Wilson, I wished to see your stage business," Lizzie babbled. "I wished to learn."

"Bosh! If you weren't William's little girl...." His face clouded with thoughts of atrocity. "I'm killing myself out there for king and country, and you ruin it! Don't you ever do that again!"

Lizzie felt God could not possibly have more humiliation in store, but she was wrong. When she joined the final tableau to drop a curtsy to the Hammersmith playgoers, they booed.

Of course, Aunt Peg had waited up, with a pot of precious chocolate made to celebrate Lizzie's expected success. William was up, too, physically present, at least. Her father's helplessness and the cruel disappointments of the preceding nights set Lizzie's large eyes to watering tears over the mahogany table.

She took her father's hand. "I was on stage acting in a comedy tonight, Papa, with Dick Wilson. He only put me on because you are his great friend, and I ruined the whole thing."

"Surely not," Peg contended soothingly.

"No, he said so. I'll never forget it. Of course there was no time to rehearse, but I didn't even understand the plot. I thought I knew about acting, but I don't. My voice was awful. I spoke through the other actors' laughs and they hated me for it. I moved during Dick's comic turn, and he was furious. I have been humbled. No, mortified. You always made everything look so easy, Papa, but there is so much to learn."

The handsome actor gazed into an unfocused distance, saying with commiserating comprehension, "Comedy is hard."

"This will take your mind off things." Thrusting a bonnet at Lizzie, Aunt Peg was tying on her own in the kitchen of Longsatin House. "Look, Noddy's hopping up and down to be off."

Peg had saved up her egg money for an outing to Bartholomew Fair. It was her reward for taking care of William all summer, while her niece had been having such memorable times at the Wells. Maria Mantino had arrived to watch Lizzie's papa for the afternoon, accompanied as always by her five contentious, screaming little ones.

The very name Bartholomew Fair had become a euphemism for all things ragtag and rowdy. Jessie Trumpet had forbidden her children to attend the famous old gathering of mountebanks and peep shows where every thief in London spent three profitable days pick-pocketing through the milling throngs.

Miss Pegeen never missed attending. She always brought home gingerbread to nibble while describing the puppet shows and phantasmagorias. The old lady forbade Lizzie to indulge her blue devils anymore. "Just go, darlin,' and enjoy yerself!"

Noddy escorted them proudly to the center of Smithfield Market where the largest tents and theatre booths were crowded side by side. Hundreds more spilled into Giltspur Street and Cock Lane as entertainers competed vociferously for attention.

"Miss Pegeen, there's the Roundabout. Look at the Whirligig!" Noddy waved a puppy-chewed three-cornered hat at the rides, excitedly. Peg let the gangling youngster join a line for the agitating Up and Down, sure it would dislodge his breakfast.

An African musician in orange vest and striped stockings fiddled before a bank of canvas-walled extravaganzas: Saunders' Tragic Theater, the Fire-Eating Flambeau Family, Flockton's Famous Musical Clock—composed of over four hundred moving parts and exhibited three times before Their Majesties. Ribbon-sellers, bare-footed Irish children, and the ubiquitous gingerbread-hawkers pressed in all around them.

Under the marquee of Gyngell's Grand Medley seated at a raised table, General Jocko, a huge baboon, munched figs and plums from the crowd with his left hand while using a quill pen to write autographs with his right. Miss Pegeen dragged Lizzie with her for a closer look at the accomplished ape. Beside him, a spangled husky sort was imploring the populous to spend "a measly two farthings to view the Young Hercules" appearing inside.

"That will be Belzoni, Aunt. I never thought to find his booth in all this tumult."

The Hercules tent stank of slaughterhouse overlaid with rampant humanity. Five men from the audience had paid an extra sixpence apiece to be carried around the stage by the Italian in a greasy parody of his pyramid act. They clung to his flesh-colored costume and laughed beerily against his cheeks.

"I want a ride on *Bells Only*." Aunt Peg started towards the stage, but Lizzie restrained her.

"No, Auntie. He only carries men to show his strength." Lizzie wondered how he could stand being pawed by the public and cried, "Bravo, Belzoni!" to show her sympathetic support. Giovanni recognized her and responded with a Mediterranean shrug that seemed to say, "Why was I born?"

"I do twenty shows a day. It's-ah too much." Belzoni told Lizzie and Peg after his performance. He was striving to speak English as he took a sip of barley water. "You like-ah the ape? He is a general. Grimaldi, he said this was easy way for me to make-ah money. Ha!"

Lizzie could think of nothing cheerful to say, sorry to find her friend in such a spectacle, as sorry as she had been to find herself in one. "I also had work this week. Pansy made me a 'posture girl.' Whatever you've heard of such, Giovanni, it's humiliating to do. I failed on stage as an actress in Hammersmith, too."

"Did they pay you?"

Lizzie smiled ruefully. "Not enough."

"I weep for your sadness."

It was showtime yet again, and the tent was filling up with more unwashed customers, some of them clutching autographs from General Jocko. The women struggled out through the hot crowd. Lizzie kissed her hand to Belzoni.

"*Buona fortuna*, Giovanni. Don't forget me."

Twelve hours later, Lizzie heard something strike her window. She parted the blue-striped curtains to see Belzoni, with a handful of pebbles, standing in the foggy lane below.

Panting, he called up, "Lisabetta, the press gang chase me. Can I hide with you? *Prego!*"

Much surprised, Lizzie flew down the stairs in her cotton nightgown to unlatch the door; she let him in and bolted it fast.

"They must have been mad to try and knock you on the head for the Navy. You will stay the night here, Giovanni." Lizzie threw some coals into the grate, brightening the drawing-room fire. A short while later, refreshed with a drop of brandy, and looking sheepish with embarrassment, the disheveled man accepted two blankets and a place to sleep on the Turkish carpet.

"Each night when the fair ends, those Navy men...uh, how you say...sweep the grounds for drunken fellows, but this time, they follow me to my *casa*. I can no go back."

Lizzie passed a hand through her long, loose hair. "Our

employment misadventures have set my mind in a new channel, Giovanni. Do you recall the day we walked across London for your trousers?"

"*Sì, sì, bella.* One of the happiest days of my life. I wear those trousers *adesso.*" He moved to throw off the blankets in proof, glanced down at his lap, then appeared to think better of it.

"In the wardrobe of Covent Garden, we met a gentleman," she continued, oblivious to her guest's byplay with his crotch.

"The man with little feet?"

"Yes, small feet but a big reputation. His name is Eggleston; he organizes touring plays and all types of entertainments in the small cities and towns of England. He mentioned finding theatrical work for both of us, and he keeps rooms near Covent Garden. If I sought him out, could you accompany me? I would feel much safer in that neighborhood with you beside me." *A male protector of Belzoni's proportions will stop any man getting out of hand.* She raised her eyes to the very embodiment of maleness spread across her mother's carpet and saw only her trustworthy, sweet *amico.*

"It may mean touring away from home. You see, there is so little money put by, I must—" Lizzie shook her head. "I must continue to work. But a woman alone, putting herself forward, visiting a gentleman's rooms, gives the impression...."

Belzoni sat up on one elbow. "The wrong impression, *bella? Sì.* It will be my joy to take you to the Covent Garden or anywhere you desire to go."

"*Grazie, caro,*" she sighed.

Stretched out before the fire's banked embers, Belzoni was stirred by the intimacy of the moment alone with Lizzie in the darkened room. She had wrapped herself in a blanket, too, an old blue one. To him, she looked like a Madonna in a Roman church, ideal and perfect. Since the day of their first meeting, when she saved him from starvation like an angel, the girl had been constantly in his thoughts. Now, if he understood correctly, she needed him. It might mean enduring the stage and acting the strong man in extravaganzas a while longer, but how worth those indignities and stupidities to be with Elizabeth Trumpet, the darling.

He rubbed his sore shoulders uncomfortably. "The press gang is *intrepido*. You are in need of capitol and so am I. If-ah you think this little man of Eggs offers opportunity, we should seek him out." Lizzie looked expectantly in his eyes. "Is tomorrow too soon, *bella*?"

"*Domani*! *Perfetto*! Thank you, my friend." Lizzie rose to say goodnight. "Sleep well, Giovanni. I shall cook you a grand plate of breakfast in the morning." She climbed the stairs back to her bedchamber. The Italian watched her long dark hair swinging with each step, his heart a melted jelly, his penis hard as marble.

Chapter Twelve

January 28, 1804
Mrs. Pegeen Sharp
Longsatin House, Duncan Terrace
Islington, London

*D*EAREST AUNTIE,

Oh, how I miss you, my home, and Papa. There has been, rain, rain, rain, every day from the moment we arrived in Plymouth, Jewel of the Exeter Circuit. Belzoni and I are lodging at Madame La Capria's Theatrical Boarding House. Not together. Giovanni stays with the actors in the garret room on the top floor. My wee pallet is in the closet of a room occupied by four senior actresses. Cost: four shillings a week. Bathing opportunities: poor. Meals: mainly oysters—the cheapest food known to man, yet they keep me lively. I've learned to like the slippery things piled on brown bread and butter.

The Princess Theatre is three rain-soaked streets down the hill. Performances are well attended. The Royal Navy boys make up a great part of our audience. The long wool wrap you knitted for me has few opportunities to dry. Despite being cold and wet, I do feel warmed by the applause. Money will be arriving for you next week, never forgetting to put aside the sum that goes towards Papa's debts. Give him a kiss from me. I pray you and Noddy are managing. What I am earning should provide a few comforts and some months of security. I console my homesickness with such thoughts.

Your loving niece,
Elizabeth Trumpet
P.S. I assume Mrs. Mantino is reading this to you, as she has my other letters. Tell her thank you and give my greetings to all the little Mantinos down at the livery stable.

Meeting with Philip Eggleston had changed the fortunes of Trumpet and Belzoni. The showman recognized Giovanni's size and power partnered with Lizzie's beauty and energy made them magnetizing together. Enthusiastically, he sent them on a tour of provincial towns, in the popular *tableaux vivants*, which required a charming appearance and no dialogue skills.

"Will I be required to show flesh?" Lizzie asked him.

"At your age and state of abundant health, I see no problem with your flesh," Eggleston responded. "These *tableaux* will be biblical stories, tales from the Old Testament. We are bringing sacred themes to life, so don't be concerned about exposure. Your costumes will be evocative of the Levant, Miss Trumpet, sandals, beads, and so forth. Mr. Belzoni will do well to let his hair grow long. He will portray that wayward Nazarite, Samson."

"Yet again?" Lizzie said, with eyebrows raised.

Ignoring her drollery, Eggleston continued. "And you, Elizabeth, as the delectable Delilah, will cause a sensation. Where available, a donkey will join you in the cast."

So, the untried actors went on the road together as the stars of *Samson and the Ass's Jawbone* and *Delilah's Shameful Short-Cut* with various donkeys. The tour's program included other acts and rotating plays in which the neophytes had only bit parts.

In spare moments, they labored to improve themselves. Belzoni set his inquiring mind to learning the arts of prestidigitation from the Astounding Absolom, a Romanian magician, soon to return to his Gypsy caravan. Mr. Herbert Holmes Pickle, an elderly character-man who declaimed the purple narration to which Samson and Delilah entwined, had responded to Lizzie's request for acting lessons. Her only previous instruction had been under the facile Dibdin, whose terse direction "more pace and vitality" was given to cover all eventualities. The girl realized there had to be more to it than that.

Mr. Pickle had never been famous. Lizzie guessed he had faced many indignities, working for small wages in small parts all his life. Yet he was still at it and, though close to dotage, never missed a line or bit of business. She respected his stamina and pride, and sensed his passion for the stage matched her own. Pickle, in mellifluous tones, assured Lizzie that she was a beginner, no matter who her father might be. Daily, she regretted William had never shared his stagecraft with her, but believed she could learn much under Pickle's moldy wing.

On the frigid, bare stage of the Majesty's Theatre in Weymouth, while drizzle washed the streets outside, she commenced a study of Juliet. The old actor directed his remarks from the pit, emphasizing them with a walking stick.

"Consider, Miss Trumpet, the text is a lyrical tragedy. So, though the character is but thirteen, she must not be a giddy ninny like one encounters today in any draper's shop. She represents pure love as Shakespeare described it. Ergo, your Juliet must be deep."

"I wish my Juliet to be real," Lizzie offered, shivering under her shawl.

"A rightful aim. Now step down to the fore-stage and begin."

"*Madam, I am here. What is your will?*" Lizzie said confidently.

"First, Trumpet, you will drop your voice from the pitch of nature to that of a professional player. In short, lower. More pleasing. Say it again."

"*Madam, I am here. What is your will?*"

"Better. Can you hear that is better?"

"I do."

"Now, posture the first. Bevel your right knee, place your right hand with fingers curved to the center of your chest, as in obeisance to your mother."

"*Madam, I am here. Wha—*"

"Why are your eyes cast down?" he called out sharply. "Have you found a loose nail on the stage?"

"I was making obeisance."

"A touch of obeisance is sufficient. Speak the line front, distinctly, favoring the patrons. Never make it difficult for the audience to see your face. Never."

"*Madam, I am here.*"

"Eyes! I cannot see your eyes!" Pickle tapped his stick and gave a scratch to the liverish spots on his chin. "Practice that posture and line one hundred times, no less. Now run out into the house and stand in the first box stage-left."

Obediently, Lizzie rushed into the dark passage behind the first tier of boxes and fumbled through the old dark green curtains that enclosed them.

"What was that? Are you all right there, Trumpet?"

"Perfect, sir," she sang out, rubbing her knee where she had barked it painfully on a corner in the dark.

"Balcony scene. Posture the second: approach the edge there and bend down towards your Romeo, right arm extended, left arm circumspect, head cocked thus."

She followed his direction. "This feels awkward, Mr. Pickle."

"Of course it feels awkward. How many times have you done it? Now say the poetry after me, copying my tone and inflection precisely.

"*Thou know'st the mask of night is on my face,*
Else would a maiden blush bepaint my cheek
For that which thou hast heard me speak tonight."

To the best of her ability, Lizzie complied.

The decaying actor sighed. "Well, Rome was not built in a day. I assume you did no Shakespeare at Sadler's Wells." He gave a condescending snort.

"I had to start where I was engaged, Mr. Pickle," she said reasonably. "And now I'm hoping to move up."

"It is laudable to have a dream. Come back down on stage now."
She did, favoring her bruised knee.

"A bit of Act Three Scene Two. In this speech, Juliet has found love and she longs for it. Hark to the emotion in my tone.

"Come, gentle night, come, loving black brow'd night,
Give me my Romeo; and, when he shall die,
Take him and cut him out in little stars,
And he will make the face of heav'n so fine
That all the world will be in love with night."

"You speak so beautifully, Mr. Pickle." Lizzie sighed with genuine admiration.

"As will you one day, Miss Trumpet. Hear me: a picturesque posture is vital. Have you seen Mrs. Siddons on the stage? Her postures are absolute sculptures of emotion."

"My father worked with her. Did you ever...?"

"No. I have never appeared with the queen of drama. In our profession, you will learn the race is not always to the deserving." They shared a wistful smile. "However, many times I have eaten at the Shoulder of Mutton Public House in Wales, where Mrs. Siddons came into this world." The old man scratched at his chin again. "To speak of your father...I find it curious he never prepared you for a life in the theatre, since you aspire."

"No, Mr. Pickle." Lizzie found a lump in her throat where a complaint might have been. "He just didn't. May we continue, sir?"

"Very well. Let us try Act Three Scene Five, where the lovers have just heard the lark, herald of the morn, and Romeo makes to depart before they are discovered. Juliet is importuning, aroused with passion. Let me mount the steps and show you." Making nothing of his stiff joints, the old actor sprang out of the pit and positioned Lizzie in his embrace. "Look up at me, Trumpet, woo me with your new-felt lust."

"Wilt thou be gone? It is not yet near day." Lost in the music of the words, Lizzie's spirit quickened with life's poetry and possibilities.

"It was the nightingale, and not the lark,
That pierc'd the fearful hollow of thine ear;
Nightly she sings on yon pomegranate tree:

Believe me, love, it was the nightingale."

Compassionately, Pickle smiled. "That was better, Trumpet. Love must be a subject you've explored."

"Only in books and plays, Mr Pickle, I've never made it my study."

"The devil you say! What of that big Italian you spend so much time with?"

"Giovanni?" Amazed to hear such a suggestion, Lizzie looked at Pickle with blank honesty. "He and I are good companions, nothing more."

"Well, I will caution you, if you continue as his Delilah that may change. Actors, wandering the world, thrust together in romantic scenes...." He bit his lip and eyed her impishly. "Bedding seems to follow as night the day."

"Really?"

"It did with me and Mrs. Pickle."

Mulling over Pickle's remarks on backstage romance, Lizzie withdrew to a discreet distance from Giovanni. The Italian behaved handsomely as ever. He concentrated on mastering *The Sands of Egypt*, a delicate trick of magic that turned red grains into azure. Gradually the weather grew milder, and the sun emerged to show her welcome face.

In March, Lizzie found etchings of Mrs. Siddons's *attitudes* in a local print shop: Terror, jealousy, remorse. She practiced them all, always including the draping of a six-foot-long scarf that was part of every depiction. Her stage voice strengthened and deepened.When a positive critique of their production appeared in the *Weymouth Crier*, Lizzie posted it off to Phillip Eggleston, enclosing a note of effusive thanks, to which Belzoni signed his large signature as well. In time the entrepreneur replied, engaging them for the spring. Their next venue would be the Bournemouth Horse Fair.

April 1804

Above the raucous theatre district, in the elegant comfort of his Bow Street rooms, Philip Eggleston perused the latest note of thanks and enclosed clippings from Elizabeth Trumpet. Through the years, he had received many such reviews and puffs from aspiring actors he'd cast upon the waters of art. One such actor, who no longer aspired but had achieved, mounted the staircase steps three at a time and burst into Eggleston's cobalt blue foyer unannounced.

Jonathan Faversham, tall, handsome, and very full of himself, had arrived. He pushed open the bedroom door to see Neville Boone, his manager's personal servant and secretary, passing his employer a starched white neck-cloth. Pale-featured Neville had spent his early life as a dresser, dancing attendance on actors. He was accustomed to being ignored until needed, but cringed at this disruption of the inner sanctum.

"Good morning, dear boy," Eggleston said, happily surprised. "How unexpected. Let the neck-cloth go now, Neville. Fetch us some coffee."

The dresser evaporated like a dew-drop in the sun, while Eggleston gestured the gifted young dynamo out of his bedroom and towards the tall-windowed salon.

"I need a word with you, Eggs," Faversham began.

"So I gather. Will you sit?" The older man eased into a lyre-backed chair, admiring his black-haired protégé prowling around the smart Pompeian-style furniture.

Nine years before, a shabby fourteen-year-old boy named Rykes Bowtree had turned up for an open audition, unskilled in anything but defiance and gutter-speech, hopelessly incapable of acting. But the famished face above the grimy collar caught the showman's interest; the burning turquoise eyes as much as shouted, "I'll do anything to escape. *Anything.*" For one London winter that was their arrangement. Gentleman's hygiene and sexual accommodation were the first lessons the wild boy learned. When spring unfroze the roads, Eggleston sent him on a provincial tour to learn an actor's life from the very bottom. Rykes drove scenery wagons, fed horses, nailed up placards, beat drums for pre–performance parades and was a "citizen" of everywhere in crowd scenes.

MacDougal, the company's leading actor, whose tights and tunics the boy washed out, was an aging player whose memory had dimmed along with his stature. Once, he had acted all the great Shakespearean roles. Now he acted bits of them, in whatever play was on. A line from *Lear*, a jot of *Julius Caesar*, and frequently a burst of song from *Much Ado*.

"*Then sigh not so, but let them go,*
And be you blithe and bonny,
Converting all your sounds of woe,
Into hey nonny-nonny."

"Hey nonny" signaled old MacDougal was up in his lines again. Rarely, an astute member of the country audience might inquire, "Is this a new version of the old Bard?"

"Yes, indeed," clever young Rykes had answered, "and what a fine arrangement of the folio's best lines!"

After many months of touring, the boy was given a chance at playing roles. He took the bait and the hook set deeply. Living amongst the threadbare theatricals, lying down with props and scenery, and hearing applause nurtured his dreams of popularity and power. By becoming an actor, he hoped to rise from obscurity and take his revenge on a world that had ignored him. He swiftly progressed from silent super, to walking man, to jack-of-all-small-parts. The boy was gifted with more than beauty. A talent to deceive made him a natural actor, some might say a prodigy. He could change his wild dog personality to suit any situation.

Eggleston placed him in several repertory companies, moving him each season so his protégé might learn without picking up provincial actors' *stock* habits. The boy memorized twenty plays, forty, sixty, playing hundreds of characters and mastering all the traditional business that went with them. His brain was always racing. His height stretched to over six feet, his body became muscular, shoulders wide and sculptured from constant exercise. He walked with a purposeful swagger. The fine features of his face changed contours with clever make-up, but the eyes still promised,

"I'll do anything."

Enduring long journeys to such outskirts of art as Penzance and Launceston, Eggleston supported his creation with gifts of books and smart clothes all the while taking sexual pleasure in the boy's maturing charms. One memorable evening, while buttoning up after a singular tryst in a Cornwall graveyard, Phillip tripped over a tombstone. The name etched on that lichen-foxed marble was Jonathan Faversham. Rykes enjoyed seeing his mentor take an undignified fall and declared, "Faversham is a grand name, a lucky name. A new name for me!" He liked the dash of it and the previous owner was, after all, dead. Taking the view that Jonathan Faversham had sprung from his very loins, Eggleston agreed.

Being in sexual servitude to the older man was no great burden to the newly-christened Jack Faversham, only a means to an end. The first moment he stepped on stage in a leading part, audiences were captivated by his fire and intensity. Women thrilled to his animal style. In dressing rooms, private coaches or behind a tree, the actor satisfied as many of his admirers as there was time for.

Jack played violent, passionate characters brilliantly, and Eggleston made sure he played them often, but frequently had to smooth the troubled waters in companies when Jack's aggressiveness and selfishness roiled the cast. As Faversham's artistic success rose on the more important circuits, Eggleston's income rose as well.

Faversham's London debut as Paris in *The Doom of Troy* had launched him splendidly. All the critics said his Mark Antony in *Julius Caesar* was a highlight of the Haymarket's summer season. Phillip Eggleston had orchestrated all of it, cultivating the friendship of Kemble at Covent Garden where Jack was now on the roster for six plays in the season ahead. The boy who had indeed done "anything" was poised to become the next darling of the London stage.

However, in Eggleston's salon that morning, words of gratitude and satisfaction remained unspoken. The bronze clock ticked in silence below the figures of Ganymede and Jupiter ascending. Neville pattered in with the silver coffee service. He haughtily poured fresh brew into two Wedgewood cups, served Phillip, twitched the yellow draperies and pattered out.

Jack stopped pacing to bend over his aging mentor. "Did you know, old cock, what my roles at the Garden are to be?"

Phillip winced at the familiarity. "Of course, dear boy, Mercutio will be wonderful for you."

"I should be Romeo."

"You should be just where I've put you, Jack." Eggleston added sugar to his cup.

Jack strode to the gold cheval mirror. "Kemble is shaking in his boots."

"Look what an impact you made last season with Paris. Mercutio is a vastly better role."

"A secondary role." He shot his cuffs and raised a wing-like eyebrow at himself.

"Careers take time, Jack."

"How many years have you spouted that? You may be pleased with my arrangement at the Garden. I am not." He whirled on him. "Is that clear to you?"

The manager stirred his coffee and drew in a lungful of the rich mocha fragrance, ignoring the tiresome show of temper. "I was just reading a note of thanks from two young persons I sent out on a tour of the Exeter Circuit. Both are inexperienced, but amiable and quite attractive. Their humble gratitude for coming engagements strikes me as wise and appropriate."

"And good luck to them, poor sods." Jack threw himself onto a chair and collected his coffee. "I've proved my gratitude for nine years. And here I am in a slavery contract to John Philip Kemble—a hack if there ever was one."

On the edge of true annoyance, Phillip warned, "I trust you are keeping such debatable opinions to yourself, for all love."

"I should be running Covent Garden."

"You forget, in that contract you call slavery, Kemble is giving you three performances as Iago." In irritated disquiet, Phillip began to tap a light tattoo with his foot.

"Not enough."

"Patience, dear boy; don't get above yourself so quickly. Your talent is acting, not theatre management."

Jack eyed the ceiling, washing his mouth with the coffee.

"You always find more inspirations than are quite necessary, Jack. It makes things difficult for others sharing the stage with you. I advise you to avoid instructing Mr. Kemble in his own theatre."

"Kemble and his tribe haven't had a new idea in centuries. That stale self-serving family is the past. I am the future."

"Smugness is such an unattractive quality."

"You've spent too much time with middling actors, old cock. Sycophants, like those fools writing thanks in the penny post for a job in bloody Exeter."

"The Bournemouth Horse Fair, actually."

"Ah, I can smell it from here. But, I'm not them. I have a vision." He slammed down the Wedgewood cup, chipping the base.

"You may have vision, Jack, but I suggest you frame it with some charm." Faversham made a gagging sound at that, but the older man believed in what he was saying and enjoyed getting some digs in. "An actor does not exist without a company around him. To triumph in the famous roles you must have the ensemble players' goodwill."

"Cack. When I'm on stage no one else matters. And your opinion doesn't matter in the least, so the lectures are over. I don't care to listen anymore." Faversham stood up threateningly then leaned down to growl into Eggleston's sagging little face. "From this day on, you can stop poking your nose up my arse. Your services are no longer required." He exploded towards the door.

"I made you an actor!" Eggleston followed him, laughing to cover his shock, shaking like a butterfly impaled on a pin. "Just tell me, what is it you know about the theatre that I haven't taught you?"

"That again! Are you frightened of losing the money I bring in? Or frightened of losing my love?" Jack spun on his heel to hurl his sharpest bolt. "You tired old prick, what makes you think you ever had it?"

Stunned, Eggleston asked with the wonder of a wounded child, "Why such words to me now?"

"Because you think you know better than me, Eggs. Well, you fucking don't." Faversham exited with a telling slam that rattled the door bolts.

"So, we're shot of him at last. Born to be hanged, that one," Neville Boone whispered to himself in the tiny pantry, furiously polishing a silver punch-cup and overhearing every word. He had known Faversham of old and found him a loathsome ornament to Eggleston's life. *Good riddance to bad rubbish.* In private celebration, he poured a brimming pony of brandy for himself, then one less full for his master. A moment later, he tip-toed into the salon with a spotless napkin, should Eggleston require it to dry his eyes.

Chapter Thirteen

Early June 1804

"MADAM, I have come back stage specifically to meet you. I mean no discourtesy. I am confounded that there is no one in this confusion of horses and riders to introduce me. Let us forego the prescribed etiquette and present ourselves. I detest informality myself, but am quite aquiver to congratulate you and begin our acquaintance. I am Frederick, Lord Dampere."

The fat young dandy doffed his beaver hat to make a formal bow, forcing a creak from his corset. Squeezed into a modish black frock-coat over gold silk vest with black ribbon trim, matching buff breeches tucked into the turned-down tops of shiny black boots, this quintessence of fashion was under thirty and smelled of cologne. His friendly, full moon-face was blotched pink with excitement as it erupted from the strangling imprisonment of his impeccable linen neck-cloth.

Lizzie was pink herself, from the exertion of riding circuits of the show-rings on a long-tailed Arab, under three blazing five-hundred-candle chandeliers. The audience at Astley's Amphitheatre, in London, admired the arts of equitation. Following the grand finale each night, some wanted to meet the horses and finger the tack. Here was *a man of the first stare*, well-spoken, who wanted to meet *her*. This enthusiastic gentleman was a bona fide follower, the first of her career.

"My Lord," she said, dropping a curtsy, "I am Elizabeth Trumpet." *God in heaven, I know him. Viscount Landsdown's mansion, Pansy on the tabletop. He stood by Octavia's side. How could he not remember me?* Lizzie suddenly felt like one of the nearby horse-plops.

Lord Dampere babbled on. "Last evening, three of my particular friends, sporting fellows all, attended this grand festino and were enthralled by your death-defying performance in *Last of the Caesars*. Appropriately, there was nothing for it but to see you myself. *Ma foi*, it is exactly as they described. You made your entrance as the captive prize, gown shredded, hair flowing, thrown to the dust with riot all round, steeds criss-crossing to wild music, those Roman boys hard at it."

"Yes, it required quite a bit of rehearsal." *Why do the enthusiasts always need to explain the show to the performers?*

"There you were, under the churning hooves, frightful enough, when this hairy fellow, driving matched chestnuts, galloped by your prone body and, with one mighty arm, swung you into his flying chariot. It was *spectacularis*, as we used to say at Eton. I was so taken, I simply had to speak with such a daring darling."

Giovanni had been mad to learn the running chariot pick-up when they watched it at the Bournemouth Horse Fair. How many twisted necks, wrenched arms, and dislocated vertebrae it had cost Lizzie were beyond counting. No matter, they had beavered on to mastery, and the trick had gotten them this engagement at Astley's.

"I am glad you enjoyed it, sir. It is dangerous, but Mr. Belzoni, the charioteer, is very strong and does not miss. My arm hardly hurts at all."

"Extraordinary. Utterly." The man's plump cheeks shook again at the wonder of it all. He peered into Lizzie's face, with pleasure but no hint of recognition. "Damn me, but you're a fine-looking girl. I missed a few charms from the distance of my box. But even through that barbarian eye-paint, I see a face quite prime, utterly prime."

"My Lord, I don't know what to say." *Say goodnight. Retire before the man's memory improves.*

"Say you will be my guest tonight at Vauxhall Gardens for a cooling slush. Your work must make you very hot. Gad! So many female performers are low, utterly low, but your charm is unique. There, I've said it. Now may I whisk you off in my carriage, as the charioteer did?"

"You flatter me, my lord, but I beg to be excused tonight. I have an important rehearsal early tomorrow morning."

"Oh, very well." He smiled, not a bit put off. "I will excuse you tonight, but I shall return soon and frequently. I shall bring the fellows, and we will show you the town. There is not another girl like you in all London. I must know you better." Dampere bowed smartly. His head of ash-blond curls looked soft as a baby's. "*Au revoir!*" He left, slapping kid gloves against his plump thighs and whistling a jaunty air.

Equally jaunty, but with relief at not being recognized, Lizzie high-stepped through the horse turds to her dressing room.

Late July 1804

"Miss Pegeen, I've brought you some laudanum for your poor wrist. It will help you forget the pain." Octavia Onslow, gorgeous in a Spanish hat of purple velvet turned up at one side with a spray of ostrich plumes, placed a corked apothecary vial on the sturdy kitchen table.

Before Octavia's arrival at Longsatin House, Peg had been moaning in her chair with her arm trussed up in a sling. Three weeks past, the old lady had come a cropper of a skittish red hen in the yard and fallen disastrously, fracturing her right wrist.

"In all my seventy-four years, I've never tripped over my fowls," she had wailed, when Noddy and Lizzie pulled her out of the mud. "Jesus, Mary and Joseph! To be done in by a chicken!"

"Only one fall in seventy-four years?" Lizzie had tried to sound optimistic. "I'd call that the luck of the Irish, Aunt!"

"I never had a pain so sharp since back in County Antrim, when that explosion I set for the Protestant bastards went off before its time."

"Tell me about it."

"Not now."

How Aunt Peg came to have such a loping limp had always puzzled the Trumpet children, but they'd been warned to never ask. In her agony, Peg was letting things slip. Lamenting she was "robbed of all her abilities," she could not even dress herself at the moment, an indignity that led to tears. Pumping water took two hands, cooking meals, tending to William—all the tasks Aunt Peg had carried off without complaint while Lizzie toured—were impossible for her now. With a heavy heart, the girl watched her gallant little relative grow instantly older.

Now Lizzie had two invalids to care for. Aunt Peg and William were both too fragile to leave alone with only fumbling Noddy to nurse them. The girl could hardly step outside for fear that something might go amiss with the people she loved most.

For an hour, Octavia read racy gossip from *The Post* to William, but the day was a bad one and he did not respond. She patted his knee sadly when Lizzie called her to the dining room, where a bread-and-butter tea awaited.

From her new experiences, Lizzie had learned there were precious few ways for a female to make the money that life required. The saved wages from her Exeter tour and weeks at Astley's, stashed in the squat white sugar bowl, were dwindling rapidly. Her hesitancy towards Octavia had turned into gratitude after the incident at Hanover Square. Onslow had shown loving concern for William for so long that Lizzie now counted her a true friend, someone she could speak with candidly.

"I'm sorry to offer you something so simple, Octavia."

"It looks splendid, Elizabeth. Making tea was not necessary. I fear you are running yourself ragged these days."

"Well yes, I'm close to being at the end of my tether, but Aunt Peg has loved and cared for the Trumpet household all my life. I'm happy to do for her now. Thank you for that tincture. I just put a *soupçon* in her tea. How much should she have?"

"Oh, no more than three drops at a time. I take it myself on occasion, to drive the blue devils away. It is opium. Imbibed too often could cause a change in her manner."

Lizzie frowned, remembering the teaspoonful she'd stirred into Peg's cup. *Too late now.*

"How did she happen to fall?"

"Memories seemed to vex her," Lizzie confided. "A letter arrived from my grandparents in Ireland, the McGintys. A cold hard crew, I've been told. They cut Mama off as though she were dead when she ran off with Papa. Well, this letter was a brutal demand for money. When I read it, Aunt Peg waxed into a perfect fury. She tossed it into the fire. Then she went out to chop off a few chicken heads, and came to grief. It appears long ago my aunt was an Irish patriot of passionate, not to say violent, disposition."

"That's probably to her credit, Elizabeth. And who are we to judge?" Octavia cut a slice of bread and crowned it with a dollop of fresh-churned butter—Boozel the Guernsey's faithful contribution to the family larder. "Milkmaids selling on my street never have butter sweet as this. A cow of your own is a true luxury in wartime." Lizzie added hot water to the teapot, as her guest sipped. "How is your brother Georgie doing with his military studies?"

"Progressing well. I long for his company, but I fear his studies might change his character. He's has been reading *The Art of War* by Macchiavelli, some shrewd Italian with a villainous reputation. Do you know of him?"

"Never heard the name. And I thought I knew everyone with a bad reputation." She smiled and put down her cup. "Now tell me, Elizabeth. When will you be appearing on the stage again?"

"The bill at Astley's has changed. In the new extravaganza, *Rape of the Sabine Women*, every girl is required to stand on a galloping horse. Unfortunately that trick is not in my repertoire."

"What about Sadler's Wells again?"

"If I apply there, Mr. Dibdin will assume his overtures are welcome. Which assuredly, they are not." She squirmed in her chair.

"I do not speak of musical overtures. So I'm growing poorer by the day."

"I sympathize. But you must take action," Octavia said matter-of-factly. "I know. Get a lodger. That's the thing."

"I have considered it. But I'm wary of sharing our home with a stranger."

"An older bachelor of quiet habits would be best. Do you know of any?"

Immediately, Lizzie's mind turned to Carlo Tomassi, the jolly conductor who never pestered the girls at Sadler's Wells. "I may at that." She hesitated, pained to bring up a subject more delicate than finances. "Miss Onslow, on another matter. Have you, uh...chanced to meet with Lord Dampere recently?"

"I've not in several weeks. Have you?"

"He saw me at Astley's, but thankfully didn't seem to remember our first encounter, when...."

Octavia took Lizzie's hand to put her at ease. "Yes. I hardly remember myself. Do go on, Elizabeth."

"He wanted to entertain me, and returned so many times I at last agreed."

The redhead's expression sharpened with interest. "Where has he taken you?"

"To Vauxhall Gardens twice, very lovely. Once to a cello concert— he fell asleep. Once to a private gambling hell near Saint James's."

She chuckled appreciatively. "He is showing you the outer edges of the upper crust."

"I have met some of his old friends from Eton."

"How did you find 'the bucks?'"

"Rather silly. Like rude boys who think they own the world. They dragged us to a cock-fight in Southwark and behaved in a most blood-thirsty manner. But I was Dampere's guest, so I did not complain." Lizzie looked up to see Aunt Peg in the hallway, glassy-eyed and cheerfully leaning on the door-jamb.

"Tell her the nob gave you a Kashmiri shawl with all the India colors in it. Go on, tell her!"

"Yes, he did, and it's beautiful as a garden. Are you all right,

Aunt?"

"That tea tasted very strange, but my wrist feels better. Tell the Whore of Babylon I'm obliged to her." Miss Pegeen cackled and staggered back to the kitchen.

"Oh, Miss Onslow." Lizzie stood up in hot embarrassment. "Your tincture hasn't changed her manner yet. I'm so sorry."

Octavia was more amused than offended. "I've taken sharper darts than that, dear. Be at ease, Elizabeth, and tell me your thoughts of Dampie."

"Since Aunt Peg's fall I haven't ventured out with Lord Dampere, but he writes daily with expectations. I am both flattered and reluctant. You know him; please tell me what you think."

Octavia squared her velvet-covered shoulders to answer frankly. "He is more courteous than his rowdy friends, as you have seen, and very generous. Quite besotted by anything to do with the theatre. But you must prepare yourself, Elizabeth. Once you accept a man's favors, even a dullard will propose payment of some kind. All men do."

Fall 1804

Lord Dampere's friends, the "bucks," behaved as was their custom in the theatre, peering through quizzing-glasses at the audience from their box, making witless jokes to each other and ignoring the Covent Garden stage altogether, where Othello was writhing in jealous agony, not fifteen feet away.

Lizzie was leaning forward in her expensive seat beside Lord Dampere, transported by the performance of Jonathan Faversham. As the calculating Iago, he fairly slithered with delicious evil in silk tights that lapped over his well-shaped legs. Jack delivered Shakespeare's dialogue in a natural way, compelling and fresh. She had felt the same novel excitement the night Faversham played Paris to her father's Tyndarcus. *That voice. The look of him. He has it all.* Mr. Pickle would have scorned Faversham's Iago, but Lizzie found it a revelation. The girl's imagination and sense of possibility were awakened by the lithe actor. *What would it be like to have a man such as that in my life?*

Lord Dampere, the heavy young "pink of the ton," who actually was in her life, squeezed against her all evening. Underpinned by his boned corset and adorned with jeweled rings, he was certainly a contrast to Faversham.

Aunt Peg had healed enough to manage a few tasks, so Lizzie said yes to an occasional outing with Dampere. She had grown used to the pudgy peer's effusive company. Wednesday last he had taken her to a fashionable sculpture gallery in Old Bond Street where the works of John Deare were for sale. It seemed erotic art was another Dampere passion. He had a collection of stimulating pieces, hoping some day to join the Society of the Dilettanti where privileged men honored art and the Roman god Priapus—he of the oversized phallus.

A raised-marble panel of Venus reclining on the body of a goat-headed sea-monster proved irresistible to Lord Freddy. The monster's curving horns were inclined back in ecstasy, while his thick, snaky tail cuddled the nude goddess of beauty. Cupid shot off an arrow above the scene. Lizzie starred at it demurely, clutching her reticule.

"You see, the *putto* circling Venus with a flaming torch? That's passion," explained Dampere, sweat dripping from his brow like sap oozing from a tree. "What do you think of it, Miss Trumpet?"

In the presence of so much sex on the wall, Lizzie was hard pressed to answer appropriately. "Wonderfully carved. The goat looks hairy and the water looks wet."

"Do you like the subject?"

Is he asking my inclination to bed? With reticence, she averted her eyes. "It is inspired, I'm sure."

"Spot on, Miss Trumpet. Utterly prime. You see that Venus has dropped her shawl? Her fingers touch the flesh of her thigh, pressing it in just so...prime. Yes, I've got to have her."

Since that day, Lizzie hadn't given a thought to sculpture, but in the theatre box, watching Faversham's riveting Iago, she was delighted to study a perfect masculine form. The last thing on her mind was the growing leviathan curled up in Dampere's satin breeches.

⚬❧

Spring 1805

"Open your throat as if you are swallowing a big porky sausage." The musician stretched his mouth to demonstrate. "Relax your jaw; those *ahs* need room to resonate."

Carlo Tomassi, the musical conductor of Sadler's Wells, had become the upstairs lodger at Longsatin House. He fitted Octavia's description—a quiet bachelor. As to his habits, it was unlikely he would try to smuggle women into his bedchamber. Dwelling near his work at Sadler's Wells was ideal for Carlo. Rent money in the sugar bowl cheered Miss Trumpet. The musician had taken to Lizzie from the first audition. Now he was providing her with gratis vocal training, and accompanied Lizzie on the pianoforte as she sang her scales in the grey salon of home.

"Well," Carlo offered, after she easily achieved a high C, "not to put too fine a point on it, my dear, if you work hard...." She nodded vigorously. "One day you will be capable of really singing. I mean opera. You have a fine voice, perhaps even a great one."

Lizzie thrilled at such a promising evaluation. Between arpeggios and vocalises, they gossiped of the theatre, Lizzie dwelling on her enchantment with Faversham, the rising star, and her continued wooing by Dampere, the swollen aristocrat.

"Lord Freddy has written a play of sorts to be performed by himself and 'the bucks.' His old Etonian chums. It stars me, as an Indian princess of Virginia. He promises the elite of the elite, those persons he calls 'slap up to the echo,' will attend. It's to be in some lavish venue near Saint James's, God help us all."

"About this Dampere...." Carlo fanned himself with a Monteverdi score and spoke in his avuncular manner. "How does he behave in your company? Treat you with decency?"

"He looks ready to pounce all the time, but hasn't so far."

"I conceive by now you know the ways of importuning men?"

"I learned a bit about them at the Wells."

"My congratulations on escaping Dibdin's clutches. Heigh-ho!" Lizzie gathered Carlo was a keen observer of backstage intrigues. "Speaking of that musical stud, did you know Charlie's building a water tank for spectacles? We open with *The Siege of Gibraltar*."

"No more clowns and dancing?"

"Oh, more than ever. Just imagine, all his girls must dive into this artificial sea and climb out, soaked to the skin. They'll look stark naked in their wet fleshings. Now they have to please Charlie and avoid drowning as well. You're well out of it, my darling. Belzoni is engineering most of the hydraulic devices, going to fill the tank from the New River. He's put up a maze of piping under the stage. Your Italian friend is tireless."

That explains why Giovanni has been out of sight. Glad to know an engineering project was in the works for him, Lizzie smiled. *That will make his spirits soar.* "Good for Belzoni."

Carlo stopped fanning himself and looked serious. "You must do the Dampere play, even if it's dreadful."

"Dreadful it is."

"Do it, regardless. His Lordship has written it for you, and that's a great compliment, even if he is a hopeless twit." Carlo plinked the keys of the pianoforte. "You'll learn much from the experience!"

Lizzie folded away her music. *That's what I fear.*

Chapter Fourteen

June 1805

V AUXHALL GARDENS was sultry that summer evening. Nevertheless the best people in their best clothes were parading the formal pathways, rounding the cooling fountains, posturing under the trees. Lord Dampere and Lizzie stopped to sip peach slushes by the beloved statue of George Frideric Handel. On the balconies of the music pavilion, string players in old-fashioned powdered wigs scraped away on the composer's *Water Music*, but Lizzie was too destroyed with fatigue to enjoy it.

The last rehearsal of *The War Whoop: or La Belle Sauvage* had transpired earlier in the evening. It was just like the first rehearsal: a shambles. Dampere had thrown together his ridiculous entertainment solely to stoke his own vanity. Lizzie was to be his "discovery" as La Belle Pocahontas in a fluff of feathers. His Lordship played John Smith in a compressing Jacobean breastplate, while the bucks portrayed savages, as suited their natural gifts. Not one of the old Etonians had learned a speech or a song. Instead they made Dampere the butt of their witless jokes. The foolery didn't seem to bother his good nature. The baby-faced young gentleman was having a high old time. Since arriving at Vauxhall, he had accosted every person he recognized to invite them to tomorrow night's "one and only performance."

Trying to forget the theatrical horrors that lay ahead, Lizzie was bending to admire the hydrangea bushes when her escort called out, "George. I say, George!" to a handsome man and a satin-swathed woman, just turning into the pathway.

"Well, Freddy, it's you, I see," the impeccably dressed gentleman answered, removing his hat. "I was just telling Julia about your exquisite jasper snuff-box that I'm planning to steal one day. Now I see you've acquired something more precious than a snuffbox. Who is this little bird clutching your arm so amicably?"

"This is Miss Elizabeth Trumpet, daughter of William Trumpet the actor, and now an aspiring actress herself. Elizabeth, may I present Mrs. Julia Johnstone and Mr. George Brummell."

Lizzie curtsied. *Why, this is the most famous whore in England...and the great style-setting dandy Roger is always talking of.* "Beau" Brummell looked stunning in a white cravat and pique vest, under a sharply cut black tail-coat—a triumph of understatement, down to his plain black pumps.

"Howje do, Miss Trumpet." The arbiter of fashion evaluated Lizzie's gown with a raised eyebrow and smiled. The white silk cut low in the neck with an overlaid tunic of silver-shot net, was a gift from Dampere. Lizzie had accepted it reluctantly, but now was glad to be well-dressed in such company.

"Delighted, I'm sure," she responded, tucking in a wisp of loose hair that had escaped from her Greek-fashion twists and braids adorned with pale roses.

"Fortunately your escort has stopped wearing jeweled buckles on his shoes and waistcoats that hurt the eyes." Brummell resettled his hat on his clean clustered curls. "I've been at him for at least two years, saying let the peacocks wear their blinding colors, but God spare dear Freddy."

The men carried on about their clothing, chins thrust up by collars so stiff they reminded Lizzie of two herons squawking in a swamp. *Mrs. Johnstone is no particular beauty, except for a wealth of hair...and a solid bosom.*

A humorous twinkle lit the Cyprian's black eyes as she appraised

Lizzie appraising her. "I've met your father, Miss Trumpet, a most charming actor. Is he appearing this season?"

Lizzie had to say no, but offered no details to this stranger.

Dampere seized the topic of acting as a cue to gush about his *War Whoop*, urging the couple to attend. They made a noncommittal reply and swanned away.

"My Lord, I am near to fainting, and the evening grows late." Lizzie's stays were biting into her ribcage. *Oh, to be home with my feet up.*

"I was just of a mind for a cold collation. Sustenance is a wonderful idea. I cannot return you to Islington in a state of faintness." He propelled her to a lantern-lit table, summoned a yawning waiter, and ordered marzipan cake and compotes of *fraises de bois* with champagne. "There is a matter I'm burning to discuss with you." He thrust his glowing face unusually close to hers and lifted her hand from the pink tablecloth to give it a moist squeeze.

A hoarse laugh from a party of strangers broke into their privacy like a cannon shot. A dozen people, bursting with gaiety, descended on the adjoining table. Lizzie caught her breath to see Jonathan Faversham himself was playing the host. His merry crew, from the King's Theatre Haymarket, were celebrating the closing night of *School for Scandal*, choosing to raise a glass in the Gardens' romantic atmosphere before facing unemployment the next day.

Being a devotee of the theatre, Dampere was delighted by this intrusion of actors. He jumped up to congratulate Faversham on his "utterly *spectacularis*" performances as Joseph Surface in *Scandal* and Iago in *Othello*. Then he proudly introduced Lizzie and invited Faversham to join them. The wolfishly handsome actor sat down and never took his eyes off her.

"Your Iago, so unique, such an insightful portrayal, Mr. Faversham. I felt privileged to see it," Lizzie, no longer near to fainting, hastened to say.

Stroking his velvet lapels, Faversham purred his thanks. "May I beg one of your strawberries, Miss Trumpet?" The actor plucked a fat one from her silver dish and slowly licked it before tossing the morsel into his mouth.

"You made a vivid impression as Paris in *The Doom of Troy*. At Covent Garden? If you recall my father was also—"

Jack cut her off, not listening to Lizzie's words but paying great attention to the lips that spoke them. "These strawberries and a crumb of cake are measly fare for a lady of such good taste. Why not have the Vauxhall sandwich, with the ham cut famously thin?"

She looked at his flirtatious face. *What is he saying...so charming...something about a sandwich?* She shrugged helplessly.

"What say we share one and judge for ourselves." Faversham snapped his fingers. "Waiter, more champagne."

Gazing at this fascinating man, Miss Trumpet's huge green-brown eyes glowed bright as the candles on the table, the lanterns in the trees, and brighter by degrees than the stars above the night's incipient fog.

Lord Dampere had been occupied paying the bill, but his voice cut straight through Lizzie's pleasure when she heard him say, "*Par bleu*, Faversham, you might enjoy coming to see a performance at the Cuckoo's Nest tomorrow night."

"The private salon near White's?"

"You know it? Excellent. I and my friends are acting in an amateur theatrical." Faversham nodded, barely distracted from watching Lizzie. "And our leading lady for the evening will be Miss Elizabeth Trumpet!"

She clutched her wine glass. *Oh, nooooo!*

The handsome actor, suddenly all attention and good manners, turned to Dampere. "My lord, I shall certainly make my way to the Cuckoo's Nest to see...what is it called?"

"*The War Whoop*," she muttered, the joy gone out of her voice. *Stop him, stop him....* "But, I'm sure Mr. Faversham has no time for amateur entertainments."

"You are no amateur," Dampere asserted with pride.

Before Freddy could embarrass her with tales from her resume, Faversham spoke up with decisive charm. "I will enjoy everything, I'm sure. Until tomorrow then?" He bowed graciously and returned to the forgotten group at his table.

Dampere poured the last of the champagne into two tall flutes.

"Now, Miss Trumpet, for that most important matter." He pushed back his chair and beckoned her to rise.

"Yes, my lord." *What a serious tone...and all at once such...dignity.* Lizzie followed him down an empty path to a small fountain where they sat on the cool marble rim, listening to the splashes and twirling their glasses.

"Elizabeth, I find you an utterly splendid girl. I would like to engage you for more than just a play." He set down his glass. "I am offering you a formal written contract to go into my keeping." Lizzie wished she had not heard, but Dampere rushed on, self-consciously. "*Carte blanche*, as the saying goes. I will provide a house, servants, clothing, jewels, funds to care for your father and aunt, a gig or curricle for your own use, theatre tickets and a box at the opera to indulge your love—our love—of the stage. I will also supply an annual stipend, agreed upon by you, me, and my solicitor, so you may live in style and put something by for your future." His tone softened. "These comforts and accommodations can be yours if you will become my exclusive mistress for as long as we both enjoy each other's company. Also, I will give a prime bonus, in gold, for your virginity. If I am not too late."

There it was. The proposition, just as Octavia foretold. Though the proposal was cold-blooded, Dampere obviously was not.

Her mind raced. *This is the way of the world. The rich and powerful always dally with the poor and powerless. How powerless I was at Lord Landsdown's.* She averted her eyes to the gardens, still teeming with the careless and wealthy. *There would be more such nights, entertaining "the bucks," without pretense of romance and love. Mama lived for love, pined for it, and what did it get her?* She raised the glass to her lips. *Georgie forgave me the Wells, but would he support my whoring? Not likely. But, in exchange for giving myself to a man I could never love...I could provide for my father. Is that what I must do?*

The surge of excitement she had felt in the presence of Faversham would never flare to a flame with Dampere. Yet? In exchange for reputation...security. In exchange for the stage...this sweating booby.

"You surprise me, Dampie." The name slipped out. Lizzie had

never called him that aloud. "I didn't realize you thought so much of me." *Does he think anything of me at all? A golden bonus for my virginity? Dampere found me in an arena, what could I expect?* She composed herself to look at his round hopeful face. "Though I have no personal experience of such...contracts, your offer rings of generosity."

Dampere's expression grew more hopeful. He began to loom in for a kiss. It would be their first.

But she raised a hand to stop him. "It is nearly impossible for me to imagine such a change in our situation. First we must perform your play, then I will give you my answer." She finished the champagne; it had gone flat. "I shall need a day alone to decide."

Thirty-six hours later, Lizzie and Noddy labored in the side yard of Longsatin House, boiling wash in the cast-iron pot over a popping fire. This day Dampere expected an answer, but her thinking was as disheveled as her appearance. Lizzie, running with sweat, hair shoved under a limp old cap of Aunt Peg's, stirred the laundry with a broom handle. Steam had soaked through the cotton slip and thin chemise she wore for the wet work.

"Hail, Pocahontas! Hail, great Indian princess!"

Looking up from her task, she saw Jonathan Faversham, bigger than life on a glistening chestnut, riding round the oak tree and into the yard.

He raised his hand in salute and said, "How."

Oh, my God. In her surprise, Lizzie dropped the broom-handle into the bubbling smallclothes.

Faversham laughed heartily and eyed her breasts through the sopping chemise. As he dismounted, the kitchen door flew open.

William Trumpet, wearing a rusty Spanish helmet and brandishing a sword, ran toward the stranger, yelling hoarsely, "Touch not my Dulcinea! Aback, muleteer swine! Aback!"

"Papa, no!" Mortified, Lizzie made a dash for her father. "Noddy, help. At once!" The kitchen boy dropped a basket of clean sheets in the dirt to grab at Trumpet, who swung his sword in righteous froth. William's daughter and servant wrestled him back into Longsatin House.

Faversham coolly observed the argy-bargy while tying his horse to the oak tree. He flipped the tails of his coat and sat to wait on the stump where so many chickens had entered paradise.

Lizzie tore off Aunt Peg's unflattering cap, ordered Noddy to keep William occupied, then returned to the yard alone. "I do apologize, Mr. Faversham. My father once played Don Quixote."

"And so he did again today," the actor said kindly. "I was in no danger then. He is very devoted to you."

"And I to him, Mr. Faversham."

"Please, call me Jack...if I may be permitted to call you Elizabeth?"

"You see me at my worst, sir." She picked up the dropped sheets, her loose hair falling in wild waves over her shoulders.

"And I've seen you at your best. I was in the audience of lay-about lords on those little gilt chairs last night at *The War Whoop*. The others in the cast were at their worst. Not you."

Dear Lord. She cringed. "I can't imagine why you came."

"To see you. Not to watch Dampere fall down and be unable to get up in his armorplate, thrashing about like an upended turtle. Your Pocahontas had convincing dignity and, against all odds, determined concentration." She set down the laundry basket to take in this shower of praise. "Movements graceful, voice modulated when speaking those atrociously written speeches. You sang the songs in perfect pitch, too."

"Oooh, my." Such an unexpectedly good review from so talented an actor overwhelmed Lizzie. She could not meet his turquoise eyes and, looking down, discovered her drying chemise had glued itself to her nipples. Hastily she crossed her arms.

Jack removed his hat. "Elizabeth, I came here today to apprise you of my next endeavor, and persuade you to have a part in it."

"You have my attention, sir." *Did I hear correctly?*

"Jack, remember."

"Oh, yes, of course." *His smile, his smile.*

"I am about to create the finest company of actors in England."
He paused, dropping the words into a perfect silence of expectation.
"I propose to hire you for that company, to make you a true actress—
the actress I know you can be."

Oh, God of heaven. Lizzie forgot to breathe.

"The Faversham Players will tour the best theatres. You will learn
all the leading roles from the great plays under my instruction and
direction. Then, when you are ready, you will work opposite me."

Lizzie felt like toppling over. "You believe in me so much?"

"I do," he said so emphatically the dark curls of his shoulder-
length hair shook with sincerity. Jack had been thinking of nothing
but Elizabeth Trumpet from the moment of their meeting. Here was
a girl bursting with life, a natural leading lady, yet an untried actress
who would be no competition to him. He could mold her into a
perfect partner onstage, and without doubt, bend her to his will
offstage. Jack knew all beautiful women longed to be taken seriously,
so cannily, he did not praise Lizzie's striking looks, though that was
half her charm. He played the card of art and sacrifice.

"Elizabeth, you must perform. I will teach you a style of acting
that is revolutionary. You have seen my work. You understand the art
I worship."

She took a step closer. "Since I was a child, watching my father on
stage, I longed to be there with him." Jack watched Lizzie struggle to
go on. "You have just described the dream of my life. There is nothing
I want more, but...Mr. Faversham—Jack...I am not free."

He reached for her hands and pulled her down beside him on the
stump. "Explain why you are not free."

In a long and tearful soliloquy, Lizzie told her story of the past
year. She was too candid for propriety and too wrought-up by his
presence to withhold anything. In this soulful state, she was so
beautiful and vulnerable that Jack had to fight to keep his hands off
her.

"You need, as in a play, an ailing uncle to leave you a great
inheritance," Jack suggested with sympathy.

"Indeed, I have just been offered 'protection' by a gentleman."

"It must be Dampere, the creature! I guessed as much! That's why

I broke in upon your privacy in such haste. Listen to me, Elizabeth. I promise you a weekly income, not of shillings, but of pounds. From the sound of it, your first concern is caring decently for your family. Join me, and you will be able to provide for your father and aunt and whoever else you are carrying on your lovely back."

The emotional girl looked at him as though he were a god.

Jack turned on his serpent-of-Eden charm. "Why take up with that toad Dampere? Come with me and live your passion while you keep your reputation. I can turn you into a real princess, Pocahontas—a princess of the stage."

That did it. Dazzled, Lizzie said something irrational that meant yes: "The honor...do all I can...prove your faith." It was the grateful garble of a person saved.

Satisfied to have gotten his way, Jack sealed the bargain by taking her head in his hands and kissing her full on the mouth. "Gad, we'll be good; I know it." He bowed and strode to his hired horse. "I have urgent business in the city. Be glad, Elizabeth. I certainly am."

He leaped into the saddle and cantered away. Actually, he was off to a backstage intrigue at Covent Garden. Waiting in his dressing room, another would-be actress of no performing ability whatsoever was ready to audition what talent she did have on the chaise lounge.

Lizzie watched Faversham until she could see him no more. A freshening breeze lifted the leaves of the oak tree. She touched her tingling lips and thanked God for escaping a sordid life. *He is my savior.*

Frederick, Lord Dampere
10 Park Place, London
My Lord,
You have given me many memories to treasure. I thank you for all your attentions, but, after careful consideration, I cannot accept your offer. My performance in The War Whoop, *which you so graciously wrote for me, has resulted in my being engaged for the new theatrical company of*

Jonathan Faversham.

Being a lover of the drama, I know you will rejoice at this turn in my fortunes. Truly, I belong on the stage, and you will always be the most appreciative gentleman in the audience. Though my answer to more intimate acquaintance is no, I earnestly wish for your happiness. I hope I may still count you as my friend. I will always remember you as mine.

Gratefully,
Elizabeth Trumpet

Chapter Fifteen

Spring 1806

"STOP! STOP, all of you! This is agony. I can't stand it. You call yourselves actors?"

Throwing down the script, Faversham exploded at his cast from the front row seats. They were rehearsing in the empty echoing Old Salop Theatre, where perpetual twilight lasted till the evening lamps were lit. The new-made company had struggled around the lesser theatrical circuits of Britain to Shrewsbury, where Jack was adding *Pizarro*, a popular historical drama, to their repertoire. He was manager, paymaster, sometime playwright, and promoter. Starring as Pizarro, the black-hearted Spanish adventurer, he excelled.

"What are you all doing up there, posing for holy pictures? Though you may not have lines in this scene, you are nonetheless *in the play*! Your faces are as blank as a flock of bloody sheep," he ranted. "Thinking about your suppers, are you? Well, think again. I'll drop you from this company like a shot if you don't show me some imagination. Who are the characters? Why are they here? Why are *you* here? You look like ass-scratching *amateurs*! Nothing but a tribe of stupid birks. The Jonathan Faversham Players will be known for excellence if I have to beat it out of every single one of you."

The twenty-odd souls on stage endured the blast in silence, as usual. Those who could not bear Jack's harangues had packed up their dignity and departed weeks ago.

"Mr. Kelly and Miss McKay, take your pitiful selves to the green room and run your scenes. I remind you the Peruvians are noble souls, crushed by a conqueror, not three-year-old, thumb-sucking brats throwing a tantrum. Imagine some grandeur of spirit." Jack shook his head. "I shouldn't have to do it all for you!"

Kelly and McKay, young and unformed in personality, slunk away, commiserating, as their tormentor sought out another of his minions in need of guidance.

"Where is the child? Junius Brutus Booth!" he thundered. A small person of ten years and some sensitivity crept to the center of the stage. "You are an ignorant puppy, child."

"I am, sir?"

"Live up to your name!"

"Booth?"

"Silennnnnnnnnnce! Are you not named for Marcus Junius Brutus, assassin of the great Julius Caesar? Do not reply. Did I not choose you to play my skin parts? Do not reply. As there are no skin parts in *Pizarro*, I have created one for you." He spread his arms wide. "You are a bird, Junius, an *eagle*, not a long-tailed tit. An eagle *soars*, it does not *flap*. The eagle is power. The eagle is *freedom*. Do you not catch the symbolism?"

The child shifted his weight in his scuffy shoes and took a brave breath.

"Did I see you move? When I, your manager speak, you do not so much as scratch your ear." He dropped his voice dramatically. "There is more, a matter so elemental I should not have to explain it to a professional actor." Faversham looked to heaven and spread his hands as if to ask, *Why, Lord, why?* "When I tell you to take stage, I mean for you to command the attention of the restive audience. Divert them from the scene-change going on behind the curtain, the inevitable groans and squeaks. You are to do this by engaging the audience with your eagle's soaring flight, conveying the desire of our Peruvian protagonists for *freedom*. Could that be any clearer? You may reply."

"Clear it is, sir." The young Booth bit his lip dolefully, regretting he had not run away to sea, or America, which he heard was a land of freedom.

"Let me hear it!"

"Clear, sir! Thank you, sir."

"Character women!" Faversham grimaced. "You will not amuse yourselves at your director's expense. You may be surprised to know this is not a comedy. Your roles are patrician wives, albeit Indian and feathered. You are not women of the town, or pirate frumps; don't think I can't hear your improper adlibs, in Cockney dialect. Fuck all! We may be in Shrewsbury, but we're going to give our audience the best of London acting. Better than London, if I have ought to say about it. Get off the stage, all of you, and run your lines. Not you, Trumpet."

In the blooming beauty of nineteen, Lizzie awaited her moments with Jack, alert and alive. Within his company, Faversham had given her the attention she'd always craved from a talented artist. She believed making scenes and raging was a proper style of coaching. She thought Jack's cutting remarks to the actors witty and memorable, instructive, not cruel. Even when the barbs were aimed at her, the girl remained devoted.

Jack spoke in a softer tone than he used to the character women, but a cool one still. "Stop grinning, Trumpet; you disappoint me. I gave you Elvira because I believed you were ready to play a woman of the world. A conquistador's mistress. A female with spine and bottom. I have yet to see either."

"Sheridan's speeches are...."

"This is not a conversation, Trumpet. I am instructing you."

"Of course."

"Do not blame the author of the play. You should know better." He sat on a bench. "Now. Act Three, Pizarro's tent, the confrontation scene. Consider that Elvira so loved Pizarro she sacrificed everything and sailed to the New World with him. Imagine such courage! She loves him that much and yet.... Here is the drama. The *conflict*! She has seen his intemperate rage, heard him swear a terrible vengeance on the Peruvians. She is appalled, and tells him so. The lines are there. Say them."

Lizzie took a moment to gather her forces.

"*My soul is shamed and sickened at the meanness of thy vengeance.*"

He clapped his hands loudly. "What are you doing there?"

"What?"

"That fist against your face." He mimicked her pose. "What is that supposed to be?"

"A gesture."

"Inappropriate. Totally unbelievable! Would this be a last remnant of your asinine Pickle-postures? For the love of Christ, put that old fart's style of acting out of your mind. Elvira speaks for all women tortured by the failings of the men they love. She...." Jack leapt up on the stage, crossed his arms, and turned his back on Lizzie, ordering, "Speak to me!"

"*Pizarro, be not the assassin of thine own renown. Thou knowest I bear a mind not cast in common mold, not formed for tame, sequestered love. My heart was framed to look up with awe and homage to the object it adored.*"

The girl believed this speech described herself.

"*My ears to own no music but the thrilling records of his praise, my whole soul to love him with devotion! Make him my world! Pizarro! Was not such my love for thee?*"

Lizzie slipped into the moment, living it as two people. Was Elvira speaking to Pizarro or Miss Trumpet to Mr. Faversham? She jerked him around roughly, forcing him to look at her. Her voice commanding, anger and tears rose in her throat.

"*Thou man of mighty name but little soul. I see thou prefer to stare upon a grain of sand on which you trample, to musing on the starred canopy above thee. Fame, the sovereign deity of proud ambition, is not to be worshipped so!*"

"Ah-*ha*! Finally!" Jack shook her by the shoulders. "Had to pull it out of you, but that is my Elvira! Smoldering like Vesuvius!" He kissed her hugely. "One day, Trumpet, you'll be my worthy adversary. Sheridan himself shall say so when we play *Pizarro* in London!"

Once again, Jack became the inspiring acting partner, warm and charming—his best character. His praise meant more than gold to Lizzie, and the promise of a London triumph, when he made it, had to come true. The actor manager, tyrant, and star shared his personal philosophy with his acolyte.

"As to that last line, you'll see. There's nothing wrong with worshiping fame when you're at the top of the bill."

October 12, 1806

Miss Octavia Onslow
15 Buckingham Street, London
My Dear Octavia,
What pleasure to hear news of Papa and the Longsatin household. You are very good to look in on everyone and send me word. With all our traveling about, it is a rarity for me to receive mail. I thank you for such thoughtfulness.

Since you mentioned having a rather restful season of late, I dare to suggest a change of scene. Would you enjoy spending more hours at Longsatin House? As we tour, I'm able to send home coin of the realm, not as much as I expected, but enough to settle all my father's accounts at last. That much at least I have done for him, but the watchful presence of a caring heart I cannot provide. Since September last, I have been home so infrequently I am perpetually concerned for Papa and Auntie. Could you attend them occasionally? My father so enjoys the sight of you, and Peg has learned you have many virtues, if not the ones she emphasizes.

Islington is green and restful. Our lodger Carlo Tomassi is a charming person, always at the theatre and never in the way. Noddy will do exactly as you tell him, if you tell him frequently. Should you wish to withdraw from being on display in town, our home is open to you.

As to my life, Mr. Faversham has at last chosen me for some dramatic roles. Touring these smaller towns, I shall learn and of course make my mistakes, but far away from more discerning audiences. Jack is a stern taskmaster, and I am certainly not treated as his pet. I have yet to achieve one performance entirely pitched to his ear for truth, yet I feel my powers increasing. Others of our band complain and disparage his directions, but I welcome them all. Acting with him lifts me to the very realms of the sublime.

In private, his charming attentions are a delight. What I feel for Faversham is quite overwhelming. I understand there are consequences for a passion indulged, but it is more difficult each day to maintain a cool detachment. His presence in a room draws the breath from my lungs and the sense from my head. I long to offer him every intimacy, yet fear that is the surest way to lose his good will, my standing in the company, and my reputation. Yet how am I to act the part of passion when I know nothing of the act of love?

Octavia, could you advise me of the fulfillments of the flesh? Daily, I grow more weakened with desire for this whirlwind of a man. No other female has my confidence or your experience of the world. May I follow the inclinations of body and heart?

I look forward to your reply.

Elizabeth Trumpet

April 1807

"Good afternoon, ladies and gentlemen. Welcome to the Nottingham Assembly Rooms. I am Michael Evans, your master of ceremonies, privileged to present to you Benjamin West's incomparable painting of...*The Death of Nelson*. Please stay in line. Maintain proper decorum mounting the stairs and walk this way."

In the April wind sweeping Old Market Square, the dour-faced, bespectacled Evans addressed his remarks to dignitaries of the town, families of substance, ambulatory veterans, humble folk, and the Jonathan Faversham Company of Players. The painting, like the players, was touring the country. Reverence for Admiral Nelson, the fallen hero of the Battle of Trafalgar, was universal. Nelson's fleet had saved the country from invasion.

Climbing the crowded stairs, a peg-legged oldster pressed against the fetching Lizzie. "Didja know, miss, King George took this painter chap down to Spit'ead and 'ad the 'ole fleet maneuver for him so's 'e could sketch a picture." The actress gowned in red made polite noises to the veteran tar as he stumped up the stairs beside her. "'Ad the admirals firin' off broadsides so's West could paint the smoke, 'e did."

"Quiet there." This from Evans, who had led his visitors into the ballroom, where stucco cupids in the moldings stared back at the people herded against one flaking spring-green wall. In the close atmosphere, Evans positioned himself in front of the velvet drapery protecting the painting. "Benjamin West was born an humble Quaker in rural America. He taught himself to paint, first mixing his colors as the red Indians did, from river-clay and bear grease. He traveled to Italy, subsequently immigrated here to England, where he excited the particular interest of our King George. With the support of His gracious Majesty, he founded the Royal Academy, to the greater glory of British art."

Lizzie attended Evans with fascination.

"Get on with it," came a voice from the rear.

Evans sniffed, grasped the curtain pull and slowly revealed the grand painting. The public gazed in hushed silence at the scene of tragedy on the HMS Victory. The work was crammed with figures, Marines in their red coats, sailors in battle attitudes, some stripped to the waist, and clusters of officers in blue uniforms, their faces anguished. Stretched ghostly pale, a bleeding Nelson lay on the quarter deck, amongst his men while French guns bombarded from all sides, with plenty of fire and exquisitely-rendered smoke.

"What's this then? 'E died down on the orlop deck." The voice from the rear again. "'Orrible dark it was, deck that deep in blood. I was there, kissin' *adieu* t' my leg." It was Lizzie's sailor, of course. "I seen Nelson die meself. Oh, 'e died in agony, poor gent."

Evans drew a paper from his embroidered waistcoat with which to quash the critic. "We thank the veteran for his first-hand account, so devastatingly true. And I have here the artist's own justification for his staging of Nelson's death in this painting. I quote: '...to excite awe and veneration, and to show the importance of the hero. No schoolboy would be animated by a painting of Nelson dying like an ordinary man.'" The people nodded and peered around each other's hats to get a better look. Miss Trumpet was moved to tears.

"West should have hired an actor to portray the admiral," Jack Faversham proclaimed, from deep in his diaphragm, using tones that carried all over the room. "Horatio looks too peaky. England won the battle. He should be transfigured with joy."

"Are you an art critic, sir?"

Seizing this opening, Jack stepped out of the crowd and threw himself onto the Persian rug beneath the picture. "Here's how Nelson should have been posed: thus, smiling proudly in victory, noble profile turned towards the light, his dying expression sublime."

He demonstrated with his own strong profile while the crowd gasped and laughed. Some applauded. He rose to make an exquisite leg to the town-folk, who were no longer looking at the painting. The patriotism of the hour had been eclipsed, and the hero of the afternoon was turning out to be not Britain's most gallant seaman, but Jack.

"My friends, we are the Jonathan Faversham Company of Players, tonight presenting that naughty satire *The Country Wife*. Not David Garrick's gelded version, but William Wycherley's own witty words brought back to life. I, Jonathan Faversham, will play the lecherous stallion Harry Horner. And Miss Trumpet, there in your midst in the appropriately scarlet bonnet, will portray the lusty country wife herself." He bowed with a semblance of humility. Lizzie waved. Kelly, McKay, and Booth, produced playbills to press upon the crowd. The adolescent ladies in the room awakened from their art-induced stupor to beg Faversham for an autograph.

Lizzie felt conspicuous, but obviously this was what the troupe was there for. Jack's performance on the carpet was a fine way to advertise their show. She believed all his choices were the right ones. After all, Faversham had chosen her for his leading lady. Following Octavia's advice to keep a distance between herself and this man, who commanded her every thought and dream, was fearfully hard.

Making her way down the stairs when Evans dismissed the visitors, Lizzie heard a female behind her say, "That man was unpardonably rude. I came to see Nelson, not some common strutting actor. My son died at Trafalgar." She glanced back to see the matron was shedding tears. "That man in the play has no feelings. He ruined the day for me."

The remark struck Lizzie like the quick touch of a foil, a stab of unexpected pain. It left a bruise of doubt in Jack's perfection, then faded, and was almost forgotten.

January 1808

Illyria Aflame: or Betrayed by Love was an exciting theatre piece Jack had written to wear down the virtue of his prize actress. The small-scale spectacle, set in sometime BC, cast Lizzie as a princess of Illyria, overwhelmed by Roman invaders, generaled by Jack.

Act One: The fair princess battles the Romans, declaiming speeches strikingly similar to Prince Hal's in *Henry the Fifth*. Nevertheless, she loses the war. Act Two: Now a captive, the princess continues to resist the enemy, singing a plaintive lament while chained to a pole. Act Three: Still combative and nearly nude, the feisty princess wrestles the general on his camp bed, her virtue betrayed by the love she has felt for her conqueror all along. Act Four: Abundant sex and servitude brings peace at last. Epilogue: Princess gives submissive speech, strikingly similar to Kate's in *Taming of the Shrew*.

The daring bit of nonsense gave Faversham a chance to be masterful and irresistible, the way he perceived himself, while Miss Trumpet in her pre-Christian wardrobe got flung around the stage and revealed delicious limbs that Jack knew would sell tickets.

The climactic tussle on the camp bed kept audiences in a state of tumescence. Being human, this excitement was shared by the actors. One night in Cheltenham, Lizzie felt particularly human as Jack rolled over her in his leather kilt. Their baiting dialogue, staged with slaps and caresses, was going so boldly, Cheltenhamians, in the rear of the theatre, had stood up to get a clearer view.

The curtain call placed Lizzie center stage with the company, as Faversham stepped forward to make a speech of thanks and take the only solo bow. After the curtain fell, Jack grabbed Lizzie's wrist with a hot hand. Assent was in her eyes at last. He pulled the girl into his little dressing room in the wings and bolted the door.

"You will remember this always," he breathed into her pulsing throat, kissing her shoulders and grasping a hard-nippled breast.

"I want to remember." Lizzie was turning to liquid, ready to be loved, more than ready to surrender. Faversham's wooing had been constant, his pursuit of the prize unflagging. The general's leather kilt dropped to the floor, a pink gown and the crown of Illyria followed when a sharp knock shook the door.

"Miss Elizabeth, it's me. Noddy! Are you in there?"

"What? Go away!" Jack growled.

"It's Noddy, sir, from Longsatin House. I do for Miss Elizabeth."

With apprehension, Lizzie pulled on Jack's dressing gown and unlocked the door. Noddy stood outside, cap in hand, looking most miserable. "Yes, Noddy. What has happened?"

"Miss Octavia sent me. Put me in the mail coach 'erself. Regrets to inform you.... Oh, Miss Lizzie!"

"Just say it, Noddy, whatever it is."

"Yer ol' pa 'ad a fall. Died this mornin', 'e did."

Chapter Sixteen

January 1808

"THERE MUST be a wake," Aunt Peg insisted, "so all the people William spent his life amongst may gather to remember and tell you their tales of what a fine and shining man he was."

Remorseful that she had been far away in her father's last hours, devastated that he had never seen her once on any stage, Lizzie cried and cried at the kitchen table. "But the circumstances of his death were so lowly and sad, Aunt."

"You would not see such a soul as William put in the ground without songs and stories of his glory days? The gathering will help to ease your grief." The old lady laid a wrinkled hand on her heartbroken niece's cheek. "Dry your eyes, Lizzie-darlin'. He knew you loved him. That he did."

On his last night, William had sleepwalked from bed to go searching in his costume trunk for the royal robe and crown he used to wear in Hamlet. Octavia was roused by the sound of his opening the kitchen door into the garden, then the scraping of a ladder, as he propped it against the house. In the cold beams of moonlight, he had climbed to the roof and begun to moan and declaim, striding across the slate tiles towards the steeple of St. Mary's. Octavia had rushed into the dark garden, shouting to wake him, but to no avail. William was the ghostly king on the battlements of Elsinore one last time. He cried, "*Adieu, adieu,* Hamlet; remember me," and fell to his death.

Lizzie consoled herself by telling Octavia, "Every actor wants to die on stage. What matter if the theatre and the audience were only in his mind? My father's ending must have been a happy one."

These sentiments were no comfort to Octavia, who had seen William fall. She let Lizzie believe what she wished. The demi-rep knew from her career in the chambers of love that desire and delusion go hand in hand.

Georgie had galloped home from High Wycombe, deeply shaken by his father's passing. Ted Wentworth, the polished son of Sir Henry Wentworth, accompanied him. The cadet had become Georgie's best friend. A steadying presence, Ted felt proud to stand by his brother-in-arms.

Once more, the front door of Longsatin House wore black crepe. William Trumpet's open casket rested—center stage—in the grey salon. Tapers blazed around him in bright silver candelabra. Octavia had provided that silver and some fortifying drams for herself and Aunt Peg before the guests arrived. Georgie had sprinkled cloves to smolder in the fireplace. Carlo Tomassi's order of claret and roasted joints of beef from the Old Queen's Head waited on the mahogany dining table. Peg had fricasseed a whole flock of chickens to serve.

In the kitchen, Lizzie slid a black armband onto Noddy's clean sleeve. His wingish ears were flushed from hard scrubbing. "Go stand ready by the door and say, 'Welcome to the Trumpet home,' as people come in. Take the ladies' wraps and the gentleman's hats, and...." The lad looked lost. She whispered, "Thank you for all you did for him, Noddy." She patted his shoulder. "Look sharp now."

Carlo eased into the good-smelling kitchen and took her face in his hands. "Darling girl. Take a deep breath." It was his advice for every situation.

In her ears sparkled her grandmother's little diamonds, worn this day to give her strength. The case-clock struck two as mourners began to appear.

The Mantinos arrived first, without a whiff of the livery stable clinging to their best clothes. The entire family crowded around William's casket, even the littlest children shy with solemnity. Meg and Dick Wilson greeted Georgie with an embrace, remarking on how he was turning into a "handsome fellow." Toby Carey entered with threadbare gravitas. Dozens of actors and actresses from Drury Lane and Covent Garden, speaking in hushed voices, filled up the house. John Philip Kemble ponderously made his way through them to the head of the casket. Thomas Jupiter Harris found Lizzie in the crowd and kissed her hand. She turned to discover the dapper Phillip Eggleston, who made his condolences to her. Octavia, stunning in deep purple and all her jewels, offered him a libation.

Performers from a much less dignified theatrical world—little Grimaldi and large Belzoni—also squeezed into the room. "Lizzie, dear," the famous clown said, "we bring sympathetic greetings from Old Dibs, who is having a bit of a financial emergency in the City today. My own heart weeps for your loss."

"Oh, Joe, I thank you." Lizzie hugged Grimaldi as Belzoni gazed at the beautiful girl in black with circumspect devotion.

Lizzie saw Sidrack and Roger Sloane come in, respectfully removing their silk hats. Somehow the sight of Roger brought to mind all the sweet summers of their childhood. Her playmate had become a serious young man, and her uncle was leaning—ever so slightly—on his arm. Noddy collected their hats as she embraced father and son wordlessly.

"A tragedy, Lizzie," Roger murmured into her ear.

Sidrack took her hand, all three feeling a tide of sorrow that made words unnecessary.

"Father has just returned from South Carolina, Lizzie."

"What news of my grandparents, Uncle?"

"In good spirits. Of course that will change when they hear of this. William was their prince."

"Father and I have been talking," the young man said. "He thinks your grandfather is exhausting himself in the Charleston shop."

Sidrack gave his son a cautionary glance. "Ricardo just doesn't want to slow down though he's sixty-five. I'm thinking of sending my son off to America one day, to help him."

"If you go, Roger, Nana will be happy to have you close at hand," Lizzie said, thinking how her Nana and Papi must be growing frail, too.

"It would please me to be of help, but this moment may not be the best time to sail for America. You may not be aware, Lizzie, but this war is straining our trade on both sides of the Atlantic."

"Because of Napoleon?"

They were interrupted as Georgie shouldered through the actors to greet the Sloanes and introduce Cadet Wentworth, explaining, "Ted is the son of the very man Papa won the fortune off years ago, God bless him."

"Happily, my father is still in funds enough to pay for my commission." Ted laughed. "But you gentlemen were speaking of Napoleon?"

In a heartbeat, Roger sensed the confident, fine-boned Wentworth was sharing Georgie's life more completely than he, a tailor, ever would again. He pulled in his stomach, which was no longer soft, and stood tall in his boots.

"Yes, the Corsican Ogre," Sidrack said, "is excluding all goods from entering what he calls 'Fortress Europe.'"

"All ships that call on British ports are now designated enemy vessels. You see, he's trying to break our trade, so we must blockade him," Roger rushed to explain.

"We heard at school that the Royal Navy is starting to seal off the American coast," Georgie said.

"They've already confiscated hundreds of American merchant vessels," Ted added, "and pressed thousands of American sailors to man the British blockade of France." At the fearful word "pressed," Belzoni turned to listen. "HMS *Leopard* hailed some American ship...."

"The *Chesapeake*, I believe," Roger spoke up.

"Yes, the *Chesapeake*. Any road, the American captain refused to heave to, so the Leopard opened fire, killing some, wounding several."

"Dear God, I had no idea." Lizzie gasped, always aware her

brother was destined to be an officer. "Are we going to be fighting two wars? Are we to be cut off from America?"

"We are already, Lizzie," Georgie said. "I'm intrigued, Uncle Sidrack. How the devil did you sail into Charleston Harbor and back through the blockade?"

Sidrack glanced around the crowded room to see the theatricals engaged in their own conversations. "Children, it would be best if you kept this to yourselves." Lizzie and the two cadets leaned in. "Roger, tell them, lad."

"A few years ago, I made the acquaintance of a fellow named Owen Lewis at Sergeant Mento's Parlor of Self Defense."

"A flash type?" Ted asked, eyebrows raised.

"No, no, hardly a criminal." Roger laughed at the thought. "A sparring partner to me. His father is a surgeon who moved his family from Wales to South Carolina where, as it happens, Doctor John serves as physician to your grandparents, Lizzie. Owen is a tip-top sailor. He captains a small merchant schooner."

"This Owen is a daring young man." The elder Sloane took over the narrative. "Enterprising, if you catch my drift. Cruises back and forth across the Atlantic, carries a British passport and flies American colors, too. He has a crew of many nations, with the foreign lingos to obfuscate any interrogations."

"A smuggler?" Georgie hissed, amazed at his old friends.

"'Blockade runner,' Owen would prefer. Adam & James could not do business these days without...*Redbeard*," Roger whispered.

"Makes my heart thump," Lizzie said. Upset by the rush of world events, she drew out of the men's circle to catch her breath.

Eggleston was at her elbow in a moment. "Kemble there looks ready to make a speech. You know he's famous for orating at funerals. So, if you and your brother wish a word before everybody gets too tiddley to pay attention...."

"Thank you, Mr. Eggleston." Lizzie took Georgie's arm and they moved to William's casket. Noddy refilled their glasses. The room grew quiet.

"Ladies and gentlemen," Georgie began. "Thank you for coming today. Papa always wished to have a gathering of his family, his neighbors, and all you theatricals under this roof—a high old time with songs and sentiment, you might say. So, we know his spirit is happy and welcomes this loving assemblage." Lizzie gripped her brother's arm tightly. "Since our mother's passing, Papa was unable to rejoin his friends on the stage. These last few years, he was parted from his proper mind. But his heart was with the theatre to the last. Elizabeth and I treasure each memory we share of him. We now invite you to drink...to our beloved father...William Trumpet." They raised their glasses and the company responded.

"Hear him."

"To William."

"Dear Trumpet."

"Rest in peace."

The toasts were solemnly drunk.

Dick Wilson cleared his throat and stepped into a shaft of afternoon sun, pouring through the window. It glistened on his balding forehead like a spotlight. "A thousand nights and more William and I shared the stage." The comedian's voice was unsteady. "Superb in any part, he was an actor's actor, playing poetry, drama, comedy, and all of them perfectly. Sang like an angel, tenor or baritone, whatever was needed. I always got the laughs and gallant William won the fair lady at the final curtain. How many times we saved each other's arses when things went wrong, and shared the applause when things went right. Meg and I stood with him and the beautiful Jessie on their wedding day." He looked into Lizzie's misting eyes. "We never saw a man more bewitched by love than William was by your mother, children. I know it for a fact. As a man, he did the best he could. Like all of us. Elizabeth and George, he loved you dearly. I shall miss him, always. My hope, my expectation, is that in another day we'll meet again to join the Lord's celestial acting company, touring the stars of heaven with some nice fat parts!"

There were cheers and tears aplenty after that. Kemble sensed that his "out, out, brief candle" reminiscences would not be needed. Before any of the other actors could eulogize, a pale young man, unknown to them, raised his voice.

"If I may? My name is Roger Sloane and, as a tiny boy, I played in this household." He solemnly moved to a corner of the casket.

Lizzie turned to her shy friend and listened with emotions flowing.

"You see, my own mother died when I was born, so while my father went to business, the Trumpet family would look after me. Georgie's grandmother helped me take my first step, so they tell me. What I do remember very well was that Mr. Trumpet was always so kind to me. He was like a comet in the sky to us children—dashing in, full of excitement, leaving us all wanting more of him. I want to say, it is a fine thing that his daughter is following his path. Splendid, too, that my friend George is to serve our country. My father and I are proud to know them and to have known their father. We shall never forget him." He raised his glass. "I give you William Trumpet."

As the mourners drank, Lizzie's eyes met Roger's in gratitude. Aunt Peg's chirp broke the silence. "Georgie-darlin', will ye not play for us?"

"Only if my sister will sing."

Carlo opened the pianoforte and struck some sweet chords. The theatricals settled themselves to listen as Georgie took up his violin and announced, "Our father's favorite song."

Lizzie moved to Carlo's side. Imagining her parents together in their loving days was all that made it possible for her to sing.

"'Twas there, while the blackbird was cheerfully singing,
I first met that dear one, the joy of my heart!
Around us for gladness the bluebells were ringing,
Ah! Then little thought I, how soon we should part."

Lizzie faltered. The haunting melody of "The Ash Grove" was striking deeper than words, and she could not manage more. The music ended as Georgie encircled her with fiddle and bow in his strong supporting arms.

The Wilsons applauded, then departed with Kemble in Harris's carriage, all bound for the performance at Covent Garden. Other horses and conveyances waited beneath the oak tree. The Mantino Livery hands kept watch while their owners lingered and settled in for the duration of the afternoon, eating and conversing in little groups. Some guests eyed the woman in purple having a good cry on the stairs. Uneasily, Roger leaned against the newel post, listening to Octavia's lament.

"There'll never be another like William, not for me. He was such a passionate, caring gentleman." The tender confession flummoxed Roger, who was unaccustomed to dealing with ladies uncorseted by wine. "Even in his days of deep confusion that man always called me 'beauty.'" Her swollen eyes welled up once more. "Beauty. Such a kindness, now there's so little reason for it."

"Oh, Miss Onslow, you're a lovely woman still." He offered her his handkerchief.

In the dining room, with the actors, Ted and Georgie held forth behind the roast beef, discussing Napoleon's recent victories. The young cadets were the only men in uniform attending the wake.

"Positively numbing," Ted said, passing a plate to Grimaldi. "Rome, Barcelona, Madrid—he's taken them all. But Boney can't get a grip on the Spanish countryside."

"When you are commissioned, where do you expect to be posted?" Grimaldi asked.

"We have no idea, but we're hoping to get into the Peninsula fight," Georgie confided, carving a great slab off the joint for Belzoni. "Hardest days are waiting for graduation."

The Italian shook his head in wonder at the untried cadets' appetite for war and watched Lizzie join Sidrack on the scroll-armed love seat.

"I see you wear your Nana's ear-bobs today," Sloane said. "Your grandmother sends her love and gave me a recipe for you—benne seed biscuits." He reached into his striped vest pocket.

"Baking? I've no time for such domestic arts on tour, Uncle. I'm living a different life entirely," she explained with patience, assuming the older person could not fully grasp the scope of travel, dedication and drudgery required of a leading lady in Jack Faversham's company of players. "Such experiences. You cannot imagine!"

The survivor of many world travels nodded with amusement. "You will be returning to your tour then?"

"Oh, yes." Lizzie nodded emphatically.

"Ah, well." He withdrew his fingers from the vest pocket. "I'll just keep the recipe till your life is more settled."

"And how is the London shop faring?" she asked out of politeness.

Roger, arriving with a plate of supper to hand his father, was eager to answer. "Adam & James prospers, despite the war."

Lizzie gave him her attention. He had surprised her twice this day.

Innocently, Roger launched into a subject of unsurpassed dullness to the girl. "Mr. Beau Brummell purchased a pair of moleskin trousers Monday last, fitted tight as a sausage casing. Then His Highness the Prince of Wales appeared on Thursday requiring the same trousers, only five times as large. He was quite gracious to me, even charming. He ordered thirty silk handkerchiefs from Turkolu, too. His Highness is not the gluttonous ass cartoonists make him out to be."

"So, Roger, you are waiting on the Prince. What could be better?" Lizzie rose to speak to Toby Carey and left Roger on the loveseat, feeling there must be something more for him in life than fitting a fat man for a set of trousers. It was no consolation the fat man would one day become King of England.

"Time for more music," Aunt Peg ordered, imbibing yet another dram in the soft depths of William's chair. "And this time something jolly, Carlo."

Belzoni suddenly came to life. "Sing that tea song, Joe!"

Everyone wanted to hear Grimaldi do his star turn from Dibdin's latest harlequinade. They clapped as the agile clown somersaulted to the pianoforte and opened his very large mouth to sing.

"Mrs. Waddle was a widow, and she got no little gain.
For she kept a tripe-and-trotter shop in Chickabiddy Lane;
Her next door neighbor Tommy Tick, a tallyman was he,
And he ax'd Mrs. Waddle just to take cup of tea."

Enjoying several antic verses, Aunt Peg cackled like one of her own chickens, then burst out singing herself.

"An ol' man come courtin' me, O for to marry me;
Maids, when you're young, never wed an ol' man!
He has no faloodle, he's lost his ding-doodle;
Maids, when you're young, never wed an ol' man!"

Belzoni hurried to Lizzie's side whispering, "Lisabetta, your little Auntie is not herself. Do you want me to carry her to her chamber?"

"No, Giovanni, don't be shocked." She took a sip of wine, happy that Peg had risen to the occasion and was her old saucy self. "This sort of thing happens all the time amongst the Irish. Excuse me. There's someone rapping at the door."

The late arrival was Jack, turned out handsomely in his finest, laughing at Lizzie's surprise. His arms were full of wine bottles, which he placed amidst the depleted stores on the dining room table as the guests cheered Miss Pegeen's singing debut. At the sight of Faversham, Phillip Eggleston departed, slipping out through the kitchen door.

"Ladies and gentlemen, it warms my heart that so many of you have come to pay respects to the one and only William Trumpet," Jack began, entering the salon and projecting his manly baritone, by way of taking over the party. "He was an inspiring actor, and I'm proud to have shared the stage with him." He made his way around the casket to obscure a clear view of the deceased. "He also gave the world an outstanding daughter who joined my company just two years ago; Elizabeth has her father's gifts of charm and talent."

Lizzie stood breathless at the back of the room, thrilled to see Jack in her home, saying respectful things about her father. His words meant more to her than all that had gone before, because they came from him. She overflowed with tears and wine, love and sadness, vulnerable as a newborn babe.

"Miss Trumpet has all the qualities to make a brilliant career in our profession. I speak as the one who teaches her. She works diligently and makes me proud. So proud, I've chosen to make an honest woman of her, if she'll have me."

Miss Trumpet felt struck with a thunderbolt, suspended in air. Everyone turned to the wide-eyed Lizzie, but before she could think or speak Jack was upon her, dropping to one knee, hand to heart, addressing her and, of course, the guests.

"Elizabeth, before your family and friends, I ask your hand in marriage."

"Oh Jack, you love me, you really love me." It was all she could say, for this moment was perfect proof. *He wants me for his wife.*

"Alas, our parents have all joined the angels, so we must pledge ourselves without their blessing." Jack gripped her hands, looking into her glowing eyes with tender soulfulness. His speech continued at higher volume. "I offer you the life of an artist of the stage, the most splendid existence on earth. Is it not so, ladies and gentlemen?"

The players present, much disguised in wine, cried, "Huzzah!" Georgie, Belzoni, Roger and Sidrack all watched with dismay as Jack swept on to a grand finale.

"Let us resolve, the moment our schedule permits, to become one—forever." The actor rose from his tableau to seize Lizzie in a passionate embrace, kissing her as though they were thoroughly married already.

When he released her, she burst out, "You have made me so happy, my darling. I love you, too, with all my heart. And I always shall, darling. I...."

"Time for that when we are alone," Jack whispered. "Now you must give your answer." He moved Lizzie through the crowd to Aunt Peg, then kissed the old lady with a hearty smack.

Aunt Peg rocked back in her chair. "Lizzie, darlin', do you know this man? Really know him?"

"Yes, Auntie, I know him, and I adore him." Her eyes met Jack's with joy. Triumphantly, she raised her arms to proclaim, "Jonathan Faversham, I accept your hand in marriage!"

The performers understood such a moment called for affirmative applause and clapped appropriately. Faversham whirled her around the press of people. With less brio than before, Carlo took his cue and began playing another Dibdin tune.

"Sister!" Georgie made a grab for the dancing couple, pulled Lizzie out of Jack's arms and into the kitchen, firmly shutting the door on the protesting actor and several inebriated guests. He held his sister by the wrists, sputtering with anger. "What just happened? Do you plan to run off without a word to me? How does this fellow dare presume...?"

"Georgie!" Taken aback by his outburst, she answered, "I am surprised, too."

"He can make so bold with you before our father's very coffin?" His face reddened. "Where does he come from? I've never even met the man. Who are his people?"

"Calm yourself, Georgie! It's just Jack's way."

"Well, you're not going to marry him, by Jupiter. I will never allow it." He dropped Lizzie's wrists.

"Please, please, brother, listen to me." Lizzie wanted him to understand the match was right for her. "Jack is a great actor. He has been teaching me and guiding me."

"I can guess to what end."

"No, Georgie!" Her voice rose. "We are not lovers."

"Penniless, is he?"

"He is an artist of genius, a rising star. He has created his own company and provides for them fairly. No actor is wealthy. You of all people know that." Lizzie caught herself shouting, took a deep breath and spoke in a more normal tone. "As for the Faversham family, he has no one; they were all carried off by the smallpox when Jack was a lad."

"His complexion seems singularly untouched."

"Jack's the protégé of Phillip Eggleston, a man of fine reputation, who was here today."

Georgie crossed his arms, unimpressed.

"And why do I have to defend Jack to you, when the important thing is I love him and he loves me?"

"Marriage is forever, Lizzie. Listen to me, please." Earnestly, the cadet brought up the past. "Do you forget how stormy our parents' marriage was?"

"No, I do not. And that is the difference exactly. Jack and I both love the stage. The life. The art. It is a perfect partnership and all I want."

"At least wait. Give yourself time to consider."

"Why? I know him through and through."

"There has been no courtship."

"Oh, Georgie, you are such a boy," she said with a toss of her head. "He has courted me onstage these two years past. And I want to be married."

"You say he has a great talent. I can see he has a great ego, but what is he really made of, sister?" He would not give up.

"I know there is no man to match him, and you will grow to see all his fine qualities, too." She spoke calmly. "Brother, it is my life, not yours. Besides, I just said yes before all the world. So don't rage anymore. Please. Just give me your blessing and be happy for me."

Georgie emerged from the kitchen with a troubled heart. He met with Faversham and did, with some grace, as his sister had asked. Roger was stunned to witness the cadet giving way. He looked at William's picture on the wall, sick at heart, with a terrible feeling Lizzie was dancing away from them forever. Octavia alone knew the girl's secret feelings, how completely besotted she was with Jack. The redhead gladdened to think Lizzie would be a proper bride. A beloved wife. She wept afresh. Quite unnoticed, Belzoni stepped out the front door, forgotten and lonely, but glad to escape the clamor love had caused.

Chapter Seventeen

Spring 1808

"WE SHALL do the deed in Salisbury," Jack whispered to Lizzie during a scene change in the backstage darkness.

"What?" Her head popped free of the pink costume. She fumbled to buckle the golden girdle. "What did you say?"

"We shall marry in Salisbury. I've decided."

"A wedding in the cathedral? Oh, how grand." Jack's announcement was a welcome surprise, for in the past busy months there had been no time to plan a marriage ceremony.

"No cathedral, my succulent morsel. Something more magical."

She reached across her fiancé's breastplate to grab the princess's crown, now missing a few gems. "Well, wherever it is to be, I must tell my family and friends straight away." The curtains opened on Act Three of *Illyria*.

"My love, don't be distracted from the play. I shall manage the details. Leave everything to me." Jack left her at a run to make his entrance.

After the closing night performance at Chippenham's Yelde Hall, Faversham, with no warning, swung Miss Trumpet into a hired coach. Driving south, at reckless speed through the dark countryside, he called the driver to halt, alighted on a grassy plain, helped his leading lady down, and waved the coach away. The clouds parted before the face of the moon to reveal the great blue stones encircling them.

Only then did Lizzie learn she was to be married in the mysterious heart of Stonehenge, without any of her nearest and dearest to witness her passage into matrimony. Her mind spun with thoughts of all the absent guests. Aunt Peg, Georgie, Carlo, Octavia.... Somehow, she'd expected her people to appear—but there was no one at all. She looked up at Jack with huge, bewildered eyes. "Here? Now?"

"Is it not magical as I promised, Elizabeth? Ancient souls made this place sacred long ago. Our marriage will be blessed by their enduring spirits, my darling. I want our vows to be pure and holy. God shall be our witness. Don't you feel our privacy is like a prayer?"

"Yes, Jack." Lizzie swallowed a gulp of emptiness, uncertain of what he expected. "I...uh...I didn't know you had such deep feelings for religion." She started as a figure in white carrying a drooping bouquet of lilies appeared from behind a standing stone.

"Ah, here is our vicar." Jack beckoned him.

Lizzie saw with happy relief the man approaching them was wearing the spotless vestments of the Christian clergy. Aged and benign, his modulated voice spoke the liturgy reverently. In the dropping dew, the full moon touched the handsome couple with beams of numinous light. The night, the earnest poetry of Jack's vows, and most of all, the Vicar's hopeful benediction, reduced the shivering bride to joyful tears. The groom tenderly kissed them away. Lizzie was on the brink of twenty-one, Jack a seasoned twenty-eight.

Mr. and Mrs. Faversham tripped across the long damp grasses a very great distance to their honeymoon lodging, on the coach road to Salisbury. Jack signed the register at The George Inn with a flourish: Jonathan Faversham and bride.

The newlyweds mounted the worn wooden stairs to the room, appropriately called *Lune de Miel*, where Jack locked the door behind them with a huge iron key. They beheld a nest of a chamber, the ceiling so low Jack's curly head nearly brushed it, the soft wide bed so large, there was nowhere else to sit.

Lizzie shook, damp with cold and hot excitement. She took off her bonnet and spencer. Against all odds, her virtue remained intact. In a moment, she would give her treasure to the man whose presence was like water to her thirst. He had taught her to act with passion and love. *How wonderful that Jack will teach me the act of love.* Passionately, she wanted to learn. This disrobing meant submission. After all the displays of her body onstage that only tantalized, this one would end in surrender. *How right it is that marriage sanctifies my desire.*

Jack ceremoniously lit two candles on the tiny mantelpiece and closed the window shutters on the world. He removed her shoes, stockings, and frock at the slow tempo of a ritual. Lizzie stood in her thin shift and turned away to unpin her hair before a dusty looking-glass. Behind her, Jack began to undress. How happy, how frightened, how ready she was. The dance began.

"Now then, Miss Trumpet."

"Mrs. Faversham, if you please."

"Venus, Isis, Goddess of Love."

"Vestal Virgin, more like."

"You are totally unsullied?"

"Unto this very moment."

"But willing?"

"Heart and soul."

"You've seen a penis, I expect?"

"My brother's in the bath when we were little. In dressing rooms, by mistake, from a distance."

"Have you beheld a rampant penis?"

"'The Stone of Tara,' as Aunt Peg calls it?"

"How apt."

"Yours, husband, will be my first."

"Are you ready for your introduction?"

"I confess to wetness between my legs."

"You may unbutton my trousers."

"Hmm. Very like my brother."

"Take him in hand and say how do you do, Alf."

"Ooh. He's growing."

"You may now call him Alfred. I want you to reveal his crown, thus."

"Oh, astonishing."

"You never saw your brother do this?"

"I never caught him at it."

"What a ninny you were. Now slowly continue."

"I love you, Jack."

"Behold. Alfred the Great."

"I take the metaphor."

"Sweetheart, I presume you've never witnessed a masculine climax?"

"Indeed, no."

"Reveal the crown of Alfred at speed."

"Like this?"

"You are a gifted girl."

"Let us see the marvel of love."

"Faster would be good."

"Are you in pain, Jack?"

"Shhhh."

"You grimace."

"'Tis ecstasy. Here it commmmmmmmes!"

"Oh, glory!"

"Ummmm."

"It shot four feet. Do you always do that?"

"I am a great gusher of spend. Not to say famous for it."

"The king is looking deflated."

"A temporary retirement. Stretch out on the bed."

"Is it my turn now?"

"As I kiss you here, and here, and here, think of the Stone of Tara."

"Oh Jack, I feel...I feel so much. Oh. Ohhh. Ohhhh. I love you, Jack."

"Of course. And Alfred the Great is now ready to salute his delicious subject. He must dress for the occasion."

"What is that?"

"A French letter—a condom—made from the lining of a sheep's

bladder."

"What's it for?"

"So you won't get pregnant."

"Well. Who'd have thought?"

"So, are you ready, little girl?"

"Yes, I love you. Yes."

"We shall fly to the moon together."

"And you are the man in the moon, Jack."

That night the Favershams made four celestial trips.

Chapter Eighteen

September 20, 1808

"You BROKE my heart, darling girl. I wanted to come to your wedding." Carlo Tomassi tossed the score of Mozart's *The Marriage of Figaro* onto the cupid-painted pianoforte in the orchestra pit of Covent Garden. In the empty theatre, three charwomen collected forgotten gloves and discarded orange peels. On the stage, men were striking the scenery for Cesare Borgia: or *The Scourge of Rome*, the play Faversham had starred in that evening. After his curtain call, the new husband told his bride he was off to Brooks's, that most exclusive of gentlemen's clubs, to "make some vital social contacts."

"No one was at the ceremony, dear friend. You were in York, Georgie at school, and Aunt Peg can scarcely get about anymore. Jack arranged everything. I expected Gretna Green, but he said that was for tradesmen and questionable elopements. We were alone in the night, witnessed by ancient ghosts and the magicians of Merlin's court. Whoever it was that raised those rocks at Stonehenge."

"No church? Have you become a Druid?"

"Don't be a goose, Carlo. We said our vows before a proper vicar, without a worrisome to-do. We met the company in Winchester the next evening, after the honeymoon night, of course." She gave her old friend a look that spoke sensuous volumes.

"Such tidy efficiency." The conductor leafed through the score looking for "*Dove sono*," the Countess's Act Three aria. Tomassi had become Lizzie's confidant, possessing worldly experience and rare good humor—the sort of person one could tell anything to. Well, almost anything. "So, how do you find married life, Mrs. Faversham?"

"I don't like it." She paused for effect. "I *love* it!"

Carlo roared at her infectious gaiety.

"What joy it is to never be apart from Jack. We have such happy times together." *He always wants me.* Her cheeks grew pink. "Rehearsing together. In our lodgings. Or the countryside." *Once under a tree, in the open.* "In the theatre carriage." *Bouncing over those rutty roads with the curtains pulled down.* "I usually prepare a supper for us after the performance." *Eaten in bed.* "Now we're in London, he's thrilled to be working again at Covent Garden." *Last night, in his dressing room, we made love between Act One and Act Two.* "Now I know what Dibdin meant by 'rapture.' I am the luckiest of wives."

"I'm happy for you, darling."

"We've taken rooms in Rose Street, just by the Lamb and Flag, to be near the theatres. Jack will be doing several roles this season."

"What about your season? Any plays for you?"

"Nothing yet, but Jack assures me that will come in time." She gave a careless shrug. "I'm keeping house with the simple contents of my traveling trunk. No new possessions except Jack's books."

"Jack reads books?"

"He has a collection of rare ones, Carlo, all concerning the arts of love."

"Poetry?"

"Positions. The positions for love. There is one Italian book by Aretino that's full of amazing etchings." She smiled with eyes cast down. "We are attempting every one."

"I collect your husband is enriching your education. Well, tomorrow my rehearsals begin early, so we'd best get on with Mozart."

"Am I not a trifle young to play this sorrowful old countess?"

"How old are you now?"

"One and twenty."

"Was anyone ever one and twenty?" Carlo sighed. "The first Countess was played by a soprano of twenty-three; Mozart chose Luisa Laschi himself. So, the lady isn't old. She adores her husband and laments his unfaithful ways. Here, translate da Ponte's words starting with '*Dove sono.*'"

"*Where are the happy moments of sweetness and pleasure? Where went the vows from those lying lips?*"

"I hope you never have cause to sing such words from your own experience."

"Oh, no, Carlo, I will never be neglected as my mother was, or mistrusted as my father was. Jack adores me. But I can imagine what the Countess feels."

Lizzie sang for Carlo. He suggested, for a softer timbre, she pronounce the e vowels on her high notes with a short i in the tones, "like the i in tits, darling girl." She adjusted the sounds and tried again, putting her soul into the beautiful aria. The maestro sat back on the satinwood music bench. "Hard work on the road has been good for you, Lizzie. The *voce* is much stronger, and you never showed such passion before." His round face looked like a naughty baby. "Could it be the Aretino?"

"You devil. My grandfather Trombetta would be pleased if ever I sang opera. So would I. Papi was a tenor in Italy, long ago. I wish you two could meet." She stretched both arms to the ceiling. "Of course, my grandparents are in America now."

"Does he sing there?"

"Oh, no, he runs Adam & James of Charleston for Sidrack Sloane. He gave up his dreams of music to make a living selling clothes. I'm told the southern planters love the English style of tailoring."

"But how can he get English cloth, with Mr. Jefferson's Embargo Act preventing imports?"

"Papi has resourceful partners, one of whom is a blockade runner they call Redbeard. Evidently, at sixty-five, my dauntless grandfather is determined to stay in business."

"We should all have such spirit, eh? Let's have another go at '*Dove sono.*'"

She picked up her music and put it down again. "Carlo. Do you smell smoke?"

Suddenly alert, they peered into the darkness around them. The stage hands and charwomen had left. Beyond the circle of candlelight in the orchestra pit was the vast theatre space, two thousand empty seats, four balconies, corridors, salons and stairways. Behind the proscenium opening lay the rabbit-warren of scene shop, machinery and wardrobe rooms.

"Yes, I do."

She looked up into the wide open flies over her head. "There. I see it." Twenty feet in the air above them, a slide of smoke was rising from a huge red curtain bound up with ropes.

"Call for help, Lizzie!" Carlo bounded to the side of the stage where the guy ropes were, trying to find the one that controlled the smoldering curtain and lower it to the stage.

She carried her candles to the huge elephant doors and pushed with all her might to open one. "Fire!" she screamed into the dark deserted street. "Fire in the theatre! Help!" She returned to see Carlo struggling on a ladder with a long gaff in his arms, trying to pull the now-flaming bundle down to the stage.

"Get the wet blankets. On the prompt side."

Lizzie stumbled to obey, tripping over the buckets of sand, always kept ready for such emergencies. The curtain dropped to the stage, nearly striking her. She dragged a blanket over the flaming fabric and ran to get another. Carlo dumped two, three, four buckets of sand, but the stage floor's rough boards had begun to burn. They beat at the flames around their feet.

A drunken man wandered in from Henrietta Street. "What's this? Fire? Oh, bloody hell." He swayed, turning to get out.

Lizzie roughly grabbed his shoulders and shook him. "Run for the Charley, sir. Sound the alarm. Please, right now."

Up in the flies, the ropes and beams were beginning to burn, sending sparks in every direction. All efforts to smother the stage boards could not keep ahead of the creeping conflagration. A stack of canvas flats leaning against the back wall flamed up with a booming sound, ignited by the wind blowing through the open stage door.

"Christ, it's going to go!" Carlo shouted in panic. "Get out of here! God, oh, God, what can be saved?"

Jack's theatrical trunk was in the bowels of the building with all his costumes, props, and manuscripts inside. Lizzie knew it would ruin him to lose it. With her candles, she plunged into the wings and down the circular stairs to her husband's dressing room. She located the latched trunk and shoved it into the basement corridor a few feet at a time, trying not to give way to hysteria. It was heavy as a whale. She was ready to scream with frustration in the smoke when Carlo appeared with a wet handkerchief to press over her nose. The big man heaved the trunk up the stairs for her, puffing out, "Stay calm, darling. I've got it." Men's voices above them testified the watch had arrived.

The theatre was aflame back to front. The doors were all open now, oxygen feeding the fire. Actors and theatre employees still in the neighborhood ran in to help, yelling like banshees.

Once outside, tumbling the trunk before them, she and Carlo made their way through crowds of gawking Londoners. The narrow streets around Covent Garden were a turbulence of frightened folk and ringing alarm bells. Lizzie turned back at a booming sound to see fire had reached the roof of the building. A dozen men pulled a water-pumping wagon down the street. A frightened horse reared on the cobblestones directly in front of them. Its tall rider jumped off and made a dash towards the holocaust, oblivious to the hot orange sparks peppering the neighborhood.

At King Street, a wild-eyed Faversham, dark locks disheveled on his shoulders, ran past them, heading for the blaze, then whirled around. "Trumpet! Are you all right?"

Lizzie nodded and hugged Jack as though he were the one whose life had been in danger. The actor pointed to the fire. "It's the devil's own pandemonium over there. My trunk, I...."

"She's saved it, Jack." Carlo wiped his sooty nose. "She thought more of your career then her own life."

"Wondrous girl." Jack realized the maestro was sitting on the trunk, and laughed with relief. "What a woman, eh?"

"Glad you appreciate her so much. I'm going back to help." The exhausted man hurried off without saying farewell.

"It was really Carlo who saved your things, Jack."

"He's a good old sort. Let's get you out of here, sweetheart."

Faversham hurried up the stairs to their modest lodgings in a celebratory mood. With his theatre trunk safe and Lizzie unharmed, he had made the purchase of a sloshing bucket of ale at the Lamb and Flag.

He poured two monstrous mug-fulls of the golden brew, while Lizzie huddled in a chair, arms wrapped around her knees. "Drink up, Trumpet. My Elizabeth is a proper heroine." For the first time he noticed the ashy, filthy state of her. "Good God, look at you. You're positively bedraggled. But you're safe, and home with me. Why so sad?"

"It was terrible. Frightening." Lizzie pushed the drink away.

"Don't think about the fire. There's nothing to be done." Jack placed the mugs of ale on the nightstand. "I know what will put you right." He pulled the tin-bathing tub out from under the bed. With a splashing flourish, he poured warm water from the big copper kettle hanging over the fireplace into the moon-shaped tub, found a cake of precious French soap in a drawer, and burrowed for a bit of flannel. He stood Lizzie on her feet to remove her reeking clothes, then eased her into the waiting water and washed all of her slowly with the soap that smelt of lavender, then stretched her, clean and limp, across the bed.

Below them was chaos in the street, people screaming, as the walls of Covent Garden Theatre shot flames a hundred feet into the sky. Behind closed shutters, in their tight brick lodging, Faversham ignored the disaster happening four blocks away, more inclined to lament the loss of his job than the theatre. He opened the Aretino etchings for perusal. His index finger twirled in the rosy orifice between Lizzie's sweet buttocks. Her eyes had closed.

Jack whispered into her warm ear. "Perhaps tonight we shall try...'The Wheelbarrow.'"

Next morning, Londoners learned more of the great fire. The blank shot from an actor's pistol in the action of Cesare Borgia had set a stage drapery to smoldering. Whether that pistol was Faversham's, no one could say.

Sheridan's piano had been saved. Mrs. Siddons's writing desk. Precious little else. A library of priceless manuscripts, Handel's scores written in his own hand, exquisite scenery, mountains of gorgeous costumes, all went up in smoke that night. More irreplaceable, twenty brave souls who had entered the flaming building trying to save those treasures perished when the Theatre Royal Covent Garden collapsed around them.

Chapter Nineteen

March 1, 1809
689 King Street
Charleston, South Carolina
United States of America

*D*EAREST NANA,
Thank you for the Christmas letter with the margins blooming in watercolor flowers. Charleston must be an Eden. That magnolia blossom! To emulate your exquisite artistry, I am taking up my paint brushes again.

Uncle Sidrack tells me he is sending Roger to South Carolina to become Papi's partner at Adam & James. Splendid! Now Grandpa can work less and spend more time singing love songs to you, perhaps on that white porch you described.

My husband appeared at the Royal Theatre Drury Lane, in the Christmas pantomime Cinderella. He played the wicked stepmother. Papa's old friend Dick Wilson was an evil stepsister. In England audiences love to laugh at men playing ladies. I managed to get on the famous stage as a mouse transmogrified into a footman. Since I never appeared without large ears and whiskers, I shall not consider it my London debut. I joined the traditional gathering in the Green Room on Twelfth Night, the one Papa used to describe. With cups of punch, Wilson toasted the memory of old Robert Baddeley, the pastry cook turned actor. The man was a lowly supporting player in Garrick's day who made a bequest in his will to treat the actors of Drury Lane to a cake once a year in his memory. When I plunged my fork into the marzipan treat, called the Baddeley Cake, I pretended my father was with me. Like a good little mouse, I ate every crumb.

Then tragedy struck on your birthday, the twenty-fourth of February. Impossibly, Drury Lane Theatre burned to the ground. Our theatrical world has turned upside down with both venues gone. It will surely be more than a year before either the Lane or the Garden can be rebuilt. So, lacking the royal playhouses, London actors are taking to the roads.

Dear Jack is plotting a tour for the Faversham Players as I write. So, soon I will be acting again and it's goodbye to our Rose Street rooms. Here I have learned to cook out of one pot over the fireplace, an essential skill for an actress. 'Tis a glamorous life, vero?

The better news is that, after so many years of training, Georgie will graduate and receive his commission next month at the Royal Military College. Your grandson is expecting to vanquish "Old Boney" immediately. Aunt Peg will attend, making her first pilgrimage out of Islington in years. The day will mark the fulfillment of George Mario's dreams. I shall wear your diamond earrings to the ceremony, Nana.

I pray for you and Papi always, and send my love across the sea. Where has the time all gone to?

Your granddaughter,
Lisabetta

April 1, 1809

"Our triumvirate has broken apart, Miss Pegeen. Lizzie married and about to become a famous actress, Georgie a lieutenant going off to who knows where, and me being moved to America. I feel so old."

"Old! Hoo! What would you know about being old, Roger Sloane? You're no more than a boy still, under that tall stiff hat."

Roger was escorting Aunt Peg, pushing her in a home-crafted chair on wheels through the grounds of High Wycombe's Military College, where Georgie had spent so many years training for his career.

"Where are we now, Roger me boy? I've lost my bearings." The old lady was invigorated by the sights around her, commenting on everything, quite her old self.

"Outside the barracks. I'm determined to find a good place to set you down for the ceremony."

In the shivery spring weather, ivy was just beginning to ascend the Spartan new brick buildings of the college, called "The Shop" by its cadets. Roger's collar points drooped in the damp, matching his melancholy over Georgie's right of passage. He felt a perfect noodle amongst the uniformed men crunching along the gravel paths in their heavy black boots.

"You have no cause for distress. Lizzie and Georgie will never forget the friend of their childhood." Peg gave him a sharp look from under her lace cap. "Your affection for them is returned; no need to feel old or left behind. You are beginning a new life, too, going off to a new country."

"I shall try to look upon it as a new life, Miss Pegeen, but truly, trousers are only trousers, wherever you find them."

"Then you must have an adventure for yourself, Roger. You'll be free of your father. It's a chance to re-invent yourself."

"I'm pleased for the responsibility, but I shall pine for old Londontown." He looked at Peg with his heart in his eyes. "And the people in it."

"I expect you'll do more with this opportunity than you can

imagine. Here, don't push so fast. What is our Lizzie about, a ways off there?"

Roger craned his neck to watch his friend meandering in circles, deeply moved as ever by this young woman, so wide awake to life. "She's talking to herself, Miss Pegeen, or praying perhaps."

"And why didn't her husband come today, I'd like to know?" Peg twitched her shoulders. "For all his acting airs, I still wouldn't trust Jack with the silver. If I can see it why can't our precious girl?"

"Lizzie explained Mr. Faversham has pressing business elsewhere." *What business could that irksome actor have that was more important than his new wife?* Roger found Jack insensitive to his own good luck in catching Lizzie, and pretentious in general. A mounted platoon trotted by in the mist as Roger tucked a thick plaid blanket over Aunt Peg's knife-like knees. He straightened up to watch the clouds passing overhead. "I believe it's going to rain soon."

The young woman in coral pelisse with the becoming tassels on her shoulders had attracted the gaze of every man in the mounted platoon. When a little half rainbow appeared over the quadrangle, Lizzie gave herself up to reflection. *Are the spirits of Mama and Papa hovering in the colored air? If they are angels...surely they must be near, rejoicing for Georgie this day."*

A man's cultured voice broke into her reverie.

"Miss Trumpet? Or rather, Mrs. Faversham. How do you do?"

Lizzie turned round to discover a worthy red-nosed gentleman of fifty and some summers bowing to her.

"May I take the liberty of introducing myself? Sir Henry Wentworth. A name not unknown to your family, I collect?" The man's blue eyes twinkled in his weathered face with rare good humor.

"Oh, Sir Henry. Your name is legend. Legend in our home. It is indeed a pleasure, sir. You who have made my father's wishes for Georgie come to...come to...."

"Fruition? The finest wager I ever lost. Trumpet had an angel on his shoulder that night, make no mistake." Lizzie thought of her own angels and softly smiled. "Such luck! He beat me double-or-nothing five times! Fortune's cornucopia!" Sir Henry rubbed his gloved palms together with reminiscent pleasure. He gestured to include the people walking up to them. "May I present my patient and gentle spouse, Lady Cecile." The ladies exchanged curtsies. "My eldest, Percy." The heir bowed with a modicum of grace. "And our little niece from Sheffield, Miss Emily Widewell."

A petite girl with blonde bangs and enormous eyes made her bob to Lizzie. "We are here to see cousin Ted become a Royal Hussar. We met his friend, your charming brother George, but an hour ago!" Emily bubbled, evidently excited by the introduction. Her little pointed chin quivered as she beamed at Lizzie.

Sir Henry, positively spewing goodwill, shepherded the Trumpet party to some excellently placed chairs on the parade ground, directly in front of a platform festooned with flags. Dainty Lady Cecile seemed on the brink of tears, though the ceremony had yet to begin. Percy, dressed in the latest "kick of the mode," said little, perhaps due to his pronounced overbite. Altogether, Lizzie liked them at once.

"My son Ted will be joining the Prince of Wales's Own Royal Tenth Hussars." Wentworth confided in the actress's ear that his grandfather had served with the Tenth, "fought at Culloden in '46. It will be your brother's regiment, too. Damn fine."

"The Tenth Hussars were created in 1715," gushed Emily, who had made a study of it. "It's the most elite regiment of any."

There was a crash of martial music. Mounted officers trotted into view, followed by the band, then the cadets marching in stiff ranks to their seats on benches, well behind the Wentworth party. When the graduates appeared, dressed in the uniforms of the regiments they were to join, Lizzie immediately spotted Georgie and Ted Wentworth, in dark blue jackets trimmed with rows of blazing silver braid. Officers of the faculty with attitudes of gravitas had gathered on the platform. A grandly bewhiskered man, using a cane, approached the podium.

"The Commandant, there, left France to join the fight against Napoleon," Sir Henry informed Lady Cecile. "Damn fine man."

The starchy ex-patriot opened his notes and began. "Distinguished guests and visitors, I bid you welcome. I am Commandant François Barry. We gather to present the ninth class of graduates at Royal Military College High Wycombe." He brushed up the bottoms of his mustache and began to bark out names in the order of their divisions—infantry, artillery, heavy cavalry, and light cavalry, which included the Tenth Hussars. Smartly, each young man marched up onto the platform, received his commission, saluted and acknowledged the applause of his proud family.

Barry took up the last parchment. "I now commission our valedictorian, the highest achieving graduate. This cadet passed with excellence through years of rigorous training in the arts of war and the sciences of peace. I call upon...Lieutenant George Mario Trumpet."

Lizzie forgot to breathe, her heart exploding. Georgie had told no one. He walked towards the general on a wave of cheers, a heavy sabre swinging at his side.

"Has our boy been singled out?" Aunt Peg asked.

"An honor, Auntie. He is judged the best."

"Ah, well, we knew that."

A horse whinnied in a far off stable. Gusts of wind snapped the banners and ruffled the feathers on hundreds of shakos.

"General Barry," Georgie began, in a powerful voice like his father's, "distinguished faculty, comrades, friends. This day is so long awaited by your graduates, so hoped for and hard won, that each man-jack of us shall never forget it."

Lizzie squeezed Aunt Peg's tiny hand. "What a man he has become," she whispered.

"We pray God to guide us as we execute our sacred duty to king and country. My brothers-in-arms join in thanking our splendid instructors. Sirs, our glory shall be yours."

"Hear him," shouted out several voices.

"I offer this morning's scripture from Chaplain Mitchell's homily: 'Yea, though I walk through the valley of the shadow of death, I will fear no evil; for thou art with me, thy rod and thy staff they comfort me.'" Georgie's voice rose with emotion. "We swear to protect our homeland to the death. Be ye friend or foe, attend. We are Christian soldiers, unafraid. We shall defend our beloved England from conquerors and our cherished people from harm. We shall preserve our English way of life, the rule of law, and the justice of peace." He pulled his saber from its new shiny scabbard and held it high. "We. Shall. Prevail!"

"Hoorah!" roared the assembled gentlemen and apple-cheeked boys, never doubting only victory lay before them. The sun appeared, making their metallic braid sparkle like a field of stars.

Commandant Barry once again assumed the podium. "Gentlemen, Lord Castlereagh has just ordered Lieutenant-General Arthur Wellesley to Portugal, to assume command over the allied Spanish, Portuguese, and British Armies. All of you graduates, likewise, will be posted to Portugal, to depart in fourteen days. Together, you will prevent the Bonapartists from swallowing up the whole of Europe by making a stand on the Iberian Peninsula. You will accomplish this against the odds of a mere...three to one."

One of the senior officers coughed in the cold air.

"Lieutenant Trumpet has sworn you will serve England with honor. Some of you will unquestionably see the valley of the shadow. You are young gentlemen—very young to me—but within each of you beats a courageous heart. I know you will make us proud. Go with God, gentlemen. Dis-missed!"

The new officers cheered three times three, breaking ranks to cherish their emotional families. Aunt Peg seemed to be doing a jig in her rolling chair, receiving Georgie's kiss with purest joy. Lizzie embraced her brother, while Roger pounded the immaculate lieutenant on the back, saying nothing coherent. The Wentworths engulfed Ted. Over and over, Sir Henry told Georgie his speech was "damn fine."

Lizzie drank in the sight of her dazzling, well-spoken brother in his tight white trousers and tall busby hat of grey. The gloss of his black boots could shame Beau Brummell. *His red sword-belt's thick enough to stop a bullet...or is it?* Georgie leaned over Emily Widewell to hear her congratulations, a smile of pleasure on his handsome face. *When did he become so beautiful? Protect him, Lord.... Off to war in some foreign land I can't imagine...to a world of carnage I imagine all the time.*

A black storm cloud threatened from the west, the breeze

freshened. Emily handed her umbrella to Georgie, who struggled to raise it over them as plops of rain began to fall.

Is it possible my darling brother could die? Lizzie chanced to look into Lady Cecile's fine green eyes and saw that, like her own, they were streaming tears.

Chapter Twenty

July 1809

B Y HIGH summer, the Jonathan Faversham Players had presented *The Caliph Robber* to grateful audiences in Haleworth, Woodbridge, Sudbury, and Eye, modest centers of culture where stock company actors slogged through repertoires of Shakespeare, old chestnuts, and bastardized romances. When Lizzie and Jack played these towns, their beauty and excitement in each other slew the local competition.

The dark-haired leading lady was still Miss Elizabeth Trumpet on the printed playbills. The euphonious name of Faversham remained exclusively Jack's. When the subject came up over toast, Jack prophesied, "You will make your own name famous, Trumpet. Look at Mrs. Siddons, forever saddled with the identity of her husband, a forgotten actor of the second rate." Adding lashings of butter, he scoffed at the thought. "No, no. You won't need to borrow my thunder. Earn your own renown."

Sunday provided the one morning for sleeping late. Faversham had never entered a church or mentioned his religious faith since their wedding. He expected his leading lady to repose at his side. On such a restful Sunday, Lizzie awakened in Lowestoft, a fishing town on the Suffolk coast where they had taken a room with a view of the water.

Jack opened their balcony doors to let in the morning sunlight rising out of the North Sea. Wrapped in a soft plum dressing gown, merry as a grig, he was picking at a plate of herring while Lizzie remained beneath the covers. "Morning has broken, Trumpet. Care for a herring?"

"Bless you, no." She yawned and stretched. "Perhaps later."

Suddenly Jack straightened. "You there!" he shouted from the balcony. "Stop that!" Lizzie heard a yelp.

"Get stuffed," was the response from outside.

"You stop beating that dog this moment, or I'll treat you to the same!"

"Shut your gob!" A piercing howl.

"By God!" Favercham flew out the door. Lizzie wrapped herself in the sheets she traveled with and crept to the balcony, peering down at the unfolding scene in the street.

A large man in a worn cap was holding a little black and white terrier by the collar and striking it with a quirt. Jack rounded the corner at speed. Before the dog owner could look up, the actor was on him, wresting away the quirt and whipping the man across the face with it. "I said leave off!" The stunned man fell on the cobblestones as the actor captured the dog and held it to his chest.

"Be off with you," Jack thundered, again raising the leather, now spotted with blood.

"Jesus," the man whimpered, touching his cut nose.

Faversham gave him a tremendous whack across the buttocks, threw the weapon in the wet gutter, and marched back to his lodgings, cradling the black and white bundle of fur, shouting, "He's my dog now!"

Lizzie had never seen Jack reach out to help the helpless before. When he reappeared with the shivering dog, she kissed him. "Well, well."

"No man has the right to beat such a little fellow. I can't abide it." Jack was still worked up. "Can you find a towel?"

"Here, darling." She tossed him one.

He petted and dried the terrier, while Lizzie poured water for the mistreated beast into a saucer from Jack's tea.

"You hurt that man."

He frowned righteously. "Deserved it."

"Yes." His outrage had moved her. "Are we really keeping this dog?"

"A well-trained animal always fascinates the public, and is less trouble to maintain than an actor." Jack rubbed the dog's head, which was lowered submissively. "We could use him in comedies. I think, yes, we're keeping him. Let's see if he fancies herring." He reached for his breakfast and set it on the carpet. "Here, boy. This is yours if you wish it."

They watched the pooch nose the salty fish around Jack's half-eaten plate; finally, choosing feast over famine, he chewed it up.

Faversham stretched before the shaving mirror. "Trumpet. What was the name of that fat friend of yours? The moist one I saved you from?"

"Dampere, as you very well know. Frederick, Lord Dampere. Do you plan to name the dog after him?"

"Never. This creature's too starved. Cassius with his 'lean and hungry look' is more like."

"Then what of Dampere?"

"I'm going to propose that his lordship invest in the Faversham Players. He has the blunt and a panting enthusiasm for you. Let us make the most of it."

"If it hadn't been for Dampie, we might never have met." Half-wrapped in sheet, Lizzie sauntered back to the balcony. "I might never have acted in lovely Lowestoft, never seen the local views. We could stroll around Lake Lothing today. Walk the dog. What say you?"

"I say no. I have seen and heard all I care to of this place."

The night before, they had played the old classic *Damon and Pythias*. Just as Jack was making his favorite hot-blooded speech, a baby in the audience commenced to howl. The infant's piercing cries grew and grew, overwhelming sanity. Finally, Faversham walked downstage and raised his hand to say, "Ladies and gentlemen, the play must be stopped or the child cannot go on." The crowd gave Jack an ovation. The wee screamer was carried out.

"Making a joke of the disruptive baby was the thing to do,

darling."

"I couldn't let him ruin our play." Jack folded Lizzie in his arms. "But, one can't make enemies of the babe's family; they bought tickets." He squeezed her buttocks for emphasis. They walked back to bed and nestled under the quilts. The dog wagged his tail and watched closely, head tilted, ears up. "Although...I would have preferred throwing the little fiend down a well. I don't mind dogs, but infants do not belong in a theatre."

"You'll feel differently when we have our own little boy."

"No children. I want no family to wear me down or spoil your beauty."

This came as more of a surprise to Lizzie than Jack's striking the man in the street to save the dog. She had been glad her husband was fastidious about preventing pregnancy. Comforted to know he wanted her health and youth preserved, although many fecund actresses appeared on the English stage whilst "increasing," even into their ninth month. Mrs. Siddons's mother, who was also an actress, delivered her at The Shoulder of Mutton Pub directly after giving a performance.

"Jack, you mean you don't want children?"

"Indeed I do. Look at the poor hack actors you've known, shackled to tribes of snotty-nosed brats. A dynasty, they call it, when they just couldn't bother to fuck with a sheath on." Idly, he reached around to stroke her breasts. "Sheer stupidity. Understand, I'm making my place in the world. I want fame. For you, too, of course. But, I don't give a monkey's ass about another generation." He turned on the pillow to look into her wide hazel eyes. "We have each other and the stage. It is enough." He pressed an ardent kiss into her parted soft lips. The little dog whimpered.

Faversham drew on a fresh French letter, then burrowed his handsome head between Lizzie's thighs. While the locks of his hair caressed her skin, she tried to think. *Jack wants no heirs to his name...unusual, but he is unusual...a genius.... Oh! Certainly a genius at this.*

She had no passion for babies and little knowledge of children. *Without a family to raise...more time for this.* Jack's mouth was voracious. *More is...oh...wonderful.* She turned her head to watch their reflections in the round shaving mirror. *What a delicious couple we are...agile as models in Aretino's stimulating book.... Ah, ah.* Lizzie lifted her hips, stretching her legs wide, bending each knee.

"Ha! That's the way, Trumpet. Open for me. So pink and smooth. I shall spend the day right—" Jack pushed and mounted, "here!" He settled deep for a long, wet ride.

⠒

August 1809

During their final week in Wells-Next-the-Sea, Faversham learned the new Covent Garden Theatre building was completed. John Philip Kemble had begun assigning actors for the fall season. Straight away, Jack paid off his weary Faversham Players, packed the theatre-carriage, and traveled home to London. Lizzie and the rescued dog, named Cassius, were to open up the Rose Street rooms while her husband made his first stop: Kemble's office.

"Ooh, letters from Georgie. Thank you, Lord," Lizzie said aloud. She pulled off her Italian straw bonnet and immediately sat down to read the mail waiting on a dusty table-top. The black and white pooch sniffed excitedly around the old furniture. "What a fine homecoming, eh, Cassie?" The letter crackled as she broke the wax seal.

Georgie's words to her were full of pride and excitement at being in the thick of things, at last fighting Napoleon's army. He had left Portugal and crossed into Spain with the staff of Gen. Wellesley, a man he respected and was apparently directly serving in the Peninsula Campaign. He described the Battle of Oporto, now long over. Of more interest to Lizzie, he mentioned corresponding with Emily Widewell, Ted Wentworth's blonde cousin, whom he described as a "splendid girl" who "writes to me frequently in a lively, charming style."

In the stack of letters, there was an ivory envelope from Sheffield, addressed to Elizabeth Trumpet in an unknown hand. It contained a pleasing note from that same Miss Widewell, hoping to renew their acquaintance and "exchange news of your brother." Instantly charmed, Lizzie vowed to reply.

From Spain, Georgie wrote enthusiastic paragraphs about his horses, the meticulous leadership of Wellesley, and praise for the Tenth Hussars. *Hot dry and rough here. I have a hard seat in the saddle. Almost no seat at all, really, because Wentworth and I are existing on raw onions, can you believe?* In a cooler mood, he admitted being the son of an actor disadvantaged him in a regiment where so many officers were highborn. The fighting he touched on lightly, but there was plenty of it. He made no mention of wounds. A fat envelope bore the latest date.

> *August 8, 1809*
> *Dearest Sister,*
> *Very good news. Look closely at this envelope and rejoice. I've been made captain. Huzzay!*
> *We were deep into Spain the last week in July, preparing to attack the French at Talavera. We faced the enemy outnumbered two to one. The ground is densely forested with cork and olive trees, so Gen. W. elected to climb a tower to survey the terrain. While we were at it, some French skirmishers appeared right below us. Did we scurry. As Wellesley was running for his horse, I charged the French, driving the lot of them into the forest. Zig-zagging back to my general I was fired upon, but dodged every shot.*
> *On 27 July, with only 20,000 men, we forced the French to retreat. Boney's jumped-up brother Joseph, the puppet king of Spain, was put to route along with 40,000 Bonapartist troops. Talavera was a murderous battle. Gen. W. thinks it the hardest fought of modern times, and I believe him. He did not stay safely back from the fight, but rode close to the fray, shouting commands, and me at his side acting as messenger, carrying orders to his generals.*
> *At the end of the second day, I was summoned to his tent where he gave me a field promotion. Incredibly, I am now a*

captain and it did not cost me one quid. We have retreated back to Portugal for food and supplies. The sight of some money would be a fine change; haven't been paid in months. That is a small matter.

We learned W. has been created Baron Douro of Wellesley and Viscount Wellington of Talavera, after the two great battles. Now I shall address him as General Lord Wellington Sir. The men call him Nosey, after his profile. I do not.

Gen. W. says our relations with Washington continue to worsen. I know Roger is in America now. Does he still use the smuggler's ship? Does that make him our enemy? I pray not. How could he ever be? What about Nana and Papi? Have you heard from them?

I am unhurt by all this war, but my thoughts are often dark. It's not all glory, infant. When I get the rare chance to sleep, I always dream of Longsatin House and our little family as we once were. I never expected to feel such tender longing for them. Please write, Lizzie. News of you and home is precious indeed.

Your loving brother,
George Mario Trumpet, CAPTAIN!!

The news from Georgie put Lizzie in high spirits. She washed her face and fell to unpacking, expecting her husband's return with good news from his meeting at Covent Garden. Hanging her red frock on a wall-peg, she heard Faversham's quick step on the stairs. Cassie's tail began to wag. The door flew open to Jack, making a bold entrance with customary drama.

"Damn Kemble!" His fine silk hat from Lock's of St. James's Street, a major investment, flew from Jack's hand across the room, knocking Georgie's letters to the floor.

"What happened?" Lizzie asked, more than surprised.

"He's an ass! A fucking ass." Jack dropped into a chair and stuck out a leg. "Boots." She knelt to tug them off as he roughly unwound his neck-cloth. "No agreement on anything. Not one role for me! Any actor who works for Covent Garden this season will be getting less than half his old wage."

"No! For heaven's sake, why?"

"Kemble and Harris were 'under-insured.' They borrowed to the skies to rebuild. So all I heard was, 'the cupboard is bare,' blah, blah. Harris wasn't even there, supposedly prostrate with pains in his chest. Kemble said, 'We make no profits till the debts are paid off.' In short, a load of cack." Jack bolted up, shed his green frock coat, and tossed it in Lizzie's direction. She caught it, trying to see beyond this tirade to the facts.

"Who is he hiring?"

"Not me. What a self-important old fart Kemble is. My name draws crowds. Does that bastard think people pay money just to see new plaster and paint?" Faversham was on his feet, changing into old clothes and shouting, "Does he think they'll cheer some supernumerary from Mousehole? He wouldn't know a star from a scarecrow!"

"Have the other actors accepted this?"

"What? Yes, so he says. Well, Black-Jack Kemble can kiss my arse. I haven't come this far to work for slave wages in London. I told him to send for me when the cash is countable. He took my point."

Lizzie still held his best coat, feeling her stomach drop to the floor. What a blow. She'd hoped to make her London debut this season. *Jack encouraged me...he said it is my time.* Faversham was slamming drawers in the bedroom chest-on-chest, looking for a shirt, paying her no mind. She set the coat aside. *I have no quarrel with Kemble. I want to work...but I must tread carefully.* Controlling her voice, she asked, "Jack? Did you mention me to Mr. Kemble?"

"God, no, your name never came up."

Seeking his attention, she moved to the bedroom door. *I must speak up.* "I would work for cut wages, darling, if all the other actors are going to. I don't give a fig about such things, and it would show our support for the theatre."

"Work without me? You most certainly will not." Jack retrieved his hat. "That would be disloyal and very, very stupid." He gave a slightly contemptuous look. "What are you thinking?"

"You and Kemble parted brass rags?"

"What of it?" Jack rushed to leave the room. "That bastard's raised all the ticket prices, too. Well, good luck to him, stupid old sod. That's a sure way to ingratiate the Londoners." He snapped his fingers to the dog. "Come on, boy! I'm off to get a bloody, fucking drink."

Lizzie watched them go, coloring with anger. What she had set her heart upon was not to be. To fight off the blue devils of disappointment, she began a reply to Georgie's letters, meaning to write of Emily and Aunt Peg, but instead found herself describing the time Boozel the Guernsey had given a pail full of sweet milk and willfully, sullenly, stepped in it.

September 18, 1809

John Philip Kemble's new Theatre Royal Covent Garden looked rather like a Roman temple. Fronting on Bow Street, between the Muses of Comedy and Tragedy in their tall niches, a Doric-columned portico opened to a gilded foyer. The architect Robert Smirke had spent a hundred eighty-seven thousand pounds on the project. On opening night, the audience gathered, absolutely wild to see what the interior would look like.

Suitably awed by the wealth on the walls, Lizzie and Jack climbed the grand staircase bordered with black Ionic columns to a domed anteroom. A large marble Shakespeare brooded on his pedestal beneath the lofty glass oculus. Around the Bard, irreverent playgoers of all classes made negative comments on the new ticket prices. Crowds in satin breeches and ostrich feathers headed for the private salons where champagne quenched the thirsty elite.

Carlo Tomassi had provided gratis seats for the Favershams in the horseshoe-shaped auditorium. On this great occasion, Kemble would make a speech to open the theatre, then follow in *Macbeth*, starring himself and Mrs. Siddons as the Scottish murderers. Lizzie opened the playbill, excited to be there, though she had to remind

Jack to smile. "You look as though I'd dragged you to a hanging."

In the very full house, dozens of chandeliers hung from poles attached to cast-iron pillars supporting five tiers of boxes, designed expressly for the ton. The private sanctuaries were hideously expensive but, with anterooms behind, were commodious enough for assignations. Jack remarked acidly on the classic plaster wall decoration, the sound-absorbing fabric on his seat and the "god-awful" color of pink paint chosen for the mahogany-trimmed boxes.

The new monstrous audience-space held thirty-six hundred seats, plus the usual benches in the pit and galleries above, called 'pigeon holes.' Standing room spectators crowded up against the coffered ceiling, designed to resemble the Pantheon of Rome. For the actors working on the raked stage, no subtlety would be seen or delicacy heard. Techniques that worked in intimate houses would have to be thrown out.

Once seated, the crowd was restless, even rowdy. Kemble's remarks of welcome went unheeded and un-applauded. Carlo's orchestra played "God Save the King," then a bit of stormy overture music. The curtain rose. The three witches in hag makeup skittered on like roaches.

"When shall we three meet again,
In thunder, lightning or in rain?
When the hurly-burly's done,
When the battle's lost and won."

Before the next witch could speak, the audience began whistling, stomping and making a terrible racket, unfurling banners in the galleries, that said, *No New Ticket Prices*, and *Go to Hell, Kemble*.

Jack grew intensely animated, loonishly pleased, shouting, "What did I tell you!" into Lizzie's jeweled ear.

The playgoers in the pit turned their backs to the stage, chanting "Old prices! Old prices!" Someone tooted on a coach horn as customers banged their shoes against the iron pillars. A pig was carried in and set to squealing. Macbeth and his clan continued over the chaos, unheard. Finally some Bow Street Runners took the stage to read the Riot Act to the misbehaving Londoners. When vegetables and bottles began to rain down from the boxes, the Favershams made for the aisle and out. Passing through a salon, Lizzie saw a rotund man under a roundel of Congreve, waving at her with his champagne glass. She recognized Lord Dampere.

He approached the couple and everyone bowed elegantly, ignoring the rude noises around them. "Not an auspicious night for *The Scottish Play*, I fear?" He chuckled in Lizzie's direction. "Driven out by the unseemly fracas, Mrs. Faversham?"

"Shocking," Lizzie murmured. "So very sad."

"Oh, by the way, I perused your proposition—" His lordship squared his bulk at Jack. "As I recall, it suggested I back your little troupe of touring actors. An opportunity to support the arts directly, what? My dear Faversham, though your talent and name is known"— this with a condescending grimace—"I must very regretfully decline the invitation."

Just then two liveried employees tried to restrain a party of well-dressed young sports barking like dogs and attempting to tear the sconces off an adjacent wall.

Dampere pointed at the unpleasant scene. "Not a good year for theatre all round, what?"

The hoped-for investor in Faversham Players turned to Lizzie with an expression of wistful regard. "Elizabeth, may I say, you look surpassing fine." He bowed again, less deeply. "*Pardonnez-moi.*"

With no other word to Jack, Lord Freddy strutted away.

Frederick, Lord Dampere
10 Park Place, London
Dear Dampie,
I write to thank you for considering my husband's business proposal. Perhaps his suggestion of financial support for the Faversham Players struck you as too forward, or ill-timed. I had spoken of your great love of all things theatrical, so the error was entirely mine.
You are a man of such enthusiasm. I would wish you an enterprise of your very own some day, apart from the

demands of fashionable society. It might be anything that takes your fancy: science, government, or even commerce. What a man of your energy and respected position could accomplish! My work in the theatre brings me joy. I wish you a taste of such ambrosia one day, however you apply yourself.

Perhaps in the future our paths will cross, and Jack and I will be pleased to perform for your pleasure. We wish for your every happiness.

Your friend of old,
Elizabeth Trumpet

The 'Old-Price Riots' continued every night at Covent Garden for three months, until Kemble, facing ruin, lowered the cost of his plush new seats. All the disgraceful turmoil was a deep satisfaction to Jack. Satisfaction however, does not buy bread. The disgruntled restless star and his beautiful leading lady booked a tour of the York Circuit to pay the bills. Once more they were on the road, so long and winding.

Chapter Twenty-One

Fall 1810

THE SILENT Woman Public House in Perth was a snug spot for thawing out from the Scottish chill. A gust off the Tay River shook the rain-spattered pub sign depicting a stocky female with her severed head tucked underneath her arm.

Two young captains of the Royal Navy set foot over the jamb as a slap of wind whipped the old door.

"A dram of whiskey for the little captain here, if you please," the large red-faced officer called out in a quarterdeck voice, "and two whiskeys for me."

The place was empty that afternoon, except for one lady ensconced by a cheery fire in the private salon, munching a slice of cheese and onion pie. It was Lizzie, enjoying a moment of solitude. She had been in the eye of Jack's hurricane long enough now to forecast his storms of behavior. The passionate lovemaking was still agreeable, but when she looked around in saner moments, Jack's ruthless attack on life was coming into focus.

Much of her time was spent smoothing the feelings Jack roughed up. New members of the Faversham Players sought her out, asking for a bit of intercession between themselves and her demanding husband who treated them like furniture. Recently, the gifted young

Junius Brutus Booth had been chafing at the bit. Friendships she made with her fellow actors in the company always melted away at season's end. She pondered how to be a good wife to a man she did not always agree with, a man who relished conflict and command. In this doleful mood, the weary actress had crept into the Silent Woman to study her scenes for next week's play, glad to be away from anyone who knew her.

"Miss Trumpet? Well, this is extraordinary."

It seemed someone knew her after all. The two naval officers, carrying their whiskeys, approached her table by the fire. "Ah, it *is* she, Mangles," the sanguine man chortled.

"Madame, we are slaves to your beauty and talent." The smaller captain, a pigeon-breasted man, rushed to pull off his cocked hat, worn fore and aft, and made a neat leg.

"We can't believe our good fortune." The large captain ogled her like a trim-rigged frigate.

"We are devotees of the theatre. That is, I count myself a devotee. Old Irby, here, is just beginning to expose himself. To the art of Thespis, that is. Expose himself. *Ha!*"

"Mangles, cease. Pursue another course." The broad, sun-scorched young captain looked down on his companion. "Tell the lady she is a captivating actress, that we have attended her every performance this week."

"Every performance. Oh, my." Miss Trumpet nodded graciously, putting aside her play and pie.

"True enough. Perth would have been loathsome without you. Would you be so kind as to place your signature on these playbills?" The shorter captain drew out a handful of them from his uniform jacket. "All treasured memories, be assured."

Both men were in their early twenties, handsome in their health, vigorous and genuine. Like Georgie, they lived in the wartime world of action, yet Lizzie could see they were excited as schoolboys to be meeting an actress from the world of art. How could she help but be delighted by their intrusion? "Gentlemen, you have the advantage of me. I would be very pleased to know whom I am addressing."

"I am Captain James Mangles of His Majesty's Royal Navy, and this blustery barbarian is Captain the Honorable Charles Irby."

The big captain bowed. "We have seen you in *Who's to Have Her?* and Mangles laughed so loud, I couldn't hear some of the speeches, you were that comic."

"It's called farce, Charles. On Wednesday, we saw *The Lawyer the Jew and the Yorkshireman.* You played the three mistresses engagingly, each distinctly different."

"Oh, that was just the wigs and costumes." Irby smiled, as if tickled at the thought.

"Nonsense, Charles, that was her captivating artistry. Excuse my friend, dear lady, he was raised in the country."

"Captains, it strikes me your support has put the Faversham Players into profit this week. Please join me and tell where duty has taken you?" Lizzie gestured for them to sit at her table. "My brother is serving in the army with General Wellesley in Spain. So I am deeply interested in military careers."

Mangles raised his glass. "Let us drink to his victories." The captains sipped, then cried in unison, "And confusion to Boney!"

The navy men, friends since boyhood, spoke colorfully of the Caribbean Islands and Mediterranean Sea, where they had sailed and seen action on the frigate Diana as midshipmen. Both had been made lieutenant and served on "brig-rigged unrated vessels." This was Greek to Lizzie, who didn't interrupt. Now they were preparing for blockade duty off the coast of France.

"My ship is in Perth to re-supply," Mangles finished.

"And mine as well. That done, we shall catch the tide."

"What a lot of the world you've traveled. England is all I know, and Scotland is the farthest away from home I've ever been." Lizzie pointed to the words carved on the mantel above their table: *East, west, hame's best.* "If ever this conflict ceases, there are many English, myself included, who would love to visit France. I had a dear teacher of that nation. I'm sure I would be thrilled by the theatres of Paris."

Irby leaned back in his chair, crossing his booted legs comfortably. "When Boney's put to rest, I mean to see the fabled east—the Pyramids, the Holy Lands. By the by, Mangles, there is an exhibition called *Egyptiana* at the top of George Street. We might scrutinize it, if duty permits."

The actress couldn't imagine Jack enjoying a tour without theatrical destinations. She folded her unstudied scenes into her reticule. These intriguing men had wider horizons than any she had ever met. "Gentlemen, I must be going."

"This lady cares nothing for your musty scholarship, Charles. Miss Trumpet, we beg to pay for your pie, and tonight we will be seeing a sight more wonderful than the fabled east," Captain Mangles said, in a fine flow spirits. "Your gracious and charming self in *The Dame of the Dell*."

At this compliment, Lizzie's face had a hint of the rising sun in it. "Thank you, gentlemen. I'm grateful to know you will be in the audience again tonight. I shall endeavor to be entertaining as a pyramid."

"Trumpet, someone you know is playing tomorrow afternoon at St. Anne's Theatre." Jack pulled up his tights before the green room looking-glass, attended by Cassius the dog who gazed at him adoringly.

Lizzie spooned more honey into her glass of warm water, so essential for relaxing her throat. "And who might that be?"

"The human ladder—what's his name. Zoni. He's trying to be an actor now, in *Valentine and Orson*. Christ, what is the theatre coming to?"

"Belzoni? I shall go see him." Cheered by the very name of her supportive, uncomplicated friend, she stirred her drink smiling, pleased to know he was so close by. "Will you join me?"

"Not possible. You forget I'm holding auditions for a new juvenile, since that little cove Booth turned in his notice. Typical. Bloody typical. You had better hope that amongst these praying Presbyterians, there's someone out there to replace him who can act." Faversham stepped back to admire the snug drape he had achieved over his crotch. "Oh, I'm told your Italian friend is working opposite a she-bear. Ha! What a perfect leading lady for him."

꧁

The play *Valentine and Orson* was a romantic spectacle set in the Middle Ages. Twin boys are separated at birth; Valentine is brought up in princely society, while his long lost brother Orson is raised in the forest by a wild bear. Orson, a giant of a man, makes only unintelligible sounds—perfect casting for an extraordinarily tall actor with a pronounced Italian accent. The mother bear was always a skin part, played by a man in a fur suit, but for this production, the Perth theatre manager, lacking the funds to produce a real spectacle, had instead produced a real bear.

Sitting amongst the Scottish spectators, Lizzie judged Belzoni was doing a fine job at the matinee, costumed yet again in a nappy of tom-cat skin and his own marvelous muscles. Then the bear lumbered onstage for a tender reunion scene with her human cub. She took some powerful swipes at the half-naked Italian when he attempted to embrace her as called for in the text. While Belzoni ducked and dodged, the audience had a deal of fun at his expense.

"Laddie! Will ye nae kiss yer wee mither?" one man yelled from the pit.

"She loves ye soooooo!" shouted another, convulsed with laughter.

Greatly frightened, the bear rose up to grab her cast-mate in a genuine ursine hug, raking Belzoni's back with her long claws. Lizzie cringed, the only one in the house who understood the danger. The desperate actor dragged the agitated "Miss Orso" off to whistles and derisive laughter. Lizzie stayed on to the bitter end then slipped backstage to surprise Giovanni in his dressing room.

"Lisabetta!" he shouted, engulfing her happily despite the bloody scratches on his back.

"*Caro*, you've been wounded."

"Yes, the bear did not read the play." He set her down in the center of the room. "What you do in Perth?"

"We are working at the Princess Theatre in High Street. I was free this afternoon. Ooh, let me clean those scratches." She poured water from a tin pitcher onto a dressing-table towel.

"I knew nothing of your appearances. I have rehearse all week." He winced as Lizzie dabbed his back, which smelled strongly of animal. "You saw this performance? A fiasco. I am mortified."

"No no, Giovanni. You gave them a good show."

"Oh, it was terrible. *Terribile!*" he shouted, then calmed, removing the bloody towel from her hand. "*Grazie, cara.*" He asked about "*la piccola* Auntie Peg" and then Georgie. "Tell-ah your brother not to be a hero. Tell him I pray for his safe returning."

"As do I. He's in the real battles now." She wiped a drop of Belzoni's blood off her finger. "More happily, he's carrying on a correspondence with a charming girl named Emily. When we return to London, Georgie has asked me to befriend her."

"May she be good for him. Your husband make-ah you happy? You are in excellent looks, as the English say."

"I'm content, Giovanni." Lizzie did not feel inclined to share her new insights about Jack and gave her usual neat answer. "It is best when actors marry actors. My mother never understood my Papa, but I understand my spouse perfectly. That is important."

"Unlike-ah your Faversham, I am not born to be an actor. I tour because I must eat. *Devo mangiare.* So, I'm the strong man, do magic. Everyone applaud when I play 'Greensleeves' on the water glasses." Belzoni took a restless turn around the room that was far too small for him. "This is not my place in life, Lisabetta. Me, I have not forgotten da Ponte's words. I dream. I want to do meaningful things, *cara.*"

"You will, my friend. If I may speak my mind, you require some cheering up. Perhaps I do, too. Tomorrow, Jack will be rehearsing a new actor, and I will have a free afternoon. There is a grand scientific exhibition come to town. We could attend together. A change of scene for me. It will be like old times."

Just as some boisterous Scots had enjoyed *Valentine and Orson,*

their studious cousins crowded into the Perth Assembly Hall for *Egyptiana: A Review of the Arts, Manners and Mythology of Ancient Egypt.* The high-minded lecture and display of exotic artifacts drove out Belzoni's blue devils splendidly. Afterwards, he and Lizzie forgot their acting trials to share slices of plum cake in the colorfully wallpapered tea room next door.

"Upon my word! There's our favorite actress in the offing." It was the booming voice of Captain the Honorable Charles Irby, who, with Mangles in tow, had just come in out of the blustery, freezing afternoon to partake of some warm, fresh scones.

"How did you find the sands of Egypt, Miss Trumpet? Spiritual, I'll be bound." Signor Belzoni was introduced and the four began a jolly chin-wag as they took their tea together, breathing the satisfying aroma of baking sweets.

"Of all the Gypo display, I enjoyed the mummy best. She reminded me of your grandmother, Mangles. The lady's such a dry wit." Irby laughed immoderately at his own joke.

"Really, Charles." Mangles shook his head. "You are a trial to me, at times."

"I found it *spettacoloso,*" pronounced Belzoni. "*Molto spettacoloso!*"

"Captains, have you ever been posted to Egypt?" Lizzie passed a tray of pastry to the men who had the appetites of growing boys.

"Since Nelson's victory at the Battle of the Nile, the Navy and the Army have been needed elsewhere," Mangles explained. "Not much chance we'll see Egypt while we're at war with Bonaparte."

The door of the tea shop banged open and closed, admitting the ten-year-old call-boy from the theatre. He loped up to their table, showering the captains with un-melted pellets of hail when he doffed his cap.

"Well, who is this? Present yourself, lad," Irby ordered.

"Tarcher, sir. Your pardon, Miss Trumpet, I'm that thankful to find you. Mr. Faversham's compliments, and he says you're urgently needed to teach some songs to the new juvenile. I'm to escort you with this here umbrella. Mr. Faversham says you are not to delay, or he'll tan my hide."

Regretfully, Lizzie began to bundle on her red wool cloak. "Gentlemen, life in the theatre is somewhat like the Royal Navy. When your admiral flies the blue peter, you quit the pleasures of land and obey."

"Your ship is The Princess Theatre."

"Exactly, Captain Mangles, and duty calls. Thank you all for a most memorable tea." She took Belzoni's hand in her two gloved ones. "I will pray your next *vis-à-vis* is more cooperative than Miss Orso. *Addio*, Giovanni."

Lizzie and Tarcher departed.

Through the shop window, the big Italian watched Lizzie's umbrella disappearing down the windy, wet street. "I met Lisabetta the first day I come to London. *Più di sett'anni fa*, more than seven years past. We were great friends before she married."

ᦉ

The hail gave way to rain. Little Tarcher held the umbrella so low, Lizzie could barely see as they walked together. When they achieved the theatre, a slender male figure was standing under the freezing front portico, attended by Neville Boone, who looked, as always, miffed and put-upon.

"Mr. Eggleston! I rejoice to see you. And here's Boone, too." Lizzie joined them, shaking out her soggy skirt. "What brings you to Scotland in such immoderate weather?"

"My quest for new talent never ends. And speaking of talent, your performance in *The Dame of the Dell* quite stole my heart."

Her cold cheeks glowed at his words. "Yet, you didn't come to see me in the green room?"

"No." Eggleston wiped a crystal drop from his nose with a handkerchief then tucked the fine linen into his coat sleeve of periwinkle blue. "May we have a word alone?"

"Tarcher, tell my husband I shall join him momentarily." As the call-boy hurried out of the wind, Boone gave a martyred sniff and stepped almost out of ear-shot. Lizzie lifted her brows quizzically.

"I shall be brief, Elizabeth. You are now, this moment, absolutely ready to play major roles at Covent Garden and Drury Lane. You have been Faversham's twinkling little constellation long enough. It is time for your own star to rise. People listen to my opinion. It would give me great pleasure, Elizabeth, to speak on your behalf."

She exhaled a cloud of breath, both amazed and concerned. "Then you must advise Jack. He has always preferred I work only with him."

"What do you prefer, my dear? What do you want to do with your great talent?"

Setting aside the unexpectedness of Eggleston's proposal, Lizzie spoke swiftly and honestly from her heart. "I want to work in London, as my father did. The best acting is done there. But I would never hurt my husband; our marriage is...."

"I will drive no wedge between you. No need for me to confer with your husband, and incidentally, say nothing of meeting me. You know, of course, I cannot guarantee you a role." He smiled. "But, if suddenly you are called to London—by Kemble or Harris, or Elliston at the Lane—be surprised. Jack, that dear self-confident boy, will believe the offer is because of him. However, Elizabeth, it is *you* I want to champion."

Two tears sparkled in her hazel eyes. "I believe I understand, sir. May I ask why?"

"Because you are so very good and honest, too. Time is always flying, especially for a woman. Mr. Faversham has no further need of me. I think you do. I collect you are wanted inside?"

"Yes, for a music rehearsal."

"Attend to it. Enjoy Scotland!" Neville Boone popped up Eggleston's umbrella. The entrepreneur's seriousness melted into a wicked smile. "Remember to be surprised."

Chapter Twenty-Two

Fall 1811

"OH PAPA, I am here! On your stage. London at last!" Lizzie leaned against the Covent Garden proscenium arch, crying tears of joy into her armful of bouquets. She would forever remember each vivid-as-a-diamond moment of this night.

Out of the blue, Thomas Jupiter Harris and John Philip Kemble had indeed contacted Faversham, asking him to play the Grand Inquisitor for six performances in a new production of *The Towers of Urbadine*. Jack accepted the offer as if there had never been a harsh word between himself and Kemble. In passing, Harris asked Jack if Elizabeth was up to playing the featured role of Lady Catherine.

"I've brought her a long way," Jack replied with restrained enthusiasm. "She could do the part quite nicely."

So, Lizzie was also hired for the six performances, at a lesser salary, of course. To be prepared for the theatre's scandalously brief rehearsals, she and Jack drilled their scenes in the Rose Street flat, watched over by Cassius, who wagged his tail at everything.

Theatre Royal Covent Garden was filled to capacity opening night, a thousand candles lit, when twenty minutes into Act One, the actors were stopped mid-scene. The Prince of Wales, having been designated Prince Regent due to old King George's mental incompetence, unexpectedly entered the sumptuous royal box with his chattering entourage. He swayed at attention for the required singing of "God Save the King," dropped heavily to his seat and waved for the players on stage to continue.

As the Grand Inquisitor, Jonathan Faversham chewed up and spat out the entire supporting cast. They cleared for his first soliloquy, a description of his noble nemesis, Lady Catherine. At last, Lizzie made her entrance. At twenty-four, costumed in peacock blue satin with a headdress of emerald jewels, the tall actress walked in the prime of her beauty. At the sight of her, the audience gasped. Lizzie spoke her first line with assurance, in a voice warm as honey. Lady Catherine was as vivid in virtue as the villain was vile.

By the final act, the theatre candles were flickering down to smoky stubs. With malice, the Grand Inquisitor interrogated and judged the blameless heroine. Lady Catherine made an impassioned speech in her own defense, calling upon Christian principles of mercy. The Inquisitor executed her anyway. Strangled center stage by his long purple scarf, the dying heroine executed a graceful fall that stunned the audience.

After a moment of silence, the balconies broke into cheers, even the Prince Regent heaved himself off his cushions to applaud, and a true ovation began. Jack broke the final tableau to raise Lizzie to her feet and, hand in hand, they moved downstage to accept the adulation. Flowers were thrown over the float-lights, dropping around the actress in a barrage of bouquets and random roses. Jack eased back, allowing Miss Trumpet her first solo bow ever, then gripped her hand hissing, "Let's not overdo it," and led her off.

The prompter passed her an armload of collected blossoms when she stopped crying in the wings. "Yours, Miss Trumpet, well-earned."

"Oh, Fenton. Such excitement. Thank you."

"You have a song in the afterpiece, remember."

"I won't forget." Lizzie floated towards her dressing room, Jack at her side.

"By gad, I've turned you into a consummate actress. Well done, girl." He gave her a slap on the bum and hurried away to change.

The after-piece was an olio of comedy sketches, ditties and

dances. Lizzie sang "In Front of Your Eyes" against a garden backdrop, flying coquettishly back and forth in a swing. Her voice had the bell-like ping that made the saucy lyrics perfectly audible in the huge house. The London audience went wild over her song. It was quite a debut. Elizabeth Trumpet could do no wrong.

The green room filled with old friends and unfamiliar well-wishers. Charles Dibdin gave her a very wet kiss and offered two new verses for her song that he had been inspired to compose in the last ten minutes. Sidrack Sloane handed her white lilies. Meg Wilson had embroidered "The Towers of Urbadine" and the date into a lovely handkerchief for Lady Catherine to carry at the next performance. Noddy, in his absolute best, William Trumpet's fine frock coat that Lizzie had given him years ago, stepped on the foot of Philip Eggleston to crushing effect, while trying to settle a giddy Aunt Peg in a chair. Emily Widewell was so excited she suffered an attack of the hiccups. Percy Wentworth languidly attempted to cure them with champagne. Cassius the dog offered his paw to all who would take it. Carlo Tomassi, flushed from conducting the orchestra, pushed everyone aside to bow at Lizzie's feet and pronounce her an inspiration.

A beaming, perspiring Lord Dampere bore down on the happy actress as well. "Utterly spectacularis, Elizabeth. My congratulations. And I have the honor to deliver a message from His Royal Highness." The babble of adulation hushed. "The prince sends his compliments and invites you and your husband to share a late supper at Carlton House."

Lizzie froze. "Now? You mean this moment?"

"Oh, yes, immediately, a private and very informal invitation, to be sure." Dampere smiled like the cat digesting the canary. Jack tried to look unsurprised. Lizzie, pulse accelerating, didn't bother.

"Dampie, how did this happen?"

"I'm very pleased to tell you. I confided to His Highness that you were making your London debut and once were a favorite of mine." Lord Freddy licked his lips, ignoring Jack. "Out of sporting curiosity, he came to have a look and stayed the entire evening. The prince was utterly beguiled by that ribald song. You have, may I say, quite conquered him."

᷂

Very keyed up and hastily cleaned up, the Favershams entered the magnificence of Carlton House, the Prince Regent's bachelor digs, where for years he had decorated and redecorated to suit his taste for unrestrained splendor.

In borrowed finery from the Covent Garden wardrobe racks, Jack and Lizzie passed their wraps to a majordomo in livery of royal blue. Following another servant, white-wigged in the style of the past age, they walked wonderingly through rooms large enough to hold a tennis match, where tapering opal glass chandeliers illuminated massive gold furniture, and every surface appeared smothered in crimson damask. The performers were surrounded by a wealth of display: marble statues, chinoiserie screens, arrangements of hot-house flowers ten-feet high, swags of tasseled silk at every window, upholstery trimmed with precious braids, motifs of kingship in the carpets, golden moldings framing yet more damask behind the paintings on the walls. Lizzie had never imagined such "much of a muchness," as Aunt Peg was wont to say.

The servant led them into the famous Gothic Conservatory, a forest of rainbow-hued columns supporting a web of fan-vaulting on the ceiling. A chamber orchestra was playing the "Masked Ball Minuet" from *Don Giovanni* in an alcove.

"Mister Jonathan Faversham and Miss Elizabeth Trumpet," the servant intoned and left them to be noticed by the smartest beings in Europe—the Carlton House set.

At once, Lizzie spotted Lord Dampere. At his side was the ruler of England, his fine-featured face set in an expression of self-satisfaction under a wavy chestnut-brown wig. Stuffed into his Hussar uniform, the monarch was so overflowingly fat, he made Dampere look trim.

"Ah, my dear theatricals," the prince called out and waddled over. Dampere followed at a respectful distance but stayed close enough to hear. Lizzie curtsied deeply, the white ostrich plume in her high-piled hair brushing the marble floor. "We were most impressed with your performances this evening. We do admire artists of the theatre, God bless us we do. It is our pleasure to have you join our little soiree."

"Thank you, Your Highness," Jack blurted, bowing again.

"Your portrayal of Lady Catherine brought tears to these eyes." The prince gestured with a silk handkerchief that fleetingly reminded Lizzie of Roger. "And as for the Grand Inquisitor...well! Could you really kill such a delectable lady as this?"

Jack shrugged. "The play is not a comedy, Your Highness."

"Truly, Miss Trumpet, we were moved."

"Moved," Dampere echoed from three feet behind His Highness.

"It is a splendid part, Highness." Lizzie dimpled up at her monarch and inwardly pinched herself.

"Now I should like you to meet my friends. Do not be put off by their wicked tongues. Be warned, vicious conversation passes for wit amongst them." The prince took Lizzie by her kid-gloved hand and propelled his way like Moses through a sea of courtiers, all parting before him. He stopped beside a large lady of perhaps fifty years, her amethyst necklace clasped tight below a matched set of chins. This vision of propriety was the present mistress of the Regent's affections, fulfilling his penchant for bosomy, wise matrons of a certain age.

"Lady Hertford, my jewel, here are the actors who so charmed you this evening." Then the prince introduced two men who had strutted into their circle: a thick-set, cheerful-faced peacock of middling years and his impeccably-dressed companion. "May I present, William, Lord Alvanley and my particular friend Mr. George Brummell."

"But we have met before, Miss Trumpet," Brummell offered, "at Vauxhall Gardens. Roses were blooming in your hair, and dear Pudge was on your arm."

"Ah, yes," Dampere murmured nostalgically in the background.

"I am surprised you remember me, Mr. Brummell. Though, of course, I remember you."

"I have a question for this breathtaking actress," Brummell announced in a voice loud enough to include most of the guests. "You may answer candidly, Miss Trumpet, since we have no secrets here."

"Remember, I warned you." The prince said, keen with

anticipation.

"Tell me truly that you have not been paramoured by Lord Alvanley here. He's just been protesting to intimate knowledge of actresses by the hundred. By the hundred, mind you."

"Rest easy, Mr. Brummell, for prior to this instant I have not laid eyes—" Lizzie paused and looked 'round to include the entire group, "or any other bit of my anatomy on his lordship." She dipped her plume to Alvanley, while the privileged bystanders chortled.

"*Brava*, Trumpet." Brummell slapped his gloved hands together. "Alvanley, you obviously missed the best of the lot. No gentleman of the *haut ton* should evermore accept your claims of manly prowess."

"*Mon Dieu*, your feckless diatribe reeks of envy, Brummell. It is common knowledge that those who can't...talk." The confident old rake pressed his face in close to the uncomfortable Lizzie. "This stunning thespian at your side, this Mr. Faversham, is he a doer or a talker? Madam, share your innermost, I beg."

"Lord Alvanley," the actress improvised, "you hear how much Mr. Faversham talks."

Picking up his cue, Jack slid an arm around Lizzie's waist with a roguish wink. "It is a well-known fact there is a time to speak and a time to keep one's tongue tacet."

Alvanley crowed. "Oh, I do admire that. Does his talking onstage and performs his best acts silently with you, Miss Trumpet? Mmmm, I envy you both."

"Alvanley is uncommon loquacious tonight," Brummell sneered, "more an old rooster clucking to the setting hens than a true cock of the walk."

"You must not be swept into the inanity offered by these two bravados." The prince turned his broad back on the men. "Their bite is utterly toothless and, as Lady Hertford will concur, their tedious persiflage provokes boredom."

Dismissed, Alvanley and the Beau wandered off, more or less comparing penises in a jocular fashion. Lizzie opened her fan to cool the air and clear away the heavy perfume of Alvanley's hair oil.

"Your Highness," Lizzie looked over the Regent's diamond decorations admiringly, "the uniform you wear is of the Tenth

Hussars, is it not?"

"Your prince is Honorary Colonel of the Tenth," Dampere piped up, still hovering close by.

"It gives me joy to tell Your Highness that my brother George Trumpet proudly wears the same uniform. He is serving in the Peninsula. General Wellesley gave him a field promotion to captain following the Battle of Talavera. You have no more loyal subject, sir, than my brother."

"Damned you say! A captain in my own regiment? Dampere here never mentioned that! Lady Hertford, my jewel, remind me to put in a word with Lord Paget. Your brother's Christian name again?"

"George, sir, like yourself, though actually after your father, who is ever in our prayers."

The prince was not inclined to thank Lizzie for her prayers to prolong the life of his mad and disapproving father. "Quite. Indeed."

"Perhaps Your Highness knows the family of my brother's close friend who also serves in Spain? Edward Wentworth?"

"Wentworth. Sir Henry's younger boy?"

"The same, sir."

"Where has the time gone? We thought young Wentworth was still a lad at Eton. Ah, the sun and the moon in their orbits, what? Miss Trumpet, we shall keep an eye on your brother." The prince peered past Lizzie's shoulder with keenest interest, nostrils flaring. "I see Truffault has set out supper at last. I enjoin you to advantage yourselves of the partridge *a la Pompadour*."

"And the roast larks *en croute*, my very favorite," Lady Hertford added.

"Toothsome little birds." Dampere laughed lightly.

"Well, charming as this has been"—Lady Hertford enjoyed a long look at Jack—"we must see to our other guests, Prinny." She took the round royal arm and attempted to steer, but the regent would not be shoved.

"We would be pleased if you performed later."

"Of course." Jack sounded both eager and ill at ease. A fish out of water.

"Honored, Your Highness," Lizzie answered with a curtsy.

"*A bientôt* then!" Like a pair of gentle hippopotami, the prince and Lady Hertford waddled off through the forest of columns to their meal.

The Favershams looked round-eyed at each other, Jack surreptitiously wiping the sweat off his brow.

Lord Dampere frothed with pleasure and moisture. "It's going so well, utterly top of the tree!"

When the Prince Regent sent word that he would be enthralled to hear Miss Trumpet sing again, it was three in the morning, following a service of collations, hot and cold, arriving on silver platters by the dozens. Lizzie had only picked at the fabulous dishes and drunk no wine. The prospect of entertaining this indulged and critical gathering was unsettling to her stomach. Jack had declined the prince's favorite maraschino liqueur several times, believing he, too, was to be called upon.

The entourage of courtiers followed their prince and the Favershams into the Music Salon, a deep-blue-velvet room perfumed with cascades of carnations. The golden *fleur-de-lis* symbol of the Prince of Wales was ubiquitous, woven into the carpet, upholstery, drapery and wall coverings. Exquisite musical instruments were displayed in niches and a grand harpsichord painted with lolling muses stood in a corner. Once Lady Hertford was planted on a generous loveseat, the prince himself selected a prized mandolin from the collection to place in Lizzie's hands. It was the most beautiful object she had ever touched; a rainbow of mother-of-pearl filigree shimmered on the polished black wood. She returned her monarch's smile with an excited one of her own, and tore into the tune that had caused a sensation earlier at the Garden.

"Will she do it? Why, yes, she will do it!
And right in front of your eyes!
Oh, why do you misconstrue it?
And why do you show surprise?
Though she swore to 'ever be faithful,'

And she promised to 'ever be true,'
I'm telling you now,
She doesn't know how.
She is feminine, through and through."

Lizzie strolled round the room and sang seductively to the gentlemen she had joked with.

"You can shout, 'I forbid!' to her face,
You can fasten her tight to a tree;
If she's craving a secret embrace,
A quick tryst, or a sly vis-à-vis,
Disregard her profound protestations,
No matter how often she tries.
If her heart is aflame,
It's all part of the game,
And she'll do it in front of your eyes!"

The prince and his mistress laughed immoderately on their love seat. Lizzie shot a look to Brummell.

"Will she do it? Of course, she will do it!
She has to stay true to her gender!
Your ranting will never subdue it;
So, throw up your hands and surrender!
Now hearken! I know what I'm saying.
It's time that you realize:
There's no simple cure
For 'L'affaire de l'amour,'
And all those incipient lies.
Despite all the strife,
Whether lover or wife,
She'll do it—I mean it!
She'll do it—I've seen it!
She will do it in front of your eyes!"

The prince and all the Carlton House set applauded enthusiastically. Lizzie had hit just the right note, entertaining "The First Gentleman of Europe."

Jack stepped forward, hand to breast, and maneuvered Lizzie off into a chair against the wall. "Now, would Your Highness like to hear some immortal lines of Shakespeare?" If the prince nodded it was very slightly, but Jack launched into Hamlet's *"Oh, that this too, too solid flesh would melt...."* Not a good choice.

After two lines, the regent gave a sigh and pointed to something that had caught his eye in the wainscoting. He beckoned to a slight, balding man behind the harpsichord, court designer John Nash, always ready to hear yet another idea from his generous employer. Seeking privacy elsewhere, they left Hamlet to explore his suicidal ruminations.

Most of the fashionables also slipped out. Jack finished to applause from a few fat ladies too sated to have left their seats. Eyes stormy with humiliation, he snapped a jerk of a bow and quickstepped out of the blue salon.

Lizzie rushed after, the sound of Jack's voice demanding his hat guiding her to the faraway foyer. There would be no opportunity to find Lord Dampere and say thank you. They were leaving. Very distressed over what Jack must be feeling, Lizzie collected her fur stole from a stone-faced footman. Her husband was pacing under the Corinthian columns of the marble portico, shouting for the jarvey, many carriages down the line.

"Oaf!" Jack did not wait for the driver, but set off on foot into the foggy streets of Mayfair. Lizzie waved the hackney to follow, and slipping on the wet cobblestones in her satin slippers, half ran to keep up. The angry actor was working himself into a tooth-grinding rage.

"The Prince of Philistines, that's what he is. Swollen pimple on the arse of culture. Mound of rot. Bloated, toad-faced turd. Walks out on the greatest Hamlet he'll ever hear. Walks out on *me!*"

"Jack, my darling, I agree the prince was inattentive, but I'm sure he was called away by affairs of state."

Jack spun in his tracks with a hate-filled look. "Horseshit. I saw you fitted in perfectly, swishing your tail like a bitch in heat."

Tearing into a tantrum was usual enough, but he had never said such a thing to her before. Lizzie bit her tongue to cut off debate while her husband was so wrought up. They trudged down Chandos Street, the horse clopping behind. She could hear muffled barks from inside the hack; Cassius the dog had been neglected for many hours.

Rounding the corner into Bradford Bury, Jack stopped in his tracks, as a boy of tender years, with drawn knife, appeared out of the shadows. The fledgling thief, hoping to take down some drunken toff, had miscalculated. Here was the fight Jack's furies had been spoiling for. In a flash, he wrested the knife away from the unlucky footpad and threw him to the ground, kicking furiously with sharp pointed boots at head and groin.

When Lizzie ran up, she could scarcely credit it; her husband had the knife poised to cut the lad's face. "Jack, for God's sake."

Faversham, face inhuman, turned from the screaming boy.

"You've punished him enough," she yelled, and Jack dropped the knife to savage the would-be robber with a last kick to his head, rendering him unconscious in the muck of the street as blood began to flow from his ears. Lizzie watched the actor straighten his clothes and continue on, scuffing his heels on the cobblestones, seemingly much better for the exercise. Repelled, she climbed into the carriage, quieted the excited dog, and told the jarvey to drive anywhere. She wept against the horsehair seat, shamed and shaken by the highs and lows of her evening.

After an hour of upset, her heart stopped pounding enough to return to the Rose Street rooms and face Jack. The one-sided battle had raised Faversham's penis as well as his spirits. He greeted her triumphantly from the bed, raising the sheets to show off his erection. For the first time in her life, Lizzie wanted none of him.

Chapter Twenty-Three

January 1812

PHILLIP EGGLESTON, punctual as always, entered the Shakespeare's Head Tavern, the dark wood-paneled actor's pub off the Covent Garden piazza. Harris and Kemble had invited him for a meal. Hoping the meeting might include a discussion of Elizabeth Trumpet, the wily manager accepted with alacrity. Touching his superbly sharp collar points, he looked around for the directors of Covent Garden.

Thomas Jupiter Harris raised his furry eyebrows in greeting. "Over here, Eggs," he called out from an ancient settle. "I've ordered us winkles and whitebait. What shall you be drinking?"

Once sure their guest was fortified against the January cold with a mug of ale, Kemble got to the point. "Your Elizabeth Trumpet is a treasure, and we are grateful you brought her out of the provinces to our attention."

Eggleston smiled. "It could not have fallen out more happily."

Harris exercised his selective memory. "I admired her courage years ago when her father went out of his mind. She begged us for a job. You remember, Kemble? She was no more than a schoolgirl. You told her to bugger off."

The dignified actor looked down his considerable nose. "Gad, no,

Harris, I've no recollection of such a meeting. It's neither here nor there; in the passing years she's learnt her craft."

"We have Jack Faversham to thank for that. Ah, how I love the whitebait season!" Eggleston opened his napkin with a flourish as the waiter carried plates piled high with crisp, golden-fried fish to the table. The gentlemen began to tuck into the salty little morsels.

"I thank Faversham for nothing." Kemble sniffed. "Did you know, Eggs, in my hour of need, when I had sunk all my own monies into the new theatre and was deep in debt, he was the only actor in London who refused to take a pay cut? And besides, the man does not know his place. He consistently interfered in the production of *Urbadine*, showing temperament, making demands. I will not have such behavior in my theatre."

"The boy has always been a legend in his own mind," Eggleston agreed. He had no part in the actor's life anymore. The end of their intimacies had left a wound in the older man's heart that was yet to heal; still, seeing Jack get his come-uppance was easing the pain.

"The thing is, Eggs," Kemble flicked a whitebait head to a grateful cat prowling in the sawdust at the door, "I've just commissioned a play titled *British Glory*. Not a deep piece, but a patriotic spectacle, 'backbone of Britain fighting off the invading Roman Empire' sort of thing. We want to cast Elizabeth as Queen Boadicea. Take advantage of Trumpet's beauty and the celebrity her work excited in *The Towers of Urbadine*. What do you think?"

"Marching Britons painted in blue, winged helmets and chariots, I imagine?" Eggleston crunched a winkle. "You know, she rides magnificently and handles weapons, too. Trumpet started out at the Wells, doing a swordplay act."

"Wasn't aware. Um, um, the sword business would cut a dash, eh?" Harris was chewing up his plate of little fish. "We're casting Kemble's brother, Charles, for the Roman Governor Suetonius. An engaging young actor, blessed with the family talent."

"Zooks!" Kemble ejaculated.

"Oh, sorry, old man." Harris had accidentally squeezed his lemon into Kemble's eye. "We don't want to use Jack Faversham, at all. Of course, he'll be damned put out. Do you think there will be trouble from Elizabeth because of it?"

"Gentlemen, there isn't a troublesome bone in that girl's wondrous body." It sounded to Eggleston as though Jack's comet had burned out at Covent Garden, while Lizzie's star was going to rise in a flash of true fame. How pleasing was that? "You'll get a fine performance from her." He raised his napkin to pat some fishy butter off his thin lips. "That girl is more of a professional than her madman of a husband will ever be." Things were turning out just as he'd hoped.

Spring, 1812

British Glory became a tour-de-force for Lizzie. She led her valiant Britons from a galloping horse on a treadmill, barbarian bodice half-unlaced, sword-arm high, slashing against the wicked invaders' spears. It was *Illyria Aflame* all over again, but this time with better production and a slave-girl ballet. Over the dead and dying supernumeraries, Lizzie raised a great red banner, singing a challenge to the Roman Governor, cursing him for setting foot on her sacred isle.

The whole thing made Jack want to set foot on Lizzie's neck. As long as the lion of Jack's ego was fed, he could function with some restraint, but when he felt ignored, his inclination was to foul his own cage. Besides blaming Harris and Kemble for not hiring him, the jealous actor convinced himself Lizzie had colluded with them. He took vengeance on her by having it on with other women.

Playing *British Glory* required all Lizzie's physical strength and energy; there was not much left to entertain her puzzling, volcanic husband. Jack filled his empty hours pursuing two randy blondes in the ensemble. He often achieved a double assignation behind the scenery during Act Four. Miss Trumpet had no notion that when Boadicea raised her banner out front, Alfred the Great was appearing backstage, making a penetrating impression on others in the cast.

"I am stopping at the Wentworths' in Golden Square for a whole month. Cousin Percy escorted me this evening. Oh, Miss Trumpet, your performance as the queen general is inspiring." Emily Widewell, blue eyes glistening, could not say enough. She looked over the swords and costumes tossed helter-skelter in Lizzie's dressing room with wonder. "How pleased George must be to know you are Boadicea; he is such a student of military history."

"Is he indeed? We must compare our letters from him. Please take a sip of wine while I change out of this squalid breastplate. I am very glad you visited the greenroom tonight." She slipped behind the dressing-room screen.

Emily perched on a chair, looking the other way. The visitor was demurely dressed in palest green with a little coronet of curls on the top of her fair head.

"What is that sound? Miss Widewell, are you in distress?"

"It is nothing. I fear the hiccups are upon me again. Such excitement!" Lizzie walked around the screen in dishabille to pour Emily a glass of water. "Oh, but your arms are bruised—*hic*—Miss Trumpet."

"Yes, well, most actresses fake the action, but as you see, I do not." Lizzie gave Emily the glass. "Take twenty sips without stopping." She pressed her fingers into the girl's ears. "There, you see? No more hiccups. Now, you must call me Lizzie, because I know you are dear to Georgie, and therefore you are dear to me."

The overwhelmed girl began to relax. "Thank you, Lizzie. You are very kind." Emily returned the glass. "But, now tell me, how do you manage with all those bruises?"

"Long ago I was taught to fall in three graceful stages by an old actor named Pickle. Drop first to your knees, then hips, then shoulders. No bruises that way. All very well for a fainting lady, but Boadicea is made of sterner stuff."

"That leap from the parapet!" Emily clapped her gloved hands. "Such daring. However do you...?"

"A mattress. And on Friday, it wasn't there. So, here I am with a blue bum." The girls laughed companionably.

"I shall write to George about this evening, and I shan't forget to describe the cheers and applause for you. Would you like me to read from his recent letters? I have some in my reticule."

"Yes, please." Lizzie began to brush out her waist-length hair as her new friend drew out a thick handful of papers from her embroidered purse. "So many? I'm blessed to get one a month now. You know, most people don't bring reading materials to the theatre, Emily."

"Though Cousin Percy is very good to endure a country bumpkin on his arm, he tends to take himself off and converse with the bucks of his acquaintance. I always carry a book for such solitary occasions. Tonight, at the interval, I finished Miss Austen's *Sense and Sensibility*, a very astute novel. May I make a gift of it to you?"

"Thank you, I would truly enjoy that." *Ah, this pretty little girl has a turn of mind to books.* "Is your family visiting the Wentworths?"

"No, only me. Papa owns a brick factory in Sheffield, which is his chief interest in the world. He considers London society a waste of time." She unfolded a letter. "I confess, I came to see you in *British Glory*, not my Wentworth cousins, though they are acting as my chaperones."

"What a bold girl you are. Let us become well acquainted, as my brother wishes. Please, let me hear Georgie's missives from Spain."

As the girl read, a man new to Lizzie emerged in the letters. Captain Trumpet alluded to terrible events with manly detachment, neither boasting nor blaming. At the Battle of Ciudad Rodrigo, two horses had been shot out from under him, surely an awful day, yet he praised the heroics of his brother officers, never mentioning his own danger. He wrote of an existence he lived in his mind, where the tragedy of war could not touch him, describing the ephemeral beauties of being alive, a sunrise or a bird on the wing, pouring out to Emily a flood of observation that sounded like poetry to his sister.

Lizzie turned from pinning up her hair. "What a style he shows to you, Emily. He opens his very heart."

"Sometimes his words take my breath away, such purity of soul and high ideals. I think I love him from these letters." Emily returned them to her reticule, speaking quietly. "I do not write of love, of course, just my hopes for him and the events of the day. But, I admit to you," she paused cautiously, "I am living for his return."

Lizzie bent over Emily's chair to kiss her crown of curls. "I am glad such a girl as you waits for Georgie."

A pale, thin young man, squinting behind his glasses, offered his card to Lizzie in the greenroom. "Miss Trumpet, I am Jeremiah Brett, an artist in the studio of Thomas Lawrence, Principal Painter to the Royal Court. You know his name?"

"And his work, sir. He has done fascinating portraits of the Kemble family." Lizzie had become accustomed to strange men presenting themselves without any introduction in this public greeting place. "Is there some aspect of *British Glory* that is of interest to you?"

"Only you, Miss Trumpet. I wish to paint you—a full length portrait that will make us both immortal."

"Is that likely, Mr. Brett?" He had her attention.

"With a subject such as you? I have no doubt."

She indicated Brett should sit. As he talked, he opened a portfolio of drawings in chalk. "As so many do, I began as a scene painter for the theatre. I am expert at backgrounds, but I was not born to paint cows and crumbling architecture. Only doing drapery and trees for Lawrence year after year is driving me jippers. I paint portraits beautifully, you see. A clientele of unfashionable strivers who want to hang themselves in the dining room and impress their kinfolk give me a comfortable living." He chuckled nervously. "But I wish to be more than a middling artist for middling people."

Lizzie shuffled through the studies of portrait heads. "Very impressive, Mr. Brett. In just a few lines, these men and women seem to cry out with life."

"Thank you, Miss Trumpet. My reputation would be made if I could paint you, in the classical manner."

"Not as Boadicea?"

"Oh, *mon dieu*, no! No helmets, please. Let Lawrence do Kemble as Hamlet and dear old Sarah Siddons as the Tragic Muse. I want you apart from any role you play onstage. A goddess, perhaps, out of costume."

"How far out?"

"Completely, if possible. Don't dismiss me, Miss Trumpet. Please come to my studio, see my finished work and then decide. And may a humble artist offer to take you to supper? I understand actors are always ravenous after the show."

"No, thank you, Mr. Brett. I await my husband here, but I will give your suggestion some thought, indeed I will. Thank you for showing me your sketches, and good night."

An hour later, Lizzie was still in the greenroom, reading Jane Austen. Growing cold and lonely, still awaiting Jack.

Chapter Twenty-Four

June 29, 1812

SARAH KEMBLE Siddons was considered the finest actress England had ever seen. The night she retired from performing, at age fifty-seven, the entire world seemed to be in the theatre. Persons of high distinction had traveled from their country houses to cheer the celebration. Every actor who could walk was in the building. The paying customers filled all the seats and standing-room, and even crowded amongst the musicians of the orchestra.

For her final London season, Sarah had recreated her most famous roles, taking the stage fifty-seven times, an ovation for every year of her life. For her last appearance, Mrs. Siddons chose the play she had acted in more than any other: Shakespeare's *Scottish Play.*

To reverent silence, she played Lady Macbeth's sleepwalking scene, then made her final exit. Applause like a roaring tempest broke across the stage.

Her brother, John Philip Kemble, stepped out of the wings. Did the audience wish the play to finish? The audience did not. The curtain came down.

In a few moments, it rose again on Mrs. Siddons, strikingly handsome in her white satin robe and veil. A farewell address was customary when a favorite actor retired; the audience did not expect icons of art to go quietly. With simple dignity, the great tragedienne thanked the playgoers of England for a lifetime of faithfulness. Her arms opened in an embracing gesture. "The greatest joy of my life has been your love." Another ovation and she staggered off, collapsing in her brother's arms, emotionally spent.

In a box seat above it all, Lizzie had sobbed in sympathy. She honored Siddons for her talents, her spotless reputation, and most of all because she was of William's generation. Now they would both be only memories of the unrecoverable once-upon-a-time.

The Favershams made their way down the crowded aisles, passing the lingering, sad-faced people staring at the proscenium— people who had watched an era end and were slow to leave. Invited guests, all the celebrated of the moment, family and friends, newcomers and old-timers, gathered by the orchestra. When the public had quitted the building, the curtain rose again, this time on long tables of food and wine—a supper in silver dishes ordered in from Gunter's by the Kemble brothers at great expense. The thousands of flowers the audience had thrown in tribute were banked in sweet-smelling piles around the Macbeth throne. Waiters and fiddlers moved onto the stage. The climax of the evening had passed; now the guests simply mingled.

Lizzie and Jack introduced themselves to the handsome George Gordon, Lord Byron, the lion of romantic poetry, who was casting his sleepy eyes over some potted shrimps.

"Nothing ever was or can be like Sarah Siddons." He shook his carefully arranged locks at Jack. "Our stage will never be the same again."

"We shall miss her," was the best Jack could say.

"My lord, I have read the First Canto of your *Childe Harold's Pilgrimage*. Your hero's experiences in Spain were of deepest interest to me, since my brother is serving there with General Wellesley."

"Ah." The moody poet brightened enough to look directly at Lizzie's animated face.

"Have you ever considered writing a play?"

Byron inflated his chest. "A poetic drama, perhaps, but I have yet to be inspired." Evidently uninspired by the Favershams, he walked away, lost in his own universe.

"Full of himself," Jack muttered.

Mrs. Siddons, changed into a gown of stark and stunning black with silver brilliants, emerged from her dressing room, escorted this time by her brother Charles. Eyes still pink from weeping and with a glass of brandy in hand, she strolled to the scenery-throne in the mountain of flowers. People immediately clustered around to be received by the abdicating queen of drama.

"How her heart must ache," Lizzie said in a low voice. "The stage was her life, and she owned it."

"She owns more than the stage. The old trout earned more money than any actor in history, and she's hung on to every penny. She must have made a fortune tonight—her farewell benefit. As though she needed one." Jack tossed off a glass of champagne. "I'm going to catch a word with Harris."

Lizzie joined the gathered friends of Siddons, so many they had turned into a queue.

As she waited her turn at the throne, Phillip Eggleston pranced up to kiss her hand. "Now the granddame is gone, there'll be more room at the top for you, Elizabeth," he whispered in her ear. "Look to it!"

"Thank you, sir. Hasn't this been a year so far?" She kissed his powdered cheek with true affection. "I am deeply grateful for all you've done."

"Your success gives me pleasure, my dear. Tell me, how are the domestic arrangements faring? Now that you know Jack's history, how are you two getting on?"

"There is never a dull moment." Lizzie wondered exactly what Eggleston meant but before she could ask, he twinkled away.

Though they had both appeared at Covent Garden, Mrs. Siddons and Miss Trumpet had never actually met. Standing close to her, Lizzie studied the famous face of the star. Siddons held her head with upturned grace, but deep lines webbed her features and the Roman nose had grown quite long. Droop and decay had begun. Lizzie understood a proud woman had chosen to say *adieu* before everyone noticed her age more than her talent. Better to voluntarily step off a pedestal than be crated up as a relic. *But oh, how terribly hard the moment of goodbye.... No fortune, no blessed privacy...could ever compensate me for retirement....* Charles Kemble beckoned her forward. *Ah, at last!*

"Mrs. Siddons, I am Elizabeth Trumpet, an admirer of your great talent, and also William Trumpet's daughter."

"Oh," Siddons broke into a soft smile, "what a fine actor he was, most polished and so in love with your mother." Instantly, Lizzie was taken by the down-to-earth Sarah, who warmly reached out for her hand. "I was terribly sorry to hear of his difficulties."

Lizzie, palm to heart, was sweetly moved. "My father was lost to himself, but never lost to the stage. Even in his slippers, he remained an actor to the last!"

"God bless him. And you, Miss Trumpet, what a fine start you are making in London. You know, I've seen a bit of *British Glory*. A lovely challenge."

"I've much to learn. Seeing you tonight, I realize how much."

"Of course, dear. We learn from every audience, every performance, especially when they are fickle and turn against us. That's why reputation is so important. Love from the gallery blows hot and cold, but first they must respect you. It is the foundation of a serious artist. Respect once lost is never regained." She sipped her last drop of brandy. "When I was little, my sweet mother gave me a penny for learning her favorite passages from the Bard or the Bible."

"And what was her choice for reputation?" Lizzie asked, intrigued.

Siddons leaned forward to be heard over the festive chatter around them. "*Richard the Second*, Act One, Norfolk to Richard:

"The purest treasure mortal times afford
Is spotless reputation; that away
Men are but gilded loam or painted clay."

Siddons sat back on her throne, looking satisfied. "Doesn't that just say it all?"

"Beautifully. A thought worth more than a penny."

"But you are an impressive girl who needs no advice from me." The older actress tucked a stray wisp of dyed dark hair into her silk turban. "Enjoy your moment in the sun, dear. I wish I could live mine all over again." She signaled for more brandy as Charles Kemble led up another supplicant.

Lizzie stepped aside, feeling she had received a blessing from the high priestess of acting. She was deeply grateful for Siddons's remembrance of her father. Jack never mentioned William anymore. Lizzie had to admit her husband believed the art of acting began with his own appearance on the boards.

The fashionables had moved on to their clubs and restaurants, leaving the die-hard theatricals crowded around the diminishing food supply. Grimaldi, rather bent in the back by time and strenuous acrobatics, enjoyed some lobster patties with Charles Dibdin, who had arrived late with music protruding from his Kerseymere coat. Dibdin announced to the party that since America had just declared war on England, he was planning another saber-rattling show at the Wells called *Nelson's Victory*. Grimaldi told Lizzie he was playing Admiral Nelson. Circling her in the manner of the one-eyed hero wooing Lady Hamilton, he joked, "Are you ready for some naval maneuvers?" Snatches of music rose from the pianoforte in the orchestra pit. The spirit of after-the-show camaraderie had settled in.

Meanwhile, Jack seized his opportunity to raise the skirts of an earthy, married actress in a dark dressing room. She practically whinnied as Jack mounted and pumped into her. Abandonment aside, the actor found her disappointingly loose in the lower works. A few sharp strokes and he was off, wiping up, and buttoning his trousers. Before the dazed lady had pulled down her gown, Jack was away to find Thomas Jupiter Harris.

The performers still were entertaining Mrs. Siddons and each other.

"To the greatest living actress of our day!
To the one who's surely earned that sobriquet.
For she can help you shed a tear
Or make your troubles disappear

Just by stepping on the stage to do a play.
All say hooray!"
"*Hooray! Hooray!*"

Dibdin had passed out music sheets for his "Serenade to Sarah." The singers, foxed with drink and every man a soloist, had formed into a bellowing choir. Grimaldi dared to ape Mrs. Siddons's famous postures on top of the pianoforte. The leading voice was Miss ElizabethTrumpet's, lifted to the skies by the general joy.

"*We give her thanks for her theatrical finesse,*
For we all have been oblige to her noblesse.
We've applauded her Macbeth,
From the murder to her death,
And, as players, we take pride in her success.
All echo, 'Yes!'"
"*Yes! Yes! Yes!*"

"*She has mastered leading ladies by the score,*
Tearful heroines in tragedies galore;
She's worn trousers as the Dane,
Then went totally insane
Wearing nothing but a sheet to play Jane Shore!
All say, 'Encore!'"
"*Encore! Encore!*"

Harris had been observing his star's farewell from a comfortable box above the stage, like the original Abraham keeping an eye on his family. He had watched Faversham disappear backstage without his wife, reappear then ignore her as he began prowling through the house.

Spying Harris in the second tier, Jack sprinted up and destroyed the manager's mellow mood entirely by joining him, uninvited. "Ah, Harris."

The theatre manager coughed a cold, "Good evening."

The handsome actor made haste to say how he was about to star in *A Bold Stroke for a Wife* at the Haymarket with Lizzie, after which he was free to discuss next season's employment at Covent Garden.

Harris deflected the subject pointedly. "How was it working for yourself in the provinces? You must have enjoyed answering to no one. Made buckets of money, I suppose. Those local companies are such a fine training ground. There's talent out of town, of course. New faces. Kemble and I have been hearing good things about this fellow Edmund Kean. I don't suppose he ever worked for you?" Harris put his feet down and gestured to the singing on the stage with his glass of port. "Your Elizabeth has quite a voice. She's a splendid girl, you know." He stood, knitting his bushy brows at Faversham. "Well, I must rejoin my guests. Good night to you, Jack."

"*Now, what we really want to say is 'Please, don't go!'*
We can't imagine your finale ultimo.
But, if our pleas you disavow
And you have taken your last bow,
Then know we'll miss you and our tears will overflow.
We love you so!"
"*We love you so!*"
"Bravissimo!"
"Bravissimo!"

Chapter Twenty-Five

September 1812

LIZZIE HAD just concluded giving Emily a riotous lesson in how to waltz, that sensuous new dance that thrust ladies into the very embrace of their ardent partners. She bent over a highly amused Miss Pegeen, who had watched the fun from her chair in the grey salon. "I must be on my way, Auntie."

"Don't be such a stranger, Lizzie darlin'. Here, give us a kiss."

"I'm glad you've taken to Miss Widewell as much as I have. Now remember, if you need anything special, just send Noddy by and I'll see you have it." Lizzie gave her little relative a peck on her withered lips. "Until next week then."

Captain George Trumpet's romance by mail with Emily was flourishing so well that an understanding seemed very near. At Longsatin House, Carlo continued to be an occasional lodger, Octavia visited frequently, and Noddy served Aunt Peg. Yet Lizzie feared Peg was too much alone. She had invited Emily to forsake the Wentworths' and stay as her guest at the Duncan Terrace home, provided Georgie's sweetheart and the ancient lady could occupy the same dwelling without declaring a bigger war than Napoleon was making on Russia. Gradually, the ladies progressed from civility to genuine rapport.

"Where are you going in that fetching bonnet, Lizzie?" The little blonde watched her new friend tie on a creation festooned with cherry red ribbons.

"To meet with an artist called Jeremiah Brett. He wants to launch himself as a portraitist by doing a painting of me."

Emily's cheeks were flushed from the stimulating dance, and Lizzie's visit. "What a glamorous life you lead."

"But not a very real one. What I do in the theatre is positively useless in these hard times, with the world so topsy-turvy. Think of the dangers Georgie faces, the sacrifices our good Englishmen are making in this endless war. Oh, Emily, my life seems so trivial and meaningless."

"Well, it's no such thing, Lizzie. You have a strong character too, just like your brother. When you sang those songs in *British Glory*, it gave everyone the heart to go on. That is important. I even wrote George that I think you are just as much of a soldier as he."

"Why, Emily...." Lizzie looked down at the sweet-faced girl who was suddenly so serious. "You make me cry."

There was another cause for her tears. The Faversham union had suffered a sea change. The night Lizzie sang at Carlton House, the sight of her husband beating the little thief in the street had shocked her. Returning to the scene over and over, she realized Jack's violence was a real part of him, not theatrics. It was as though she had discovered vermin folded into a fine garment, a terrible surprise waiting to crawl out on her very skin. This new view put her ever so slightly on her guard.

Jeremiah Brett poured two glasses of claret from a cut-glass decanter shaped like a bell. "Let us drink to art, Miss Trumpet." He put the stopper down by some oily rags. "And perhaps a sip to commerce."

Lizzie held up her wine. "To fame, Mr. Brett. May she come knocking at your door."

The intoxicating smell of linseed oil and drying pigments filled

Brett's high-ceilinged studio, where tall arched windows opened to the light on Maiden Lane. The walls were hung with studies of Brett's own reedy thin face. There were finished canvases of working folk, nudes female and male, an officer in regimentals standing beside a devil-eyed horse, all impressively done. A tall easel, plaster columns, velvet swags and sundry props cluttered the back of the room.

"Miss Trumpet, may I sketch you as we talk? I do not wish to weary you with posing. I believe you have a performance tonight at the Haymarket Theatre?"

"Yes, with my husband in a comedy." Lizzie settled herself on a spindly chair, keeping her back straight and her chin high.

The artist put on his pince-nez spectacles, picked up a Conte pencil of graphite and several sheets of paper. "Let me explain myself. I wish to paint flattering full-length portraits of the high and mighty for fat fees. You are a diamond of the first water, a beautiful actress most of London has seen on the stage. They think they know you. Well, I will create a likeness of you that staggers them with insight and drama. When it is finished, my portrait of Elizabeth Trumpet will be accepted to hang in the Royal Academy Show and cause a sensation."

"You propose to make a great work of art."

"I am capable of it."

"How do you envision the sensational painting, Mr. Brett?"

"The classical world being the highest expression of art, you must represent a goddess from the Greek pantheon. It is the fashion."

"What about the insight and drama?"

"I'll manage the insight. You supply the drama."

That seemed fair enough to Lizzie. She relaxed a bit, remembering Madame Bonnet's fascination with the mythology of Olympus. "Which goddess, do you think?"

"I'm partial to the goddess of victory, the winged Nike with all her energy and gravitas, bearing the crown of glory and fame to winners in battle."

"Wings? Did she fly about?"

"Always. Imagine great gorgeous wings. Let down your hair, please, and release that neckline?" Brett tore off a sketch at speed.

"Oh yes, a Nike whirling through the clouds will be just the thing. Care for another claret?"

Lizzie opened the top of her dress with business-like modesty, undoing five pearly buttons.

"Uncover a bit more, if you please. Victory has bare breasts. That's the whole point of winning a war, eh?" The artist laughed.

"I will not uncover everything." She shook her head.

"But your bosom is part of your singular good looks, the form and abundance, so...." Brett stared down Lizzie's décolletage hopefully. "So uplifting."

"No. This display of flesh should be sufficient."

"Then we must have wet drapery at least. Your un-corseted torso and long legs caressed by the winds through a wisp of gauze—I paint gauze exquisitely."

"Doubtless you do." Her smile widened.

Brett ripped into another sketch. "Tell me about your talented husband," he requested in a charming tone. "Jonathan Faversham excels at villains. I saw him throttle you as the Grand Inquisitor."

Lizzie briefly described her marriage, dwelling on the acting instruction Jack had given her. "I am everything to him. Mr. Faversham lost his entire family to small pox when he was but a child. So, we two have a life together of unusual closeness." *And I am now closely watched. It takes so little to provoke him these days.* "I would never do anything to displease him." So saying, Lizzie closed her bodice.

"Miss Trumpet, I respect your tender feelings for your husband and I honor them. Together we shall create a magnificent 'Winged Victory.' And tonight, I shall applaud husband and wife at the Haymarket. *A bientót!*"

Lizzie's smart half-boots of yellow leather had begun to pinch, so on the spur of the moment, she returned to the Rose Street lodgings to change them. Nearing the top of the stairs, she heard unexpected sounds coming through the front door: masculine grunts of passion, what might be the bed rocking against a wall and a female's throaty cries.

Silently, the actress entered the sitting room. With her blood turning cold, she faced the sleeping chamber where the bed was indeed being put to good use. The black and white dog stood with forepaws on the coverlet, watching a girl with dirty brown hair ride astride Jack's hips, pounding towards her joy supreme. Jack bucked, squeezing her bouncing buttocks in his long fingers and making the high-pitched scream that always announced his eruption. The two had not heard the front door open, and Cassie's tail kept wagging. The girl snarled, beating her inner flesh fast on Jack's penis as he spasmed with lust.

The world dropping out from under her, Lizzie charged into the bedroom, grabbed the chamber pot and smashed it down on the mane of dirty hair. The girl tumbled to the floor. Jack was drenched in piss and turds.

"Bastard!" she yelled and whirled away, screaming like a lunatic as she torpedoed down the stairs.

Lizzie ran aimlessly into the busy streets of Covent Garden till she caught sight of her wild-eyed reflection in the window of the Shakespeare's Head Tavern. She stopped, fists clenched like weapons at her sides.

I could have killed that girl.... She touched her forehead to the cool glass, breathing like a galloping horse. *God help me...I could have killed him, too.*

A Bold Stroke for a Wife was a well-known 18th century satirical play, full of marital insult and injury. Despite what had happened in the afternoon, in the evening, the Favershams' show went on. Backstage, they never exchanged a word. Onstage, Lizzie gave an icy performance. In dialogue, belittling Jack's character, she was rewarded with a dozen new laughs at his expense. By the epilogue, she felt triumphant, but wretched.

Jeremiah Brett appeared in the green room, to pay his respects.

Lizzie could scarcely focus. Her meeting with the artist seemed to have happened centuries ago. The room filled up with followers. When Jack entered, all smiles to greet his public, she raised her voice. "Mr. Brett, I shall be delighted to pose for your painting...in the nude!"

All present turned to Faversham, who pretended deafness. Aware of the heavy atmosphere between the spouses, Brett hastened to retire, after thanking Lizzie effusively.

When the last person had said goodnight, Jack grabbed the elbow of his leading lady. "I have something to show you tonight, Trumpet. Whether you want to or not, we are going for a drive."

"Where to, guv?"

Jack handed Lizzie into the hackney coach, muttered a destination to the driver, and jumped in with an eager Cassius. The horse entered heavy London traffic. They passed several minutes, turned away from each other, listening to the sounds of the late-night streets. Nose pressed to the small round window, watching the dark outside, only the dog was enjoying the ride.

"You defiled our marriage bed, Elizabeth."

"Oh, you first I think." She cast him a steely look. "Where are you taking me?"

"All will be made clear in the second act."

Already boiling, Lizzie grew more uneasy as they entered the East End Docks and stopped in the dark passage of Pillory Lane, where Jack told the driver to wait with the dog, no matter how long.

"Prepare yourself, Elizabeth."

Before them stood a dilapidated ale-house with the incongruous name The Tudor Rose. It looked a perfect college of crime. Lizzie had known such places from plays and books, but the reality of dirt and despair was even more frightening. Half dragging her, Jack strode in to set her down at the darkest table. Rough drunks eyed them as an old crone limped up to pour two servings of the house specialty—"blue ruin"—raw gin tempered with misogyny.

Jack addressed the serving woman with his most charming smile. "Worked here long, dearie?"

"Waited table at the Last Supper, didn't I." The hag managed a wink and left them alone.

Lizzie had had enough. "Jack, in God's name what does this stinking place have to do with us?"

"Elizabeth, I'm not quite the man you thought you married." He took a short swallow of gin. "Welcome to my home. It's time you had a look at my family."

"Your family? Your family is dead."

"Well, they deserve to be. My mother is a woman of no consequence named Lucy Potts. She was a great breeder of men. Look behind you. Those three sods picking their noses back in the snug are my brothers, each one of us spawned by a different father. My real name is Rykes Bowtree, and I don't know or wish to know who my father was."

Lizzie said nothing as the revelations came pouring out.

"I grew up in this place. Truly." Jack's gaze swept the dismal room and its seedy occupants. "This is the very hearth of my childhood. I still have dreams of it, nightmares, of course. I was the baby, knocked senseless by those three brutes for no other reason, but they could do it. That old criminal wiping the bar there is my grandfather, Alistair Potts by name. I could always count on him to have a hearty laugh at my plight. Mum kept so busy with her legs spread for business and blind drunk, I don't think she knew I was alive. I learned the ways of the world here, Lizzie, the ways of this world, at least. How to get on. I mastered emptying the slops and moved on to the customers' pockets. It was expected. My original trade was thieving." He took another sip of gin and gritted his teeth. "Have you nothing to say?"

Sitting still as death, Lizzie grasped she had lived beside a phantom, a created character, a mirage of a man. The man she loved was the Jack he had invented. What of this stranger? "Go on. Tell me all of it."

"As you wish. Attend to those working girls on the stairs, Maddie and Sally. Once they were young and juicy. They would jack my growing prick to torment me. I celebrated my first whisker by having them both at once." Lizzie glanced at the two slatterns for only a second. "Now they look to be fire-ships for the clap. Astonishing they're still alive. Maddie taught me those sucking-lapping kisses you fancy so much, Trumpet. You should thank her."

Lizzie felt slapped. "How did you get away from this?"

"At fourteen I tumbled your great friend, the elegant Mr. Eggleston. He had a taste for my looks and quickness. So, instead of putting me in a molly house, he sent me off to learn the theatre-carpentry trade. I took my chance further, aspired to act, especially how to walk and talk like a gent. I'd always had a lark mimicking the customers here. When Eggleston saw I had the will to change, he taught me to read, and wash with thoroughness. Useful things."

"He saved you."

"He got his pound of flesh, believe me. Built me up to make a fortune off my talent. I owe him nothing. Would you like to meet my mother? The female who carried me in her belly and pushed me out of her body? To call her a real mother would stretch credulity. She's the creature who poured our gin. Here I sit and dear old Mum doesn't even know me." He took off his hat and looked around the room. "Not one of them recognizes me." He exhaled through his teeth in disgust. "Ah, the joy of it."

Waves of shock and anguish from Jack's confession churned in Lizzie's stomach. "Let me leave, Jack. I feel ill."

In the privacy of the hired coach, Lizzie found her voice, though it was strangled with pain. "Why did you throw your story at my head tonight?

"So you would know how far I've come," Jack answered with urgency. "I've risen out of that pit onto the king's own stage. Believe me, that's why I make such a convincing villain. I know how to cheat like Shylock, plot like Iago, and murder like Richard the Third. Part of my nature. You see, when I play a hero, that's the real acting."

"For all these years you were acting with me, too? In all our time together you never trusted me with the truth? And suddenly you do? To what purpose?"

"For your own good. You were so angry over that girl today. An afternoon intrigue is a very petty crime, I assure you." Jack petted the dog curled on the seat between them, ears up, appearing to understand every word. "It's time to be done with pretense, so you can grow up, my dear."

"I'm to grow up? What am I to make of that? What do you expect me to do?"

"Show compassion, Lizzie. With you, I'm the best person I've ever been. You stopper my temper, you inspire my art. And consider this, if it weren't for the things you've learned from me, you might still be doing chariot-tricks with that big Italian or reduced to whoring with Dampere. You've become a proper actress, under my instruction. Isn't that what you dreamed of? We are a pair, a team of steeds pulling Apollo's chariot of the sun."

"Well, you certainly made a workhorse out of me." Wounded to the soul, she lashed out, "Did you ever love me, Jack?"

"What a question. I'm mad for you, and always will be."

"Then why did you take that despicable woman to our bed?"

"You've been giving your best to the audience these days, my dear. A quick fuck with a nobody, to cool a man's blood. I tell you it signifies nothing. You are my beautiful partner. You belong at my side." He held up his hand to forestall a reply. "But, hear me now: if you are so angry over so little, so destroyed, then...." He shrugged. "I'll find another leading lady somewhere."

"Don't bargain with me, Jack. That place—The Tudor Rose—was a vile beginning, and you should have told me of it long ago. But for your past, I make no judgment. None. You have shown me the source of your furies, but whatever you were, and whatever I was, that means nothing in our lives now." She looked Jack straight in the eye. "Our marriage is precious to me. I thought it was to you, too."

"The most precious thing in my life."

She shook her head. "Jack, you take *care* of things that are precious."

"Have you never made a mistake?"

"I have never been untrue to you."

"I told you it was nothing."

"Loyalty is nothing?"

"That tart!"

"Have you had her before?"

"Never."

"Are there others?"

"Hundreds. You know my capacity."

"Don't scoff at me. You have cut me to the heart, Jack. If cooling the blood takes precedence over our sacred vows, then I need to know. I have honored our marriage. Is it over?"

"God, you're serious." He raked his hand through his hair.

"I need an answer."

Jack took her gloved fists and kissed them, holding them for a long moment as the coach swayed over the dark streets. As they passed through a lamppost's circle of light, Lizzie saw tears rising in his eyes.

"You are the only person in my life I have ever cared for. Can you name another? Not my travesty of a family and none of the souls I have used along the way. Only you, the one pure light in my darkness. I love you as much as my black heart can let me love. I've never been a good person, but with you, I wish to be. You are my passion. What more can I say?"

Her breath felt stifled. "Say you're sorry."

"Sorry indeed. I am sorry and I love you. I love you and I'm sorry, and may it never happen again."

"Absolute truth from this night on? I require it, Jack."

"I swear it. We shall have honesty." His voice choked. "Do you still love me?"

Images of Jack with Eggleston and a hundred degrading scenes were snaking into her mind, but yes, still, love was there. "Even now."

"Then all is well." Jack gave her a burning kiss. "Driver! On to Rose Street by Covent Garden!" The hack rolled through the breaking dawn as the actor leaned back at his ease again. "But, Trumpet...."

"Is there more?" She was not smiling.

"Don't ever cross swords with me. That would be a mistake."

Chapter Twenty-Six

January 21, 1813

No WOMAN wants to believe the brightest star in her heaven is a villain. With reluctance Lizzie forgave Jack, but he would never again be the god of love and wisdom her innocent heart had worshiped. A sadly flawed genius, a troubled human being, such was her husband, bound to her for eternity. She kept this new view of him private, like a tarnished locket round her neck. The fresh pain of his unfaithfulness cut too deep to share, even with Octavia or Carlo. His confessions at The Tudor Rose had moved her from anger to a cautious compassion. She became his understanding angel, yet a step apart from her old adoring self.

A tender interval of peace passed between the Favershams, until Lizzie appeared with Dick Wilson in a series of new plays in Richmond. Her father's dear friend instructed her by example in the delicate art of comic timing. Miss Trumpet loved working opposite the old master. After a happy evening of performing with Wilson, returning home to Rose Street and a cynical, spiteful Jack, so unsparing in his criticisms of other actors, drained her good spirits. As though a veil had been lifted, Lizzie saw his behavior as the jealous writhing of a thwarted ego, exhausting to watch. Needing easier companionship and brighter hours, she made more frequent visits to Duncan Terrace.

"So, Maestro, you've chosen Mozart for me?" Lizzie carried in the tea, eager to begin her lesson. Back at home, surrounded by her mother's furniture and her father's books, there was no undertow of marital discouragement pulling against her natural inclination to happiness. Carlo Tomassi's positive attitude was as comforting as a soft pillow.

"Yes, I thought about your vocal repertoire while I was on tour. Oh, tea and Savoy biscuits! How you spoil me!" In assertive good humor, Carlo accepted a lemon-laced pastry off Lizzie's tray. The musician was lodging at Longsatin House again, this morning attired in a paisley robe, his crown of platinum hair radiating in all directions like peony petals. He was choosing sheets of music in the salon, enjoying time at the pianoforte with his favorite student.

"You're really too young to sing Dido or Poppea. How old are you now, my darling, not that it matters?"

"I'm ancient, Carlo. Twenty-six."

"Nothing of the kind. Susanna or the Countess aren't in your voice at the moment, so you shall learn Zerlina first. She's fun, and the music will not tax your throat while you're so busy with the amusing Mr. Wilson out in Richmond."

"Zerlina sings 'La ci darem' with the Don, lucky girl."

"Today you'll sing it with me, even luckier. They say at the premier of *Don Giovanni* Mozart was so unhappy with Signora Bondini's cry of terror, when the Don seizes her, he hid in the scenery. When the cue came, Mozart reached under her costume to pinch his soprano on the bum. She shrieked. 'There,' the naughty genius said, 'that's how I want it every time!'"

Lizzie chortled along with Carlo, enjoying the tea and the gossip that always accompanied the scales and arias.

"Oh, before I forget, I bought a little copy of your painting. Will you autograph it to me, with a suitable sentiment?" He withdrew a sepia etching from his Moroccan leather music folder.

Lizzie perused the symbolic image of herself that was not really herself at all. "Brett said the street vendors are selling out. I have no idea if it's first-rank art, but everyone seems to love it."

As Jeremiah Brett had hoped, his painting, "Elizabeth Trumpet, as Winged Victory" had made his reputation at the Royal Academy. People stood twenty deep at the exhibition, drinking in the scandalous image, executed with such touchable reality. The Prince Regent had purchased the original painting for his private collection. Lord Dampere commissioned Brett to execute a copy for his collection as well.

Lizzie had posed with one breast exposed, descending from the sky, a victory palm in her right hand, a crown of gold leaves in her left. Rose and blue cords tied beneath her bosom held the transparent drapery that caressed hips and thighs. Zephyrs blew across the background's golden clouds, lofting her magnificent dark hair. From her naked back sprouted feathered wings, pink-tipped to match the hard nipples of her breasts. Indeed, no one could confuse this creature with an angel. Lizzie's reputation was also made. In the *Gentleman's Magazine* and news-writings of the day, Miss Trumpet was always referred to as "the Winged Victory."

"Are you making the most of the sensation you have caused?" Carlo asked, admiring his own paper copy, now inscribed "to my true, beloved friend."

"I have some roles coming up at Covent Garden. The new manager at Drury Lane, Mr. Arnold, also wants to talk to me."

"And how is the volatile Jack adjusting to your flurry of fame?"

"He is resentful. My current celebrity gives me a little power; I can request that he appear with me, but I'm not successful every time. Jack has not always made friends."

Carlo merely nodded, but Lizzie could see he thought the worst.

"Between us, Jack has ceased to be the main attraction. I can no longer cross a street unnoticed, Carlo. This is hard for him and, thus hard for me, when he is so constantly unhappy. Our rooms are the scene of tempests every day."

"Enough. Put that out of your mind." He touched the ivory keys.

"Singing will drive the blue devils away. To work, Miss Trumpet!"

⚬

"So, where is Georgie now?" Lizzie held the pin with a twist of light blue ribbon tied to it. Low fires burned in the downstairs rooms as the women in their wool dresses worried over a campaign map of the Iberian Peninsula Emily had made and mounted on the dining room wall.

"I'm guessing your brother is here, in north-central Spain." Emily pointed to a line of red pins that stood for battles and skirmishes. "See, here is Burgos, where he fought the battle, then the army fell back and finally General Wellesley repositioned his army here at Ciudad Rodrigo."

Lizzie pushed the blue pin into the map.

"When did you last hear, Lizzie?"

"My last letter was dated 'late August in the year 12.' Georgie wrote about his general's arrival in Madrid. He said there may have been something of the sort when Jesus entered Jerusalem, roses raining down on the officers, tossed by the señoritas from their balconies, crowds crying hosannas of praise for chasing the French out of the capitol, all very gratifying. The Spanish royals gave Wellesley the Order of the Golden Fleece, something akin to the Garter. I've received two letters since then."

"Did he mention wounds, Emily? When I see returned soldiers in the streets, missing arms and legs, I fear for him. After so many years of fighting, it seems the chances of—"

"Don't speak of it. If he had suffered a wound, we would be the last to know. You know he makes light of the hardships. Look here." Emily thumped a finger on a pile of newspapers tied up with string. "I've marked all the stories about General Wellesley and kept them for you, starting in August with the Prince Regent raising him to Marquess of Wellington."

The women saved Captain Trumpet's letters and every scrap of war news the press offered. Hostilities with America had been mainly confined to the Canadian border regions. Roger Sloane had hastened to assure Lizzie, in an October letter from Charleston, that her grandparents were safe for now. Trying to make sense of how the grinding conflict against France was going, Emily and Lizzie shared all they knew. Bonaparte's huge drive into Russia had halted in Moscow, but that didn't concern Georgie. What did concern him was the attack on Wellington's leadership from the Whig opposition in Parliament. Some MP's were crying for the general's recall.

Seated at the mahogany table, Lizzie read aloud from Ponsonby's speech in an old copy of *The Times*: "Our being in the Peninsula is a waste of English blood and treasure. The military power of England is not competent to drive the French out of Spain." Lizzie slapped the paper down. "Treasonous toad!"

"'Not competent?' George would throttle him if he heard that." Emily scratched her wrist in agitation.

"Damn the surrendering Whigs! The Crown and the people want the French finished off."

Emily looked soberly at the map. "In one account I saved, Sir Francis Burdett told parliament the withdrawal from Burgos was a disastrous defeat and a waste of life!" She ferreted out a letter from a separate file. "Now, listen to what Georgie wrote about Burgos: 'Our English troops were outnumbered four to one, with overextended supply-lines and no twenty-four-inch guns to withstand a siege. Wellesley, of course, retreated to a defensive position. Ciudad Rodrigo is a fortress town on a mountain.' If George makes that clear to me, what's so difficult for those bone-headed men in parliament to understand?"

"Emily, you already talk tactics like a soldier's wife. It is my dearest hope someday we will be sisters, but may I give you a bit of advice from a married woman?"

The blonde girl was returning her newspaper collection to the chest-on-chest. "Anything you say to me is of the greatest import."

"Then I suggest—just suggest, mind—that you take time to know Georgie as he really is before you pledge your life to him. There can be surprises, Emily. I was quite swept away when I married."

Eager to hear more, Emily sat beside her. "Of course you were. Mr. Faversham is surely one of the most attractive and accomplished of men."

"Yes, he is that and more, but...." Lizzie had not intended to compare her diminishing romance to the trusting Emily's anticipation of perfect happiness.

"Is there something I should know?"

"Only think, four years of war must have marked my brother. He may...."

A frosty gust of wind pummeled on the windows and doors. Outside, a horse's hooves struck the new cobblestones of Duncan Terrace.

"Did you just hear something?"

"What?"

Emily started to rise. "I'll just...."

"Anyone home?" A male voice called out as the front door opened then banged shut. "Anyone at all?" Heavy-booted feet crossed the vestibule floor. A tall man in a worn grey cape walked into the dining room. The two ladies froze in shock.

Roused by the masculine voice, Aunt Peg had left her kitchen to see who had arrived. "Well, and it is himself! You're just in time for supper, George Mario." Cool as a basket of cucumbers, she gave the obvious order. "Emily, darlin', set another place at the table."

What shouting, what tears, what kisses followed Georgie's unexpected appearance. Noddy was roused from his dozing in the cow shed to pull off the officer's muddy boots and tend to his weary horse, to stoke every fire in the house to a jolly blaze, and to "Get out of the way," while the three women tried to serve up a meal, simultaneously chiding, caressing, and adoring their hero.

"You're a major! God bless us, when did that happen?"

"Why didn't you write to us that you were coming?"

"Are you on leave? For how long?"

"I am not on leave, my dears, but on duty." The tall officer was ensconced at the mahogany table in his father's old place, as the ladies spun around him. "I am to serve Wellington here in London for a time. For this mission, he raised me to the rank of major."

"What is the mission, brother?"

"I doubt that you ladies are aware of the politics, but our effort in

Spain is being attacked by the Whigs in Parliament." His voice began to rise. "Well, the general has had enough, and has sent me to stop the rot. Representing him, I am to speak to those members who have raised public distrust to such a pitch. What do those damn fools in government know about tactics?" Georgie's exhausted face flushed. "So, I'm to collar these half-wits and bring them up to scratch."

Georgie had brought the battlefield into Longsatin House. Lizzie saw his nerves were ragged as his uniform cuffs, the flesh of his cheeks dark tanned, with not an ounce of extra flesh upon them. He had aged and hardened and was wound up tight. Her heart went out to him, whispering, "You bear a grave responsibility."

"I do. Usually the general prefers titled men to represent him."

"If Wellington is such a high-in-the-instep aristocrat, darlin', why did he choose you?" Peg removed his scraped-clean dinner plate.

"I have been in every battle with him and know the conditions. Auntie, I hesitate to repeat the fine things the general said to me at our last meeting, but he judges me trustworthy and exceptionally well spoken. I can thank Papa for that." He glanced warmly towards his sister. "Perhaps he wants me to talk to those MP's because I'm not a titled gentleman, but a plain soldier. This army has gone from one battle to another with never a pause to restore itself. Officers and men alike sleep in the saddle and drink far too much. Many have no idea where they are and care less, some stop speaking to curl up like knots in wood or stones in a fire. Men can tremble for days from the shock of the great guns. I'm probably here just because I don't shake." Georgie's voice died away.

Lizzie spoke up brightly to cover her concern. "You'll be surprised how much we do understand, brother. Cast your tired eyes on that map. Emily made it. The blue ribbon on that pin stands for you."

"What a topping map!" Georgie kissed the little hand that was clutched in his. "By Jupiter, you are a splendid creature." Emily was in a daze. Lizzie could tell the porcelain-faced girl was holding her breath to suppress a cannonade of excited hiccups. "I have delivered General Wellington's dispatches, now I must get hold of the Whig speeches calling for his head. I'm behind the times and it's vital I get to the key men. I must not lose a moment."

"Oh, perhaps these can help you? The worst attacks on the general began in November; Sir Francis Burdett had much to say." Emily got up to unearth her collected archive of newspaper articles from the chest-on-chest, putting the tall stack beside Georgie's elbow.

He read the first page with rapid intensity. "This is precisely what I need. Emily Widewell, you are a wonder."

"We all think so," Aunt Peg said, pouring her nephew coffee with an unsteady hand. He took the coffee absently, his gaze never leaving Emily.

"Tell us, how is the war going?" Lizzie asked.

With a snap, Georgie turned his head. "Napoleon has deserted his army in Russia to flee back to Paris, just as he ran away from his defeat in Egypt years ago. The *Grande Armée* is retreating over lands they just destroyed. Those troops are from his conquered territories, most don't even speak French. They are boys and girls as young as fourteen, not trained soldiers at all."

"Girls?" Emily gasped. "I cannot imagine...."

"Yes, girls! And, of course, camp followers always travel with armies to service the soldiers and for the supposed adventure of a great invasion, but more often because it's safe. Marauding stragglers between the lines of battle can do terrible things. The invaders of Russia have been dying by the thousands since the winter closed in. I'm told the French are digging mass graves in the snow along the line of march."

An ember popped like a gunshot in the fireplace grate. Major Trumpet flinched at the sound. "So, Napoleon is desperate for more troops, you see. Our war in Spain is bleeding him, tying down a quarter million soldiers, keeping them from joining his command. We've fought so well, and lost so many men. We can't stop now. I've got to make those fools in Parliament see it. Bonaparte will never be satisfied; he will keep fighting until every soldier and horse in Europe is shot to pieces. There will be more battles, more carnage." Georgie had been shouting then his face went slack, the images of suffering rising in his mind.

"Excuse me, Major. Some port, sir?" A freshly cleaned-up Noddy held a tin tray with a glass of wine at the officer's elbow.

"Ah, Noddy, my man, I see you are full-grown and dutiful. Yes, leave the bottle, and I'll need more light to read by," Georgie commanded in a tone new to the ladies, as his eyes poured over the newsprint.

Peg and Lizzie cleared the supper away. Emily went to fetch lights. When she returned with fresh candles, her intended's blond head was resting on the mahogany table, pillowed on the pile of clippings. Georgie was fast asleep.

With his letters of introduction, Major George Mario Trumpet moved through St. James's and the halls of government as Wellington's voice. Serious meetings with men of power smoothed down his battling-soldier's manner. Over the weeks, he grew into something he had never expected to be, a passionate diplomat. Lean and erect in a new uniform tailored by Adam & James, the striking Major of the Tenth Hussars had ample cachet. Over time, he persuaded the querulous Commons and Lords that General Wellesley, now Lord Wellington, was England's most valuable commander.

When not attending to that urgent business, the restless Major Trumpet spent every moment with his family. He took Miss Widewell to see Lizzie in her plays. He drove Aunt Peg for carriage rides in Regent's Park, stopping by the Grenadier pub, so the officers who made it their watering hole could greet the old lady in her gad-about bonnet and drink toasts to her countless birthdays.

In the evenings, he took up his violin to play again the Italian serenades and Irish ballads his parents had loved—songs that unlocked the feelings in his heart that war had sealed away. In time, he made new music of his own: serenades to the life of "home and beauty." The point of his existence seemed to be somewhere in the depths of Emily's loving blue eyes.

That spring, Lizzie vicariously felt the stirrings of awakened passion. It was plain as morning Georgie and Emily were "swept away," just as she had been when Jack was her all-in-all. She wished them a longer idyll of joy than fate had given her.

The shy, thoughtful Emily bloomed like a flower, swaying giddily on the upright vine of Trumpet's supporting strength. Georgie was besotted with his little darling, taking her for strolls along the New River. Under the flowering trees, they exchanged kisses and promises that drove him wild.

In April, there was a wedding at St Mary's. Emily's mother attended, representing the Widewell family of Sheffield. Rather an unadventurous person, she was shocked by all the picturesque theatricals filling the groom's side of the church. Octavia's delicate history with the Trumpet family took a bit of explaining. Vicar Strahan permitted Major Trumpet to play the violin as his bride came down the aisle, on Sir Henry Wentworth's arm, carrying white lilies. After the prayers and before the vows, Lizzie sang "Believe Me, if All Those Endearing Young Charms." The lovers pledged before God to love each other until death parted them. Mrs. Widewell returned to her husband with such vivid impressions of Peg, Miss Onslow, the Favershams, and Carlo Tomassi that she was never allowed to visit London again.

Orders for Georgie to report back to his general came in August. He solemnly rode away towards the crossroads of the Angel, his bride, his aunt and his sister waving to him from the steps of home with very wet handkerchiefs. Two months later, the new Mrs. Trumpet asked her busy sister-in-law and Octavia to a ladies' tea. Peg's diagnosis was happily confirmed. Lizzie began to squirrel away money for a layette.

February 26, 1814

On the opening night of a new production, the management of Drury Lane often provided house seats to the famous actors of the day. Lizzie wished to treat the Longsatin House ladies to an evening of Shakespeare. Jack had no interest in watching other actors work, especially in the company of his wife's relatives. He professed a cold must keep him home, or no farther from it than his pub stool at The

Lamb and Flag.

The play that night was *The Merchant of Venice*, and Edmund Kean, as Shylock, made what the newspaper critics called, "the greatest London debut of all time." The audience adored the powerful young actor, brilliant as a flash of lightning. He resembled Jack, dark and lithe, villainously handsome, and hungry for fame. Overnight, Mr. Kean achieved a great reputation. Junius Brutus Booth also appeared as the comic Prince of Aragon. Lizzie was very glad Jack had missed the show.

⚜

The Ides of March, 1814
Trumpet Ladies
Longsatin House, Duncan Terrace
London
Dearest Family,
This date may have held an evil portent for Julius Caesar, but not for Major G. M. Trumpet. My news is all good.

I don't know which of my brief missives reached you over the past months, so I must recapitulate. When I took leave of you, my duty called me to return to Gen. Wellesley's command in Spain. By the time I achieved San Sebastian however, the army was on the march north. Though I was alone on a spirited horse, I had the devil of a time catching up. The first week in October, I met them just in time to cross the Bidassoa River, riding into France at the general's side. The French Grande Armée was literally running from us, dropping their cannon and supplies of food and winter clothing as they went.

We caught some of them at the Nivelle, engaged and prevailed. Repeated our success at the Nive, crossed the Ardour and took Bayonne. We've eaten in the saddle, bivouacked without shelter, changed mounts without changing boots or uniforms. Through all this, I have had nary access to private time to write. *Just three days ago, we charged into the lovely city of Bordeaux, fired a few shots for show, and planted our emblems. Wellington is now preparing to descend on Napoleon in Paris. Boney won't have a chance. The army of France is broken.*

My darlings, the end is in sight. A few more skirmishes, and I will be eating champignons in a café on Montmarte, lighting a candle in Notre Dame, and fighting off hordes of mademoiselles starved for affection. Disregard this, Emily, I'm saving all my kisses for the lips I love.

I pray you are all well. Soon, very soon, we will be together.

Your obedient,

Major George M. Trumpet

Chapter Twenty-Seven

May 6, 1814

IT WAS a bright spring morning when Carlo's bass voice swelled up the stairwell singing, "For the Lord God Omnipotent reigneth! Hallelujah!" He pounded on the door of the Faversham lodgings, thundering, "Open unto me, I have news. News!"

Lizzie, in a pique wrapper with her hair half up, raised the latch. She found the maestro in a state of heated happiness, fanning himself with his hat, his excited face nearly as red as his disordered cravat. "What in the world?"

"Lizzie, you're an auntie, that's what. An auntie to the prettiest baby girl in England!"

"Dear God, why wasn't I sent for? Is Emily all right?"

"Calm yourself, my darling. Mrs. Trumpet delivered in a flood. There wasn't even time to get the midwife. May one enter?"

"Of course." The actress hurried her friend inside. "Tell me everything."

"I was coming in from a rather late engagement. And there it was, Emily in extremis, nature not to be denied. For a childless woman, your Aunt Peg gave a lot of orders. Mrs. Mantino and I actually birthed the infant. How fortunate I speak some Italian, though 'umbilical' isn't usually in a singer's vocabulary. But there's more to tell, do you hear those bells? They are ringing all over the city. Wellesley has entered Paris. The war is over!"

"Oh! What perfect joy!" Lizzie tearfully embraced the bouncing Carlo. "And that means Georgie will be returning. I must go home immediately. I want to hold little...but what is to be the baby's name? Georgia? Georgette? Georgina?"

"Georgina has more music in it," Carlo offered.

"Yes, yes it does, Georgina it must be. I'll dress directly."

"Where is Jack this morning?"

"Last evening, he went to speak with the management at Drury Lane about next season, and never came home." Busying herself, so as not to face Carlo, she poured water from a pitcher onto a flannel and wiped her eyes. "I waited up till dawn and had just fallen asleep."

"Oh, my darling girl."

"Not unusual," Lizzie said flatly. "This has become his routine of late."

"But I cannot escort you to Duncan Terrace just now. Dibdin wants me to put together a huge chorus for the Wells immediately. I'm to round up all the usually-out-of-work singers. Charlie is writing a 'Victory on Land and Sea' spectacular as we speak."

"How like Old Charlie."

"Offered me twice my usual fee."

"How unlike Old Charlie." Lizzie laughed.

"I must be off. Try not to fret yourself over Jack too much. You may take my horse to Islington, dear. I'll stop by Longsatin House tonight with champagne. We'll all have a glass together to wet the baby's head. *Arrivederci!*" He fairly danced out the door.

"I'll sing soprano for you," Lizzie shouted out the window, "first or second, whatever's needed." Carlo waved his old three-cornered hat at her from the street. He gestured to the lamppost where his sway-backed mount Vivace was tied. The neighborhood had come alive with people heading for the Lamb and Flag to celebrate the great news. In a few moments, the actress had dressed in her riding habit and descended the stairs to collide with her returning husband at the building's front door.

"Good morning, Jack, are you well?" The actor plainly was not. Wherever he had spent the wee hours, he was in a livid humor. His dog busily scratched at a flea in his ear as Lizzie pulled on brown leather gloves. "Did you have your meeting?"

"The fucking committee at Drury Lane? Yes, I met with them. That posturing ass Lord Byron has hired Kean for all my roles. They didn't offer me one fucking play for the entire fucking season."

Lizzie was too preoccupied to make the expected noises of dismay. "A disappointment, of course. I'm truly sorry, Jack. Emily just had her baby. A girl. I'm going to see them."

"Oh, happy day for the women," Jack said dismissively, deep in his own drama. "Kean, that puffed up hysteric, that toadying clown."

She waved with an unconcerned air as a staring neighbor passed them by. "Do you really wish to discuss this in the street? I'm sure there's room for both you and Edmund Kean in London."

"Well, evidently not at Drury Lane."

"Jack, dear, stop a moment. Listen to the bells. Peace has come. This is a great day for our country. Be glad." Wild to go, Lizzie turned away.

Jack grabbed her wrist and spun her around, answering in a voice that echoed off the brick walls of the narrow street. "Well, if that's all you care about my career...*which should fucking interest you*...I'll find someone who *fucking* does!"

"Find her and be damned, husband!" Lizzie jerked her wrist free, untied the waiting horse, mounted, and rode away.

In the celebration of peace, the English let their feelings pour forth like a dam giving way. People of all classes greeted each other in the streets with joy. Civilians thanked veterans, and every returning soldier was a hero. Toasts were drunk to total victory at the Admiralty. The war chiefs were so glad Napoleon had abdicated they refrained from shooting him in the head. To rid the world of "Boney" in a gentlemanly manner, he was exiled with a pension to the insignificant island of Elba. Now nothing but a prize prisoner—

perhaps he would go mad, madder than he always had been. Good riddance.

At Longsatin House, toasts were drunk to new life in the name of Georgina Trumpet. Healing possets were brewed for Emily, while Carlo, Aunt Peg, Octavia, Noddy and all the Mantino next-door neighbors enjoyed champagne.

Childless, Lizzie marveled at how sweet it was to share the mothering tasks of rocking, changing, burping, bathing and cuddling the fascinating baby. She moved back home to be of help.

It was the happiest of times. Toasts were drunk to the Prince Regent. In the heart of Mayfair, his design committee quaffed exquisite claret. They planned the National Victory Celebration that Prinny expected to outshine Moses' parting of the Red Sea and the Assumption of the Virgin into Heaven.

Giovanni Battista Belzoni, former strong-man and theatrical hydraulics expert, was commissioned by the prince's design committee to create festive water displays. The Italian yearned to share his elation. Da Ponte was long gone to America to escape his debts, but Giovanni believed there was someone who would share his happiness. He would search out Lisabetta.

Belzoni lowered his head to enter the Lamb and Flag. He enquired of the publican in attendance if perchance he knew where Jonathan Faversham lived? "I have heard he and his wife keep rooms somewhere in this Rose Street."

"And who wants to know?" growled Jack emerging from the gloom, his face and linen damp with sweat. He had been sparring all afternoon in the pub's upstairs room where pugilists in training often knocked each other's brains out. "Oh, it's you. Her old fee-fie-foe friend." He gave a condescending nod. "If it's Trumpet you want, *amico*, she's not here. Gone to care for her new little niece in Islington. Her brother's spouse had the baby while he's off with Wellington playing the conqueror. You Italians love *bambini*, I collect?"

"Yes, oh yes. Buy you a drink?"

"Can't waste time with you, *amico*. Just on my way to Covent Garden. I'm needed there to carry out an English theatrical custom: giving the retirement oration for some hack actor." He put down a coin and picked up his silk hat. "Toby something. Anyhow, *paisan'*, it's Islington you want. Miss Trumpet has moved back there. Come, Cassius!" He whistled up his little spotted dog, brushed past the giant and was gone.

Belzoni stayed to finish his claret. *So the Favershams are living miles apart?* For some reason he did not examine, that news added to his happiness. He tipped the publican generously and joined the uproarious crowds filling the streets.

A few blocks farther on, Belzoni saw Jack again, striding ahead, silk hat set at a jaunty angle, the dog quick-stepping on his short legs to keep up with his master's pace. A heavy-laden lorry was bearing down on them, but in the chattering celebrating crowd, crossing the street in several directions at once, it was making slow progress. Cassius paused for a second to lift his leg. The lorry driver, intent on avoiding a passing caleche, swerved his draft-horse team to cut a corner and a big iron wheel passed over the urinating dog. Crushed in two, Cassius yelped, and could not rise. Belzoni watched Jack turn at the sound and run back to his dog.

"Cassie! No!" Faversham picked up the wounded animal, screaming, "You've kilt my dog!" as the lorry rolled away. Cassius whined in pain, his eyes searching for comfort from his master. "They've hurt you. Oh, my little friend." Cassius tried to lick Jack's face. "My sweet little one...oh God...oh Jesus." Jack pressed the body of his treasure to his chest while people passed around him. The bundle of mangled fur shivered in his arms. "Don't die! Oh, Cassie.... Please, God!" The dog shook terribly and went still. "Nooo!" Faversham sobbed in the street like a heartbroken child, his tears flowing into the little animal's faithful, loving face.

Belzoni's heart ached for them both, but truly, there was nothing to be done.

The Italian stepped round to Islington that afternoon. At Longsatin House, he received the greeting of a prodigal son. A detached observer would have seen Belzoni's pleasure at being in Miss Trumpet's company again. The affectionate inclination of his head and the bumptious energy of his manner revealed where his feelings lay. Lizzie asked him to take a turn around the garden with her, for the day was warm and she wished to breathe in the soft spring air.

"What a commission! I had to tell you, Lisabetta. I shall create such a fountain for the celebrations!" Imperfectly, he tried to hush his booming voice for baby Georgina's sake, as Lizzie promenaded her in a pink blanket up and down the vegetable patch.

"Your dreams of hydraulics will be fulfilled. Now you can put da Ponte's mathematical book to some use."

"I have memorized each word, it's true. The largest fountain is to be by the steps of Carlton House."

"Filled with champagne for the Regent's guests, no doubt?"

"No, you joke. A great water display. My head is bursting with ideas."

"Mind the lettuces, Giovanni." The giant gave a little hop to avoid the nubs of rocket peeping up from the soil they strolled through. "Tell me of your adventures since I last set eyes on you."

"Touring, always touring. I was Samson again." He shook his head. "Who else, eh? I connived to get a Spanish passport and played sacred dramas in Portugal and Spain, after the armies moved on."

"How enterprising. But dangerous, surely."

"I was popular, *cara*. I even appeared at the Royal Court in Madrid."

"Remarkable. You prospered?"

"Not to excess, but I didn't starve. I went back to Scotland and worked as an actor, then traveled to Dublin and Cork, too."

Lizzie patted the baby, trying to imagine herself traveling the world. "What plays? What roles?"

"*The Algerian Pirate*, I was the pirate. *The Mountain Witches*, I was a witch. And...you will laugh."

"I am ready for a laugh," she admitted quietly.

"*Macbeth, King of Scotland*, I was the old rascal himself."

For friendship's sake, Lizzie managed to contain her amusement. "So, you really are an actor now."

"Acting is for you, Lisabetta. I have retired. My last performance was at the Blue Boar Inn in St. Aldgate's. I called myself 'The Grand Sultan of all Conjurers' and did magic tricks. The crowd was appalling. But now I'm recognized for my scientific mind."

"The world is going your way." They walked under the oak tree's shade. Georgina had fallen asleep in Lizzie's arms.

"And you, Lisabetta? Playing London shows, the celebrated painting. 'Winged Victory,' the 'British Nike.' My little friend is famous." Softly he asked, "You are happy, yes?"

"Of course, and it gladdens my heart to see you." She gave the Italian a reassuring smile, but offered no details of her present situation. "How did you know I was staying at Longsatin House?"

"I looked for you in Rose Street, and saw your husband at the Lamb and Flag."

"Ah," she said, with a flicker of unease. "How did you find Jack? Well?"

"Oh, yes. Capitol, as the English say. But, Lisabetta, I should tell you I saw him later in the street with his little pet dog."

"Cassius. The Faversham pride and joy. He's trained him wonderfully, even more thoroughly than me," she added wryly.

"There was an accident with a lorry. I saw it happen. Jack is safe, but your husband's dog was killed, Lisabetta. I am so very sorry."

"Cassie is dead? Oh, *caro*, how cruel life is." Tears sprang to her eyes. "Poor Jack." She clutched the baby and looked away, grieving for a long while. "This is no small thing. He will suffer so."

Chapter Twenty-Eight

June 23, 1814

IN EARLY June, Major George Mario Trumpet was posted to London to help coordinate the huge celebration for the Duke of Wellington's victorious return to England. Baby Georgina cried the longest and the loudest at her father's appearance. Thin and tense, speaking with authority in his voice, Georgie was polished with the patina of a warrior's experience, and the more precious for it. Oh, how many times he kissed his wife and babe, his beautiful sister grown thin herself, and his ancient Aunt Peg. Nothing would do but the old lady should try on his busby hat, a tower of grey fur and red feather rising two feet tall. And so she did, looking rather like a monkey in a Gillray cartoon.

Holding his daughter in his arms, Georgie stood before Emily's map that had grown to include France. Many red ribbons marked his recent battles there. Of course, the women wanted a story for each ribbon, so Georgie told of the colorful events, not the slaughters too unspeakable to mention. How Wellington captured the silver chamber pot of the upstart King Joseph, the taking of Pamplona with the Spanish allies, the entry into beautiful Bordeaux.

Wearing her kitchen apron, Lizzie listened at the mahogany table, attempting to paint a watercolor portrait of her brother as he spoke.

Georgie showed them his ink drawing of the excellent bridge Napoleon had built over the Garonne River. A few weeks before, he was riding there with Wellington when a French sentry fired at them from close range. "That ball went whizzing by my ear like a bumblebee. You do not know it, ladies, but there is an unwritten understanding that pickets never fire upon one another. The French sentry's superior was so scandalized he rushed forward to apologize! 'A thousand pardons, General, this idiot is a green recruit.' Wellington laughed, but I did not."

"You never wrote about that." Emily moved to embrace her husband yet again, drunk with the pleasure of his presence.

"There was no time to write, my dearest. Napoleon's marshals fought on even after the Emperor had abdicated. At Easter, we were in a fierce dust-up at Toulouse. When we dispatched the diehards, Wellington and his staff—every last one of us—went to the theatre. What do you think of that, Lizzie?" He barked a laugh. "So damned civilized."

"What was the play?" Lizzie asked, mixing her colors with a sable brush.

"*Richard, Coeur de Lion.* All in French, of course. Then Wellington was made a duke and Ambassador to France. I rode in his train when he entered Paris to review the troops with the new French king, Louis the Eighteenth. Well, not altogether new. Old Louis is rather a decayed specimen of the ancient regime."

"I thank God you are done with the war at last, my darling," Emily whispered, her dread that she would never see her beloved again quite vanished. Reassuringly, Georgie pressed his lips to the crown of her head, breathing in the sweet fragrance of her hair.

Lizzie saw Georgie's face suddenly transformed into a mask of tragedy. "So many of my comrades are gone, turned to corpses, row upon row, lying in formation just as they marched into the cannon's mouth. The mad ambition of Bonaparte caused it all. I smell the stench of death in his very name. He is Satan on earth."

Lizzie's brush stopped moving, leaving a puddle of carmine on her picture. She had never imagined such fury smoldered in her brother's heart.

The revealing moment quickly passed as Georgie smiled once more. He kissed baby Georgina, who looked up at him with round, innocent eyes. "Don't fear, little one, now your father's duty is nothing more arduous than planning a parade."

‹6›

July 11, 1814

All the population of England seemed to be pushing towards Pall Mall to witness the show of shows, the National Victory Celebration. Major George Trumpet was giving the people a sight they would remember all their lives.

Emily had a well-situated seat in the grandstand close to Carlton House. Octavia Onslow perched in the window of an old acquaintance above Charing Cross. In the crowd thronging Piccadilly, Jack Faversham could be seen finishing off a bottle of spirits in the open air.

Leading the parade was an honored drum-major, a ginger-mustached sergeant, gorgeously turned out in a long green coat crusted with silver lacings, white trousers and gloves, magenta sash and cuffs, topped off with a bicorn hat, plumed in white. He strutted out to lead a hundred musicians, keeping time with a tall mace of sterling silver. After the flourish of music, mounted officers from every regiment that had seen service followed on their gleaming saddles and embroidered blankets of "horse furniture." They were a rippling sea of red coats and bouncing gold epaulettes.

Allied officers passed in less familiar uniforms: Austrians in grass green with square yellow czapka hats; Hohenzollerns in tall Roman-style helmets; Russian Cuirassiers in neck-to-girdle black armor and the eight-pointed star of St. George; Prussians in dark blue jackets with black plumes and a golden eagle on their shakos; Spanish Dragoons in yellow tunics. The whole mass was interspersed with Scottish and Irish bagpipers playing to wake the dead.

There were nearly as many veterans in the crowd as in the parade, cheering the swallow-tailed guidons of their passing regiments. The noise quite drowned out Emily's hiccups when she spotted her husband riding with the staff officers in the final guard of honor.

The volume of frenzy grew as thousands caught sight of Wellington himself, mounted on his mighty chestnut Copenhagen. "Huzzah! God bless ya, Ol' Nosey! Hip Hip Huzzah!" The deity of war received this adulation with guarded dignity, perfectly matched by the sangfroid of his well-traveled war-horse.

Before the steps of Carlton House, dressed to out-dazzle the heroes of the day, the Prince Regent waited with all his ducal brothers, on a sturdy platform.

Once Wellington came into sight, a tall man, pacing at the corner of this structure, waved dramatically to a toothless workman crouched beneath the platform. "*Cominciare!*" The workman waved back, drunkenly. Belzoni shouted, "Turn on! *Adesso!*" The Italian gesticulated wildly. "Cue la *fontana*! Now!" At last, the fellow began to crank a handle and drops spurted into the air from a hidden pool. A fountain behind the royals came to life, waters flashing higher and higher in the three-plume insignia of the Prince of Wales.

"Oooh," cried the crowd and the royal brotherhood.

"How stupendous!" said the prince, then took out a silk handkerchief to dab where the cascading spray had hit him in the eye.

When the Iron Duke arrived and began to ascend the carpeted stairs, sunshine broke through the clouds. In the name of his father King George the Third—far too deep in madness to attend—the prince presented his general with a baton of victory, cobalt blue enamel worked in gold and diamonds, personally designed by the regent.

Wellington attempted to voice his thanks. "I want words to express...." But the duke was too deeply moved to go on.

The prince, whose own face was awash in happy tears, said instead, "My dear fellow, we know your actions and will excuse your words, so sit down." And, so saying, the fat man seated the great man on a chair only a few inches lower than his own. The crowd jubilated.

A slender, handsome gentleman in simple black appeared on the platform. He was an actor from the Royal Theatre Drury Lane. Edmund Kean's recitation of the Ode of Victory received thunderous applause.

The conductor of the orchestra tapped for attention. As well as penning the Ode, the prince had chosen the music. Now his favorite soprano stepped out from amongst the dukes to sing. Elizabeth Trumpet, in crimson satin and borrowed jewels, nodded to Carlo Tomassi. Above the instruments and the spraying fountain, her voice soared in the most triumphant lyric from Handel's *Messiah:*

"*Rejoice, rejoice, rejoice greatly,*
O daughter of Zion;
Behold, thy king cometh unto thee.
He is the righteous Savior."

Georgie stood in his stirrups to better see his sister. In her color and plumes, the infant is a true bird of paradise. He felt as though his body was lifting up over the crowd. *I am quite light headed...I see everything. The great round world and all its people—myself included—as God must see this wonderful day. Thank you, Lord, for peace on earth...as it is in heaven.* Such pride and satisfaction touched his heart, the colors before him began to swim through his tears.

"*And he shall speak peace unto the heathen;*
Rejoice, rejoice, rejoice greatly!"

Jonathan Faversham had shoved his way quite near Major Trumpet's horse. The actor's sight was also blurry, but not from the joy of peace or pride in Lizzie's singing.

The Duke of Wellington dined that night at Carlton House, the most honored guest of the Prince Regent, in the company of England's greatest.

Nothing pleased Prinny so much as hosting a grand party. He engaged Vauxhall Gardens to accommodate his overflow guests, the not quite so great, but nevertheless renowned. That seemed to include everybody. There were hundreds of tables, thousands of flowers, towers of food and gushers of wine. Candles, lanterns, and a few new gas lights shone on the beautiful women and even more beautiful men promenading up and down the paths under the cool green trees. Battalions of hard-pressed waiters served amongst clowns on stilts, jugglers, ballerinas on ponies, tumblers and rope dancers. Grimaldi was there amongst the theatrical guests, but entered into the carnival spirit of the evening to do an occasional back flip and sign autographs.

Belzoni circulated, hoping to encounter Lizzie, but instead was congratulated by many people he didn't know. The most interesting of these strangers was a mature snuff-colored gentleman in a green turban who introduced himself as Captain Ishmael Gibraltar, agent of Mohammed Ali, Pasha of Egypt.

"Sir, the government I represent wishes to modernize our country. I admired your fountains of spectacle today." The Egyptian bowed his turban, so tall it nearly bumped the Italian's chin. "I believe a man of your hydraulic skills could be of great help to our Pasha's ambitious plans. Do you have a moment to discuss the science of water?" Giovanni confessed he would like nothing better. The two men conversed for some time.

In a dressing room tent, pitched on the damp grass and somewhat apart from the merrymaking, Lizzie changed out of her red satin. She powdered lightly around her stays and bosom, then donned a costume of white silk and crystal beading. This creation of transparency and lights had been designed by the prince, whose taste was everywhere in the day's celebration. Her solo had gone so successfully, the actress was allowing herself a moment of solitary pleasure. Wellington himself had thanked her. This was the life of fame indeed, even though no one had provided a maid or dresser, and she was changing alone in a little tent. She was scheduled to sing in the gardens later, after the fireworks. As she stood on a scrap of oriental carpet, smoothing out the gauze and ostrich feathers of a fantastic headdress, someone coughed outside.

"Excuse me, Elizabeth. It's Uncle Sidrack and party. May we enter?"

"Goodness, yes, and welcome." Lizzie opened the tent flap to see Roger Sloane standing beside his father, with a pert red-headed girl on his arm. "Roger! The American has returned." She gave her childhood chum a gleeful hug. "It's been years. How changed you are!" Indeed, the chubby, ill-at-ease boy was transformed into a well-muscled, good-looking beau any woman would be happy to claim.

"Lizzie, you are more beautiful than ever," Roger said excitedly. "You must meet my bride." With shining eyes, he introduced the girl in apricot muslin. "May I present Susannah Lewis Sloane."

As the ladies curtsied to each other, Sidrack explained, "These children are on their wedding trip thanks to Susannah's daring brother. Come inside, Owen." He pushed aside the tent flap to reveal a compact, beaming young man that could have been Susannah's twin. "Elizabeth, this is Owen Glendower Lewis. Perhaps you will recall I spoke of a business associate who sailed through blockades like wind through a net?"

"Redbeard himself?" Lizzie laughed and gave her hand to the sea captain after he removed his hat to show off rusty side-whiskers and a head of flaming curls.

"My adventurous brother wanted to give us a wedding gift I would never forget..." Susannah began.

"...so he swam us through the British blockade of South Carolina and on to London as though he did it every day," Roger finished.

"Which I do. Practically," Roger's brother-in-law added, with a snap of his fingers. "What a time to arrive in London, eh? History being made. Banquets. Balls. Victory parades."

"All these formal occasions, Uncle, they must be good for your tailoring business." Lizzie laughed. "Is this your first trip to England, Susannah?" She wanted to put the girl at ease and gave all her attention to Roger's American bride.

"Yes. But my family, the Lewises, came to America from Wales. So this is a homecoming in a way."

"How are you finding London?"

"Enormous. It makes Charleston seem like a village. I'm quite dazzled by all the people. And I had no idea you were so famous, Elizabeth!"

"Not so famous as all that. I was honored to be chosen for the ceremony."

"Well, you are famous to me, because Roger says you grew up

together, and Major Trumpet was his childhood companion. Your grandparents confirm it."

"Do you see Nana and Papi often?"

"We were taking tea on their piazza just before our voyage here, and we have letters from them for you Trumpets in our traveling trunks."

"Well, thank you, Susannah. Roger, how did you meet your delightful bride?"

"Through music, Lizzie. I heard her singing in the choir at St. Michael's Church. Like yourself, she is a magnificent soprano." Susannah squeezed Roger's arm and shook her curls at Lizzie in protest. "No, it's all true," Roger went on, "I attended for months before I had the courage to speak to her."

"Being Welsh, we Lewis children grew up singing," Susannah explained. "At Christmas, all the family performs Mr. Handel's *Messiah* for our private amazement, gathered around the sitting room, wailing loud enough to frighten the horses in the street."

"Susannah's father, Doctor John, said if I was going to make such calf eyes at his daughter, I had better learn to make music," Roger admitted. "I can hold my own with the tenors now."

Susannah winked at Lizzie. "He cuts quite a figure in the choir."

It was plain as a pike-staff to Lizzie, this straightforward lively girl had put some go into Roger. Or was it being in a new country? The once bumbling boy, who fumbled the buttons of her fencing jacket and never ventured to raise a foil of his own, now looked quite capable of negotiating his destiny.

"I shall have a dinner for you at Longsatin House," Lizzie said impulsively. "I wish there were chairs in this little tent to accommodate you all...."

"Is this where they put you up, sister? I thought I'd never find you." Major George Trumpet, in the glory of full-dress uniform, with Emily in tow, entered the crowded tent. "Uncle Sidrack! Roger! Well, this makes it the happiest of days." Introductions were made, and good feelings abounded. "What say we all leave my sister to rest and go to the Grenadier for a jolly supper? I want to introduce Emily to my brother officers, and they are sure to be taking a dram there." The suggestion was taken up with enthusiasm. Georgie graciously maneuvered the visitors out, then turned back to kiss Lizzie's hand. "While I was knocking French heads, you've become an artist, sister. By Jupiter, you have! We'll return after supper to hear you sing."

As the young married couples strolled away, the actress heard Emily say, "Our tomorrows shall all be made of happy days."

Lizzie rested on a stool with a wet towel around her neck, trying to relax. *What has become of the Faversham's happy days?* In the flurry of rehearsals and fittings, Jack was not uppermost in her mind, but she had expected to hear something from her husband when she sent him word of her appearance. There had been no answer. No word that he was proud or pleased or gave a tinker's damn. Whispering the lyrics for the evening concert, she put on her grandmother's earrings. Full dark had fallen, but there was time enough to take a breath of air. She stepped outside in her shimmering beaded dress.

"Why wasn't I given that Victory Ode?"

Lizzie turned to find Faversham standing behind her, unshaven and looking much the worse for drink. "Jack! Are you all right?"

"Why did they give Kean the honor?" His bloodshot eyes hardly focused on her.

"I'm sorry, they just didn't engage you."

"Why you and not me?"

"I don't know. The prince planned everything. I had no hand in it."

He scowled at her, unsteady on his feet. She felt the unbridgeable distance between them widen like an ocean. His presence frightened her. *What topic is suitable, when your husband appears like a ruffian from a nightmare?*

"Did you hear me sing? They introduced me as the British Nike."

"I heard you." Without warning, he slapped Lizzie hard, knocking her back into the dressing room. Grabbing her at the waist, he whipped her face back and forth with his big hand. "So high and mighty." He struck her throat with his fist.

"Stop!" she screamed, but there was too much din outside to be noticed.

"Shut up, whore!" He tore her bodice open, the crystals flying, then turned her round and yanked up her gown. She tried to strike at him, but he was far too strong for her. "Bitch!" he shouted in her ear. "Ungrateful bitch! I'll show you what you need." He lifted her body and threw it over the dressing table, spread her buttocks and jammed his penis like a weapon into the tender flesh.

He thrust and thrust, beating her on the head and shoulders all the while. He pulled at her hair with a vengeance as he ejaculated, struck her once more and shoved her to the ground. Buttoning up his trousers, he kicked a terrible blow between her legs. Finally satisfied, he lurched out of the tent, unnoticed by anyone.

Scarcely breathing, Lizzie lay motionless on the carpet. *So this is pain. All the times I played a victim, I never could have imagined.... How awful....* Her face was swelling and a river of blood ran between her thighs. She drifted in and out of consciousness.

"Ahoy, Miss Trumpet." A masculine voice woke her. "Captains Irby and Mangles here. Do you remember us?" It was Irby speaking outside the tent. "We met in Perth."

"Is she in there?"

"We're on leave and saw you perform," Irby spoke more loudly through the canvas. "You sang wonderfully on the platform with Kean and all. Well...we do not mean to disturb...."

Lizzie cried out in a broken voice, "Help. Help, please."

"I believe she replied," Irby said to his friend. The captains entered the tent.

"Dear God. Miss Trumpet, what has happened?" Mangles knelt over her. Lizzie tried to cover the evidence of her rape.

"Where is your husband, Miss Trumpet? We shall take you home." The men were appalled at what they saw.

"No, not home. I must not be seen." A thunderous salvo shook the ground. "Take me away from here, please...please." Fireworks were beginning all along the Thames, but Lizzie heard nothing more. She had fainted.

"Get her into a carriage," Mangles said to his tall friend, wrapping his cloak over her. "We must do as she asked." Irby lifted the British Nike off the bloody rug and carried her into the exploding night.

Chapter Twenty-Nine

July 11, 1814
The Trumpet Family
Longsatin House, Duncan Terrace

*D*EAR ONES,
The wealthiest man in England has invited me to his country house. His wife wants to arrange theatrical evenings with the family, and is paying me a grand fee to coach them all. My spur of the moment departure from London is their secret. Heigh-ho, the glamorous life! Who can fathom the peculiarities of the rich? Perhaps a mysterious disappearance will add to my reputation. I am undertaking this adventure without knowing precisely when I will return, but, worry not, I am in the best of hands. A friend is writing this for me.
    In haste,
    Lizzie

Captain Charles Irby had written this letter in his clear hand, with many flourishes and serifs. Her family was surprised and concerned, but only Octavia suspected it might be the work of pure mendacity.

⟜

August 1814

The Raptor was a tight little two-masted schooner, a Baltimore clipper some would call it. The ship was privately owned by Captains Mangles and Irby, men of gentle birth and some fortune. The adventuresome young navy officers, on temporary leave and half-pay since the outbreak of peace with the French, had sailed from the Pool of London down the coast of France, around the Iberian Peninsula and through the Pillars of Hercules into the blue Mediterranean.

Mangles tapped on the cabin door of his female passenger. "Does Miss Trumpet feel like taking a turn on deck this morning?"

"Miss Trumpet does, but later, please," Lizzie answered softly, afraid for the damage she still felt in her throat. Her body and her spirit had not yet recovered. The captain's doses of laudanum induced deep-healing sleep, but called up troubling dreams. In the fantasies, she was a child holding her mother's hand, watching William Trumpet move through pools of light onstage. She'd run to jump into her father's arms, but he was tantalizingly tall, out of reach, moving into a last bit of light, then gone. Lizzie would awaken under a twisted sheet, always unfulfilled, then crushed to realize she was hurt and far from home.

She pulled on the clean white shirt and patched trousers folded by her bunk. Purposely avoiding the mirror, she braided and tied her hair in a sailor's queue. Jack's beating haunted her. Her mind dragged over and over the same rutted road of bad memories. *How could he have treated me so, done such a monstrous thing? I gave Jack all the love I had. If I put myself in his hands again, I'll spend the rest of my life cleaning up the disaster he is making of his.*

She opened the cabin door to draw in a blue china bowl of potable soup the captains offered at the start of each day. Thoughts of past escape and the future kept her company as she ate alone, without relish. What were the chances that two admirers of her acting would carry her off by sea? Bless them, they never asked who treated her so savagely. *They saw me in my shame. What they must think of me? Far better to never speak of it again.*

With effort, she left the refuge of the dim cabin. Clean air, bright sun, and ruffles in the moving water shining like handfuls of diamonds greeted the risen invalid. A chair, placed out of the wind, waited on the scrubbed deck. Nothing was required of her. Days at sea were free to watch the migrating birds cross the horizon or count the dolphins dancing in *The Raptor's* wake. She could sleep hours away beneath the towering fore-and-aft sails or gaze at the ever-changing clouds and let her mind go blank, but it would not. As time passed, she asked Irby to teach her seamen's simple tasks and applied herself to learning the ropes and names of sails. When strength began returning to her legs, she climbed the rigging with pent-up energy, hand over hand, fearlessly reaching towards the sky. The crew gaped up at her, an enthralling sight, silhouetted against the sunsets.

On the Italian shore, in a quiet cove east of Portofino, Captain Irby convinced Miss Trumpet he could teach her the valuable skill of swimming. "This warm salt water will feel like bliss," he promised.

In her white shirt and sun-bleached trousers, she walked into the surf, clutching Irby's big hairy hand. After an hour of struggling in the azure waves, Lizzie felt she had learned enough to stay afloat, gurgled her thanks, and waded out, exhausted.

Leaving *The Raptor's* company gamboling in the surf, the girl ambled alone down the beach, scrunching her toes in the wet sand. What if she'd never be able to go onstage again? She couldn't imagine facing an audience as she was. *Is the best of my life over?*

Just beyond her, a small flock of shore birds marched in line through the lapping tide. *Did Jack ever love me? I was his obsession, not a partner at all.* Her mind scampered on like the shore birds feeding in the ripples. Why did she love him so long, so blindly? Why not leave him? Be shot of him forever? *Why not?*

"Miss Trumpet! Come back!" The men were waving and calling out. Lizzie had not realized she'd walked so far.

⚬♪

The gibbous moon had risen like a lamp of weathered pearl. At a table on *The Raptor's* deck, set with linen and silver, Captain Mangles sliced through fresh-baked swordfish. Irby poured wine into Lizzie's glass as the ship rocked gently at anchor.

"I believe you will enjoy the taste of this, Miss Trumpet." Mangles served her a mighty portion. "More like beefsteak than fish."

"I'm not wearing shoes now, Captain James. Call me Lizzie as my family does." Her unguarded words proved some inner healing had taken place, and the men looked at her with pleasure, not to say enthusiasm. "My brother himself could not have cared for me more thoughtfully than you both have. And it is as brothers that I think of you." She knew, from the dimming of the light in their eyes, this was not the kind of intimacy the captains had hoped for. They were young and vital men, and despite her fading bruises, she was an object of desire, but no man could entice her now. Her own lusts had been trampled on. The thought of sex and its consequences made her soul recoil.

Do they understand I do not wish to come between such true comrades? Cause a romantic competition that would bring me no happiness and surely give them much pain? Men are so reckless....

"Nor do I have a favorite. I love you equally." *That should quash any ideas of triangles and intrigues....* "I have seen you are true friends as well. A closer bond than family, is it not? Sometimes, we are lumbered with our families, but choose our friends from all the population, and hold them precious." *Are they listening to the sense behind my words?*

"Well said...Lizzie." Wryly, Mangles raised his glass and met her gaze.

"Hear, hear! To friendship," Irby added.

Lizzie drank deeply of her wine, relieved.

"Our destination. It's time we discussed it with you." Mangles put his elbows on the table and laced his fingers beneath his chin. "We are in the Mediterranean for a reason. As it happens, Irby's mother is a dear old friend of Neil Campbell's mother."

"Colonel Neil Campbell," Irby corrected.

"Yes, of course. Colonel Campbell, I meant to say...."

"One should actually say Colonel Sir Neil Campbell."

"Thank you, Charles. Don't be tedious. Campbell is serving on an island off Tuscany, not far away. His mother required us to deliver a pack of letters to him, also an article of clothing sewn by her own hands. A silk shirt, I believe."

"Muslin small-clothes," Irby corrected again.

"Good God. Well, Irby here, being a good son himself, agreed to the dear lady's wishes. And, since we both are on post-Napoleon leave, and this island is much in the news, we planned to do this favor and see a *curiosity* at the same time."

Irby leaned across the table, moving the candles in their hurricane glasses absently. "However, the night we were to depart London, we found you at Vauxhall Gardens...in some distress."

"In much distress." Lizzie passed a hand across her forehead. *Please say no more.*

"Well..." Mangles went on, "rather than draw attention to your distress, or leave you with strangers who might not provide proper care, in the heat of the moment we just brought you on board. Perhaps you recall dictating a letter to your family? Your mind did not seem perfectly clear that night, and you slipped into a deep unconsciousness. So without a plan of any kind, we simply sailed away." A seagull squawked overhead. "Kidnapping was not our intention."

"Of course. Rescue. It was rescue," Lizzie whispered, with lowered eyes.

"Get to the point, James." Irby coughed. "Our destination."

"Colonel Campbell is on Elba."

"The...Elba?"

"There is only one. Campbell is serving as Commissioner of Elba, where Napoleon Bonaparte is now living like a fish in a bowl."

"Napoleon is the 'curiosity' you mentioned? The captive emperor?" Lizzie looked up at the moon. *So much for Bonaparte's reputation...the scourge of civilization has become a curiosity.*

"The very one," said Mangles.

"Is he open to view?"

"Yes. In fact, he welcomes company that brings him news of the world."

"Well! My darling brother, the major, wouldn't like it, but what an experience that would be." Lizzie laughed at the thought. *And suddenly I am inspired to rhyme...like Old Charlie Dibdin...how should it go?* She sipped her wine, then stood up, saluted them and said, "Gentlemen. Attend.

"*It was a famous Frenchman, who sought the maiden's heart,*
A gent of small dimensions, and his name was Bonaparte.
He was emp'ror of the nations, 'til the English knocked him flat,
Without a crown or cannons, he was nothing more than fat.
'Make your exit,' cried the maiden, 'you shall never play the part.
You were vain, but now you're vanquished.
I don't give a fiddler's fart!"

The captains exploded with laughter, pounding the table.

"Poetess extempore!"

"Hear, hear!"

For a moment, Lizzie felt quite her old self.

"Gentlemen, if we were in a play, and don't you think we are? And if I were the heroine, and I believe I am. I would say...'Who's for Elba?'"

Irby's pink face shone with delight. "We sail at dawn!"

"What a wasp-nest of spies this island must be," observed Mangles, as the three loyal subjects of King George the Third toured the seventeen-by-eleven miles of mountain and hill that was thorny little Elba. Irby estimated they'd seen a thousand French troops scattered amongst the olive trees. Four British frigates were anchored in the harbor. The packages for Colonel Campbell had been delivered. The guardian of Napoleon's exile was quite nonplussed to receive motherly advice and nainsook drawers at this distant station.

"Campbell seems a bit testy from protecting the peace of the world," Irby mused, urging on the hot mule pulling their cart. "Heavy duty, I imagine."

"I'd be testy," commented Mangles. "Wouldn't you?"

Permission had been granted for them to be received at noon at the Villa dei Mulini, a decaying old pile that once was two windmills and now the Official Residence of Emperor Napoleon Bonaparte. The Treaty of Fontainebleau had given him the island, the guards, a decent allowance, and his own flag. British sailors had made the emblem to Bonaparte's specifications on his voyage over from France. That flag—white with red diagonal band and three busy gold bees— flew over the villa as Lizzie and her Navy friends tethered the mule and climbed up broken steps to the unprepossessing door.

The native Elbans were discovering the meaning of the new flag. They were to be the energetic bees for Bonaparte. In hopes of starting a silk industry, the defeated dynamo had men planting mulberry trees on neglected hillsides around the wind-swept stone town of Portoferraio. On the Corsican's orders, garbage was collected daily by old men carrying baskets on their backs. Formerly, the locals had passed a morning doing nothing more than gossiping at the doorways and swatting flies. Those sleepy days were done; all was improvement now, like it or not.

Waiting in the glaring sun for the villa door to open, Lizzie adjusted her soft yellow sleeves. During a supply stop in Genoa, a gifted mantua-maker had sewn her a new cotton gown. The captains looked brushed and distinguished in their dress uniforms with ceremonial swords. Mangles scratched at his collar and cleared his throat with suppressed excitement.

A butler in blue livery opened the door. "*Bon jour, madame et messieurs*," he said, bowing economically. "*Entrez-vous, s'il vous plait.*"

Sounds of hammering and shouting came from above. Two men with buckets of plaster and rolled sail-cloth mounted the staircase as the visitors were led into a wide salon with a low ceiling. Plenty of ebony cabinets and chairs trimmed in golden sphinxes lined the walls, but no other guests were sitting in them. Beneath the chandelier with a few crystals missing, bicorn hat under his arm, stood history's exclamation point, Napoleon Bonaparte.

The butler introduced, "Captain the Honorable Charles Irby and Captain James Mangles, both of the British Royal Navy, Miss Elizabeth Trumpet of the Theatre Royal Covent Garden."

The Emperor engaged them in rapid French like a man with no moments to waste, appraising the beauty in yellow with a discerning eye. "Good day, *messieurs. Et madame.* As you can see, we are renovating our Imperial Palace. Permit me to inquire when you left your homeland?"

"We departed London in July," Mangles answered in such tortured French that Lizzie winced. *Madame Bonnet would have kept James after class.*

"Ah," continued Napoleon, "And what is the state of affairs in your country?"

"Experiencing the usual post-war difficulties. The expenditures for war have been great, and now there are more men than jobs."

"There is unrest?" Napoleon placed his hat on a malachite credenza.

"We are no experts on the economy of our nation," Irby hastened to say. "My friend is a simple captain"—he gave Mangles a disapproving look—"very simple. Britain is happy for the peace."

"Tsk." Lizzie sighed over Irby's equally appalling accent and studied the eagle motif in the stucco ceiling. The hammering continued overhead. Bonaparte conversed with the Navy men in the style of a police interrogation.

"What do your sailors drink?"

"Uh, beer or brandy.

"French brandy?"

"English."

"Does it taste different?"

"Why, yes."

"When the sailors get paid, I suppose they drink wine?"

"Beer is preferred, actually." Mangles looked surprised at this choice of subject. Napoleon turned his verbal guns on Irby.

"Have you ever been to Paris, *capitaine*?"

"Yes."

"What did you eat?"

"Veal, I believe it was veal."

"How much did it cost?"

"Too much."

Napoleon paced the room hardly seeming to listen, but taking in everything, especially the silent Lizzie. When he circled around her, she dropped a graceful court-curtsy, perfected for player kings. He seized her hand and gave it more of a nip than a kiss.

"*Enchanté, mademoiselle.* You wear the color of summer, or perhaps I should say of lemon sorbet."

"I have heard you are a connoisseur of feminine costume, Highness," she answered in Italian, thinking fast.

"You speak the language of Dante, *signorina?*"

"My grandparents are Italian, living in America."

"America is twice as large now, thanks to me."

"I'm sure my grandparents are very grateful for the purchase of Louisiana," Lizzie answered carefully, as she studied the physical persona of Bonaparte, a compact man with thighs of overdeveloped muscle and a baggage of middle-aged flesh softening his face and stomach. His eyes were as singular as Jack's. Even more compelling...freshly shaved, smells of cologne. His armies had devastated Europe.... *Is it possible he feels no guilt for the death he has caused? No remorse? Such coldness...he might be the Devil himself.*

"But you are an actress, *signorina.* I find the art fascinating. Mademoiselle Georges, of the theatre, is a particular friend."

With a nod, Lizzie acknowledged the discarded mistress of the Emperor.

"I am building an opera house at this very moment. Some licorice, *signorina?*" Bonaparte foraged in a pocket and pushed a piece of black candy between Lizzie's surprised lips. The captains didn't notice. Pauline Bonaparte, the Princess Borghese, had joined them.

Napoleon introduced his sister, saying, "Pauline has accompanied me here with a loyal heart. Her presence makes my court beautiful."

The princess was indeed beautiful, possessed of a flawless

complexion, dainty figure and dark, bright eyes. She'd dressed to receive visitors in a sheer gown remarkably low in the neck. Lizzie admired the matched bracelets of Burmese rubies on her wrists. The captains admired her ruby nipples, plainly visible in her décolletage. Like her brother, she circled the room to be admired and circled the captains to judge what they had to offer.

"We are improving and decorating this heap we call a palace," the princess said to them in French. "My Palazzo in Rome was a jewel box of colors, but here in this rustic atmosphere," she rolled her eyes at the men, "I find I cannot decide on the tones to paint my bedchamber. Would you advise me?" Her white hand absently brushed her own breast.

"Pink," Irby mumbled, obviously thinking of something else.

"Ah, but you must see it, gentlemen, a very private place at the top of the house. I have such interest in English tastes. I burn to show you my little nook, and see what you would do with it." Pauline's eyes were dancing between the men, hips twitching as she moved to leave. She looked coquettishly back over her shoulder. "You will ascend with me?"

"Delighted, Your Highness," Mangles answered before Irby could stop him. Two Bonapartes in one room seemed to have broken the British line. Irresistible as a praying mantis, the lady took each captain by the arm. Irby raised his eyebrows to Lizzie as if to say "she cannot help herself," as he was dragged away.

"Pauline amuses herself with men. She will examine the English taste for some time." Napoleon smacked his lips. "Now we shall amuse ourselves as well."

Good God, he means to have me. Lizzie took several steps towards the gardens. "Perhaps a walk in the fresh air, Highness?"

"I will introduce you to my horses; you English are mad for horse-flesh, I believe?"

"I should enjoy that, of all things."

"Bring your parasol, the sun is hot." The Emperor bolted through the garden doors, eagerly pulling Lizzie after him. *Did he take that for an invitation? Introduced as an actress...stables...beds of hay— damn the captains for leaving me to this fate!*

When they achieved the ramshackle stable, the volatile Emperor did not make the feared lunge at her, but gave his caresses to the horses instead, telling the names and histories of all his beasts. Much relieved, Lizzie stroked the nose of a pretty Andalusian.

"Ah, you like Córdoba? That is the Empress's horse. I expected my pretty Marie Louise to join me here by now." His dark eyes took on a look that in a lesser man Lizzie might have called sad. *Or was he dissembling?*

"Circumstances have kept me from my spouse, too."

"The war?"

"A kind of war, yes."

Napoleon showed no curiosity about Lizzie's marital problems and moved to another stall. "This handsome fellow, called Taurus, was given to me by the Czar." The Emperor reached into a hempen bag. "Let us give him a treat."

Lizzie pressed her cheek into the horse's neck as the mighty grey lipped a carrot. Bonaparte bent to scrape some dung off his shiny boot.

"Did you know we English actors perform French plays in London? Translated and re-titled, sometimes only a few days after they've opened in Paris."

"Perhaps you should create some entertainments for me?"

How would "Commanded to perform for the Corsican Monster" look on my theatrical resume? Lizzie wondered. "The captains are departing today, Highness."

"We can at least read a play together! I enjoy the classics for amusement after dinner each evening with my staff. They are only amateurs, but you...." His eyes took liberties again. "You do read French?"

"*Mais certainement.*"

"You must see my opera house!" The Emperor of Elba called for a valet to bring them two copies of *Folies de l'Amour*.

The afternoon light had lowered to long rays across the theatre steps. Within, seated on the edge of the stage, Bonaparte and Lizzie read scene after scene. The Emperor was enjoying himself, speaking all the parts in a swift-paced monotone, no different from his usual speech. Lizzie supplied all the color and variety until her voice grew tired, and Napoleon closed the book with a clap.

"Let us talk about you, *signorina*. What do you think of my performance?"

"I believe Talma, the greatest of French actors, has coached you?" Lizzie had no wish to offend.

"He showed me how to carry myself like a Caesar."

"But, you mastered that perfectly. Of course, if you want to do comedy well, where the characters are not always the famous men of history.... Do you really want my opinion?"

"Yes, your honest opinion."

"Most people in an audience will not grasp the ideas as quickly as Your Highness. Too much haste and the comedy is blurred. Think a trot not a gallop, as it were. A good actor lives in the moment of his performance. He does not rush forward."

"This is new advice for me. Thank you, *signorina*." The Corsican Monster grabbed her ear in his right hand and gave it a painful tweak, his customary manner of showing his pleasure. "This husband of yours, he is an actor?"

"Yes."

"Famous?"

"Not as famous as he wishes to be."

"Of course. Is he any good?"

"He is magnificent." Lizzie had to give the devil his due. "At acting."

Chapter Thirty

September 1814

*T*HE RAPTOR put to sea again with the evening tide. Lizzie and her captains stood on deck, watching the rocky cliffs of Portoferraio recede in the distance, all three hesitant to speak of their afternoon with the Bonaparte family. The two men were relaxed and covertly smiling at whatever shared experience this little port would be remembered for.

Lizzie had changed into her sailor's rig—striped trousers and blue jacket—happy the tension of being in "Boney's" presence was over. "So, gentlemen, tell me, I beg, how did you find the Princess Borghese on close acquaintance? You both were in her chambers for hours. Well, was she amiable?"

"Oh, in every respect." Irby smirked, putting a spyglass to his eye for a last glimpse of Elba in the luminous gold of sunset. "Pauline Bonaparte has the manners a lady and the appetites of a—"

"A very forward woman," Mangles finished for his friend.

"I was going to say...." Irby took down the glass to look at his passenger's inquisitive face. "The appetites of a female cat."

Amused, Lizzie raised an eyebrow at Irby. "Did you ever keep a cat, Charles?"

"Certainly, they are excellent ratter's on board a ship."

"How did the princess enjoy your English 'taste'?"

"Couldn't get enough of it, wouldn't you say so, Mangles?"

"Yes, we gave her a sample of how things are done in Britain." Mangles turned as red in the face as his perpetually pink comrade. "She was gratified, poor thing. Starved for masculine...conversation."

Gorgeously, the sun's disk settled into the far watery horizon. The three went quiet, to honor the turning of a memorable day into calm night.

"What did you think of the Emperor, Lizzie?"

The actress paused to review her impressions before speaking. "Powerful, compelling in his masculinity, brilliant about many things, perhaps all things." *And who am I really describing*? "Charming as required, blind to his own faults, brutal, vain, and fearfully threatening." *Just like Jack!*

"What is that aroma coming out of our galley, Irby?"

"It's garlic." Lizzie laughed. "Don't tell me you've never heard of it, Captain James. A traveler of the world like you?"

"Smells very foreign."

"The Jesuit is making our dinner, Mangles, by way of thanks for taking him aboard. Miss Trumpet was very pleased," Irby chortled, "even if the ship's cook wasn't."

"My nana used to make delicious Italian dishes with garlic. When my grandparents immigrated to America, my Aunt Peg dug up all the garlic bulbs in our garden. She favored less exotic fare. It was good of Father Mancini to offer to cook. You will love the supper tonight, I assure you."

Father Mancini had accosted them in Portoferraio, at the foot of *The Raptor's* gang-plank, seeking any ship bound for Palermo. Irby was disinclined to add a strange passenger, but Lizzie liked the man's gentility and grace. She discovered the balding ascetic priest wished to see his gravely ill sister and prevailed on the captains to let him join them, since the Navy men were sailing by Sicily, anyway.

Mancini proved to be a fund of information over dinner, telling them of ancient Greek ruins including a theatre the captains should see. After the convivial meal, the officers went topside to privately recall their stimulating encounter with the Borghese femme fatale.

Lizzie lingered over the table with Father Mancini who raised the subject foremost to an Italian's heart: *la famiglia.*

"Are these officers your brothers, *signora*?"

Say yes, it is the easy answer, and they nearly are. "Yes, father."

"Are you sailing to your husband, *signora*?"

How hard it is to lie. "No, father. Away, in fact. You see my husband is...." *How to describe what Jack is to this good man...?* "He is an unhappy man, quite unacquainted with God."

"Then it is up to you to teach him of God."

"I cannot imagine that, father."

"Has there been love in your marriage?"

"A great love in the beginning." *Once I believed Jack's need for love was his strongest characteristic. Now....*

"Then pray for him, *signora*. God is always working in our lives to lead us to heaven."

Next morning, *The Raptor* sailed into the tearing wind of a Mediterranean levanter. Before first light, the ship heeled violently to starboard, throwing Lizzie from her bunk. Buttoning on her seaman's trousers, she climbed the hatchway ladder to a wet deck where the barefoot frantic crewmen were aloft reefing canvas and setting stays against a dawn sky of red and inky black. Spindrift splashed her face with force.

"Get below, Lizzie!" Mangles yelled over the weather. "We're in for an uncommon dirty morning."

Father Mancini, looking rather green about the gills, called up from below to ask if he could be of help.

"Get the *padre* back to his cabin and stay in yours!" Irby shouted, the power of the ship's bow-wave nearly knocking him down. "Stay below, by God!"

The Raptor plunged through tumultuous seas all day and into the night. The pumps worked heavily, spewing water, to little avail. Down in her dark cabin, Lizzie heard the storm speaking with all its frightful voices: The rigging wailed chords that rose and fell like the screaming of the furies, the thunderous ocean battered the wooden hull like the kettles of hell, and water sloshed ominously on the very deck beneath her feet. The priest's suggestion that she had responsibility for Jack's soul had unleashed her blue devils again. Imagining shipwreck, Lizzie rolled about on the bunk, trying to pray, remembering speeches from plays, remembering Jack and Bonaparte, deciding they were both sons of Satan and be damned to them.

Since Faversham had beaten Lizzie's throat, fear of further damaging her voice had kept her from vocalizing, but if this was to be her last moment on earth, why not? *I shall sing, by God, I shall; if I'm to die, at least I will die with music.* She tried something from her days at Madam Bonnet's, a few soft bars of *Plaisir d'amour.*

"Plaisir d'amour ne dure qu'un moment;" The joy of love lasts but a moment;

"Chagrin d'amour dure toute la vie." The heartache of love endures all your life.

She stopped, hand to throat. *No good. "Plaisir d'amour" is a poor choice.... A melancholy...mournful...mewling choice.... Music is the divine language, Papa said, and if I'm to meet God tonight, I will show Him my spirit. He will hear me coming...unafraid....*

Lizzie recalled an old Italian song that suited her mood. The sound of the words against the shrieking darkness made her courage rise. She sang with growing power.

"Vittoria, vittoria, mio core! Non lagrimar più!" Victory, victory, my heart! No more tears!

"E sciolta d'Amore la vil servitù." My vile slavery to love is at an end.

"Nel duol, ne' tormenti io più non mi sfaccio;" I am no longer ruined by grief or torment;

"E rotto ogni laccio, Sparito il timore!" The snare is broken and fear has disappeared.

"Vittoria, vittoria, mio core!" Victory, victory, my heart!

❧

"The Raptor is more tempest-tossed than sea-worthy," Irby

informed his passengers, once the ship was safely tied up in the port of Palermo. "She'll need some repairs before we can go on. Mangles and I are off to the shipyard for new canvas." He stepped on the gangplank and turned back. "You didn't really think we were done for, did you?" The beautiful sun-washed morning made the past night's stormy terrors seem like a distant dream to all of them.

"I think you are fine seamen," Lizzie said with grateful sincerity. The Jesuit begged her to translate his thanks.

"Father Mancini is saying he kisses your hands. Do I go with you or stay with the ship?"

"Stay and be guarded by the crew. Do not set foot off The Raptor by yourself. We shall get our business done and return shortly. Tell the padre we hope his sister recovers." The men left and it was clear Father Mancini in his buttoned cassock and wide black hat was anxious to be gone as well.

"I owe much to your charity for bringing me home, signora. An unforgettable journey, eh? I was praying every moment."

"I'm sure that made all the difference."

"There is one thing I must say to you before goodbye. During the storm, my heart was full of fear."

"As was mine, father."

"Then I heard an angel singing, or so I wanted to believe, but it was you. Beautiful. Your song reminded me, no matter how life engulfs us, God is always near." Tears filled Lizzie's eyes. He took off his hat. "Use your great gifts and God will be with you." In blessing, Mancini made the sign of the cross over Lizzie, picked up his battered, round-topped trunk and stepped off the ship. "*Arrivederci!*"

Lizzie watched him go. *In all my time with Jack, I lost track of God. I believe I caught a glimpse of Him last night. I will need the help of heaven if I'm ever to be...to be right again.*

November 1814

Mangles and Irby sailed The Raptor into the Harbor of Gibraltar a few weeks later. Most proudly they showed off the wonders of "The Rock" to their precious female passenger: the great guns, the honeycomb of defensive tunnels, the huge shipyards and everywhere men of the Royal Navy.

"These streets are home to the greatest defense force in the world," Irby said, with much satisfaction as they walked up the steep odorous alleyways towards the top of the town, "a perfect little Britain."

"What a snob you are," Mangles chided.

"I naturally enjoy hearing English spoken again."

"Are you both quite determined to see these Barbary apes?" Lizzie twirled her parasol. "I worked with monkeys at Sadler's Wells. They are very forward creatures at best."

Irby insisted, not taking her hint. "You should see everything, Lizzie, and from Gibraltar's summit, you can observe Africa and Spain in one go, a remarkable viso. Ah, this exercise to the limbs is most invigorating." Choosing a vertical path, he puffed, "The climb will do us good."

At Monkey's Cove, all their friendly overtures to the apes amongst the rocks were ignored. One husky beast eyed Irby then defecated with intent. The tailless primate's surly attitude did not surprise Lizzie. She led the officers away to a patch of smooth ground where they flopped down to rest their exercised limbs.

Mangles fixed his spyglass on The Raptor, a toy ship on a sapphire sea at this distance. "Everything's as it should be; all's right with the world."

"Well, not entirely right." Lizzie counted five gulls circling far below. "I wish to speak of something that's been troubling me."

"Certainly, Lizzie. Ah, look at that ape with the large red bottom coming towards us, Irby. The nasty fellow is about to throw a turd at you."

Too late, the pink-faced captain jumped to his feet. "Wretched beast!"

"Don't throw it back, Irby. You'll set a poor example."

"Gentlemen, please. May I have your attention? First, I wish to thank you for taking such splendid care of me all these months, I am in your debt and I wish to repay you for the your kindness."

The captains hastened to mumble and shake their heads dismissively. "No, no, no...."

"Now don't make those noises. I must repay you, but I left England without a penny. So, my dear friends, how can I contribute to this voyage?"

"Well, let us consider...." Mangles raised his glass again to look over the busy town below them. "The largest number of British sailors in the world are gathered in this port, and sailors are famously starved for entertainment. So, the question would be—"

"The question is," Irby interrupted, "could you perform?"

"Here on Gibraltar?"

"Why not? A concert by the renowned 'British Nike,' Miss Elizabeth Trumpet, would be well attended, without doubt."

"An all male audience?" Lizzie pictured what that might mean. *Men in uniform. Daunting...remember those eager boys in Plymouth long ago? They* were *the best audience....*

"A benefit for you, Lizzie." Irby seemed to think she had not understood. "Not to repay us, but to refurbish your fortune."

Mangles better knew her mind and asked with concern in his eyes, "But, tell us, are you ready to sing again?"

She took her deepest breath. *All men are not like Jack, right?* Decision made, she put hands on hips and replied with gusto, "Yes, Captain James."

"Hallelujah!" Mangles exclaimed, jumping to his feet. "Ah, Lizzie—Miss Trumpet...I would be obliged if you let me arrange everything." Irby was happily scrambling to be upright, too. "Assisted, of course, by Charles here, this rather squalid captain, sporting a monkey turd in his hat."

⚓

Officers and men by the hundreds gathered for the open-air concert in the vast cobblestoned oval of the South Parade. With her heart beating in quick-time, Lizzie mounted a torch-lit platform-stage to the warmest reception of her life. She wore the yellow gown so admired on Elba, with ribbons of gold worked into her piled-up hair. The captains had assembled a mismatched orchestra of sailor musicians: violins, drums, accordions and flutes, ready to rip into any improvisation.

She opened with a comic song, "Laid Up in Port," followed by a very good impression of Mrs. Siddons's sleep-walking scene. A lucky one-eyed boatswain's mate from the front row jigged while she danced and sang "*Scacciapensieri,*" the Trumpet family tarantella. A medley of Irish ballads was warmly received, and when she ventured "*Roll Me into Your Arms, Love, and Blow the Candle Out,*" the sailors took to it like a double portion of grog. Irby and Mangles played a scene with her from *The Rival Tars.* Their acting was stiff as two posts, but the men-a-wars-men adored it.

LIzzie then sang a lament the flute player had recommended.
"*Here lies poor Tom Bowling,*
The darling of our crew;
No more he'll hear the tempest howling,
For death has broached him to.
His form was of manliest beauty,
His heart was kind and soft.
Faithful below, Tom did his duty,
And now he has gone aloft."
Were that not sentiment enough, Lizzie closed with "The Lass That Loves a Sailor." She managed to finish without a sob, but it was a very close thing. During her bows, The Raptor crew passed the hat for their lady, then carried her round the jammed parade on their brawny shoulders. A violinist from the orchestra stepped forward and began to play "Heart of Oak," and as if it had been planned, the thousand men in the audience sang to her.
"*Come cheer up, my lads, 'tis to glory we steer*
To add something more to this wonderful year,
To honor we call you as freemen not slaves,
For who are so free as the sons of the waves."
There was no stopping Miss Trumpet's tears then.

"I am as proud as if I'd been made Admiral of the Blue," Irby confided. "No, prouder, by God." Still charged with excitement, the star of the evening and her entourage of two were alone at last in the salon of the Hotel Mediterranee.

"Charles, James, did you know David Garrick wrote 'Heart of Oak'? To think an actor wrote those words years ago, for a panto." Lizzie toasted her friends in the champagne they had insisted upon ordering. "Oh, that song...that song!" She was clinging to the halo of happiness that surrounded the night.

"Your tribute, madam, for an inspiring performance." Mangles dropped a heavy purse into her lap. "For our own British Nike, our own Winged Victory!"

Lizzie reached out to squeeze the hand of each man. "Oh, my dear, dear captains, with all my heart, I thank you for showing me so much of the world, and for this night. You have given me back my life." The choking truth of it came clear in her mind. *The ugly battle with Jack is behind me. My confidence, restored.... Thanks be to God...I am Elizabeth Trumpet once more....* "I insist you keep this purse. We will discuss the matter no further, and please, when it is quite convenient for you both...I am ready to go home."

Chapter Thirty-One

December 1814

THE NEW-planted plane trees along Duncan Terrace were shaking off their last leaves in the sharp breeze. Two horses pulling a hired coach trotted past a tall woman in brown traveling clothes walking from the Sign of the Angel. If Lizzie had looked up, she would have noticed the coach was filled with the very people she longed to see: Emily, flourishing a fur tippet, little Georgina under her first silk bonnet, Octavia, a few pounds heavier and more decidedly red-headed, Noddy in charge of a brazier of coals to warm their feet, and Miss Pegeen bundled under a mountain of rugs and wraps against the winter weather. Aunt Peg had demanded a drive around London to celebrate her eighty-fourth birthday.

Lizzie carried a set of mosaic buttons to give her for the occasion, packed in a sea bag along with a rag doll she had made herself for Georgina, and her precious watercolor pictures of the Mediterranean. She opened the heavy front door, expecting the place to be full of family, and was surprised to see not a soul. She shut the door and took a good deep breath of home. A ghost of bacon in the air drew her to the empty kitchen, where a Stilton cheese stood alone on the scrubbed table. Opening a cupboard for a plate, a thudding noise from the garden startled her. Peeking out the kitchen window, she saw the back of a fair-haired man throwing a knife at Aunt Peg's chopping block. Georgie!

"Brother, I'm home," Lizzie shouted and flew out the kitchen door to jump on his broad back, exactly as she had when they were children.

After this greeting, tempered with hugs and kisses of relief, Georgie demanded, "Where the devil have you been keeping yourself?"

"And why the devil are you out of uniform?" she answered with spirit.

"This is my last day of leave. Tomorrow, I rejoin Wellington's staff in Paris. Shall we go inside?"

"No, I like being out here with you. Let's have a good chin-wag like old times. Where is everybody?"

Georgie explained about Aunt Peg's outing. He had stayed behind to prepare for his journey to France. Lizzie wanted to tell the truth to the brother she'd always loved, and this was the first time in years, the siblings were alone together.

"I was not at a country house giving acting lessons to the richest man in England, whoever that may be, but I did give an acting lesson to Napoleon."

Georgie sat on the stump amazed, while Lizzie recounted her months at sea, the Mediterranean, the captains, her impressions of Elba's emperor, until he asked, "Where was your husband in all this?"

"I have parted from my husband, Georgie. I've loved him, he's full of talent and imagination, but he cannot imagine anyone better than himself. He's gone mad with jealousy of Edmund Kean and was taking my small success quite badly. The night of the Victory Celebration, after you left me at Vauxhall Gardens, Jack turned up savagely drunk. He gave me a round beating, struck at my throat, and...." She shivered. "Well, he was very rough. I was too hurt to sing. I could barely speak."

He bolted up. "If I had known this I would have called him out. I would have killed the...."

"Of course you would, and ruined your career. The captains found me, too bruised to be seen and afraid to go home, so they took me under their protection. I had no idea where I was going."

"Where is Faversham now?"

"It's over, Georgie. I'm not going back to him."

He stared at her fiercely. "Did those navy chaps treat you decently?"

"Yes, oh yes. Those two were on their mettle, believe me. I had such blue devils, Georgie, thinking I could never appear on a stage again. You need so much confidence to carry on in the theatre, and I had lost mine. Then Captain Mangles organized a benefit for me on Gibraltar, and I was able to sing again for the whole fleet, or it felt like the whole fleet. I made some money to repay the captains and.... Oh, Georgie, it's so good to see you. Can you forgive me for lying to you all?"

He embraced her for a long time. "For all you've been through, dear sister, I am so sorry. What would you like me to do now?"

Lizzie noticed Georgie's weapon, still embedded blade-deep in the old stump. *How handy for defense, should I ever....* "Teach me how to throw your knife."

"What?"

"Some day I might use it for a piece of stage business, when I act again." She shrugged. "It's a skill I could use. Really. Please, brother."

He eyed her with baffled admiration. "How unlike Emily you are. Very well. Hold the dagger thus. Soldiers call it a dirk, Lizzie. Throw it evenly without a jerk." He did so, striking the stump from two meters away. "See? It will spin, once in every meter. Now you try."

Lizzie took the weapon between her thumb and first finger. "Tell me what you think of Wellington while I practice."

"Oh, the general is a great commander who, like a mighty oak, casts a wide shade." Georgie paused and grew more serious. "But when the peace is finally hammered out, I'm going to sell my commission."

She pitched the dagger to see it bounce off target. "I thought you loved being a hussar."

"I'm done with it. I've seen battle and diplomacy up close and both are bloody hell, I can tell you. I've played a part. The general values me. As the new ambassador to France, he promises he'll set me up for life in a government post where I can serve England out of uniform. He's made me a diplomat, by Jupiter. One day soon I expect we will be going on to Vienna, where all the greedy governments are going to divide up the land and treasures of Europe." The flying dagger sank into the stump with a smack. "Ah, excellent! Now throw it that way again."

"Such wonderful expectations, yet you sound positively wretched."

"My God, Lizzie, all those dead men, millions of lives ruined and nothing settled."

"Not settled? We won a war."

"Yes, and the government and allies are all at loggerheads over Poland and Saxony. These monarchs and dozens of petty princes are just as greedy as your friend Napoleon."

"He's no friend of mine, Georgie."

"He must be bottled up for good. For the peace of the world, the tyrant must never rise again." Georgie marked an X on the stump with a stick. "Put it right there." Lizzie did. "Formidable minx! You've got it, done and dusted!"

"Tell me how you received that wound above your eye, brother?"

"A skirmish with French cavalry."

"What happened to the man who cut you?"

"I killed him." Georgie saw his sister's eyes widen, and added with more gentleness in his voice, "That is what soldiers do. War is murder on a grand scale."

"But it was your duty, not your nature." Lizzie handed him back the dagger. "I could never kill anyone."

"If Boney had invaded England, who's to say what you might have done? I've seen Spanish ladies fight like amazons to defend their families."

"I'd rather play Lady Macbeth than be her."

"And I'd rather stay home with my girls. I'm done with soldiering, sis. Once a year I'll go to Brighton for the regimental dinner, maybe play a game of skittles at the Grenadier with Ted Wentworth and that will be enough."

"Truly?"

"As a boy I wanted to be more of a man than I thought Papa was. Such youthful blindness. I was mistaken in everything. Whatever I was proving to myself, at least I served England and I'm proud of that."

"Thank you for caring for me when we were sprouts, brother. Papa was gone so often, a slave to his work in the theatre; Mama was heartsick and far away in her mind, but you were always here. You included me in your life. I played at warfare like a boy because you wanted to be a soldier." Eyebrows raised, she gave him a wry look. "That was the only reason Dibdin hired me, you know, because of the fencing."

Charmed by her lack of vanity, he laughed. "Not because of your beauty or your courage?"

"No indeed. There are always pretty girls who are desperate and daring. It was the fencing that made me special." Her throat closed up with emotion.

"And now you're learning to throw a blade, by Jupiter. Let's go inside and have a glass of Christmas cheer to celebrate your homecoming. It's too cold to stay out here with the chickens."

In the kitchen, they warmed themselves by the banked stove fire. Georgie opened a bottle of port. "Emily and I have been working very hard on making a brother for Georgina. My wife is the best girl in the world, Lizzie. She loves you, too. Soon I'll finish my duties for the king, then no more wars for the Trumpets, real or theatrical." He poured two glasses full and put one in his sister's hand with a flourish saying, "I see the future clearly now."

"Do you, Georgie? Tell me what you see."

"You'll live here with us and be welcome forever. I'll support my girls in style. You will never be saddled with Faversham again. If you wish to be the busiest actress in England you may, or if you chose, you can just lie about Longsatin House, watching Aunt Peg petrify and my children grow up. What do you think of that?"

"I think it will be wonderful brother. Let us drink a toast to home and beauty." Their glasses touched with a merry ring.

"To home and beauty!"

Chapter Thirty-Two

Late December 1814

PHILLIP EGGLESTON was enjoying chops "hot and hot" at the Shakespeare's Head Tavern, off the busy piazza of Covent Garden. The wintry air had quickened his delicate appetite, and he chewed rapidly with his eyes fixed on the plate. This usually discouraged opportunistic actors from sliding up to his table for a keep-me-in-mind encounter, but not always.

"Eggs, you old sodomite, how goes the battle?"

Lifting his exquisitely pomaded head, the sixty-four-year-old manager beheld an insouciant Jack Faversham, dressed in last season's black velvet coat, a bit shiny at the back and stained at the cuffs.

"My calendar is full," Eggleston said dismissively, without getting up. "And yourself?"

Nonchalantly, Jack sat down uninvited as Eggleston wearily wiped his mouth on a napkin. Ignoring the cold reception, Faversham plunged in. "I hear they're doing *The Duke and the Devil* at that little Majesty's Theatre in Richmond. I've worked up some clever new twists on the Duke, and am available to play him again." He motioned to the pot boy in his long apron for a pint of ale. "I was a terror in that, remember?"

"Terror, yes. I've been hearing that word associated with you a good deal of late, Jack."

"What? Fined for farting in the Drury Lane green-room?" Jack shrugged. "You're joking, of course."

"I am not. In *The Dark Tower*, you nearly put out Dick Wilson's eye."

"The old comic made a great story of it, Eggs. He'll dine out on it for years. The important thing is I set a new style of realistic drama that thrilled the customers, left them absolutely panting for more."

"It was the prompter's wife you left panting, and the company at each other's throats." Eggleston picked up his fork, with a hard look at the actor he believed was behaving like an adolescent brute. "Consider, Dick Wilson is beloved by his peers and the whole of London. Do you think anyone is going to take your part? Word has it that Jack Faversham no longer knows his lines, ignores the rules of backstage behavior, and is recklessly rough onstage. What do you say to that?"

"I say I'm the best actor in England, as you very well know." Jack crossed a leg, accepted his ale from the pot boy and took a long pull at his glass. "Truly, nothing is more dependable than jealousy."

Eggleston had heard such blather before and did not pursue it. "Where are you hiding your Lizzie these days? She missed contracted performances and has just disappeared. I've heard nothing of her for months."

"Nor I." Jack shook his head. "She may have joined the great mystery, for all I know. What a waste of my training. But she was only a supporting player."

Eggleston started back at the heartlessness of Jack's remark. "Too bad you feel that way. She was just coming into her glory days, and the two of you made a formidable partnership."

Jack licked the ale from his lips and cocked a black eyebrow at Eggleston. "Who can understand women?"

"Well, *The Duke and the Devil* is cast, Jack. More to the point, you have earned an odious reputation, certainly not the one I planned for you." Faversham opened his mouth to speak, but little Eggleston cut him off sharply. "You are unemployable in London, unless you are ready to beg for minor parts. I doubt you could stomach being a torch-bearer for Edmund Kean. His looks and style are similar to yours and, sorry to say, he has surpassed you. Of course, our ties were severed long ago, and you haven't asked my advice in years, but for your wife's sake, I will make this suggestion." The elegant manager wiped the grease off his fingers, and threw down his napkin. "Stop playing the villain in life if you ever wish to play one again onstage."

January 1815

Lizzie settled into the scroll-armed chair in Eggleston's salon, where the furnishings were smart and small in scale. The manager himself reminded her of a watch-fob. He had listened to her account of the night at Vauxhall Gardens with no comment. In hopes he could find her work out of London despite the closing in of another bleak winter, she finally brought up the subject that could not be avoided.

"What do you know of Jack these days? I can hardly expect to never cross paths with him, if we are working in the same business."

Eggleston had welcomed her back enthusiastically, feasting his esthetic taste on her beautiful slender face, the enormous eyes like jewels beneath her wing-shaped brows. *A face made for drama with a persona at ease in comedy...what a creature.* He asked shrewdly, "Are you going to divorce him, Elizabeth? You should, you know."

"No. I don't have the money or influence to go through the courts for a proper divorce. But, I will never live with him again. I want to make my own way as an actress. You understand, don't you, Phillip?"

"Perfectly. And, I must say, this is the time to be free of Jack, if you seriously want to act again. It is to your advantage you never took his name."

"He was loath to share it. His wish for singular fame was ferocious."

"Whether you're aware of it, his mercurial reputation has made him an outcast to the theatre community. He is feared for his violence and bullying. No company will hire him. And with all the drunken geniuses and curious behavior our profession excuses, that is saying a lot."

"Poor Jack," Lizzie reflected, looking at the collections of plays filling a glass-faced cabinet. "He is the assassin of his own renown."

"What?"

"I quote *Pizarro*."

"Ah. We can be grateful you never picked up his habits. I took him up from a tribe of thieves and turned him into an actor. He was a beautiful boy then, with a great ear for speech and a talent for dissembling."

"I know his seductive charms, Phillip," Lizzie said levelly, thinking how she and this man had both enjoyed Jack as a lover, and what a unique experience it had been.

"Quite." Reading her meaning, he paused. "Well, to let you know, he approached me a few weeks ago, looking much the worse for wear and talking a lot of cocky nonsense. I set him straight. Since then I've seen and read nothing of Jonathan Faversham. If his money has run out, I'm guessing he's returned to the criminal life, using his skill at disguise."

"Oh, dear God."

"So, you are a leading lady again," said Octavia, carrying Lizzie's soaking wet half-boots to dry out by the fire. "Shall we all throw flowers and make a great to-do?"

"I'm to be a leading lady in Cornwall." She reached for a cup off the mahogany dining table, where her family gathered round the teapot to learn the outcome of her meeting with Eggleston. "Philip has found places I can work immediately." Grateful beyond words for the chance to act again, she tasted her tea with thirsty pleasure. "And, if that means being the toast of faraway Worms Head or Great Grimsby, so be it."

"Your work is your salvation," Aunt Peg piped up. Sitting amongst them, she could hear very little of the conversation, but had guessed the cause of Lizzie's lightheartedness. The soon-to-be-employed actress hugged her ancient aunt and cheerfully passed the sugar bowl to the full-blown rose of a woman across the table.

"Octavia, darling, do you think I'm too old to play innocent maidens?"

"Worry not," the expert laughed, "you can still pass for one and twenty, in the dusk with the light behind you."

"We were just getting accustomed to your face around the house again; we shall miss you so," put in Emily, pouring milk for little Georgina from the earthenware jug decorated with figures of a soldier and his sweetheart sadly parting, above the motto "Love Subservient to Glory."

Lizzie mulled over the sentiment. It spoke of all the Englishmen who left home to fight for country, for something greater than themselves. And then there was Jack, who got it all wrong. Nothing was subservient to Jack's glory. *The man I loved is now despised, perhaps a criminal.*

She tapped a fingernail against the milkjug, her mind drifting out of the ladies' conversation. She shivered, despite the warmth of the room. *Pray God, I never meet him again.*

February 1815

"Now Emily, you must pass on every scrap of Georgie's news from Vienna. Write each day, and I'll do the same when I'm not rehearsing or performing for those barbarously accented Cornishmen."

"Every day," replied Emily. "Depend on it, dear."

Lizzie supervised Noddy, who was hoisting her portmanteau to the top of the great diligence. In the confusion of the Sign of the Angel inn-yard, he had almost forgotten to see her belongings securely tied to the heavy public coach. For the third time, the inside passengers rearranged themselves, but the beautiful actress in tawny brown wool always was positioned at a window seat. The still-devoted and helpful street-sweeper Simon had seen to it.

An idler watched the spectacle of departure from the third gallery of the Angel. This fellow did a great deal of watching these days: Visitors to London, lost and vulnerable in the traffic of nine hundred thousand souls, drunken dandies staggering out of their elegant clubs, decidedly inelegant as they vomited in the street, ladies in pairs, stepping aside the importuning vendors, beggars, and ragged children running errands for adults. The idler knew where people went, what they did and what they had. The street was his theatre these days, where he made a comedy of theft, a drama of assault.

When the coach made its way out of the inn yard heading west, Peg, Emily, Octavia and little Georgina all waved madly to the departing actress. To the bleating of the long copper coach horn, Lizzie threw kisses to her family, not noticing the idler tipping his hat to her, a fine silk hat from Lock's of St. James's Street, now rather spattered, dirty and worn.

Chapter Thirty-Three

February 25, 1815

*D*EAREST LIZZIE, beloved sister-in-law,

How unfortunate that you are wrestling with the elements in faraway Chester. There is plenty of winter here, too. Father Thames has frozen solid, and ice on the river is thick enough for a Frost Fair. Georgina and I went out with Noddy to see the marvel. The hawkers set up booths that stretch from bank to bank, which makes it remarkable. Someone was roasting an ox, which, though my stomach is settling down, I dared not partake of. Aunt Peg orders me to brew strange possets for my health. She sleeps much of the time now, and when she wakes, worries about all of us. Georgina chatters in her baby language every moment. The great news is that God has blessed me and Georgie again. I am happy to announce soon another little Trumpet will be tooting around Longsatin House.

Roger Sloane writes that your grandparents in Charleston thrive, having survived the war between England and America unscathed. He sent his particular greetings to you. His wife Susannah has livened Roger's days in America with her bright manners and domestic command. I read between the lines that he is happy as a new husband can be.

Lord Dampere has visited Octavia twice this month. She bids me tell you this has to do with a new business, not her old one. His lordship is looking for productive occupations to fill his time. She says he's realized a gentleman can have other pursuits besides gambling, gossip, or racing his caleche. With his usual enthusiasm, he asked about your performing in what he called "the hinterlands."

Carlo has signed a contract with the Royal Opera. He will be coaching all the hot-tempered Italians and doing some conducting, as well. This means he will need to move his lodgings back into the city. He also found a friend in one of the singers there, a Mr. Grey. They will be sharing rooms to save on expenses. Mr. Grey is a jolly Irish tenor. I have never seen Carlo so happy.

We are saving the Gazette and Journal articles you sent from Exeter and the small towns in Cornwall. Such fine things they wrote about you in The Rivals. I'm decorating a box with spool-work to keep your clippings in.

George arrived on February third at the Congress of Vienna. Wellington has replaced Lord Castlereagh as England's lead delegate, a powerful responsibility. My husband believes old Louis the Eighteenth has no ability to heal France. The diplomats spend most of their hours at balls, dallying with diamond-covered ladies hosted by diamond-encrusted heads of state. He writes they dither about protocol rather than making a just peace. The abolition of slavery, freedom of the press, and the rights of Jews are all topics the Congress is wrangling over. Who would have guessed?

I'm sure George isn't able to tell me half of it. Wellington cannot spare him yet, but I dream he will be home in time for my lying-in. If I have a boy, what do you think of the name Arthur? George tells me it is a military custom to *name a son after his father's commander.*

Thank you for the gifts, but your presence is more precious than any monies, Lizzie. I miss your good company. Come home to us soon.

Your ever-loving sister,
Emily Trumpet

March 1815

Lizzie was delighted to be playing Thomas Otway's *Venice Preserved*. Everything in Chester was delighting: The spacious theatre, new friends amongst the actors, walking the old walls and attending services in the beautiful cathedral.

The local company's style had been *competitive histrionics*, unguided by anything but precedent. After years of working together, it was every man for himself. The actors were committed to attention-grabbing nonsense that had nothing to do with the text. Rather than complain about such unprofessionalism, or try to change it with a brutal critique, as Jack would have done, Miss Trumpet ignored their *improvements*, devoted herself to the truth of the play, never complained and treated everyone with respect. The cast came to love her.

For the first time, Jack was not directing her performances. Lizzie thought much of her father, who always said "the audience tells you true from false." She acted as she felt, and felt more than ever before in her life. In the pure air of her selfless devotion to the play, members of the cast gradually let go of their mannered habits just to keep up with her.

March 17, 1815
Phillip Eggleston
Eggleston Theatricals, London
Dear Phillip,

I wish to thank you for the engagements you have made possible. I know the London season is bright with new plays and fine actors, yet I cannot imagine a more rewarding experience than acting Venice Preserved *in frozen old Chester. I will travel anywhere to continue doing such work. Yes, anywhere. If you hear of Mister Faversham, I hope it isn't in the criminal courts.*

Wishing you continued prosperity,
Elizabeth Trumpet

March 17, 1815
Dear Roger,
News of you has reached me through Emily. I am touring again, living the life of an unmarried actress. Do you shudder at the thought? Of our old trio, two playmates made fine matches, and mine unraveled completely. Nevertheless, I am happy, alone with my art. Rest assured my reputation is blameless. I remember that concerned you deeply when I first stepped on the stage, and how angry your interest made me. I have lived a bit since those uncertain days, and believe your concern for my welfare was driven by affection. I thank you for it now, and should have then. I wish you every happiness, Roger, and the blessings of an honorable life whose foundation is built on love. Perhaps one day when we are crisscrossing the world we will meet for a fine catch-up.

May I give a bit of "sisterly" advice to a newly married man? Praise your Susannah for making you so happy. A woman yearns for the reassurance she is loved, in words as well as deeds. I rejoice that you are content, and wish you what I wish for Georgie, a home full of children for me to visit and spoil. But, for the nonce, I must be off to rehearsal.

Your own,
Lizzie

❧

March 30, 1815
Dearest Carlo,

Are you finding all those divas to your taste? We are hardly doing music on such a grand scale here in Ipswich. In Shakespeare's Othello, *I do make the most of "The Willow Song." As Desdemona, I pour my heart into that. I warm up in my dressing room with "Caro mio ben," to remind myself of you and me working at the pianoforte in Longsatin House. Sometimes I change the words to "Carlo mio ben." Ha-ha! Does your Mr. Grey appreciate the personal coaching you are giving him? Enjoy the music you make together.*

I had the most extraordinary experience doing George Colman's The Wags of Windsor *last week. These bits of comic fluff are unfailingly popular on provincial stages. One must do the lighter properties to keep the theatres open, don't we know? But to tell my story: in Act Two, when I am alone onstage, there is a droll bit of business with a key that should raise a laugh. However, no matter how I played it, emphasizing it or throwing it away, no one got the joke. The business was set at downstage left. On one particular night, as the moment approached, I felt something, something like the presence of a person, pushing me downstage right, directing me gently as a ballet master would set a dancer in position. Well, I got the laugh. Was some ghost of an actor helping me? My father, perhaps? It made me feel less lonely, and strangely loved.*

Speaking of love, I have not sought a replacement for Jack. Eager fellows offer their devotion for a night or even the length of an engagement, but though the fashionable world thinks nothing of it, I refuse to become so casually entangled. Consequently, I am chaste. I don't think the rapture I felt with Jack will ever happen to me again. Such passion came at a great cost, and there are other delights in life. Certainly to be a free woman, working on her art is a great joy. The price is loneliness. The reward, peace. Who but you could completely understand, dear friend?

A gentleman from the Royal Theatre Bath was in the house last night and, following the performance, treated me to an oyster supper. He may be only an enthusiast, but vowed to recommend me, with no wrestling in the blankets required. Joining the company at Bath would be a leap-up in prestige. I never speak of possible engagements until they happen, as you taught me, but if the offer does come, I shall write you first of any.

How I long to see you.

Addio,

Lizzie

April 1815

Elizabeth Trumpet was announced to play the title role in *Jane Shore* at the Royal Theatre Bath. The old Roman spa town had a discerning population, the most discerning outside London. People of wealth enjoyed the wonderful new architecture of the Royal Crescent, the socially polarizing gatherings in the assembly rooms, and the theatre most of all. The fashionable audiences of Bath could make a star of an actor but to fail there was to fail indeed.

The eighteenth-century drama by Nicholas Rowe was the greatest test for a dramatic actress of the day. The historical Jane had been torn from her husband and forced to become the mistress of King Edward the Fourth. His rival, the Duke of Gloucester, accused her of witchcraft, and she was condemned to be outcast until death. In soaring poetry, the playwright depicted Shore as a woman of honor, unjustly punished. The plum part required a marathon of emotion only a gifted actress dared attempt.

Lizzie prepared, rehearsing with the company and alone every waking moment, thinking of nothing else, sustaining herself with the stomach-filling buns from the Sally Lund Tea Shop, and pot after pot of strong tea. She was making her own acting choices, and fear of failure haunted her.

Opening night, Lizzie's nerves quite paralyzed her when the prompter rapped on her dressing room door. The backstage veteran had seen such hesitancy in overworked leading ladies before. Brooking no nonsense, he picked Lizzie up like a piece of scenery and carried her to the side of the stage.

Once she was set down in the wings, blocking her way was, of all people, Frederick, Lord Dampere. "Octavia advised me this night could be a turning point for you, Lizzie," he hastened to say, perspiring in his black evening clothes and spilling over with delight in the situation. "So, I have brought my old Eton boys from our *Belle Sauvage* days to cheer you on. We can't wait to see your Jane. So very proud." He kissed her icy hand. "This is your dream, is it not? Now, my dear, show them how it's done."

Her knees shaking and eyes about to overflow, "Oh, Dampie," was all Lizzie could manage to say.

"Please, my lord, we really must begin," the prompter intruded firmly, and hustled Dampere's large presence away.

In their long medieval robes and towering headdresses, the cast clustered about nervously, anxious to begin. A string ensemble throbbed the first passage of dramatic music, and the curtain rose. The corrupt Duke of Gloucester strode on. Lizzie tensed, but as her cue was spoken, she inhaled opportunity, remembered she was William Trumpet's daughter, and entered with a firm step.

The audience appraised the actress, giving her beauty and dignity the attention it demanded. What she had learned from William, Jack, Carlo, and even Mr. Pickle, was in her bones, framing the perfection of her own choices. Smoothly, the plot moved forward, every nuance heightened by her performance. At center stage, she spoke the lines all female hearts could understand.

"Mark by what partial justice we are judg'd;
That Man, the lawless libertine, may rove,
Free and unquestion'd through the wilds of love;

While Woman, sense and nature's easy fool,
If poor weak Woman swerve from virtue's rule—
If, strongly charm'd, she leave the thorny way,
And in the softer paths of pleasure stray,
Ruin ensues, reproach and endless shame,
And one false step entirely damns her fame;
In vain with tears the loss she may deplore,
In vain look back on what she was before;
She sets, like stars that fall, to rise no more."

By Act Three the audience was so moved, they sat quietly through the interval, hardly talking. Everyone in the theatre realized this was a rare night, when actors and audience experience the drama as one.

By the last scene—Jane's death scene—the audience was wholly with her. Lizzie had drained the cup of tragedy, lifting her hands to heaven in prayer.

"'Tis very dark, and I have lost you now;
Was there not something I would have bequeathed you?
But I have nothing left me to bestow,
Nothing but one sad sigh. Oh! Mercy, heaven!"

Members of the orchestra wept as they played the final cadence, and the curtain fell to a hushed silence. Everyone there wanted to keep the memory in their hearts forever, and did not dare to shatter the spell. Lord Dampere finally rose to his feet and began to applaud, joined lustily by the Etonians, then by every living soul in the audience. When Lizzie stepped through the curtains to receive her ovation, her heart was beating high.

Chapter Thirty-Four

May 1815

MAJOR GEORGE Trumpet had been right about Bonaparte. Napoleon escaped Elba and made straight for France. Once the daring general was back on French soil, the army was dispatched to recapture him. Face to face with his veterans of the Imperial Guard, Napoleon ordered them to fire on him or "salute their Emperor." As if in an opera, those veterans burst into sentimental tears, threw down their guns, and embraced the bloody-minded tyrant who had given them so many victories. How frighteningly theatrical, Lizzie observed, when she read of it.

The war recommenced. European armies reshuffled themselves to march against Bonaparte, and the Royal Tenth Hussars were again assigned to Wellington. Emily received word from her husband in Antwerp that a decisive battle was expected soon.

June 1815

Clasping her bonnet to her head, Lizzie ran down Duncan

Terrace, calling out to Longsatin House before anyone could possibly hear her, "Emily! Aunt Peg! It's over! The battle is won!"

Emily's pregnant, billowing figure appeared at an upstairs window. "Lizzie, you're home from Bath?"

Lizzie stopped in the street to call up to her. "I just arrived at the Angel, and a coachman gave us the news. A smashing victory!" Windows opened all over the street as neighbors leaned out to catch the wonderful words. "Napoleon's *Grande Armée* was crushed at some place called Waterloo!"

Emily dashed down the stairs and into the lane, carrying Georgina in her arms. Lizzie embraced them, so very glad to be home. Their lives had been framed by nineteen years of war, fear and conflict—now ended. The English women cried with relief and clung with joy. Maria Mantino and a gaggle of children joined Lizzie. The little ones began spinning each other in circles and shouting. The bells of St Mary's Church rang and rang.

The Trumpet household was serving tea and cake to Carlo in the grey salon. On his weekly visits to the ladies, the round musician always brought a basket of delicacies from Gunter's. Aunt Peg had called for music from Thomas Moore's *Songbook of Irish Melodies*, and Carlo's friend Mr. Grey complied with a tune that showed off his lyric tenor.

"The Minstrel Boy to the wars has gone,
In the ranks of death you'll find him;
His father's sword he has girded on,
And his wild harp slung behind him."

Emily held the letter Georgie had sent from Flanders a few days before. He was with Wellington, and the women expected to hear more any hour. The window's afternoon sunlight passed through the pages, making the letter glow like a living thing. As Mr. Grey sang on, Octavia answered a knock at the door.

"Mrs. George Mario Trumpet?" the soldier on the doorstep asked.

"This is her home."

He presented a letter, saluted, and clicked his heels. Not staying to meet her eyes, he hurried back to his mount and cantered away.

"A letter has come," Octavia said, joining the circle of friends with the bit of paper in her shaking hand. Emily reached for it. The music stopped. Emily tore at the envelope and read aloud.

> *19 June 1815*
> *Dear Madam,*
>
> *In the final moments of the Waterloo Battle, at approximately 7 p.m. yesterday, near Plancenoit, Flanders, Emperor Bonaparte's Imperial Guard fiercely attacked my position. Round-shot from French guns quickly cut down four of my staff.*
>
> *Major George M. Trumpet, with the utmost gallantry, thrust himself between the point of fire and myself, thereby taking a ball meant for me, his commander. Know that Major Trumpet died bravely and instantly in an act of supreme heroism and sacrifice for his country. Know also that no soldier ever distinguished himself more highly.*
>
> *I cannot express to you the regret and sorrow with which I look round me and contemplate the loss which I have sustained, particularly in your husband, who had been at my side every day for six years. The glory so dearly bought is no consolation to me.*
>
> *I am sorely grieved,*
> *Arthur Wellesley, Duke of Wellington*

Emily collapsed in Lizzie's arms. The women sobbed as Peg began to keen and wail.

Carlo closed the lid of the pianoforte and quietly slipped out the door with Mr. Grey. They wandered slowly towards the New River, the leaves of the young plane trees shimmering green and yellow above them. Carlo thought aloud, "Those ladies must face whatever comes without their protector now. Napoleon's Armageddon has taken away their future."

July 1815

It may be Georgie's love was more dreamed of than experienced, but it had sustained Emily through loneliness and uncertainty. To Miss Pegeen, he was forever the good and beautiful boy, forgiven every mischief. To Lizzie, he was the steady, loving brother she could trust and be proud of in every circumstance. To Georgina and the baby soon to come, he was father, the source of their existence.

Ted Wentworth delivered her husband's sword to Emily, with the engraved gold watch from his grandfather, and a small military chest of his personals, now so very precious. Wentworth had watched his friend die, on the open rolling pastures of Waterloo, along with his English comrades by the thousand.

The ladies made a shrine to Major Trumpet on the wall by William's chair. In the center was the watercolor Lizzie had painted of her handsome brother in his dress-blue uniform, his blond hair perhaps a bit more wavy than in life. His medals, so dearly won, and the battle-scarred sword hung above it. His violin and bow rested in silence. Emily had included Wellington's letter in the shrine. She kept her husband's last message in a silk envelope worn against her heart. "All my love to my precious girls."

On the night Octavia first lit a candle under the portrait, Aunt Peg quietly said a rosary before Georgie's image. She asked the little family to help her to bed, announcing, "I need to rest, my darlin's."

As Lizzie put a glass of water at the bedside, her Aunt Peg reached for her niece with a frail old hand, so worn in the care of others. The heart of love was in her eyes. "May the Lord bless you and keep you, Lizzie dear, and make his face to shine upon you."

For two days, Peg did not move or drink, but slumbered deeply, once calling out, "Georgie, come back inside and leave those chickens be!" Later she murmured, "Jessie, darlin', don't cry and spoil your pretty eyes. He'll be home soon. You'll see." Her breath slowed.

Before dawn on Sunday, in the strong voice of her younger days, she spoke one last time. "She's going to sing and dance at the Sadler's Wells! Our Lizzie! Won't that be the finest thing?"

Sobbing with a grief sharper than any before, Lizzie watched the last soul who knew her from the beginning slip away, through St. Mary's graveyard, to a greater world.

Chapter Thirty-Five

August 1815

*D*EAR *LIZZIE*,

My deepest sympathy surrounds you. The days that have passed since I heard of Georgie's death have not diminished my shock or sorrow, and for the loss of Miss Pegeen as well, a person no less dear to me. Would you put a flower on her grave in my name?

Feelings overwhelm me, as though I too have lost a brother; my heart tells me, if love and loyalty count for anything, I have. As a lad, growing up, Georgie was my ideal, always so strong and fearless, full of liveliness and generosity of spirit to me. So like yourself, Lizzie. He was the rising sun of my imagination, the man I wanted to emulate, but could never hope to match. He lived and died a true hero.

I am filled with concern for his widow Emily. How are you all getting on at Longsatin House? I can imagine the sadness of a fatherless family. Susannah and I have been blessed with our first child, a fine son. In our joy, we have named him William. My dear wife and I hold the Trumpet household in our prayers. Know that you are not alone in grief, though an ocean separates us. When you are able,

please write.
   Your friend of old,
   Roger Sloane

Lizzie folded the letter from America, glad to know her family was remembered with such love. Roger's words gave her comfort. Gazing out her bedroom window to watch a morning breeze stir the leaves of the old oak, she felt close to him, closer than she could have imagined when they played in its branches years ago.

That morning, a pair of females spread across Jack Faversham, enduring what remained of his vigor in the act of love. The trio occupied a dark and rotting room above Ave Maria Alley by St. Paul's. They had been at it since midnight. If the women had been dressed, they might have been described as blowsy tarts, but they were merely naked, slippery wet objects with openings for Jack to stuff.

The slight girl serviced him standing against the moldy wall, a "three-penny upright," while the heavy-breasted one awaited her turn to ride on Jack's unsatisfied penis. He roughly shook the derriere of the girl who grunted and gasped as he pounded away. The one on the floor sat up and bit his buttock. When he pulled out to change partners, Jack's member was dripping. He hadn't bothered with a lambskin sheath, or a linen one, or any armor at all.

Times had changed for Faversham. No one knew him by that name. No one knew him at all, for he went about in clever disguises, making his living as a thief and thug. Jack's hair had thinned, and a rash troubled his privates, but disappeared after a dosing of mercury and arsenic pills. His sexual conquests were no longer the belles of society or the fresh beauties of the theatre, but the lowest whores of the streets. These two cost him practically nothing. They were business acquaintances who had never stepped into a theatre in their brief, brutal lives.

Faversham squeezed the breasts of the fleshy one, battering deep into her well-worn interior. He still believed himself the greatest of cocksmen—the man he had always been. The disease he had picked up, when returning to his old life, he willed himself to ignore. More tormenting were his thoughts of the past. Remembering a certain face and body made his climax surge to a shuddering explosion. His eyes rolled up in his head.

"Aaaaahh...Lizzie!"

Boozel's granddaughter lowed with relief as Lizzie set to the task she had performed so often as a child—pulling a cow's teats and watching the warm milk splash into a clean pail. Little Georgina, wearing a pink ribbon, tumbled about outside the shed, talking baby gibberish to the fascinating chickens behind their fence, just as her father used to do. Noddy bent over the lettuces, knees crusted with black soil, weeding in the vegetable patch with a trowel.

Lizzie hoped for acting work in London soon. Edmund Kean was launching his second season at Drury Lane in the fall. She wanted employment there, but needed some way to be presented for an audition that was neither too forward, nor too humble to be considered.

The arrival of Emily's baby was imminent. That morning, the mother-to-be had awakened with a rush of housekeeping energy. "Let's have a go at those windows," the pretty widow suggested and commenced to polish away with vinegar and vigor on every pane of glass in Longsatin House.

When Lizzie compared her brother's marriage to her own, common sense told her she had come up short. As a wife, Emily had been loved and had a daughter to prove it, perhaps a son, too, if God was kind. Emily could face widowhood knowing that, though their time together had been brief, her husband had been the best of men.

Faversham was another kettle of fish. Lizzie feared she would meet him in the street every time she left the house. *I ran away from him, and he deserted me, but we are married still,* Lizzie mused as she worked, enjoying the sounds of Georgina's laughter. *One thing Jack was steadfast in, never giving me a child.* Instead, he molded her into what she wanted to be, a true actress. *Now I'm left to my own devices. Well, the stage must sustain me.*

"I will shower Emily and her children with love, and everything they desire, if I make some money," Lizzie whispered to the family cow. "And I shall love them always, just as if they were my own children. What do you say to that, madame?" She slapped the square bovine rump for emphasis.

Out of the corner of her eye, she saw something fall from a second story window at the back of the house. Running into the yard, she found Emily's earthenware bowl of vinegar broken on the ground. She set down the milk pail and flew into the house, taking the stairs two at a time to find her full-blown sister-in-law standing at her bedroom window in the middle of a great puddle, like a ship on the sea.

"Oh! You gave me such a fright. I see you've just spilled the cleaning water. I'll mop it up directly." Lizzie turned to get more rags.

"I would prefer that you first send for Mrs. Sewell. That's my water on the floor," she hiccuped. "The baby is coming."

Lizzie rushed to the window, yelling down to Noddy, grubbing in the garden. "Go fetch the midwife! And be quick about it!" He trotted off, seeking beyond the boundary of his usual excursions, became hopelessly lost, and failed to find the redoubtable Mrs. Sewell. When he stumbled home to tell Lizzie of his circular adventure, she sent him off again, frantically this time.

Lizzie put Emily to bed, watching her thrash in a quick volley of labor pains. The veins of her neck corded like ropes with effort; she gasped, moaned, and still had the grace to tell Lizzie not to fear. After an hour, the actress knew no help was coming. Do or die, the delivery was up to her.

Georgina had crawled up the stairs crying at her mother's distress. Told in urgent tones to be quiet and sit still, she watched big-eyed from her little blue chair as Lizzie followed Emily's panted orders.

Before there was time to talk about it, the baby's head was crowning. Emily pushed, Lizzie pulled and, in a gush of bloody fluid, a new child slid into the world—a healthy, reddish boy. Lizzie cut the cord with Georgie's dagger and tied it off. With shaking hands, she wiped the tiny person clean and set the treasure in his mother's arms. Lizzie cried, telling Emily how magnificent she was. Georgina saw it all, amazed her mother had been keeping a baby brother under her apron. The three females rhapsodized over the infant, kissing his fingers and toes, admiring his wondering eyes and round pink mouth.

"Like a rosebud," his mother said. "Our son is Georgie's last gift to me." She looked in Lizzie's happy flushed face. "To all of us."

Hours later, when Noddy at last hoisted a distraught and breathless Mrs. Sewell up the stairs, they found Emily, serene, lying in a clean bed, her arms encircling two little ones, and Lizzie cuddled protectively beside them all.

"Well." Mrs. Sewell crossed her arms over her spreading bosom to look at the flummoxed Noddy accusingly. "Well, I don't know, I'm sure."

⌒૭

"Kean, isn't it? Savior of the Royal Theatre Drury Lane?"

Edmund Kean, in the Shakespeare's Head tap room for a solitary fortification of alcohol between breakfast and rehearsal, turned his head. "Sir?"

"I've been a happy observer of all your triumphs on stage these past months. I am Phillip Eggleston, of Eggleston Theatricals."

"Ah yes, of course." Kean smiled slightly and returned to his liquid solace.

Eggleston's lodgings overlooked the local watering-hole. Many a morning, he had spied the most popular actor in London, slipping in like the eel he resembled for a quick bracer. Today, the showman hoped Kean's thirst was going to be Lizzie's opportunity. Out of affection for her, and the old desire to put Jack in his place, he had plotted this chance encounter. "I give you joy of the success of your *Richard the Third.* You breathe such vivid life into the poetry of Shakespeare."

"And, best of all," Kean confided matter-of-factly, "the Lane will turn a profit next week. I shall be famous and rich. Rich, at last, after knocking about for a lifetime out of town. Now my son will go to Eton!" The man's words rang with pleasure, his skin exuding the juniper perfume of frequently imbibed gin.

"A blessing on your head, Edmund," said Eggleston, in the unreserved manner of friendliness peculiar to theatre folk. He called to the proprietor. "Guillam, another bumper for Mr. Kean and a tot of sherry for me."

Kean bobbed his head with tempered gratitude. "A neighborly gesture."

"I am a neighbor, as a matter of fact. From my window, I can see both Drury Lane and this happy establishment." He checked his cuff for lint. "Edmund, I know of an actress who would add a breath of air and light to your company."

"A niece of yours perhaps? Or a particular friend?"

"No, no, nothing of the kind. An accomplished professional. Her talent could never match yours, of course, but together the two of you could strike sparks."

"Have I seen this Ariel onstage?" His brow wrinkled with only tepid interest.

"I'm speaking of Elizabeth Trumpet."

"Oh, Jack Faversham's delicious wife. 'Winged Victory' she was called, or something of the sort. Yes, of course, I know her."

"You have announced Hamlet for next season." Eggleston looked Kean straight in the face, daring a direct approach. "She would make a memorable Ophelia."

"She's a bit luscious for what I have in mind for my Ophelia. She's a gifted singer, but her forte is comedy, I believe."

"Her beginnings were the illegitimate theatre, I grant you—burlettas, harlequinades." The pot-boy delivered their drinks. The older man hastened to put down coins from his waistcoat pocket. "If I recall correctly, your first important role was a skin part in *The Monkey, the Monk and the Murderer*."

Kean had to laugh at that. "Good of you to remember. Yes, I was the cleverest of apes in my little fur suit. Captain Jocko ate his heart out over me."

"My point is one must begin somewhere," pressed Eggleston,

raising his glass to Kean and taking a sip, "if you haven't seen Trumpet of late, you can't imagine the honesty she brings onstage."

"Can't I?" Kean's black eyes half closed. His foot beat nervously over a crossed leg.

"She's been doing classic drama in the northern counties this year, had some drama in her real life, too. To put it squarely, she is finally shot of Faversham. The managers of every theatre she's played write me pages about her new style, how she puts the companies on their toes, how audiences weep and cheer. Her *Jane Shore* in Bath was extraordinary. I saw it. She is unlike any other."

Kean's glance darted impatiently towards the theatre across the piazza. "Isn't Trumpet rather tall? When I gave the victory ode at Wellington's celebration, I noticed her on the platform. She was somewhat majestic."

"That was merely the fashionable attire, plumes and high heels," Eggleston lied. "She stands just to your brow."

"Very well, but I promise nothing." Kean stood up. "Send her by to read with me." Speaking in a cautionary way, he added, "If she impresses...well...."

"Her acting is something to relish," Eggleston quickly put in.

"Then perhaps, sir, I might spread her across my...*ham*...*let*," joked Kean. The compact actor downed his gin, grabbed his hat off its peg, and touching index finger to brim in a gesture of parting, made his exit.

Eggleston toasted himself with the dregs of his drink, satisfied. Lizzie's triumph was assured.

Chapter Thirty-Six

January 1816

THE POPULAR cartoon by Gillray of a slender dark-haired Kean carrying a theatre on his back had been framed to hang in the tap room of the Shakespeare's Head. The star was the greatest attraction of the day. All over London, broadsheets announced: "Tonight at Drury Lane Mr. Edmund Kean as...Hamlet, son to the late, and nephew to the present king." Listed farther down in the cast: "Miss Elizabeth Trumpet as...Ophelia, daughter to Polonius."

Who would have thought a girl who did horse-tricks at Astley's could rise so high? No longer an acolyte of Jack Faversham, coached to death and often crowded off the stage, Lizzie had become her own creature. Eggleston, who had seen her in rehearsal, expected that tonight, after Ophelia's mad scene, she would be proclaimed the new queen of English drama.

Lord Dampere was attending, of course. In the crowd of fashionable carriages arriving outside the theatre, he was the solitary whip to his own ruinously expensive yellow caleche, pulled by a magnificent piebald, eighteen hands high. Three thousand seats were sold for Kean's exciting Hamlet, and this the first performance by his new leading lady. Most of the audience was actually seated by the second scene of Act One, appreciatively listening to Kean's compelling voice.

"*How weary, stale, flat, and unprofitable*
Seem to me all the uses of this world!"

At the back of the top gallery, disguised in grey wig and grey coat, a feverish Jonathan Faversham listened to the soliloquy most intensely of all, mouthing the words in perfect cadence with Kean:

"*Fie on't! Ah, fie! 'Tis an unweeded garden*
That grows to seed; things rank and gross in nature
Possess it merely. That it should come to this."

Envy, palpable and sharp, twisted like a knife in Jack's gut. In recent days, he had felt the first headache pains and weakness of syphilis. That blow had unhinged him, and the blame for all his misfortunes must fall somewhere. Unnoticed by the attentive patrons, he left his seat to creep through the house.

In the wings, Lizzie awaited her first entrance, beautiful in Ophelia's red silk overdress. Her dark hair was unbound, hanging below her waist. She felt assured and excited; she had achieved her dream. Kean had praised her in rehearsals, Dick Wilson was her Polonius, and the company was welcoming. Drawing in a steadying breath, she noticed a strange man in an old-fashioned wig standing in the shadows of the opposite wing. Startled, she thought this might be the famous Ghost of Drury Lane, the "Man in Grey" actors had watched moving through the house during performances for decades. If it was he, she took it for a blessing, but the sight distracted her, a second before her cue from Polonius. Lizzie entered, disturbed by what she had seen.

POLONIUS. *How now, Ophelia! What's the matter?*
OPHELIA. *O, my lord, my lord, I have been so affrighted!*
POLONIUS. *With what, I' the name of God?*
OPHELIA. *My lord, as I was sewing in my closet,*
Lord Hamlet with his doublet all unbraced;
Pale as his shirt; his knees knocking each other;
And with a look so piteous in purport
As if he had been loosed out of hell
To speak of horrors, he came before me.

Over Dick Wilson's shoulder, Lizzie saw the man in grey step closer to the stage and the prompter spring up to stop him. *So, it's not the ghost.* The intruding stranger suddenly whipped a fist into the prompter's face, dropping him to the floor. Shocked, but still playing the scene, Lizzie checked the wings for help. No other stage personnel were in sight.

POLONIUS. *Mad for thy love?*

OPHELIA. *My lord, I do not know;*
But truly do fear it.

POLONIUS. *What said he?*

OPHELIA. *He took me by the wrist and held me hard*
Then goes he to the length of all his arm;
And with his other hand thus o'er his brow,
He falls to such perusal of my face
As he would draw it. Long stay'd he so;

As she spoke, Lizzie crossed upstage to alert the cast of danger. When she passed by him, the man in grey tore off his wig and coat. *Jack! My God, it's Jack!* His mad, malevolent gaze locked with hers. She turned to Wilson and the audience, speaking with genuine fear.

OPHELIA. *He raised a sigh so piteous and profound*
As it did seem to shatter all his bulk
And end his being; that done he lets me go;

Lizzie looked into the wings again, but Jack had disappeared. Out of her sight, he had seized a lighted torch from the upstage scenery wall. Continuing the scene and all unknowing, she moved quite near him, the hem of her long train within reach of the torch. His arm stretched towards the red silk. The fabric gave a soft hiss as it caught fire. Lizzie walked downstage, small flames creeping up the back of her costume, till she smelled the smoke and felt the heat. She whirled around, pulling at her skirt. Now the audience could see the train was burning. Lizzie screamed.

"She's afire," Wilson yelled and threw her to the stage, beating at the flames.

The prompter had recovered his wits enough to grab a wet blanket from the pile kept close by and ran into the set to throw it over her writhing body. "Hold still," he ordered, trying to smother the flames, blood still running from his smashed nose.

As no one had lowered the curtain, the horrified audience shrieked, gasped, and stood to watch. Cast-members rushed out with buckets of water and sand to extinguish the blazing fabric. Flames had licked up Lizzie's leg. She screamed again in pain and shock.

Kean knelt down and breathed into her ear, "It's all right, girl. It's all right." Then, speaking in full voice, announced to the house, "The fire is out. Be calm, everyone, all is well. I say, be calm."

But Lizzie could not be calm. Jack had just tried to kill her. In a rage unimaginable, she kicked off the blanket and unhooked the blackened gown. Ignoring Kean and the others, she staggered towards the pit in her tights and ruined bodice. The excited audience applauded and cheered.

"Ladies and gentlemen," she said, barely in control of her voice, "your pardon, this spectacle was not a part of our play. My costume was set ablaze deliberately by my own husband. You all are witness."

There were jeers from the gallery and the whole crowd of patrons pushed forward to hear. Wild to strike back, Lizzie rushed to Kean and pulled Hamlet's foil from his belt. "Come out, Jack," she screamed. "I know you stayed to see me suffer. Come out and face me, coward! Bastard! I challenge you. I call you out!"

As though this was the cue he had been waiting for, Faversham leaped onstage. He shoved Kean out of the way and grabbed a foil from the actor playing Laertes. "Bitch, you'll die tonight. Make a good end to a bad performance." He hooked the epée into an iron stanchion and yanked the protective nib off the blade. Lizzie quickly did the same, and the two circled for position.

Someone yelled, "Ring down the curtain," but the wings were jammed with actors, and frightened spectators crowded every exit.

The Favershams began to fight center stage. Jack rushed forward, trying to overpower with his greater reach and strength, but Lizzie turned lightly away, parrying and whipping the point of her blade into Jack's side as she returned to her fighting stance. Jack was pinked, bleeding through his shirt, but too crazed to notice. He charged over a fallen chair, slashing right and left; he cornered her in a false archway then pushed inside her defense. As they grunted and separated, he slashed down to cut a rip in the flesh of her arm. She was hurt, but more focused on revenge than pain. He slashed low and slit the side of her calf where she was burned. He slashed again; she thrust, turned and parried, *seconde*, parry, *tierce*, parry, *ballestra* and...Lizzie flipped his blade. Jack's weapon flew out of his grasp into the air, clattering to the stage fifteen feet away. Her blade penetrated the cloth of Jack's shirt right at the heart. He fell on his knees and opened his arms. She froze.

"What's the matter, ducks?" He gasped. "Can't you do it right?"

She had him. *I can kill*...she thought wildly, but hesitated. In that second, she could not bring herself to plunge the blade for a mortal blow. She pulled the foil's point back from his chest. Like lightning, she stabbed between Jack's legs, right through his penis and scrotum, skewering his body to the stage. He howled, clutching his crotch.

A great gasp filled the theatre. "Jeeesusss Christ," someone wailed as Jack writhed in pain.

"Elizabeth!" A fat man yelled and charged up out of the pit, knocking all aside. He grabbed the bleeding actress by her slashed arm and dragged her off-stage, as pandemonium erupted. "Make way. Make way, you sods." He elbowed through the pole-axed crowd out the stage door to the street.

Faversham was left clawing at the shaking foil in his bloody groin, screaming, "Kill her! Kill the bitch!"

The actors and Kean tried to stop the spectators rushing towards Jack's thrashing form. The roar from the house carried to the steps of Drury Lane, where Lord Dampere lifted Lizzie into his caleche and used his whip to clear a pathway out. The piebald horse whinnied and nearly trampled a pair of footmen as he raced round the corner.

"Now that's what I call a night in the theatre," snorted Dampere, whipping the excited horse and trying to keep his passenger from falling out of the little contraption.

Lizzie was shivering. "Dampie, it's you. Oh God, oh God."

"Are you badly hurt?"

"I don't know." The pitch of her voice was hysterical.

Her rescuer fumbled a lap robe towards the half-naked actress. "Where shall we go?"

"Home. Duncan Terrace." She pressed the wooly robe against her bleeding arm, as Dampere turned the horse north.

"Oh, what have I done?"

"You settled the hash of that villainous bugger. But, now, my dear, you must disappear immediately, even if you're the hottest ticket in London." He laughed his little snorting laugh. "Dueling has become a capital crime."

"You mean, I could die for not killing Jack Faversham?" Lizzie touched her burned hair. "He set me on fire."

"So you say, but the audience could not see him do it. I know I did not. I was amazed when you accused him with such vehemence. I believe you, Lizzie; however, the whole of society heard you call him out. They saw that wicked thrust. Delicious it was, but perhaps unwise. Certainly unwise for a woman." He slapped the reins. "Legally, you have committed attempted murder. The crown can't have it, oh my no. Your Jack will certainly die of that wound. May be dead already."

She huddled in the scratchy lap robe, her painful wounds throbbing. "Then I have to run. Oh hell! Calamity. I have no money for escape."

"Oh, I'll give you the blunt to get away, Elizabeth. You must take ship out of the country, I'm afraid." The piebald clattered on the cobblestones as Dampere coaxed him on. "I doubt you'll get another leading man to perform with you for a while." Amused at his own wit, the large man fairly fell off the seat with laughter.

"I'm done with the stage forever," Lizzie groaned.

Once home, she described what had happened to the astonished Octavia and the weeping Emily, while they cleaned and dressed her wounds. In William's old wardrobe trunk, she found clothes to disguise herself as a man. While she gulped down a cool drink of water in the kitchen, Octavia slipped the dagger from Georgie's shrine into her traveling case.

In a few moments, Lizzie stood in the lane of Duncan Terrace, filled with regret, fervently kissing Georgina and baby Arthur. The goodbyes choked her. "What will you do without me? Christ, am I leaving you all to starve?"

"You must think of yourself," Octavia said coolly. "I shall see the children and Emily are provided for. The wages of sin pay interest, I have money in the government funds."

"Forgive me, Emily." Lizzie held her sister-in-law close. The consequences of her actions were beginning to sink in. "I never meant this to happen. Somehow it will come out all right. I love you all." It was a fugitive's litany.

Hours later in the dark interior of the hired coach, the actress relived the long night behind her. The burns and cuts reminded her she was lucky to have survived, but the future loomed uncharted, black as the night. *I have destroyed my own life*, she realized, watching the cold stars sinking in the sky.

Rowlandson published a drawing of Elizabeth Trumpet, half-naked on the Drury Lane stage, plunging her epee into Jack Faversham's manhood. When the print went on sale at Ackermann's Shop in the Strand, it was mobbed. "He Takes Her Point" sold out. Who could resist buying such a caricature? Nobody.

Street singers loudly bellowed bawdy songs about Lizzie that drew laughing crowds. The Prince Regent's chef Careme created a dessert named "The Trumpet Voluntary," Nesselrode pudding in a cherry sauce with a stake of cinnamon bark thrust through its mound. Journalists of the lowest sort surrounded Longsatin House expecting, begging for, and then demanding a glimpse of the perpetrator. Emily steeled herself to deal with them, and in the dealing never hiccupped again. Dampere was assumed by his old Etonians, with much winking and sly-dog innuendo, to have secretly sequestered the beautiful actress on some country estate. Kean denied any foreknowledge of Lizzie's duel and, for the sake of actors' reputations everywhere, felt it his duty to denounce her. The law moved majestically in her direction.

In one performance, Elizabeth Trumpet had acquired universal notoriety. Set ablaze in public by a husband crazed with jealousy and disease, she had become famous for being wild, and nearly deadly. With a single stroke, any chance of Lizzie being taken for a serious actress in England was over.

Jack survived. Once free of the pinning blade, he had scuttled under stampeding feet, avoiding the Bow Street Runners in the uproar. Like a wounded, snarling dog only a fool would try to comfort, he made his way to Wapping and the East End docks, where he disappeared. The proud actor cringed to hear his name become a colossal joke.

June 1, 1816
Maestro Carlo Tomassi
Royal Opera House
London, England
My dearest friend,
I hasten to assure you I am in good health and earning enough to stay alive. Cognizant that I am a fugitive, I hope this travels from my hand to yours with no one the wiser. When you show these words to Emily and Octavia, caution them to be circumspect for their own sake as well as mine.

Following that most harrowing night, I traveled on a slow vessel to Malta, where I stepped ashore along with her cargo of oak timbers, cordage, and a tonnage of tar for the English naval base. Most King's ships bound for the Mediterranean pass through Valetta's Grand Double Harbor to re-supply.

By recommending myself to a tavern here, I was engaged to serve spirit-lifting libations to the officers and men frequenting the port. I also sing. The clientele at the Carlos Quinto has never included the gentlemanly Knights of Malta. The pianoforte appears to have been in a shipwreck, but it allows me to accompany myself as well as the drunks when they feel the need to entertain each other.

These musical interludes are often punctuated with manly contretemps, matchless dialogue, and blood-drawing mills, whereupon I withdraw to my closet/room above stairs. Though I feel safe enough with Georgie's dagger strapped to my thigh, I'm happy to report I have never yet used it for protection. So, this singer is not quite ruined entirely, dear Carlo, and my repertoire of salty songs is growing by the day. Such an opportunity!

I long for my loved-ones terribly and the world I left behind.

Pray for your involuntary exile,
Lizzie T

Chapter Thirty-Seven

December 1816

THE DAWN was breaking over Cleopatra's city, where she loved Julius Caesar and Antony so well. Lizzie stood again between her two young captains, Mangles and Irby, facing the most beautiful golden shore she had ever seen.

Over a glassy sea, they sailed into the harbor of Alexandria on a morning painted with new sunlight. To their left the great lighthouse once stood, wonder of the world, now only a low shore where fig trees and a few domed buildings cast reflections on blue-green waters. On the quay, sea-spray slapped a square fortress whose stones seemed made of golden ether. A plentitude of bold and husky rats were strolling over some faded boats, nearly tripping the women buying fresh-smelling fish from the morning catch. The schooner drifted past scattered structures that looked like ruins but seemed to be inhabited. Date palms stirred, dust billowed up, and men in long loose clothing haggled while a camel peered towards The Raptor with disdain.

"Welcome to Egypt—classic ground," Irby said, tying up to a weathered bollard. "We shall go ashore and reconnoiter."

"And, Irby, you listen to me," Mangles cautioned as he reluctantly buttoned on his coat in the shade of the sail. "Whomever we turn up in the way of English speakers, say not a word about our private passenger. You know how loose-tongued you get."

"I know what I'm about, James."

"Am I to be smuggled off in a carpet like poor Cleopatra?" Lizzie asked. She was eager to be off the ship, no matter how big the rats were on shore.

"Stay on the vessel, Lizzie. Discretion suggests we first find how a beautiful woman can safely present herself here at the end of the world. Charles is apt to forget...."

"Oh, Mangles, stifle yourself." Irby started toward the nearest structures.

The decommissioned captains, their wars behind them, were embarked on an adventure. The Royal Society had charged them to deliver a letter to the renowned explorer and eccentric John Lewis Burckhardt. After sailing their private ship and crew to Egypt, they intended to proceed to the Holy Land. Both men were primed and ready for a long journey filled with scholarly discoveries. When they achieved the bustling port of Valetta, a fellow officer had recommended the musical entertainment at the Carlos Quinto in Urbino Street. The tavern nightingale turned out to be Lizzie, destitute and much put-upon. Having no plans to return home, the actress willingly sailed away with her young comrades.

Alexandria was free of plague for the moment, so Irby and Mangles wandered about under the sun. Rag-tag children and dogs followed them at a distance. The captains did not speak a word of Arabic and carried themselves like the proud commanders of creation, English gentlemen, lost in the heat of the day.

Impatient of their return, Lizzie spent the hours on deck with her watercolors, painting the harbor sights. Thoughts of plays and stages came rushing up, but her anger and regret over Jack was changing in her deepest being, like a cooling fire turning to ashes. *To escape from violence, the Holy Family came here; and for the same reason, so have I.* Her seeking eyes widened to take in the blueness of the Egyptian sky above the crumbled city. On such a morning she believed her journey was a providence. *Am I here for a reason?*

"*Oui, messsieurs. Pommard, c'est moi. Votre servant.*" The former French soldier emerged from behind a curtain of beads, wrapping a purple turban over his unkempt hair.

"*En englais?*" said Mangles, hopefully. The past week had been a touch too exotic for him. The air in the souk was pungent with unidentifiable smells.

"I speak the British. How is King George? Still crazy?"

The officers ignored this pleasantry. "Listen, Pommard, we are captains Mangles and Irby of the Royal Navy. We are having the devil of a time locating Mr. John Lewis Burckhardt, the itinerant Swiss scholar."

"For God's sake, just ask him if he knows the fellow," muttered Irby.

"Now, Pommard, word has it you are acquainted with the gentleman. Do you follow?"

"I am like a brother to Monsieur Burckhardt. Your search is over."

"Well, then, sir, where is he?"

"It will be impossible for a stranger to find the location in this old city, *mon capitaine, c'est vrai*. But for a very small price, and because I would have to leave my shop in the hands of inept assistants, I will guide you myself to Monsieur Burckhardt. But first...." He clapped his hands and shouted in Arabic to someone behind the beads. "You will drink a glass of tea, *n'est-ce pas?*"

"Yes, most gratifying," sighed Irby, resigned to the ways of the East.

Following Napoleon's defeat at the Battle of the Nile in 1798, Jules Pommard, along with the French Army, had been abandoned in the sand by his Emperor. This particular soldier adapted to the climate and embraced the local customs by marrying several Egyptian ladies. He slept away most days in his fly-blown shop, selling copperware near the free-standing column known as Pompey's Pillar.

Enjoying the company of fighting men, even his old enemies, Pommard reminisced about his past army duties, among them protecting the gaggle of natural philosophers who accompanied Bonaparte's invasion of Egypt. After an hour of drinking sweet tea from dirty glasses, the Frenchman owned that Burckhardt, between trips to Syria, Mecca and, recently, Mount Sinai, could be found recuperating in a gated rest-house on the edge of the city.

Mangles purchased an old-looking silver bracelet for Lizzie from one of the black-veiled wives and offered up the money with a large tip to Pommard. Finally, the Frenchmen led his customers out of the sleepy souk, continuing the story of his life.

One day, by the Nile Delta village of El Rashid, he had found a broken stone inscribed in three languages. "Rosetta" was the misunderstood name for this place of discovery. By treaty, what came to be known as the "Rosetta Stone" was handed over to the English government as a spoil of war. In return for this prize and other antique loot, the Royal Navy shipped the stranded army and scholars back to France. Pommard, who loved a certain Fatima and her sisters, had no regrets. The French government had many regrets, however, especially over the lost Egyptian treasures.

By sunset, the captains were reclining on an open rooftop, coats discarded, drinking *karkody*, a crimson brew of hibiscus flowers. A fine-featured Somali girl in loose trousers and a vest embroidered with amber beads cooled their brows with her ostrich feather fan.

Burckhardt had received them graciously. The letter they delivered confirmed his commission by the African Society of London to join a caravan heading southwest to Timbuktu, then explore the upper reach of the Niger River. He was elated, although no European had penetrated that country and lived to return for a thousand years.

Burckhardt, who had renamed himself Sheikh Ibrahim Ibn Abdallah, drew on a bubbling water pipe filled with honeyed hasheesh. Below an emaciated, tanned face, his limp beard flowed over a red sash. Mangles thought he looked frail for his thirty years, as the scholar confided how he had spent the last decade of his life. He had become fluent in Arabic, immersed himself in Islam, and embraced the Oriental life. The lovely Somali girl Y'lemba he had purchased in a slave market.

When the captains spoke of their projected expedition into the heart of Egypt, Burckhardt warned them of the hazards he had witnessed: the *khamsin* sand-storms that smothered every living thing, the mysterious eye-disease that caused temporary blindness, the invisible horse-hair leeches that attached themselves inside human throats, swelling and strangling men to death. When Irby happened to mention their private passenger of the fair sex, Burckhardt set down his pipe in a concerned manner.

"Do you plan to leave this English lady on your ship, protected by your crew?"

"Oh, we couldn't leave her," said Irby, as the skies above them blushed carmine. "Oh my, no. She will accompany us."

"Is she a relative?"

Irby paused. "A sister."

"A beloved sister," stressed Mangles.

Burkhardt eyed the men over his bent, smudged glasses. "If she is to travel rough, across deserts and up the Nile, as you plan...." The captains nodded brightly. "Dragging an English female through this country would be a great inconvenience to you, a misery and danger to her. I caution you, slavery is a way of life here. She would be a prize trophy in a rich man's harem. So even in your company, she must dress as a boy. I would suggest the costume of a Mameluke boy, boots and turban, always carrying a dagger in the sash. Such boys are much admired by the Egyptians." The helpful scholar lowered his voice. "Even Mameluke women dress as boys." Irby and Mangles nodded again, less brightly. "Can she truly bear hardship?" He paused to give a fresh pull on his water pipe. "Did I mention the scorpions?"

March 1817

In the center of Cairo rose the Citadel, a twelfth-century magnificence surrounding the Gawhara Palace occupied by Mohammed Ali, the jumped-up son of Albanian tobacco merchants. By succeeding in wars of aggression for the Ottoman Empire, by bashing religious fundamentalists and, most recently, by ambushing and decapitating forty enemy princes he had invited to dinner, the short general had become Pasha of All Egypt. He planned to do away with barbarism. He liked to think of himself as a modern man.

Captains Irby and Mangles stood in a dark hallway of the palace, waiting to be presented to this paragon. They were attended by their Mamaluke serving boy, who of course, was Lizzie.

British Consul Henry Salt was there as well, to make the proper introductions. He whispered the Pasha's history to pass the time. Salt, in his young, self-important way, gossiped with the captains and totally ignored their servant. Lizzie had taken a mild dislike to the man. As a diplomat, he was far cry from her elegant, honorable brother. She turned from his dish-shaped face and empty round eyes to admire the colors around her; the geometric dazzle of green, blue, and yellow tiled walls, and red patterned carpets piled five deep underfoot. In the midst of this decaying wealth, a fragment of Pharaonic sculpture served as a doorstop.

A servant, golden-skinned as a twist of tobacco, beckoned them on. His head was topped off with a jaunty red tarboosh that reminded Lizzie of Aunt Peg's flowerpots. They hurried over more carpets, through several arches, up a stairway carved in the Moorish style into a terrace room blessed with ventilation and a view over the Nile's palm-lined banks.

Compact and muscular, the Pasha was sitting in cross-legged ease on his throne, a new purchase, massive with gilded lions on the armrests. He was a vigorous forty-seven. The same age as Wellington and Napoleon, as he pointed out to every guest. Salt and the captains made a leg and Lizzie her newly learned *salaam*, graceful as a ballet step.

Speaking French, Salt addressed the throne. "May I present His Britannic Majesty's government's greetings and good wishes to His Highness Ali Pasha! Blessed be the name of Allah."

Ali responded in halting French. "I am most gratified by my English cousin's friendly message. Please to sit." Lizzie sank into a cushioned divan set against the wall in shadowy gloom. The captains had begged Lizzie, with respect, to call no attention to herself.

"With the gracious permission of the Pasha," Salt continued, "I shall explain who these two gentlemen are and why they have journeyed to your country."

Ali inclined his head and gestured to the tobacco-twist servant for coffee.

"For the past ten years, Captain the Honorable Charles Irby and Captain James Mangles have served England in active duty, engaging Bonaparte's Navy on several occasions."

"Bonaparte, that son of a dog," spat out the Pasha.

"These distinguished men wish to see the magnificence of ancient Egypt and the progressive achievements of the new Egypt, brought into this modern age by your august self."

Ali broke in. "With the blessing of Allah, I shall transform this land from a forgotten backwater into a mighty empire of the East. Knowledgeable tourists are welcome. Do the captains and their"—the Pasha gave Lizzie a critical eye—"companion...bring practical suggestions? What use can I make of these British?"

Irby respectfully said they hoped to see ancient engineering marvels. Mangles was a botanist, and they would be honored to make useful scientific suggestions after touring the Pasha's domain.

The fragrant coffee arrived, a thick, sweet Turkish brew served in tiny cups. While the servant poured, Mohammed Ali caressed his round, red beard. "I recall an engineer, possibly an amateur, whom I recently invited to create a water-lifting device to improve irrigation on the Nile. He was a tall Italian who had lived in England. I had him build his machine in the gardens of my Soubra Palace, where I go to shoot birds and escape the Cairo dust."

Lizzie sat up. *No, it couldn't be.*

"Though I liked the fellow's manner, I was apprehensive of his invention. It lifted a great deal of water, but would have put too many men out of work. So I rejected it, and we continue irrigating as we have for five thousand years, with oxen and sweat." The Albanian laughed from his throne and the visitors joined in politely. "What happened to that fellow anyway?" he asked the consulate.

"The man labors for me now, as a kind of assistant," Salt answered. "Your Highness, would it be possible for the captains to receive a *fermin* to ease their travels through the towns beyond Cairo? This official document would introduce them as your guests and be extremely useful."

"Granted." The captains bowed their thanks. "I have given many such *fermins* to French explorers in past months. Philosophers and scientists. Clever men who despised Bonaparte as much as I did. These French are helping me plan the modern cultivation of cotton, which will double our country's income."

Lizzie appraised the wily Pasha. *Plainly he's speaking of the French so glowingly to torment us English. Does he play one country against another?* Ali shot a glance toward her, making sure someone in the room took his point. His lips were smiling devilishly behind his beard.

She turned away to face the Nile. *Is Ali referring to Belzoni? Very tall, English speaking, a kind of water engineer.... How many of those do you meet of a Sunday?*

Once the precious *fermin* was in hand, and the English party crammed into a small carriage returning to the consulate, Mangles asked Salt about his Italian assistant.

"Captain Ishmael Gibraltar introduced him to me. The fellow calls himself a hydraulics engineer, but made his living as a circus strongman in Europe. Belzoni by name."

Lizzie's breath stopped.

"When his water-lifting device failed to captivate the Pasha, he was quite destroyed." Salt brushed a fly from his nose. "No money to leave Egypt, close to starving. I hired him, out of Christian charity."

"That was a kindness," observed Irby, half-asleep.

"At my order, he transported a huge stone head called 'The Young Memnon' out of the desert and down the Nile. The Frenchies were mad to have it, but couldn't budge the thing, even with dynamite. But, damn me, if Belzoni using his own muscle and few dozen *fellahin*, didn't drag it with ropes over a track of rolling palm trunks. Tons of solid granite. Remarkable." Salt laughed. "Today that head is bound for the new British Museum in London. Great coup for England, and me."

Heart in her mouth, Lizzie heard Mangles ask, "Is he in Cairo now?"

"No. Gone. I sent him up to Nubia, rough country, far past the First Cataract. Burckhardt suspects there is a huge temple there buried under a mountain of sand. I expect him to pick up any antiquities he might find for my collection."

Lizzie finished brushing the dust off the captains' wool coats on the balcony of their rooms. The night was buzzing with insects and the soft talk of Egyptian gentlemen drinking tea in the café below. Irby and Mangles in their rumpled shirts were full of excitement and anticipation, charting their Nile journey, discussing logistics and studying Salt's oft-folded maps of Africa, spread over a table inlaid with camel bone. Concerned for her safety in a desert wilderness, they had decided to leave the actress behind, secure and secluded in Cairo. Lizzie had decided otherwise.

She stepped into the circle of candlelight on the table to interrupt them. "Charles. James. I wish a serious word." The men put their maps down and gave their attention as though to a beloved child. "When you began your journey, you had no idea I would turn up singing in that Maltese tavern. You have stood between me and disaster more than once." They demurred with their usual male noises indicating it was nothing. "Grateful as I am, I must insist on remaining in your company. Ali Pasha could certainly tell I was no boy servant. God knows what he might decide to do with me after he thinks about it." She looked them in the eyes. "I shall go with you."

The captains sat back in their chairs. "Lizzie, dear, we want to strike out for Philae Island, a most dangerous place. Everyone tells us to go heavily armed," said Mangles.

"Wild natives, crocodiles and the like," added Irby. "This is one time James is right. We only have a few guns. There is no reason to expose you to such risks."

"You should take me along because it *is* dangerous." She paced around them. "My skill with swords and rash behavior is what got me here in the first place. I will never complain or hold you back. And I suggest you go farther than the Philae ruins. I suggest you find my old friend Belzoni. Go all the way to Nubia. What if there truly is a temple in the mountain of sand? Don't you two want to be the first to see it? Now that would be a real expedition!" *How could I tell them of being a girl at the Wells, dreaming of greatness on the stage? Belzoni was part of that lost long ago.* So many people from her early, hopeful life were gone, but it seemed the ambitious Italian was still standing. Why not travel a thousand miles up the Nile to see him? Her empty heart had never needed a purpose so much. It was folly, of course, but Mangles and Irby were bound to run into folly whether she went along or not.

"Come now," she said seductively, "we faced the Bonapartes together." The men exchanged knowing looks, remembering the Borghese princess and how well that turned out. "You two get hold of a riverboat, and we'll sail to this place together. What's it called?"

Mangles raised the candle to find the spot on the map. "Abu Simbel."

Chapter Thirty-Eight

July 1817

"MY SONS, you are men; row away stoutly!" chanted the boat-captain.

"Allah and Mohammed!" the oarsmen answered.

"The river runs swiftly!"

"Allah and Mohammed!"

"The wind is against us, but Allah is for us! Row on, my sons, for supper is cooking!"

The First Cataract of the Nile lay behind them, a great tumble of crystalline sandstone boulders in the wide river, and now the waters were smooth again. A boy with round cheeks was swimming a camel across the flood. Two ostriches chased their long-legged shadows in the distance. The rented *dahabeeyah*, a flat-bottomed wooden craft, was being crewed by five brothers and one troublesome brother-in-law, a roguish band and none too steady. They had sailed, rowed, and poled the English passengers hundreds of miles south, beyond all the places called Egyptian into the wilder country of Nubian chieftains.

The Royal Navy officers were half-stupefied with heat and the monotony of flat-river sailing. Dozing in the shade of the on-deck cabin, they no longer gazed on the pale gold hills and sky, or the golden water, looking so still between the far banks. Lifting a sleeve bleached at the shoulder from endless sunlight, the riverboat captain pointed his arm forward. No one noticed but the milkable goat, tethered in the bow. Lizzie, who had been petting its scraggly rough head, turned to look up.

The Island of Philae, sacred to Isis, could be seen ahead. A tranquil refuge in the center of the Nile, green with papyrus plants, wild palm and acacia trees growing amongst a cluster of apricot-pillared temples, the island was mirrored on the surface of the slow-moving waters around it. Oars dipped and dipped, a measly breath of wind nudged their triangular sail.

"Isis, goddess of love, has always been worshipped on the Island of Philae," Mangles had told Lizzie. "I got it from Burckhardt, who seemed to know. Hers was the last temple of the old religion to fall before Christianity."

The rich colors of cobalt, emerald and carnelian were still clinging to the lotus-bud capitals of the columns. It was all so bewitching Lizzie decided to salute the sacred spirit of the place before the men woke up and the spell was broken. She knew the ancients worshiped love, and gave love the form of a beautiful goddess, who listened to the prayers of women. *Could that goddess be listening still? Here, in this silent place at the world's end?* Carlo had taught her Cleopatra's aria from Handel's *Giulio Cesare* that began, "Calm thou my soul, oh Isis." The words suited Lizzie's prayer.

"Convey me to some peaceful shore,
Where no tumultuous billows roar,
There, free from pomp and care to wait,
Forgetting and forgot, the will of fate."

"Oh, Queen of Heaven," Lizzie whispered, "What is love that I may find it?" She smiled at her own fancy. *Better not let the Navy boys know I thought the pagans might have something to teach the English.* The breeze pushed the sail hard for a moment and on the land, a bearded figure walked out from between the painted pillars.

Mangles shook Irby awake and they started giving orders, shouting to the shore. The figure on the island waved slowly and ambled over the broken monuments down to the bank. Lizzie could make him out clearly now. The boat's bottom was touching sand when she impulsively slipped over the side and started wading in, soaking her thin cotton gown in river water. On solid footing, she began to run towards the tall figure, her wet drapery instantly as clinging and transparent as ever Jeremiah Brett had imagined.

"Giovanni! *Son' qua! Ecco Lisabetta!*" she screamed.

The jabbering boatmen watched the two meet with whooping greetings, as the man lifted the beauty over his head to spin her around. Like a piece of precious porcelain, he returned her to the earth, saying over and over, "*Cara* Lisabetta, this must be a dream."

When things had settled down, the English party dined at Belzoni's campfire in the temple ruin. They feasted on pigeons, a very local delicacy, split and roasted to sizzling crispness. The milkable goat had been in jeopardy of becoming dinner, but Lizzie begged to preserve her for companionship's sake.

"Remember where we met you?" asked Mangles, addressing his bearded host, then immediately answered his own question. "In a drafty Scottish assembly hall. We all had come to learn about Egypt."

"But, of course, I remember." The Italian was smiling all over his face. "Lisabetta said I should go to the exhibition, to take my mind off a very rude bear."

"And here we are, assembled in Egypt ourselves!" Lizzie glanced around her, happier than she had been in many months. Giovanni's presence gave her a sense of confidence in this fantastical journey.

Irby stood up to stretch his legs. "Pray consider of it. We are about to join in Belzoni's great endeavor to unearth a lost temple. Picking our teeth on the porch of Isis. All Miss Trumpet's idea. Damn, what pleasure!"

"We expected to find you up river, Giovanni, at the Abu Simbel village," Mangles added.

"That village is not much, my friends. I chose to wait in these more pleasant surroundings for the gifts Mr. Salt promised to send to the village chiefs."

"We have the gifts aboard. The consul insisted for safety's sake we bring along an armed janissary. He's guarding the vessel now." Mangles shook an intrusive ant from his trouser leg. "He's an Italian Muslim named Finati. Fluent in the local lingo."

Belzoni instantly called his *paisano* to join them by the fire. Finati, of Ferrara, small and mustached, was another ex-conscript of Napoleon's army, a soldier of fortune who had converted to Islam during a peripatetic career.

"Gentlemen, your presence will be a tremendous help to me." Belzoni took Irby's hand with unbridled Mediterranean gratitude. "Men of action impress the raggedy-assed bandits who call themselves chiefs hereabouts. *Scusi*, Lisabetta."

"Then let us impress their asses by honoring King George's birthday tomorrow," suggested Irby, full of patriotic zeal. "Raise the Union Jack. Fire off a twenty-one gun salute with our pistols at sunrise. Terrify the camels!" The men found this a capital idea.

When a procession of stars rose in the sky, Lizzie retired to sleep away from the others, beneath pillars carved with the face of Isis, beautiful as the crescent moon spangling the Nile. Her mind was filled with Giovanni, wildly attractive in the native garb he wore. *He is a romantic at home in this oriental wilderness...my giant, still seeking to do great deeds.* On the shore, he had embraced her with unguarded feeling. *It felt wonderful to be in a man's arms again, but I must be careful...careful.* The captains were dear, boyish, attentive, but she had no inclination to take either one for a lover, and what a nest of vipers it would be to welcome both to her bed. Dry celibacy served her well during those days on Malta. In this dangerous country, the mere sight of an unveiled woman could end in mayhem. She grew drowsy remembering how Giovanni had pulled her into a racing chariot, how they had toured with rope dancers and acrobats. *And now...together again.... What would Belzoni's circus be like?*

"Where's the temple?" Lizzie asked, shading her eyes with both hands. The beauty and the captains were standing in their little boat facing a massive pile of sandstone cliffs jutting up from the Nile bank.

Belzoni pointed at the great expanse of nothing, a tower of blown sand, mountainous against the cliffs.

"Just there at the top, Lisabetta. A cornice with a row of apes' heads looking west. Do you see them?"

"Ah, yes, apes."

"Everything below them is the temple?" Irby focused his small brass telescope at the cliff.

"Pish. Everything below them is sand, Charles." Mangles wiped his wet brow. "It's not a place. It's a landscape."

The boat-captain's brother-in-law, Hassam, called the "blue devil" by the English for his cerulean galabia and mutinous ways, slithered up to Mangles with his hand held out. "Baksheesh," he said, pointing to the shore, "*baksheesh!*"

"What's this then?" Mangles turned to Finati for clarification.

"He wants a tip for showing you such an amazing sight," the janissary reasoned.

"Tell him he's got it wrong. His sight is covered in sand. Say I will not charge him for the more magnificent sight of two Royal Navy captains. Tell him to be off."

⚬⚬

A herd of gazelles grazed on a millet-patch planted near the riverbank, ignoring the straw hyenas villagers had raised to frighten them off. The mud and grass village of Abu Simbel was a squalid sort of place. In its weedy center, the *raggedy-assed* chiefs, Dawud and Kahlil, had seated themselves on the ground to parlay with the English visitors. They accepted Belzoni's gifts: two turbans, a pair of guns, coffee, and some small mirrors for any women who might turn up. The Nubian villagers, wearing their hair in the bob-cut style of old Egyptians and the loin-cloths of direst poverty, gathered to stare suspiciously at the Europeans from a distance.

Reposing on a scrap of rug behind Belzoni, Lizzie regarded the villagers. The Nubians had next to nothing and assumed the visitors were rich. Since any visitors were precious few, every one must be squeezed dry. She knew, despite this dignified meeting, her friends had traveled beyond the rule of law. Coins changed hands. Belzoni paid for the services of a hundred village men to clear sand away from the promising mountain. All agreed, when the door of the temple was reached, if there was a temple—and if there was a door—the chiefs could claim a lion's share of the treasure they assumed the English were seeking.

The next morning, eighty workers arrived at the cliffs, carrying rake-like boards for dispersing the mountain's sandy summit. Khalil and Dawud made a tremendous show of driving them, then relaxed in the weeds to study their complexions in the mirrors supplied for the women.

Up on high sand, the village men began to sing. Lizzie, ever interested in music, paused in milking the goat to ask Finati the meaning of the workers' song. The janissary translated: "It is a very good thing to get Christian money. We will get as much as we can."

The Nubians raked under the apes for a few hours and then departed to sing about something else. The next day fewer men appeared. The next, Dawud and Khalil needed the workers to rob a Moorish caravan in the vicinity. The sand at the summit had only gone down about six feet.

"Only ninety feet to go," Mangles opined, with a wry grin.

Lizzie watched Belzoni stay reasonable, tireless and firm. The Samson of Sadler's Wells had become a strong man indeed. Calmly, the Italian received the Nubians' invariably bad news. Hourly, the locals demanded more gifts. Not to be outdone, the hired boatmen threatened to leave if they did not receive more largesse. Another day Khalil presented Belzoni with a watermelon and announced Ramadan was about to begin. For the next month, all his men would be unavailable for work.

In the shade of two towering date palms, Lizzie cut the watermelon. Georgie's dagger was proving a useful tool.

Belzoni passed around the dripping slices to his friends seated in a companionable circle on dusty carpets. "There is one word you will often hear in this country: 'baksheesh.'"

"Often indeed," Lizzie agreed, smoothing a piece of sweet-fleshed melon over her dry lips.

"It means money, but more than that. It means the money you must give me now, immediately, because I demand it. That was the first word I learned in Egypt, along with '*Inshallah*,' if Allah wills it." He took a huge wedge of melon. "Without baksheesh, I can tell you, Allah never wills it. There will be more demands from the duplicitous Dawud and Kahlil before this is done."

"With each mile we travel up river, Mohammed Ali's *fermin* carries less weight," Irby observed.

"Those two-penny despots control every fly on every sodding donkey." Mangles sighed.

"Can't argue with that." Irby tossed his rind over his shoulder. "I doubt the villagers will ever see their pay."

Finati patted the gun he cradled on his lap like a dancing girl. "You know the workers get their wages in millet. Grain for porridge. Look around you. What would they buy with money?"

"Pharaoh had labor problems, too, gentlemen. I seem to remember a major unpleasantness with Moses." Lizzie sheathed her brother's dagger and turned to Belzoni. "So, what is to be done, *caro*?"

"It has come to this: we must do all the work, and do it alone." Belzoni straightened his back, his white teeth flashing in a grin. "Would you like to help me move a mountain?"

⚬

In the cool before dawn, Belzoni, Finati, the captains, and Lizzie started climbing the dune towards the cornice of apes. Each footstep sank them to their knees in shifting sand, fine as powder. For every inch raked away, it seemed two came falling back. The sun's reflected glare against their chins felt as if they were standing over a skillet of coals. By nine in the morning, heat drove them off the mountain and under the shade of the boat's sail; there they rested until three in the afternoon when the mountain itself cast a shadow over their toil.

They labored on until Venus appeared in the sky with her court of lesser lights. The boat crew was amazed to see the Europeans work with such mad industry. After two days of fascination, they offered to assist and were paid for it, except for Hassam, the blue devil, who had a genius for hysteria and shunned work of any kind. He urged his brothers-in-law to murder Belzoni, but a dousing with Lizzie's dishwater ended his mutiny.

With each hour of toil, more of the carving on the mountain face was uncovered. A disk in the center of the cornice became visible, emerging from a deep niche. More digging revealed a hawk-headed man. To the right of this creature was a smooth wall, then a great projection they believed must be a colossal figure. Belzoni and Mangles shoveled sand away from the rounded shape of a classical headdress with a rising cobra in its center. The regalia of a pharaoh! Slowly sand was carted away from the forehead, the straight nose, the sloping brows, the deeply-cut lids. The open stone eyes at last looked out on the little band of breathless people, transfixed with awe.

"Today is the first of August, high summer in England, but here, ah, a foretaste of hell. The temperature gauge reads one hundred twenty degrees," Mangles announced, studying his thermometer hanging on a tent pole below the diggings.

"What is the highest temperature that instrument offers?" Lizzie asked.

"One hundred twenty. So, it could well be more, probably is," he decided with zest. "I feel quite purified by all this heat. Climbing on sand has tightened my limbs to steel. You know, Irby, struggling up a dune would make fine training for our Royal Marines. I must mention it to the Admiralty." He extended his bowl for another helping of millet gruel, the ration they all were living on. The flesh on Mangles's sun-baked arm was red, flaking and peeling all at once. But he and Irby never made a word of complaint.

With blistered hands, they had swept back tons of sand from the colossal figures. Four identical pharaohs were enthroned against the mountain, one, alas, obliterated above the knees. The shoulders of the figures were twenty-one feet across. Belzoni thought the oval cartouches carved on the statues' massive arms must contain the royal names, but he, like all the world, could not decipher the hieroglyphs.

They all turned at the sound of a scream. Hassam was running to Belzoni, crying with excitement. "Baksheesh!" The door into the temple had been found.

In the cool of the morning, Lizzie lit candles for the men and started up the slope to the mysterious door. While the Europeans dug to make a passable opening, the boat crew trudged up carrying torches and shouting, armed with swords and pointed sticks. Hassam was wailing, screaming, and pouring ashes over his head, threatening to sail their boat away if gold was not handed over instantly. The captains, who had had enough, drew their pistols. Irby reminded the boat crew to do their duty. Duty was untranslatable. Finati pointed his rifle. All was uproar.

As the sky lightened, little brown birds flew around the stone pharaohs gazing serenely over the shouting mob. Lizzie was shamed by the endlessly contentious behavior of the men. Taking her cue from the smiling colossi, she slipped behind Belzoni and wriggled through the small opening he had made in the door. In a moment, the disputatious men realized she had disappeared. They stopped roaring in mid-hysterics.

Easing down a slope of sand, Lizzie stepped into a great pillared hall, her candle barely illuminating it. The chamber was vast, a hundred fifty feet long. She could not guess how wide. Suddenly a telling blow was struck on the door, a bright beam of sunlight shot into the cavernous space, and Belzoni's long body came swooshing into the temple.

"My God, Lisabetta, you have beaten all of us! Are you all right?"

"Of course. Look. Oh, look, Giovanni!"

The light of the rising sun was touching another room beyond them and another beyond that. The captains and Finati tumbled in, exclaiming with joy. Their five candles revealed images of the Pharaoh everywhere—sculptured into pillars supporting the walls, in colorful murals charging his chariot into battle, and twenty feet tall in the temple's holy of holies, carved elbow to elbow with his gods. They gazed in wonder at the mural where the royal hero was painted so much larger than his enemies. In bright reds and blues, arrows flew in all directions, peasants fled, and the conquered of many races knelt in supplication. With one hand, Pharaoh clutched a dozen men by the hair and lifted an ax to dispatch them.

"Who was this Pharaoh?" Lizzie asked.

"Perhaps Rameses the Great," Mangles answered, "certainly the Napoleon of his day."

"I wonder how tall he really was."

Wandering about, they tried to understand what they had discovered, and guessed how many thousand years had passed since any man had stood in that place. Mangles wanted to measure the dimensions of the fourteen rooms. Belzoni planned to make drawings of the masterly warfare mural. The air was foul and stifling, they were sweating and filthy, but no matter, the captains were slapping each other's backs and laughing.

Irby grabbed Lizzie's hand impulsively. "Thank you for making us journey to Abu Simbel, dear courageous lady. We are each a part of this discovery. This moment is ours forever, and it is magnificent."

Lizzie felt a stab in her heart, wishing her family could see this. *Aunt Peg would have joked, Georgie questioned—Would Mama and Papa have been amazed?* She leaned her tired back against a pillar of Pharaoh and began to cry. Belzoni came to her there and wrapped her in his round, dusty arms.

"*Cara,*" he whispered. "Remember who we were? Vagabond actors, you and I, less important than the scenery. Well, we are something more now."

Chapter Thirty-Nine

September 15, 1817

M*Y DEAREST EMILY,*

I greet you with prayers for your happiness. Forgive the long silence from your renegade sister-in-law. Life has set me on a path I would not have chosen. The dramas and romances I performed on stage have changed into my real experiences. I have been where no news could reach me. I am thriving, but worry how you are getting on, you and your little ones, my treasured family. When it is possible, I will come home to you.

I am living as a vagabond in Egypt, protected and inspired by an old acquaintance from my girlish acting days. Giovanni Battista Belzoni was a notable theatrical for many years. He is working here, to collect works of antiquity for the British Museum, with the blessing of the British Consul, Mr. Henry Salt.

I was brought to this country, more or less as extra baggage, by the Captains Irby and Mangles, whom you must remember. They saved me from a sordid life in the port of Valetta, on Malta. The captains, those intrepid travelers, have since gone on to Palestine and Damascus without me. I had no inclination to journey farther with them, my female presence often a hindrance to their explorations. Of course, I miss their good humor, but my life is easier with only one commander in charge. Three men of forceful disposition, encamped with me day and night, such stories to tell! Egypt has become my place of refuge by chance, as you and I might run from the rain into the Royal Opera Arcade.

I am Mr. Belzoni's assistant. The man has a great gift for hard work in hot places. I am literally digging things up to earn my daily bread. He keeps a record of all we do and see. My small talent for drawing is useful. I write his words in English with the hope his journals will one day be published.

The objects we find are beautiful to my eyes, not like the classical arts of Greece and Rome that everyone admires, but of a different world altogether. I am certainly living a different life. There is no theatre here, but the Egyptians and their overlords are all fine actors, full of dignity whatever their poor circumstances, passionate in their faith.

This month, we are camped in Wadi Biban El Muluk, a narrow forbidding canyon where the walls of rock are striped in browns and grays like frozen tree-trunks above dry hills. The ancient tourists named this blazing spot the Valley of the Kings, leaving their marks on tombs that were opened and emptied long ago. Giovanni studied the writings of Herodotus, an old Greek who traveled this way before Julius Caesar was a pup. Using those descriptions, he has discovered three forgotten tombs in this valley in less than a week. Three! His perception is uncanny.

Our primitive existence in Egypt will make for amusing tales when we are reunited before the fireplace at Longsatin House. The desert has transformed my looks, my face is bronzed with sun and my feet are often bare. You, the sweet English rose, would be amazed at me. Nothing do I possess, except for a little she-goat, and even that poor creature has been looking rather peaky lately.

I often masquerade as a boy for the sake of propriety, so in a way I'm still an actress. I shall never again appear on the London stage and that wrings my heart. I do not mention this to Belzoni who hated working in the theatre and wants to be remembered only for his new accomplishments. I loved the acting and the people too much to ever forget my old life, but events have given me a different role. At least I am in the company of an amiable man of unshakable resolve. I feel needed and that my being has some purpose. It is enough.

Kiss your children for me, and forget me not. Never for a moment do I forget you.

Your loving,
Lizzie

The shooting wars between Britain and France were over, but both countries were rancorously plundering the sites of ancient empires for trophies to erect in Paris or London as monuments of conquest.

While Europeans carried off the Egyptian heritage, Pasha Mohammed Ali played one nation against the other, a *fermin* here, a privilege there. He was only too glad to give up the old stones. "They were raised in the age before the Prophet, and therefore are of little merit," he said. Antiquity inspired no awe amongst the natives. The *fellahin* sliced up thousand-year-old pillars for millstones and built their mud houses on the roofs of temples.

Belzoni's habit of trying harder than anyone before him had brought a huge reward. He found the largest tomb yet discovered: the resting place of Seti the First, Pharaoh of Egypt. French Consul Drovetti gnashed his wolfish teeth at Belzoni's luck. British Consul Salt was elated.

The spectacular tomb had been dug three hundred feet into the rocky walls of The Valley of the Kings. The place had been plundered long before Belzoni's excavation. Nothing remained, with the exception of an empty alabaster sarcophagus that gleamed like a huge milky opal. The workmen who had helped him batter into the tomb were paid and dispersed. Only a veiled female servant stayed on at his side, day after day, drawing copies of the mysterious figures on the walls.

Lizzie scratched at her hair, bound under a length of red and yellow striped cotton. *Oh, what I would give to bathe in the Nile.* She was hot enough to ignore the crocodiles, dirt, and dead donkeys she had seen in the deep brown water. *All I wish is to be cool and wet.* The tent-like black dress she sweated in had been bartered from a Bedouin woman. The back of it bellied out where the native lady had squatted in it for years. And it stank.

Lizzie named the room they occupied The Chamber of Beauties. Oil lamps on the floor flickered golden light across the vaulted indigo ceiling, painted with stars. In companionable silence, she and Belzoni tried to keep their dropping sweat from spoiling the watercolor pages of the day's work. The Italian believed he was painting the goddess Isis, grasping Pharaoh's hand as they stared at each other in profile against a saffron background. Out of her earlobe a baby cobra, that was either an earring or a real snake, looked ready to jump across the painting into the king's brown face.

Lizzie was completing her copy of two ducks poking their orange-and-black-feathered heads through a tuft of reeds. She reached inside the red embroidery at her neckline to give a good scratch at the sticky skin below her breasts.

"Can you bear this heat a little longer, Lisabetta?"

"Finish, Giovanni. If you can endure it, so can I."

The big man had removed his shirt and was sitting cross-legged, bent over his colors. The ropey muscles across his chest and back were glistening.

He could be Atlas, on a break from hoisting the terrestrial globe. Lizzie pulled the striped scarf from her head, shook her long hair, and dragged her nails across her scalp, relieved to find no tiny companions, only oil and dust in the wavy strands. To rest her back, she stretched out full length on the stone floor.

"Last night I dreamed of being in this room. The people and spirits in the murals were all alive. Snakes writhing, beetles clacking, and you were here too, Giovanni, dressed like an Egyptian, except the jewels of your collar and bracelets were tattooed on your chest and arms, all coral and turquoise."

Belzoni stopped painting. He was always interested in how he was perceived, especially by her.

"Was I playing Pharaoh in your dream?"

"You were Pharaoh. Every soul was bowing to you."

Belzoni rocked back with a laugh. "*Molto bene*! I like that."

Lizzie did not add that when she awoke from the dream, her sex was drenched with moisture and she felt near the pinnacle of desire. She well knew the excitement male and female could give each other. Sometimes her vivid memories of Jack were a torment. Lovemaking had kept her tied to Faversham in coils of lust after trust had waned. The angry ending of that love had made her self-protective as a tortoise.

In the tomb's stillness, she recalled how Pansy and the girls at the Wells had imagined Belzoni as a lover. *When I was still a virgin, Giovanni was my respectful friend. He never tried to touch me as so many did.... I was too young and stupid then to understand a man's nature—too young to know the satisfactions of love.* Her thighs opened involuntarily as she imagined being filled and flooded. *Is he my gift from Isis?*

"Giovanni, is that snake Isis wears in her ear about to dart at the king?"

"Perhaps." Belzoni studied the figures he copied. "I think this Pharaoh had nothing to fear. Notice, *cara*, how the goddess has taken his hand. She loves him."

Do I love him? I know what the snake in Genesis accomplished. Aunt Peg made it crystal clear.... "Aren't you hot, Giovanni?"

"Melting."

"I need to cut my hair short. It will be cooler."

"I can cut your locks, *cara*. My father was a barber, remember?

He trained me to be one, too. That's what I would have been had I stayed in Padua."

"I'm sure you're glad to have escaped a hairdresser's career. But do you have combs and scissors?"

"*Certo*! I have everything that's needed."

Of course he does, she thought. He put down his brush to look at her, reclining amongst the paint pots. *He is intrigued.... Should I do this...?*

"Madam, would you prefer the coiffure of an Egyptian princess, hair bobbed in a shingle, or a sculptured cut, close to the head, a la Titus?"

"Oh, the Titus style, please, Giovanni. And, if it's possible, a wash with soap?"

"This evening we shall go down to the river. The locals fear the dark, so except for the nighttime creatures, we will be alone. There I will turn you into a lady of London fashion."

I once set the London fashions.... He is so confident. Oh Isis, be with us.... "Might there be snakes in the water, Giovanni?"

"Yes, cara, but what are snakes to us?"

At moonrise, they rode round-bellied donkeys out of the hills to the Nile. The creatures' little hooves rang like castanets on the rocks. At the Colossi of Memnon, pairs of amber animal-eyes watched from the shadows. On the riverbank, Lizzie was startled when a strange deep sound echoed across the ripples, descending like a scale: *uh-uh...bu-bu-bu-bu-bu-bu*.

"*Ecco*. A hippopotamus is out there swimming in the dark." Giovanni spoke quietly, removing his shirt. "He's giving us a basso serenade."

Wearing only her thin shift, Lizzie dove in beside a mat of quivering blue water-lilies. Standing in the shallows together, Belzoni began to touch her, working a precious fragment of soap into foam, stroking the fragrant suds through her hair with his callused fingers. Lizzie relaxed with the pleasure of being clean, and floating in his gentle hands. He rinsed her with a flourish from a half-broken water jar and, leaving the river, walked to their torch on the bank. The light wind made the orange flames speak like rippling silk. He motioned her to come out of the water and sit beneath the light.

Belzoni lifted the dark, damp tangles of her hair into the night breeze, enjoying the intimacy. Gently, he pulled the wooden comb through her wild mane, using the scissors with slow care. With every snip, she became more of his creation. He swept the cuttings into a little basket. "Some Egyptians still practice sorcery. They could use this hair to bewitch you. We Italians take precautions."

Finished, he put the scissors down to arrange the short, curling tresses framing her face. His hands lingered to caress her long neck and bare shoulders.

"Do you like what you see, Giovanni?"

"*bella*," he answered. "*bella*, Lisabetta." His big hands moved to encircle her waist, easily lifting her higher than the flaming torch, then slowly, his heart racing, lowered her warm mouth over his own. The aching snake in his trousers began to rise like a royal cobra.

"Take me back to the Chamber of Beauties, Giovanni." They kissed again and again. "I want to enjoy you under the eyes of Isis."

In the light of the oil lamps, Lizzie dropped her Bedouin dress, the linen shift and turned round to show herself. She sank to the floor, opening her arms. "*Andiam'*, Giovanni." Her rosy nipples pointed straight at him, her long legs spreading wide. With a moan, he entered her paradise. Her sheath was tight and slick, grasping and pulsing. The smothered passion he had felt for years exploded with his copious climax. Lizzie shuddered beneath him.

Belzoni entered her satiny sex over and over again. He penetrated her from the back, kneeling, his hands milking at her swaying breasts, pulling on the swollen nipples as he beat against her warm buttocks. At his wish, she rode upright on his long, thick member, twisting and grinding to please herself. She was stretched, sore, inflamed and perpetually wet, sometimes groaning, sometimes crying with release.

He could not get enough of the downy lips between her thighs, toying with his fingers in the moist pink flesh, pressing his wide tongue up and down her clitoris till she screamed. He suckled at her breasts, filling his mouth until she panted and begged to be taken again.

They lay side by side, Belzoni buried in her flesh, her bosom crushed in his hands. Reposed that way, they rocked and gasped, dissolved and dozed, without ever pulling apart. Like immortals they transcended the world. And Isis smiled.

Chapter Forty

November 1817

IT WAS rumored. It was hoped. It was assumed, Belzoni had found treasure in the tomb of Seti. To investigate this windfall, Mohammed Ali sent Hamid Agha, a local lord who was his personal eyes and ears in the desert. The steely old criminal arrived on horseback at a gallop with a horde of armed men. His white, cloud-like beard and mustard yellow turban, encircled an intelligent face radiating confidence. Robed in tones of coal and flame, Hamid carried a massive scimitar in his sash. Following a decent enough greeting to the Italian, the imposing character swiftly made for the tomb's rocky entrance, his followers crowding behind.

The Egyptians ignored the hundreds of hieroglyphs on the walls. Of course they ignored the Italian's female servant—Lizzie—veiled in black with eyes downcast. They rushed past the manifestations of the soul, the sun, the dart-carrying demons of the underworld, the vultures on the ceilings, the parade of humankind, some black, some bearded, some tattooed. Looking everywhere and seeing nothing, the horsemen were clearly searching for something they had not found.

The Agha walked through every chamber, called for more light, then ordered his chattering cohorts out of the painted rooms. The lids of his eyes narrowed with a conspiratorial twitch as he addressed

Belzoni.

"Where have you put it? You can show it to me, *Effendi*."

"I have shown you everything I found, Hamid."

"Not everything." He tapped a finger to his long hooked nose. "I have heard. I know. In this place you have a big golden cock."

Lizzie, carrying in a fresh candle, heard, gave an involuntary yip, and stumbled in her Bedouin dress. Belzoni ignored her, giving the Egyptian worthy a look of appalled innocence. The Agha put hand to scimitar, menacingly.

"The cock is full of diamonds and pearls."

"No. No. The tomb was empty, Hamid. No diamonds, or gold of any kind." Eventually, the Agha was persuaded of this disappointing truth. He turned to go.

"But what do you think of all you have seen?"

"It would make a good place for a harem." Hamid jerked a thumb at the painted walls. "Give the maids something to look at. My heart weeps to find no treasure. But that slave of yours with the candles might be worth something. How much for the woman?"

"The woman is not for sale, Hamid, but would you care for some mint tea?"

"I would not." Without a single souvenir collected in his saddle-bag, the Agha and his riders thundered away, throwing up plumes of hot sand behind them.

Lizzie slipped out of the shadows to give her giant a stimulating squeeze.

"The Agha wanted to see your golden cock? He had no idea how close he was."

"Lisabetta, *carissima*, you know it is your private jewel."

The next visitors arrived by boat in an impressive flotilla. The Earl of Belmore, an affable Irish peer in his forties, was peregrinating across the Mediterranean in the company of his Countess, two sons of their union in their teens, Lord Corry and the Honorable Henry, an entourage of chaplain, doctor, dogs, and the usual swarm of overtaxed servants. Acting as host was Consul Henry Salt, on his first trip out of Cairo to actually see the places where Belzoni had been so successful.

All the travelers were astonished by Seti's tomb. "Exquisite! Superb!" They waxed rapturous in praise of the discoverer. "What deduction! What genius! What a splendid headpiece!"

Belzoni drank in all the gracious things they had to say. Lizzie, again playing the supernumerary Mameluke boy, required and received no credit. She saw her lover engaged by the attention, the happiest Giovanni had ever been amongst strangers, perhaps even happier than he was with her.

The Earl of Belmore shook Belzoni's hand in the Chamber of Beauties. "I congratulate you, sir, on this discovery. You have opened a door to the mysterious past."

"You shall be prominent in our journals, lionized from Dublin to Dingle," the Countess added. She was a cool creature, a tempered aristocrat to the bone.

Belzoni revealed the sarcophagus last. Lizzie had placed lighted candles inside so the translucent alabaster radiated a ghostly glow. The Countess ran her fingers over the incised hieroglyphs painted a delicate blue against the pale stone. Her boys gazed with adolescent intensity at the bare-breasted goddess carved inside.

Salt gasped. "Such a prize! I must get this to my collection in Cairo immediately. You'll have to pack it up directly, Zoni, it's the finest thing you've come across."

"How long has Signor Belzoni been in your employ, Salt?" the earl asked.

"I do not work for a man. I work for the British nation." The Italian was irked. His angry tone caused the group clustered around the sarcophagus to raise their heads as one.

"I have personally financed these expeditions for over a year, my lord," Salt managed to say, but Belzoni overrode him.

"I am not breaking my back for wages, but for the glory of the British Museum. I am no one's employee. I am independent!" His voice was loud in the stone room and the atmosphere had gone, appropriately, as cold as death.

Standing out of the circle, Lizzie was shocked. Evidently Giovanni had taken the word "employee" as a slur upon his honor. He glared at Salt for a long moment of awkward silence.

"Signor Belzoni, is there any chance of going crocodile hunting?" the countess inquired in meltingly soothing tones. It was a change of subject that brought the Italian to his more civilized senses. He caught Lizzie's cautionary look and calmed himself.

"Yes, *contessa*. The sport is exciting, but the meat is rather tough. On the way out, you must look in the Chamber of Mysteries. There is a crocodile-headed god on the wall, wearing a green kilt. Would you boys enjoy a hunt?"

"We are game for anything," the Honorable Henry, a near midget of thirteen, piped up. Lord Corry snapped out of his adolescent torpor, animated at the thought of killing large reptiles.

As the family left, Lizzie caught the earl saying *sotto voce* to his wife, "Thank you, Juliana. How I abhor an 'atmosphere.'"

Once the Belmores were gone, Lizzie set out a meal for Giovanni. But he could not face their usual fare of flat bread and dried dates. In a brooding mood, he heard her urge him to seek out Consul Salt and clear the air between them.

"He gave you an opportunity here when you needed one, *caro*. He has a right to take some credit. Every appearance cannot be a starring role, you know."

"Do not compare me to your husband, *bella*. *Per favore*! I have put those performing days behind me, thanks be to God."

After enjoying the sport of crocodile slaughter, the Earl of Belmore sent a message to inquire if Belzoni could use his famous "jiggery pokery" to find them a mummy pit? He and the boys would love to make a discovery of their own.

Happy to oblige, Belzoni led the party on camels to a likely spot beyond the Valley of the Kings. As they removed shovels from the saddle bags, he was at his most charming.

"I myself once fell into a nearby cave that was crammed with hundreds of the desiccated dead. I sat up amongst the mummies, breathing their bituminous stench, only to be bombarded by bats: a veritable bastinado of squealing brown balls."

In the shade of a boulder, Lizzie brewed tea for Consul Salt who told Belzoni he was only along for the camel ride, but appeared anxious to catch him in an amiable mood. His round eyes never focused on Lizzie. The Belmores began digging at a distance. A hawk screamed in the sky as, rather reluctantly, Belzoni sat down beside Salt. When he reached out for his tea, Lizzie gave him an encouraging wink along with his cup.

"To the Belmores," Salt said, raising his drink.

"*Inshallah.*" Belzoni raised his. "May they have luck."

"*Signore,* I want you to know I have high regard for you," Salt began reassuringly, with a tentative smile. "I mention you in all my dispatches to London. People know of your work here. But our arrangement is like a man who commissions an architect to build his house. The wonderful house is the achievement of the builder, but it belongs to the man who paid for it."

"Why do you take praise for discovering the Pharaoh's Tomb? You did not."

"Because," Salt answered, "I represent the crown."

"But I discovered it," the Italian insisted.

"Remember Napoleon's scholars? They took credit for discovering Egypt when it's been here all along. A question of national pride, don't you see? Look, old man, I have paid your expenses, but in the light of your great discoveries...."

"How can a man hire another to make discoveries?" Belzoni said, eyes flashing.

"My dear fellow, I will pay you a monthly wage, and a share of any antiquities I can spare. What do you say to twenty-five pounds a month?"

"I believed I was working for the British Museum."

"Yes, but only through me." Salt twisting uncomfortably in his tailored trousers, put down his tea to say more, but was interrupted.

"I say, the boys have bashed into something here." The earl loped up to them, arriving in a state of overheated excitement. "My God,

Belzoni, you really have a nose for this business, don't you?"

The large man rose up to inspect the small body just unearthed. It was only a poor female. There was no mummy case, no papyrus, no charms or jewelry, just the preserved little body. Lord Corry poked at the dry linen wrappings around a perfectly intact shoulder as his brother touched the long brown hair still clinging to the scalp.

"Papa says people used to eat these things," commented the Honorable Henry.

"Apothecaries used to sell mummy as medicine, before our enlightened times," Belzoni admitted, noncommittally brushing some curious flies off the vulnerable body.

"Well, I mean to keep mine for a curio," the boy confided, "at least the head."

Lizzie drifted closer to look. The delicate bones in their crusted grave-cloth made her want to weep. *This girl lay forgotten through the ages, with nary a trinket to prove someone had loved her.* She crept back to the teapot as the Irish family prodded the shriveled corpse. The mummy awakened despair in her heart.

Giovanni and I are living in each other's pockets, but he never speaks a word of love to me. Am I to be forgotten too? Oh, Isis…what is our future?

December 1817

"Wake up, *caro*. I have had another dream."

Belzoni had not been sleeping well, even here in the Chamber of Beauties. He had accepted Salt's money reluctantly and felt less a man for it. Now Lizzie was intruding on his rest. "What is it, Lisabetta? Was I Pharaoh again?"

"No, you and I were walking in Piccadilly."

"I haven't seen Piccadilly for years. What of it?"

"Giovanni, what if you put on an exhibition of this tomb so the whole world could enjoy it?" He turned to see his lover's eyes wide open with excitement. "I dreamed of Piccadilly because there is a huge building there called Egyptian Hall. It is a fantasy like the Regent's Pavilion in Brighton, but it already exists." He roused himself to recline on an elbow. "Think of this. We have been copying the paintings to illustrate your journal, but what if we copied everything in every room, and then built a life-size model of it?"

"Like stage scenery?"

"Exactly like stage scenery. People would be as thrilled as the Belmores were. And everyone would know Giovanni Battista Belzoni had brought that beauty and magnificence to the British people. I can see you now, standing before them, lecturing like the scientific gentlemen of the Royal Society. That is what you want, isn't it, *caro*? Recognition?"

Belzoni had listened carefully. "I could dress 'a la Turk,' perhaps, unwrap a mummy on the opening day?"

"Yes! Mr. Salt will be in Cairo, dusting his collection, while you are showing the wonders of Egypt to the world." Giovanni smiled with a far away look while Lizzie's vision gathered momentum. "We could take the show on to Paris. Did I say show? I meant the exhibit, traveling museum, call it what you like. Londoners would pay to get in, so you could profit for all your efforts, Giovanni."

"To make impressions of these carvings, these thousands of images, would be a great undertaking," Belzoni said.

"A bloody lot of hard work, but you and I are good at hard work, *caro*."

The Italian took Lizzie's tousled head in his hands. Her Titus haircut had grown out shaggy as a Gypsy and her body was warm with pulsing life. "Your dream, *bella*, it is an inspiration." His lips brushed hers. "I kiss the dreamer."

January 1818

Belzoni seized upon Lizzie's idea for a London exhibition. The tomb contained one hundred eighty-two life-size figures, eight hundred smaller ones and nearly five hundred hieroglyphs on the decorated ceilings, walls and pillars. To make a perfect model to astonish the world, he and she diligently copied the line, contour and color of every one. They worked by candlelight. The wax for the impressions ran in the stifling heat. It had to be mixed with resin and dust, making a frightful mess. Lizzie emerged from her work in the darkness, to be half-blinded by the sun.

Consul Salt had sent out another traveler to see the tomb. He was a lanky British colonel. Officers going back and forth to their posts in India sought out the Valley of the Kings these days, as an attraction not to be missed. Finati, the janissary, was making a good living guiding such gentlemen. Belzoni happily embraced his new role of authority on antiquities. The colonel was most appreciative, lingering for hours. Finati made a campfire at dusk and prepared native beans with plenty of garlic, poetically named *ful madamas.*

After the beans, the colonel mentioned what had inspired his trip into the desert. "I first read of your discovery in the *Quarterly Review, signore.* They praised your indefatigable labor. Thanks to you, the British Museum is likely to become the richest depository of Egyptian antiquities in the world." He belched discreetly. "Quickened my interest in this place."

The Quarterly Review was read by every serious scientist in England. Giovanni was keen as mustard to get a copy of the article. The colonel left with Finati when the full moon rose, promising Belzoni to mention his work to the Royal Society.

Once Lizzie and the Italian were alone, a family of fellahin from the village of Qrna crept out of the rocks to offer ancient knick-knacks for sale. It was their custom. They dwelled in the smoke-blackened caves of burial sites opened ages ago. These enterprising folk had spent generations secretly removing objects from the tombs cut into the cliffs above their village. The family lived modestly on the proceeds amongst their goats and sheep. Their penned livestock were sheltered where some grand courtier was spending eternity, forever serenaded by the neighs and baas. The Qrna supply of papyrus, scarabs and golden jewelry seemed endless. Lizzie and Belzoni had become steady customers.

A chalice-shaped drum was in the villagers' pack that night. After the trading was over, Lizzie asked for music. The eldest son took the instrument under an arm to beat accompaniment and commenced a piercing descant.

Belzoni grasped the gist of the song enough to translate: "A caravan crosses the desert. Many camels. Big desert. A camel has hurt his foot."

The tune moaned on for several verses and, when the camel's foot seemed to get no better, Lizzie begged, "Could they play something a touch more lively?"

Putting heads together, the men broke out another drum and a pair of cymbals, playing a country tune with a cheerful rhythm. The family matron got up to dance. The woman, neither young nor beautiful, was seven months pregnant and tattooed about the chin with dots and triangles. She functioned as the family workhorse, yet, as she swayed her hips in the smoky firelight, she changed into a proud and joyously sexual being. The barefooted mother, wind billowing her indigo veil, seemed to make love to them all.

Caught up in the beauty, Lizzie decided, *this dance was made for me!*

Chapter Forty-One

February 1818

"OPEN YOUR palm, like a goddess giving life." Farouze, a wrinkled old Egyptian dancer, was instructing her foreigner in a mixture of French, Arabic, and hand signals. "Lift each hip sharply as you move. The feet are not so important; create your own step. Begin."

Lizzie wished for a mirror to see herself in, but there was no such luxury in this room above a Cairo alley. The floor was slick from the unwashed feet of countless women. She tried the movement again, holding her shoulders absolutely still while her hips kept time to the beating drum: one two *three*, one two *three*.

"Slide your belly forward and pull back, forward and slowly back." Farouze directed her student as she sat playing a slow throb on her drum. Latticed light seeped through a mashrabiya-screened window. The little wooden spools of carving kept interiors hidden from prying masculine eyes.

Dressed in loose Turkish trousers, her coin-decorated belt worn low, Lizzie moved her bare stomach forward and back. So she could breathe, the bright buttons of her tight red vest were half undone. Stretching arms behind her and thrusting her breasts forward, she copied the swaying elegant walk of a camel. That afternoon she had seen a magnificent white one, crossing Cairo by the great Mosque of

Ibn Taloun. She lowered her eyelids as the animal had, remembering its long dark lashes. She slyly turned her head and extended her back impossibly far.

"*Bon, bon,*" encouraged Farouze, making the drum shudder. She wore heavy bangles of turquoise on her wrists and ankles and had long, henna-dyed hair. The enterprising creature had taught *raqs sharqi* steps to brides and prostitutes, but never before to an English woman. The foreigner's grace and dedication, along with her generous payments, made her the teacher's favorite.

Lizzie moved inside a veil of rouge gauze, showing off her eyes, playing the veil out tantalizingly, revealing a few more inches of flesh with each step. The gauze floated like a spirit in air, then settled over her rippling belly as she lay down to dance on her back. She opened liquid arms, arching her spine to offer her breasts as Salome might have done.

Farouze began to play a slower, more sensual air on the oud. Her instrument was precious, hundreds of years old, with more inlaid mother-of-pearl decoration than adorned the Prince Regent's mandolin in Carlton House.

At Edfu, Lizzie had first seen the musical instrument's ancient ancestor: A crowd of naked girls were drawn on the crumbling wall of a ruined temple, all the ladies beautiful as cats with their painted lips and eyes, and every one wearing a long black wig crowned with lotus blossoms. Some were playing pipes, some carrying cymbals, and one willowy creature stood by a harp tall as her shoulder. Lizzie was delighted by the all-girl orchestra waiting for their cue. She knew how it felt to wait in the wings.

"Finale!" shouted Farouze.

Lizzie struck her cymbals in a faster tempo. Heels off the floor, all quick steps and shimmy-shakes, she whirled in circles as Farouze ululated a high-pitched wail. She extemporized some undulating pelvic thrusts, a few leg-lifts from Sadler's Wells, and closed with a floor pose that Charles Dibdin would have recognized.

"*Ha bibi*! *Ha bibi*! You little darling," cried Farouze. "Come back in five days." And then, in Arabic, which her student could not quite understand, she asked, "Why can't more of my girls be as inspired as this English?"

Masquerading as an Egyptian wife gave Lizzie the run of Cairo. It pleased her to disappear into the exotic world and watch it from behind a veil that covered her constant pleasure in the differences and similarities to London. No one noticed another female in black emerging from the alley. Her dancing clothes were folded in the basket she balanced on her head. A solid matron gripping a tray of flat bread-loaves hurried down the unpaved street, and Lizzie chose to follow her, bobbing along behind, heading for the souks of the Khan El Khalili, the Grand Bazaar.

Houses made of blistered plaster with dry wooden balconies protruded far over the street. A flock of white pigeons suddenly rose from a hot rooftop to circle above her head. A tumble of striped watermelons lay broken against a doorway. Some passersby coughed from the silty dust that rose with every step into the hot air. Gobs of spittle dropped where men spat to clear their perpetually irritated throats. A gang of little boys in woven skullcaps nearly knocked her down dodging around a farmer with a wheelbarrow-load of cucumbers. Lizzie loved the walk as much as the dancing. *I have been sequestered amongst the ancient dead for months, God bless them. But today, ah, today I run free amongst the living!*

The woman with the tray of bread turned into the bazaar, a medieval maze of streets loud with haggling merchants. Lizzie swung around the carcass of a skinned sheep hanging by its heels. Disturbed flies lifted off the flesh to hum around her ears. *How very like the smells of Smithfield's Market. Except....* Except here everything was different. The shopkeepers were all male, chatting together, one sucking on the ivory mouthpiece of a gurgling water-pipe, unconcerned about ever making a sale. She understood many words and phrases of Arabic now, a language she thought musical, with lush singable vowels. Knowing a little kept her wary and watchful. *Give the slave market a wide berth. I've no curiosity to experience a harem.*

She sidled down a narrow lane shaded overhead against the noon sun with straw matting and ragged red linen. Here were four-foot-wide

storefronts of tailors' establishments—*the Savile Row of Cairo*? Teams
of sewing boys knotted buttons of gilt thread onto cotton gowns. At the
corner began a street of metal workers, where lustrous copper pots and
brass chargers were jumbled in every space. The lowly cousins of the
smiths sat cross-legged, polishing their days away.

Between a waist-high burlap bag stuffed with dried figs and
another full of aging pomegranates, she stopped to get her bearings.
Nuggets of resin in wooden boxes exuded the aroma of frankincense,
joining sweet spicy cardamom, musty golden turmeric and the
ubiquitous stink of human urine. A bunch of fresh mint had fallen
into the dirt underfoot. A speckled fowl pecked at it. At a sweetmeat-
seller's, a plate of pink-colored jellies caught Lizzie's eye. She pointed,
paid, and sampled. The taste and perfume of roses caressed her
tongue. Her next purchase, a mysterious looking pastry, was made of
dough and crushed almonds that leaked honey. Into her mouth,
before any flies could rise. An explosion of taste.

An immaculate white-bearded gentleman parted a clattering
curtain of cobalt beads. Here was a shop of powders, unguents, and
cosmetics. *What a discovery.* Tacked on the wall were "the hands of
Fatima," lucky trinkets of silver filigree. On a low table, tiny black and
blue bottles of kohl, the eye-paint of ancient ladies, waited for
purchase. Irresistible. Choosing three bottles of black and one of
malachite green, Lizzie paid from her household allowance. Shopping
done, she plopped everything into her basket then replaced it on her
head. To the gorgeous white-haired shop owner, a veritable Beau
Brummell of the Khan El Khalili, she sang out, "*Shokrun*," and left the
covered bazaar for the sun-beaten streets.

A wedding possession passed by. The bride sat on a flat-topped
cart, upstaged by her dowry gifts piled around her in abundance. A
hundred relatives were shouting in lusty celebration. Flutes and
tambourines were playing. Lizzie joined the spontaneous parade for a
moment, her hazel eyes dazzled by the people and the colors spinning
around them. *The living world. These people are wise to say 'God is
great.' Joy! Joy!*

While out of town, Henry Salt made the British consulate in Cairo available to his gifted partner and servant. The diplomatic residence was a lovely old Arab house. A life-size carving of Rameses II dominated the inner courtyard where citrus trees fruited and a fountain tinkled delightfully. Lizzie liked to cool her heels there in the cascading waters.

Every day, she worked diligently at the Consul's desk, transcribing Belzoni's account of his discoveries in her superior English. Around her, the library of Burckhardt—the great stack of seven hundred Arabic books and manuscripts he had willed to Cambridge University—towered against the walls.

Burckhardt had died suddenly, at age thirty-three, his life's work incomplete. Belzoni felt the loss keenly. It drove him to accomplish more and more, but trying to write in the confinement of closed rooms was impossible for the restless man. Leaving Lizzie to puzzle over his notes, he had decamped to Giza where he theorized on how to open the Second Pyramid.

Arab tales said the huge building was packed with scrolls of ancient wisdom, magical drugs and rubies big as ostrich eggs. Medieval Christians thought the pyramid was Joseph's granary. To Lizzie, the mysterious pyramid was another challenge her ambitious lover had set his heart on conquering.

Under a blossoming lemon tree, in the Consul's courtyard, Lizzie rehearsed her dance steps. She dropped her garments in the sweet perfumed air, content to be alone in an empty house. Coming eye-to-eye with the Rameses statue, she posed before his full stone lips. "Remember me, Your Highness, the girl who lifted your covers at Abu Simbel?" She struck her cymbals by the Pharaoh's ear. "When we first met, you were really big."

After a delicious bath in the evening, she stole into the bedroom to admire her own Egyptian collection. From a leather-strapped trunk, she gently lifted out a small alabaster carving of a naked girl lying on her belly, adorable buttocks in the air, her hands presenting a tiny palette. *Should I keep this for mixing my new maquillage or save it for Emily?* There was a deep blue ceramic tile, embossed with golden spirals, the blue so intense it seemed on fire. In a bit of rag, the bangle bracelet Mangles had given her, and a pale clay figure of the sacred ibis with a fish in its bill. *I have seen your grandsons, sir, walking by the Nile.* Her fingers caressed the few perfect amulets: a scarab of yellow quartz, the eye of Horus leaking a perfect tear, and a carnelian "cross of life." She opened the doors of a red and green wooden box, inside a pair of seated clay lovers held lotus flowers and each other's hands.

Lizzie drew out the largest item to set on a bedside table. She removed the linen cloth covering a terra cotta sculpture of a copulating man and woman. Giovanni had bought it "for inspiration." The man was stocky, reddish, and holding out a penis three times the length of his person. The woman was plump and white, her legs spread to ride this magnificent member like a horse. The penis had penetrated right through her to the ground where three helpful dwarfs were collecting semen in an overflowing bowl. These ancients were having a jolly good time.

"Thinking of me, *bella*?" Belzoni unexpectedly appeared at the bedchamber door, his white teeth gleaming in an easy smile.

"How could you tell?"

"Did I surprise you?"

"You always do, *caro*."

Between the kisses and queries, he invited her to ride out with him that night to Giza. "I want you to be there, Lisabetta. But, while we have this comfortable accommodation"—he settled down on the bed, pointing to the terra cotta couple—"let us imitate art."

February 28, 1818

"Take care, Lisabetta! Let me just.... Stop where you are, *cara*. This will be so much easier." Belzoni wrapped her tired arms around his neck and scrambled up the rough stones of the Great Pyramid.

"You know the way so well, Giovanni," she gasped in his ear. "These blocks are as big as my mother's dining room table at home."

In a half hour of perilous climbing, they reached the summit, four hundred and eighty feet above the Giza sands. There, on a stone twenty-feet wide, they lay against each other under the black sky, spangled with the zodiac of stars, whispering and watching for the sunrise.

Belzoni had studied the Great Pyramid for months. Over the centuries, tourists squeezed into its chambers, baffled over its making and meaning. Belzoni surmised the Second Pyramid, standing in perfect alignment nearby, might be similarly constructed. Herodotus, the famous Greek traveler, wrote in the fifth century BC that this was the tomb of Pharaoh Chephren and the structure had no opening. In modern times, Napoleon's scientists could find no entrance. There was talk in Cairo that Consul Drovetti would dig into the pyramid for the glory of France, if necessary blasting his way in with dynamite.

Hastening to beat the French diplomat, Belzoni wangled a *fermin* from one of Mahammed Ali's lesser functionaries to explore the Second Pyramid. Only Lizzie knew her lover had hired eighty workmen to secretly excavate. Financing for this mad endeavor was emptying his flat purse. If successful, the achievement would not have to be shared with Salt. The glory would be Belzoni's alone.

Ten days earlier, behind a loose block in the pyramid's north face, he and his men had cautiously entered a passage, which burrowed a hundred feet into the heart of the structure. But the debris-filled cavity was a false corridor, crudely cut by grave-robbers.

Instinct told him to try a concavity thirty feet to the east. They began digging again. Towards dusk, a huge granite block was wrenched aside to reveal two upright stones supporting a third, possibly the lintel of the true entrance. Belzoni rode back to Cairo to fetch Lizzie to the site. Tonight, his expectations were great.

Their bodies cooled down in the morning dew. Lizzie knew Giovanni dreamed of a great reputation. Good luck to him. For a circus performer, with empty pockets at the end of the world, success would be hard to achieve.

"I was in Rome the first time I touched an Egyptian stone. As a poor young man, *cara*, I lived with a wise monk called Brother

Cesare. We labored together, cleaning the city fountains."

"You told me that the first day we met, over a meat pie at the Old Queen's Head. Remember?"

"I only remember how beautiful you were, Lisabetta, and how kind."

"Go on, *caro*."

"In the Piazza Navona stands an Egyptian obelisk taken by the Romans in the days of the Empire. Obelisks were carved to guard the sanctuaries of Amun Ra, God of Light. They show a sacred ray of sunlight pouring down on earth."

"We've seen Amun Ra everywhere, always standing by the shoulder of Pharaoh."

"Exactly." Belzoni stretched his long legs and put his head in her lap. "Well, various calamities had buried several obelisks in the rubble of Rome. A few generations ago, to show their power, the mighty popes raised them again. The hieroglyphs were a mystery, as they are to us. But to the holy fathers, the Light of God was eternal, so they embraced these old monuments as symbols of faith. My lowly job at the Piazza Navona was to scrape mosses and filth from the carvings of the fountain called the Four Rivers that is the base to such an obelisk."

"I've seen an etching of it. Is it beautiful, Giovanni?"

"*Bellissima.* As I worked down in the basin, scrubbing, I would look at the wonderful marble animals around me: a horse for the Danube, a crocodile for the Nile, and the male figures of the rivers, all big strong men like me. Brother Cesare taught me all creation was revealed in that fountain. The rock in the center was the one that Moses struck to make the waters flow, the palm tree was the symbol for eternity. I came to love it. People say the figure of the River Nile has a covered face because no one knows the river's source. But, I say the old man of the river feels the terrible presence of God. One day I dared to put my hands on the ancient hieroglyphs. They were holy to me. Do you suppose God has brought me to Egypt?

"To what purpose, *caro*?"

"To help me unearth these ancient things. So man will know God has always ruled this world."

They saw the minarets of distant Cairo glow in the tawny pink beginnings of dawn. The earth was turning. The disk of Amun Ra erupted from the horizon, striking the pyramids with shafts of gold. At the call of the *muezzin*, the two fell silent. On the ground below, Belzoni's men made their morning prayers to Allah.

"If my 'pyramidical' brains have found the true door, and God lets me go in, I will know he has blessed me."

"I have no doubt of it, *bello*."

"The day has started. *Avanti!*"

As Lizzie rose, she noticed names written on the stone beneath her feet. "Look! The Belmores have been up here. They scratched their signatures. The Earl, Juliana, and...who is Rose?"

"Rose was the countess's little dog."

"They wrote a dog's name on the Great Pyramid? Good God."

"The Belmores were intrepid. Why not sign their names? It is fitting, Lisabetta. I mean to make Belzoni a great name, a name writ large. I mean to sign it every place I go."

March 1818
Mrs. George Mario Trumpet
Longsatin House, Duncan Terrace
London, England

My dearest Emily,
For all this time away from England, I have kept no diary. What began as an escape has become my life. I never thought my story material for a traveler's account, an entertainment tale of wonders and hardships.

In past months, I have been dutifully transcribing Signor Belzoni's rambling journals. They tell of his discoveries in the East. He plans to publish this account in Europe and often looks to me for a turn of phrase when his English fails. He has been the doer and I the helpful observer, but what I have just experienced I want to share.

So, this tale is for you, dear sister-in-law, my family, my cherished friend. Elizabeth Trumpet, the actress you knew, has successfully disappeared into thin air. But, your Lizzie (whose name will never appear on the playbill of this drama) has literally become a torchbearer in the pageant of Egyptian history.

The day Belzoni found the opening of the Second Pyramid (I expect you will read of this soon in the papers) he called on me to climb the earthen ramp he had made leading to a small door fifty feet up the face of the mysterious pile. We both helped his Arab workers clear rubble away from a stone portcullis fitted into the granite walls. Belzoni was able to slide a thin cane of barley through a slit above it. Poking about, he estimated that the portcullis could be raised. With superhuman effort, he pushed the stone up a few inches and wedged it with small rocks, then dismissed the Egyptians. When we were completely alone, he took both my hands in his. Often I've wondered what place I held in this man's heart. Was he about to tell me?

Before I write of feelings, let me explain. In the past, I watched Jack Faversham achieve the pinnacle of theatrical success, then poison everything by taking revenge on the world and me in the bargain. The tenderness I offered he quite threw away. But I allowed myself to be ill used. No matter anymore.

Acting is an undignified way to earn your bacon, Emily, unless you love it. I always will, but I'm not sure Mr. Faversham ever did. Jack's brief hour of acclaim was just an actor's turn after all, a strut of his own vanity, like Shakespeare's "puffball," a gossamer memory, doomed to be forgotten when a newer player took the stage. I came close to drowning in the wake of Jack's sinking the night of that unfortunate performance at Drury Lane, but, thanks to God and dear Georgie's training with the blade, I lived. When I said goodbye to you, I vowed to never be at a man's mercy again.

Yet once more I'm in the supporting cast of an opera where the baritone has all the arias. What I am giving and receiving this time is different, Emily, I swear.

Giovanni's tasks are so demanding of his strength and very soul, I can hardly feel jealous of them in the usual woman's way. I've lived at his side in this desert where each day is dangerous and exhausting. He wishes to make a name in the world for his discoveries and daring. Why not? He is a remarkable man, Emily. He deserves what I wanted most and lost forever in my own country: respect. But I have digressed.

Instead of a declaration of love, he asked me to be the first to enter the pyramid. Why? The opening was still too small for his giant's body, we did not know what lay inside, and because no other soul could be trusted if the place held an undisturbed king and all his priceless things. He did not think our lives would last long if the poor workmen were thus tempted. Giovanni placed his faith in me. So, though God alone knew what was waiting in the dark beyond, I said yes.

He kissed me then and searched in his saddlebag for two torches. I asked for a "robber's rope" to swing on in case there was a pit to trap thieves. The old tombs are full of stairs and deadly drops. For an hour he strained to raise the portcullis alone with brute strength. When it was a bare nine inches up, I pulled off every garment, lit one of the torches and slithered under the tons of stone.

I was far from composed, the skin on my back, breasts and belly bleeding from scratches. My hand shook, holding the light as I peered into the deep darkness, the air so dead and dry it pulled at my lungs. Ahead lay an open space, a clear passage cut out of solid rock. I crawled on, grasping my coiled rope, feeling the passage inclining down. As I feared, there was a drop to another level, and I tugged on my rope-end so Giovanni would hold it firm as I swung down. Here was another corridor of red granite, spacious enough for me to walk upright with my flickering smoky torch. The walls were bare of decoration. I tried to not think of the huge weight of stones above me, but it was like not thinking of a crocodile when you are swimming in the Nile. Impossible.

I moved beyond where Belzoni could hear my voice, into what I imagined had to be the center of the pyramid. In a gloom unimaginable, I reached the King's Chamber, a stone room of black unpolished granite big as a banquet hall. The ceiling was twenty-three feet high, peaked and supported by beams of stone. I lit the second torch and noticed the dark walls sparkling around me. Crusts of salt stuck to my fingers when I touched them. No paintings here or statues of gods. But I did spy a black, carved sarcophagus set into the floor, a broken lid beside it. Empty. I was not inspired to lay my nude body in the coffin and commune with the spirit of the Pharaoh. Though, perhaps the old boy would have enjoyed a visit from an undressed actress after so many thousand years alone. I returned to the hanging rope before my torch burned out. Calling in my second-balcony voice for Giovanni to pull me up, I then squeezed back out as I had entered, through the compressing stone gap.

I found him in a sorry state. During the long time I had been gone, he regretted sending me in alone and was more anxious to know I was safe than to ask what I had found. Giovanni's feelings for me were as naked as my bleeding body. In that passage, tight around us as a walnut shell, he held me in his arms, hearts beating a rapid tattoo while tears washed both our cheeks. Well, it was a moment.

I dressed and made my way into the welcome air outside. We chose four of the best workmen from the camp to return with levers and raise the portcullis enough for Giovanni to enter.

This discovery has created much excitement, jealousy and conflict. Inside the pyramid, Giovanni has etched his name and the date in letters so large no one could miss them. Salt is proving far from amiable. Alas, I anticipate discord ahead. But, for this spring, Belzoni is the hero of Giza. Huzzah, I say. My part was brief, but an adventure.

Please keep this letter in the box you decorated to hold my clippings and playbills. When we are old dames together, recollecting in our chairs, we will take it out and read it with Georgie's precious letters, and be proud all over again.

Kiss your growing babes for me.

Your loving,

Trumpet of the Pyramids

Chapter Forty-Two

January-February 1820

LIZZIE AND Giovanni sailed back to England on the *Star of the East*. The ship was an old Indiaman, creaky and leaky, but big-bottomed enough to hold Belzoni's personal collection of statues, mummies, and smaller treasures. The long voyage gave them enough leisure to nearly finish writing Giovanni's narrative. Contrary weather confined them together in their cramped cabin for endless hours.

One wet afternoon, all the pitching and yawing turned their stomachs queasy and tempers short. Lizzie put down her pen when the winds picked up. She curled in her bunk, knees up, under a heavy quilt. Belzoni stopped dictating when he had to "clap on" to the rope life-line in the damp room. Low in spirits, they returned to their old argument.

"I say again, *carissimo*, it is not a proper title. Books do not have forty-two-word titles."

"It is the perfect title: *Narrative of the Operations and Recent Discoveries Within the Pyramids, Temples, Tombs and Excavations in Egypt and Nubia; and a Journey to the Coast of the Red Sea, in Search of Ancient Berenice; and Another to the Oasis of Jupiter Ammon.*"

Lizzie raised a cryptic eyebrow. "That certainly says it all." She looked at Giovanni's handsome face with patience. "But, something simple would make for larger print on the cover. How does this sound? *The Egyptian Explorations of Giovanni Battista Belzoni*, writ in large letters of gold."

"We are not preparing a playbill," he snapped, frowning. "This is a work of science, a book for gentlemen of learning. Short titles are for ladies' novels."

"Mmm." Lizzie remembered how well titled *Sense and Sensibility* was. A large wave hit the bow. A pair of Giovanni's huge shoes *chasséed* across the cabin floor like ballet dancers. "More importantly, I'm concerned about your tone, Giovanni. You attack those men who do not support your achievements."

"You mean those spiteful, jealous blackguards who say I paid a fellow a hundred pounds to find Seti's Tomb? That I paid another fellow to open the pyramid? I want it understood I made those discoveries alone."

"I was there, too, remember?"

"For much of it, yes. Thank you, Lisabetta, of course. But you saw in the French newspapers that reached us how Drovetti belittles me. In the English journals, Salt takes credit for my discoveries, when he was never even there! We don't know what people think of me in England, or how I will be received."

"I'm sure they will think a great deal of you, Giovanni. When people see your collection they will be astonished. Filled with admiration. It isn't necessary to tear others down to build yourself up. Your words against Salt and Drovetti may, I fear, make you look small."

"Small?"

"Ungrateful. Vain. You know what I mean. In the beginning Salt did pay you, *caro*, so...."

"Rubbish! Nothing I have written needs to be changed." Bristling, he sucked in his queasy stomach.

"I've been transcribing your journals for months, never expecting any credit for it, but I do think you might listen to my opinions." Lizzie rearranged her cramped legs with a restless kick. "I want the book and the exhibition to be a triumph as much as you."

"We change nothing." Angry now, the hairs of his head seemed to vibrate.

"And when it comes down to it, Giovanni, I shall have no reception in England at all, since I will arrive in disguise. It would be wiser for me to never show my face in London. Try to understand my fears about the future."

How much they needed to get away from each other, to exit the cabin and say nothing more. But the troubled waters made that impossible.

When Drovetti blocked Belzoni's plan to open the Third Pyramid, the thwarted Italian tramped into the eastern desert, in search of something old that would be something new. With Lizzie at his side, he explored the Oasis of Jupiter Ammon, where Alexander the Great had gotten the notion he had a covenant with heaven to conquer the world. During their forty days of wandering, Belzoni suffered a terrible fall down a rocky hillside. The camels died from the many days without water, and devilish thirst came close to killing Giovanni and Lizzie both. She could not imagine a journey more intimate in misery. At the end of it, Belzoni found the windswept remains of Berenice, a renowned lost city of antiquity.

He returned to Cairo with a reputation for success so conspicuous, the jealous French took to shooting at him. Outside the Luxor temples, a gun was fired in Lizzie's direction. Giovanni, in his rage, knocked a few hired brigands off their donkeys. Drovetti watched his men dispatched from a safe distance. This final encounter and subsequent lawsuit had hastened Belzoni's departure from Egypt.

It pained Lizzie to be quarreling over something so small as words on a page. But, these words would serve to make Giovanni's reputation, and that was no small matter to him. Reputation had been no small matter to her. Once. She quietly sighed with frustration. The silence between them lengthened.

"I have asked too much of you, I see that now," Belzoni finally said in a cool tone he had never used with her. "What will be best is for me to write the book myself." He pulled himself up to stand over her bunk. I'll leave you to make sure our baggage is secure in the hold." Then his hand took her ink stained fingers in his own. "I believe you want success for me, *cara*, but we remember things too differently. *Capito*?" And he was out the door.

She pitched the pages of their work into the air with exasperation, her heart withering in her chest. "*Capito*."

⚓

Little Arthur Trumpet ran up the staircase to Emily's room. "Mother! Come quick. There's a creature in black, knocking at the door. I think it's a ghost." Message delivered, the golden-haired four-year-old hurtled back down the steps.

"A moment, please," Emily called out, crossing the worn floor.

Arthur had climbed a chair to get his father's sword down from the wall and was fearlessly swinging the scabbard against the drapes. "I'll protect you, Mother."

"Be still, darling, and stop that slashing at once." Emily pulled the boy against her side, drew the bolt, and cautiously opened the door. A blast of March wind blew the visitor's black veil and robes in the air like a dark descending angel. Emily recoiled.

The little boy lunged at the menacing stranger. "Go away. Don't touch my mother!"

In the commotion, Noddy had come out of the kitchen. "It's Miss Lizzie!" he shouted and cut a caper on the carpet.

"Emily, forgive me," the figure in black cried. "I had to cross London like this. Don't be afraid, Arthur, I'm your auntie."

Shocked into candor, Emily could only say, "My God, Lizzie, what happened to you?"

"Everything, my darlings. Everything!"

⚓

April 1820

England welcomed Giovanni enthusiastically. *The London Times* announced: "The celebrated traveler, Mr. Belzoni, has arrived in this metropolis after an absence of ten years, five of which he was employed in arduous researches after the curious remains of antiquity in Egypt and Nubia. He plans to display his beautiful tomb from Thebes when a convenient hall is located."

Such attention excited the Italian. Moving quickly, he engaged Egyptian Hall in Piccadilly for a full year and took a small room for himself in Half Moon Street. The aristocratic tourists he once guided round the tombs and pyramids were delighted to find him in town. "The Young Memnon" was on display at the British Museum and drawing crowds. John Murray, the respected publisher of *The Quarterly Review*, came forward immediately to publish Belzoni's narrative. Murray introduced his author to the cognoscenti with a new persona: "Man of Science." Giovanni, the man of the moment, entered social circles the Patagonian Samson could never have stepped into.

Miss Trumpet's role was to be a supporting branch on the growing tree of Belzoni's celebrity. Anonymously, she shouldered responsibility for the creation of his exhibition. Work and passion entwined them in Egypt, but now they were physically separated most of the time. Lizzie didn't envy him any happiness, but she began to daydream of living her old London life again.

The last man she had said goodbye to in England was the first she hastened to look up, Frederick, Lord Dampere. In the intervening years, the actress's old admirer had become the entrepreneur of a thriving brewery, in imitation of Samuel Whitbread, that generous benefactor of the Theatre Royal Drury Lane. In those troubled post-war years, the working man and so many who could not find a job at all, solaced themselves with cheap drink. As the barrels of Peer's Proud Ale rolled out, the money rolled in.

Octavia Onslow managed Dampere's entry into commerce. She kept order in the books and a cool head sixteen hours a day in the red brick building on Brewer Street, Pimlico. Since making Octavia a silent partner, his lordship had never been so rich or well taken care of. Watching the retired *grand horizontal* work so hard in a legitimate business shamed Freddy. Forsaking his old round of fashionable entertainments, he had recently taken up his duties in the

House of Lords with a seriousness that was appropriate to the times.

The lord was dumbstruck at Lizzie's return. Their reunion was toasted in generous samples of the peer's beverage. Octavia, required to attend the arrival of a wagonload of hops, left them alone in her third floor office that overlooked the brewery.

Lizzie noticed Dampere wore a black coat. The country had begun a year of mourning for the death of George the Third. Gone at last, the mad old king was warmly remembered in the public mind, especially in comparison to his extravagant flesh-pot son, soon-to-be crowned King George the Fourth. Like his royal friend, Dampere was fatter than ever. Tight-tailored over a man's corset, his guileless baby face flushed pink, he resembled a ripe-to-bursting fig. Lizzie's clothes impressed him as well.

"Are you costumed as a follower of Allah for some reason, my dear?"

"It is to make myself invisible."

"Hoo! I should think it will do rather the opposite. Walking down Bond Street in such a costume, you will stir curiosity. Let me take you to a dressmaker this afternoon and order you some pretty things straight away. Are you in need of funds, Lizzie dear? I'm overjoyed you sought me out. Your slender cheeks and bronzed complexion have only gilded former beauties." With a happy gasp, he made a move to kiss her hand. She saw a web of red veins now laced the Dampere nose.

"Dampie, please understand. If I'm a fugitive still, my face must stay concealed in public. Can you just tell me how I stand with the law? I've been gone so long, surely that nightmare with Faversham must be forgotten by now."

"Truly, Jack's skewering is something for the archives. New scandals happen every day. Let me tell you the latest." He sat her down on a handy chair and poured himself more refreshment. "Remember Princess Caroline, the foul-smelling Brunswick woman the prince found repugnant on their wedding night and never touched again?"

"I know that was the story." Lizzie sipped her ale, tasting home in every swallow.

"Well, now that Prinny is finally going to be crowned king, he wants to divorce her. She's been living abroad for years, disporting herself with a big Italian of low degree. Their household staff will be made to witness against her. Maids will tattle about how many bodies in a bed, stained sheets—that sort of thing." His upper lip was bedewed with the froth of excitement and the foam of drink.

Lizzie murmured, "Really," wondering how to get back to the subject of herself. Dampere ran on, telling of the delicious downfall of the great.

"Caroline has refused to divorce. She wants to be queen now, despite years of carrying on with this Bartolomeo Pergami fellow and being the scandal of Europe. A parliamentary Bill of Pains and Penalties is coming to the House of Lords to judge the grounds for dissolving the marriage. Then there will be a very public trial. I fear I shall have to sit in my red robes of state with the peers of the realm and do my duty. Judge the evidence of every sweaty reminiscence, don't you know? Why they don't just give Prinny his way I'll never understand."

This avalanche of information about the consequences of an unhappily married woman having an Italian lover disturbed Lizzie, but did not put her off. "Thank you for the gossip, Dampie, but I came here to inquire about my own situation."

"Ah, yes. Another glass?" She shook her head. "Well, the thing of it is...." He pursed his lips glumly. "Sadly, you are still outcast, my dear. 'Pistols for two, coffee for one' used to earn a slap on the wrist for the survivor. No more, Lizzie. Your initiating a duel remains 'attempted murder.' If you are reported at large in London, the magistrates will collect you in a trice. With so many witnesses against you, it would mean hanging. What a loss to the English theatre. So, sadly, you must remain hidden."

"Nothing has changed?" Her eyes had lost their sparkle. "Even if Jack is alive somewhere?"

"The bastard disappeared like dew in the morning, Lizzie. I tried to locate him myself, but even if he died in a ditch, and may I say, I certainly hope he did, it wouldn't take the guilt off you."

"I see." Lizzie looked up at the glass oil lamp hanging above her and felt a weight nearly forgotten strapped back onto her shoulders. "There will be no chance of being an actress anymore?"

Dampere slowly shook his head. Her cherished daydreams of returning to the theatre with a fictitious name, first doing tiny parts in outlying towns, living her career over again and coming home to Covent Garden as a reborn leading lady, had all gone awry. Elizabeth Trumpet, the actress, was finished. It was a hard blow. Lizzie's eyes showed it, though they stayed dry and were looking levelly back at Dampere.

Out of his dog-like affection, he said all the wrong things. "How I've missed discussing plays with you, Lizzie. Oh, it will be wonderful to have you with me in my theatre box again. I can't wait to see your disguises, the costumes, what role-playing you will do. The finest actress in England will be sitting in the audience." He patted her elbow awkwardly. "I am so very sorry." She nodded as if she had lost only a trifling thing. "Here's a thought. I might put on a play myself. What about Elizabeth Trumpet behind the scenes, secretly advising me at every step? What do you think of that?"

She thought very little of it, but was too heartbroken to speak.

In the silence, Octavia burst into the office, pulling off her shop apron, then crushing Lizzie in a heartfelt hug that was returned to a prodigious degree. "Well, my lord, have you told our dear friend of her part in Peer's Ale?"

"What's that?" he asked brightly, the ash-blond curls above his collar corkscrewing upward.

"The investment. You do recall?"

"Oh, of course, of course! I forgot to mention it, in the surprise of such a phantasmagoric reappearance. I'm a perfect pudding-head sometimes. Mama always said so. Cast your mind back in time, Lizzie. Once in a letter you urged me to seek out an enterprise to channel my energies. Remember that? You planted a seed, the sprout of which has come to frothy golden fruition." Dampere opened his arms wide to indicate his yeasty domain. The subject changed his demeanor, his moonish face all abeam.

Lizzie looked bewildered. "I don't understand. I have no capitol to...."

"When his lordship told me you had inspired his interest in manufacture," Octavia put in more calmly, "I suggested he make a token investment on your behalf, by way of thanks."

"Our Octavia has a fine headpiece on her, does she not? I immediately put in a hundred pounds. You will remember that was the amount your Jack urged me to hand over to the Faversham Players. Money he never saw, but to me it always had your name on it." Dampere was eager to rectify a slight Lizzie had nearly forgotten. "And, by way of being a silent partner in Peer's Ale, you will always be a part of all this. A part of my life. Utterly without obligation, you see." Stopping himself short of choking on emotion, the man asked Octavia, "What is the dividend? I confess, Miss Onslow keeps the books better than I."

Withdrawing a ledger from her upright desk in the room's corner, the redhead made several calculations with a dark blue feathered quill. She finished and turned to Lizzie. "As of this month, Elizabeth Trumpet's account has accrued over five hundred pounds sterling. These monies are awaiting you in the company safe."

Lizzie gasped, crumpled in her chair, and began to weep.

Octavia knelt before her, tenderly stroking her trembling hand. "I am pleased beyond measure to give you this news, Lizzie. You may not be an actress anymore, but take some consolation. You will never be a pauper again."

❧

"Where to next, Miss Elizabeth?" A light drizzle was falling on skinny young Marco Mantino, who had been waiting for Lizzie in Brewer Street with a small carriage. Marco had been the baby sick with diphtheria, that cold spring of 1803, when Jessie had nursed him and died herself. Now dressed in a maroon coachman's uniform, he was old enough to be a driver for his parents' livery business. Maria and Salvatore Mantino blessed the memory of Lizzie's mother and father and charged the returned traveler no rental for the modest carriage. "Back to Islington?" Marco asked.

The subdued passenger straightened her spine against the

horsehair upholstery. "Not yet, Marco. Please take me to Maiden Lane. Let us try to find a place I remember in Frances Court."

It was a short drive to a covered alley opening onto a patch of emerging green grass, surrounded by three-story houses. The alley passage was choked with the traffic of two cart-loads of furniture under canvas.

Marco jumped to assist his passenger down the carriage steps. "I'll escort you to the door, Miss Lizzie." He offered an elbow respectfully. "Don't know what kind of odds and sods might be lurking about this close to Covent Garden."

Lizzie immediately saw the house she was seeking, the blue front door wide open. Cartage and bundles of luggage were leaving the residence in the arms of three hurrying black servants. "This is the place, Marco." She chucked him under his stubbly chin. "I will go on alone from here." She could hear a rich male voice, shouting inside the house.

"What a *cock-up*! I told Timothy we would need three carts. What was he thinking? Now there is no room for the music stand. Well, I'm not leaving it behind!" A man with disarrayed white hair popped his head out into the rain and waved her away. "No Gypsies! No Gypsies today! Don't want my fortune told, thank you very much." The blue door slammed shut.

Lizzie stood still, projecting her voice to fill the gloomy grey court. "Would that be George Frideric Handel's music-stand? The rosewood music-stand you saved from the Covent Garden fire? I'll help you carry it, Carlo."

For a moment, silence, then a whoop that ascended four octaves from basso to coloratura. The blue door flew open. "Darling, darling, darling girl!" Carlo danced her into his empty house. "These eyes of mine didn't recognize you at all in that costume. You look ready to sing *The Abduction from the Seraglio*. But your timing is terrible. I'm leaving the country tonight."

"For a concert tour, maestro?"

"No, for America! I'm to be an impresario amongst the savage colonials of Pennsylvania. I've been invited to create my own opera company."

"My, that sounds too good to be true."

"Well, you may be right. I'll be starting from scratch, surrounded by Quakers who won't even sing hymns. I'll get them going with some Gluck, Old Testament oratorios, *Samson* and such."

"They should love that."

"I've signed a second contract, in a moment of weakness, to put on poetry readings at the Walnut Street Theatre, also in Philadelphia. Do you know it?"

"No, Carlo dear, I've never heard of it."

"The place is supposed to be old, well established for America. Of course, nothing is really old there."

"Perhaps that's a good thing?"

"The Yankees put great value on experience since they have none. Which means, I'm going to be well paid. Best of all, I can put Mr. Grey into the roles he should be singing instead of watching those macaronis from Naples take his parts when they don't have half his talent. The powers that be at the Royal Opera are besotted with Italian singers. It's too exhausting to bear."

"Timothy is going with you?"

"Yes, he should be at the ship now, with his costume trunks. We're off from London Dock with the evening tide."

"Carlo, I can't stand to say goodbye to you again. Could you spare just a few minutes to talk?"

"Of course, darling. Let me lock the doors and dismiss the heavy-lifting boys. I'll take you round the corner to Tom Rule's place in Maiden Lane for a bite of supper before I go. He'll find us a private room. You look like you could use a good helping of steak and kidneys."

"I could, I could."

"This will be my last meal in England. Let's order the whole menu, from potted shrimps to spotted dick. Spotted dick has always been my favorite." He laughed. "Oh, darling girl, it is sublime to see you!"

It was impossible for Lizzie to be sad in the presence of the friend she loved so much. They crammed a good deal of talk into the hour at Rule's. She told a much abbreviated version of her Egyptian sojourn then asked Carlo's news of all their old acquaintances.

Charles Dibdin had lost the Wells, and currently moldered in prison for debt. Beau Brummell had fled to France to escape his creditors, and was laid low with syphilis, dying by excruciating inches. Thomas Jupiter Harris puttered in his Wimbledon garden, recuperating from a life in show business. Dick and Meg Wilson had gone to watch the sunsets over Budleigh Salterton and grow fat on Devon cream. Phillip Eggleston lived in retirement, but would never dream of dying anywhere else than his London rooms. The officious factotum Neville Boone was still in service, pouring coffee and starching collars, strutting over Eggleston's decline, and gleefully cutting any actors who turned up in hopes of a job. The great Edmund Kean was now famous for making alcohol a part of his every characterization. Grimaldi, the king of clowns, continued to perform, hobbled and bent from a hundred old injuries. Attentively, Lizzie took it all in, till time grew short.

"Carlo, I need your help. Where can I find good painters and scenery craftsmen to make models for Belzoni's exhibition? His expectations are high, but his money is short."

"Let me give you some names, darling. I know a pair of gifted fellows painting away at the Lane. I'll write an introduction to get you back stage." He called for paper from the waiter and scratched something for her after paying the bill.

"Do you plan to go disguised as a male or a female?"

"Female. I've spent too many days clumping about as a Mameluke boy."

"Delicious! You must give me all the details some day. Here are the scenery-builders' names and my address in Philadelphia." Lizzie carefully placed it in a hidden pocket beneath her black robes. They moved together across the restaurant. Carlo told Tom Rule he was on his way to Pennsylvania. "To 'The City of Brotherly Love.' That sounds promising, doesn't it?"

Marco drove the carriage with Trumpet, Tomassi, and Handel's music stand safely to the London Docks where Timothy awaited, near to apoplexy watching the rising tide. Excitement kindling in his eyes, Carlo made Lizzie swear to sing every day. "And practice every aria I taught you." He gave no advice, but knew she wanted some word to carry her forward.

"Don't despair, darling girl. Life is full of possibilities, and your life is not over."

She choked down a monstrous lump in her throat. "I am selfish to wish Philadelphia was not so far away."

"I shall write often, Lizzie. *Lo giuro*, I swear it."

The rainy skies had cleared into a beautiful blue and gold evening as they said goodbye below the tall-ship masts. "Bon voyage, Carlo!" she shouted. *"Bon voyage*, Timothy!" She gave a last wave and stepped into the carriage.

Amongst the dock workers, a shuffling man turned his head at the sound of Lizzie's voice. As the carriage rolled smartly away, his dim eyes could just make out the discreet lettering on an outside hamper. Mantino & Sons Livery, Islington.

Chapter Forty-Three

Summer 1820

"THE SEABRIGHT brothers build with speed and accuracy, ma'am. Harry and I will have it up in a fortnight."

"I'm sure the Italian gentleman you represent will be pleased," the younger brother added.

Lizzie was meeting with the two young scenic carpenters Carlo had recommended. Belzoni wanted no part of going into a theatre to engage model makers and left this crucial task up to Lizzie. There was nothing for it that morning but to assume a new identity and present her introduction to the call-boy at Drury Lane, the scene of her *crime*. Memories of the violence she had lived through on that stage made her rigid with nerves.

Stephen and Harry Seabright were vigorous, good-humored artisans who had begun painting tradesmen's wagons, and now created scenery pieces of surpassing realism. Lizzie's drawing of a decorated pillar from Seti's Tomb, with all the dimensions neatly marked, excited their imaginations. If the plaster copy they created was accurate, she would entrust them with her wax moulds of the raised carvings of Horus blessing Pharaoh.

While the brothers wrote up their estimate, Lizzie noticed a splattered old print of "Elizabeth Trumpet as 'Winged Victory,'" tacked to the scene shop wall. Beside it was a cartoon of Nelson mounting Emma Hamilton. Both images were brown with age. *Tempis fugit, Trumpet.* She smiled to herself, drawing three pounds from her reticule. "For the cost of materials, Mr. Seabright."

Harry took her money with a waggish grin and put knuckle to forehead in thanks.

"Mind the shavings on your shoes," Stephen said, giving his hand to lead her out through the elephant doors. "Can you see your way, ma'am? It's a bit dark backstage."

Lizzie had introduced herself as Madam Abydass and spoken with the bastardized accent she had used in any plays set east of Constantinople. She wore black-rimmed glasses in want of a wipe, a dress of Emily's that was a few inches too short, a cheap grey wig with ringlets like ram's horns and a homely bonnet, round as a cave, that covered most of her face. "I am not a bat, Mr. Seabright. I shall find the exit, thank you."

No one recognized her, and she had seen no familiar faces. Certainly this was the moment to go, but the breath of backstage air, rich with dust and scenery paint had flown her back in time. She stopped to listen to the actors rehearsing Shakespeare's *King Richard the Second.* Someone had just begun John of Gaunt's famous speech from Act Two.

"This royal throne of kings, this scepter'd isle."

Gaunt was one of her father's roles. She could almost hear his dear voice speaking, as the words washed over her.

"This other Eden, demi-paradise.
This happy breed of men, this little world,
This precious stone set in a silver sea."

With a start, she looked straight at the stage. There was something familiar about the unseen actor's voice.

"This blessed plot, this earth, this realm, this England."

She stepped nearer the wings to see the man who was playing Gaunt.

"This nurse, this teeming womb of royal kings."

A prompter flatly interrupted the flowing Shakespeare. "Mr. Mallory, we are taking a cut here. Your last good line is '...this realm, this England,' then enter King Richard."

Mallory protested. "But that cuts eighteen lines, Ted—the heart of the speech!"

"The old play is long, sir. We're taking the cut. Enter Richard and his court." A band of players in heavy coats, who had been waiting in the theatre's freezing space, ambled on.

Lizzie had witnessed this sort of artistic agony thousands of times. Jack constantly cut the speeches of his supporting cast, especially when actors risked having shining moments of their own. She looked over her glasses, feeling sympathy. In sharper focus, the actor named Mallory not only sounded familiar, he looked familiar. *Well, damn me!*

Mallory was hoisted on a litter by the servants of Richard's court and carried off stage to expire. Dumped in the wings, he got up slowly, with a wounded air, and had a private seethe.

Lizzie approached him in the cold dimness to say with Slavic gutterals, "You make very fine Gaunt, Mr. Mallory."

The actor looked down his arching nose at such forwardness from a foreign woman in an ugly bonnet. Dismissingly, he turned away to rearrange his wooly muffler. "Madam, are you aware this is a closed rehearsal?"

"Is it? Forgive me. Your acting compelled me to listen." *How can he argue with that?*

"Well, thank you, madam. John of Gaunt is a choice role, though brief."

"I never speak to a gentleman I do not know without proper introduction, but I believe I know you, sir. I am Madam Abydass, but you? Have you previously been in holy orders?" The man stared blankly at her smudgy spectacles. "Did you ever serve as a vicar?"

"I have always been an actor, madam, but you have guessed the essence of the Mallory specialty: roles of gravitas—judges, Roman senators, bishops, men of the cloth. The stock character of a kindly vicar I have played with much success many times."

Lizzie was positive this was the man she remembered. What that could mean so shocked her, she nearly forgot to sound like Madam Abydass. "Where and when might I have seen you?"

"Well, the very first time I took such a part," Mallory was delighting in his own biography, "was quite strange, really. Some years ago, when I was pretty green, I met an actor who was making a bit of a name at the time, putting together his own theatrical company. He wanted me, dressed as a vicar, to meet him and some pretty ingénue by the Stonehenge monuments at midnight to perform a marriage scene. There wasn't to be an audience, mind you, but I had to wear a high church costume and never say a word out of character. He told me he was experimenting with ideas for a play he intended to write. He probably was experimenting with the ingénue, too."

"You performed a ceremony?" Lizzie's knees threatened to give way.

"Not a real one, of course. I met the bride and groom by the standing stones in my old-age make-up, alb and surplice, holy as God. I spoke some passages from the Book of Common Prayer and came out with an extemporaneous blessing that had all three of us in tears. Next morning, the actor met me in a Salisbury pot-house, looking very smug, gave me seven measly shillings and never said a word about engaging me for his grotty little company."

"Your story captivates me." She could barely control her voice. "What happened next?"

Mallory assumed she was asking about him, of course. "I felt my performance had gone so well I emphasized spiritual qualities at my next audition. Sure enough, I spent several years working in Dublin playing loveable papists in comedies at the Crow Street Theatre. Found my niche, as it were."

"Did you ever see that actor again? The one who played the bridegroom?"

"Fortunately, our paths never crossed. He acquired a very unsavory reputation. Became quite unstable, poor wretch. I can see you are innocent of the ways of the drama, madam. The audience often confuses an actor with the part he plays. I'm positive you missed my debut as a vicar unless you were wandering across Salisbury Plain in the moonlight some thirteen years ago. Ha!" He chortled at the thought. "But, somewhere else you may have seen me in one of my piety roles and an impression was made." He flashed some yellow teeth.

The dawn had broken wide open. "An unforgettable impression."

"Well!" He made a courtly bow from the waist. "Indeed a pleasure, Madam Abydass. I hope you will come see our *Richard the Second*. My benefit night is on the tenth, in two weeks." The teeth flashed again.

"What was the name of that unsavory actor? Surely, that's the most significant part of the story?"

"Oh, there was nothing significant about him. Jack something-or-other. He died revoltingly, madam. Unlike myself, he did not last."

"What's your pleasure, dearie?"

"Bring me a snifter of brandy."

Noddy and Marco were standing outside the Shakespeare's Head, watching Lizzie through the small glass windowpanes that faced the vegetable market, flower carts, and loitering whores of Covent Garden.

She sat with her back to them. Having emerged from the Theatre Royal announcing she needed a drink, she'd marched across the piazza to the tavern, the men dogging after her.

"You stay back with the carriage. I 'ave my eyes on 'er by right of seniority," Noddy said. Marco walked off, crushed as the cabbage leaves and turnip-tops underfoot. Noddy settled himself by the bow-window, happy to be in that lively part of town. He'd heard there were over a hundred brothels in Covent Garden. The sassy girls parading under the arches of the piazza were stimulating his fantasies.

Last year the twenty-nine-year-old had had a mind to leave London and become a factory worker for better wages in the north. He'd arrived just in time to see his great uncle Alex sabered by the Manchester Yeomanry at the Peterloo Massacre. The workers' uprising and violent suppression by the government had terrified Noddy. He drew a veil over his own memory of nearly being trampled. He wouldn't have believed such things happened in England. Giving up thoughts of improving his lot, he had returned to Islington, content to serve the Trumpet family till death.

When he remembered his duty to guard Lizzie, he turned back to squint through the tavern window. Three empty brandy glasses were on her table. She gestured for a fourth. "What's this then," he wondered. "Not like Miss Lizzie at all."

Inside the tap room, the actress was powerfully stirred by Mallory's revelation and the unaccustomed alcohol. *So, never married at all.* Tears began to well. *How Jack must have laughed when I was spreading my arse for him. Calling him husband. I could forgive him trying to murder me. But I can't forgive how he made a fool of me.* She sipped, swallowed, and smoldered. *Burn in hell, Jack. Mallory says you're dead, dead as mackerel. If you were alive today, I'd run you through all over again.*

By her fifth brandy, Lizzie mellowed into tipsy gaiety. Bonnet awry, she felt light of head and heart. When the waiter trotted by, his prominent Adam's apple captured her fancy. She peered at him through Aunt Peg's distorting spectacles.

"Are you musically gifted, sir?"

"Not so's you'd notice."

"Pity. I took you for a castrato." She cackled with laughter.

Noddy's face pressed against the window was the last thing Lizzie saw before sliding off her chair to the tavern floor.

⚓

Marco picked up the reins. The riotous passenger had been loaded into the carriage in every sense. "What's to be done, Noddy?"

"Take the long way 'ome. Give 'er a chance to come more to 'erself 'fore Miss Emily sees 'er."

Marco turned the sorrel mare towards the Strand. "Pa told me she's unjustly outlawed. That's why she's goin' about dressed so peculiar—in-cog-a-ni-to, Pa calls it. Do you think she's play-actin'?"

"No." Noddy sighed. "Crykies, she's three sheets to the wind, all right. And I don't know why, I'm sure. Unless somethin's 'appened to 'er back at the theatre."

The two had no way of knowing more and dropped the matter as the grand new structures on Regent Street filled their eyes. The carriage had to stop in the heavy traffic of St. James's, people and horses churning about as the men waited and fidgeted, their two behinds sharing a driver's seat built for one.

"These here are the new gas lamps," Marco said, pointing. "Supposed to be wonderful bright."

"Very pretty, I'd say." Noddy rubbed his eye where a coal dust cinder had lodged.

"Whoa, what's that noise?"

"Why, I believe Miss Lizzie is singin'."

Indeed she was, the "Queen of the Night's" coloratura snatches blending chaotically with songs of the tavern. Alarmed at such ringing sounds floating out of his passenger, Marco turned the mare out of traffic and towards Green Park. Inside the carriage freedom reigned. A window opened and bonnet, then spectacles, flew into the street.

"Boys, where are we?" Lizzie's head and shoulders pushed through the opening and the grey wig fell out, too. "Do you know I'm an unmarried woman, Noddy? I'm free."

"That's very fine, Miss Lizzie, but please to keep inside."

Lizzie unpinned her hair, singing, "Free am I, free as a beeeeeee." Marco trotted the sorrel mare up Piccadilly. Heads turned. "Freer than I used to beeeeeeee."

"Don't race the 'orse, for God's sake," Noddy yelled, hanging on to his seat and his hat. "Don't make a spectacle!"

"Too late," snapped Marco. "A spectacle is what we are."

Lizzie's long dark locks of hair were whipping in the breeze as she emerged from the window again. "Oh, there's the Gyppo Palace," Lizzie trilled as they trotted past Egyptian Hall. "Are you in there, Giovanniiiiiiiiiiiiiiiiiiiiiii?"

As the horse whinnied and turned right into the Haymarket, Marco pulled back on the reins and they slowed to a reasonable trot. Throngs of Londoners had seen the loud soprano in the careening carriage by this time, but fortunately not a single one had recognized Elizabeth Trumpet.

"I want to go somewhere else, boys," Lizzie announced, no longer singing or throwing things out the window, but rather hanging there like an overripe fruit. "Where are we?"

"Cockspur Street, Miss Lizzie. But I think we must 'ead for Duncan Terrace now."

"Not yet. Oh, no-no-no. Go left into the Strand, Marco. Is there anything you boys would like me to sing for you?" She waited two seconds. "You'll like this one; I learned it on Gibraltar.

She loved her young lodger from Kent
And his poker, so long that it bent...."

Marco cut her off. "Sing when we get 'ome, Miss Lizzie. Then Bob's your Uncle Dick."

She giggled. "Head for St. Paul's."

"Right-ee-oh."

"Marco, are you enough of a Londoner to find Pillory Lane?"

"What do you want in that place, Miss Lizzie?"

"A filthy pot house called the Tudor Rose."

"And if 'e can find it?" asked Noddy, apprehensively.

"If you love me, Noddy, on my order, you will walk up to it and piss on the door."

Chapter Forty-Four

Fall 1820

*T*HE BOY *in blue ran away from Lizzie and almost out of sight. She pursued him with all her strength, kicking against her long skirts.*

"Come back," she called, waving as she jostled strangers crowded into the lane. "He can't hear me! Oh, why doesn't someone stop him?"

She pushed into the yard of the Angel, where coaches and carts were departing in a melee of mud and noise. The boy had mounted a skittish horse that spun about, nearly trampling her. "Stay, Georgie, stay!" she screamed. The horse reared, raising him above the crowd into the failing light that touched his golden hair and silver braid. Time stood still as a spot of crimson blood blossomed silently on his tunic.

"No!" she screamed and sobbed as horse and rider galloped away.

"Aunt Lizzie."

Lizzie awoke to find herself, not in the horrifying circumstance of the nightmare, but the safe quiet of her own chamber. Standing beside the narrow bed was the boy of her dream in miniature: little Arthur Trumpet, his blond curls and adoring blue eyes a perfect copy of her lost brother. Georgie to the life.

"Are you all right, Aunt Lizzie? You cried out."

"Oh, sweeting, I'm quite all right. Here, give us a kiss."

She struggled with the twisted bedclothes, pushing the unwelcome dream out of her consciousness. The five-year-old pressed a wet peck on the cheek of the woman he was devoted to. Lizzie took a deep breath and drew her nephew close. "I was having a dream about your father."

"Oh, tell me, please."

"Well, we were running down Duncan Terrace, as we used to do when we were your age."

"I wish I could see him."

"He was a little older than you are now."

"Was he wearing his uniform?"

"Yes."

"Blue and Silver?"

"Yes, and he was mounted on a wonderful horse."

"A white horse?"

"Yes."

"Did he ask about me?"

"This is what he said to me. Tell Arthur I'm watching everything he does. Tell him I love him very much."

This was a love that Arthur struggled to imagine. The sounds of traffic passing in the lane drew him to the window. It was a day of dismal fog that muted the clopping sound of a carthorse pulling its load to market. Arthur pressed his palms against the window glass. "I wish my father was here instead of in heaven."

"I know, darling."

"I'm glad he came to see you." The boy turned from the dreary view. "Can we have sword play, Aunt Lizzie?"

"After a cup of tea and a wash, it will be my pleasure."

"Oooh." Little Arthur was enraptured by his aunt's skill with foil and dagger. Indeed, it was the foundation of his respect for her. Satisfied that his relative was her steady self again, Arthur scampered downstairs shouting to his mother and Noddy, "Clear the chicken yard. After breakfast, there will be battle!"

A wet towel pressed to her eyes felt more refreshing than sleep.

Pinning up her hair, Lizzie took a serious look in the mirror. *What had Papa said? Hard times made you strong. Hard times fired people like diamonds.*

Jack had denied her children. Perhaps his beating had destroyed her chances of ever bearing them. There was no way to know. When she tried to forgive and forget Jack, the regret she felt for her own barrenness made it impossible. Giovanni had spent measureless gifts of sperm in her, but there had never been a pregnancy. A child would have been so welcome...under any circumstances. She shook her head. *If I'm not a diamond, I certainly am an Auntie. That is precious enough.*

"Did Arthur wake you, sister?" Emily, fair and smiling, came to the doorway with a pot of tea on a tray. She had taken to wearing a ruffled white cap tied beneath her pointed chin. "I've told him to give you privacy, but I fear he thinks that's some kind of jam."

Georgie's widow had been without female companionship for so long, Lizzie's return to the house had lightened her heart. Following Waterloo, her father had suffered reverses in the economic downturn and was preoccupied with trying to keep his factory open. Mother Widewell wanted her daughter home in Sheffield on the condition that she wed a suitable beau. The beau the family found suitable proved a musty, wheezy fellow with a sock full of money to put into the struggling family business. Emily did not wish to become a human sacrifice, stiffened her spine, and said, "No, thank you."

For the funds to live on, she sold Georgie's valuable commission. Ted Wentworth had managed it for her before departing to India with his regiment. Her most generous relative, good-natured Henry Wentworth, had succumbed after a lifetime's incautious imbibing of Portuguese port. The family fortune passed to Percy, the eldest son who was gambling his wealth away in the highest style, wagering on horses that failed to place. Wanting to provide towards her own livelihood, Emily had prevailed upon Sidrack Sloane, with dignity and forceful argument, to make her an apprentice tailor. Showing a real skill, she had learned the art of pattern cutting and fine finishing, saving every penny of salary against the future. She hoped to make her money stretch far enough to educate her babes. Young Georgina was sewing samplers praising the virtues of thrift.

"You appear to be in fine fettle this morning, Lizzie," Emily offered.

I must talk Emily out of wearing that awful cap. She is making herself old before her time. "And you look the personification of cheerfulness."

Emily set the tray on the rumpled counterpane and sat down. "Our unstoppable boy is going to give you some exercise this morning, he tells me."

"Does it disturb you?"

"No indeed. His father would have given him such lessons. Arthur's been raised in a cattery of women after all. I'm thankful you're passing along the daring Trumpet heritage. You've always brought excitement with you."

"Yes, the chickens sound quite stirred up." Lizzie laughed, buttoning on a pair of trousers.

"Are you content? Tell me true."

"Perfectly content. I'm so grateful you've chosen to rear the next generation in Longsatin House. I've quite fallen in love with your children, Emily. I count myself blessed with such a family to cherish."

"Nevertheless, you must miss the stage."

"What penetration." Lizzie stopped dressing to sit on the bench at the foot of her bed. "You have caught me out. In Egypt, I could put the theatre out of my mind for weeks at a time, but here in London? I find myself yearning to perform again." Emily made a sound of woeful sympathy. "But, I must not dwell on the impossible. I was improvident and am paying the price. Fate has also given me you, and your children, whom I shall care for with a grateful heart. Don't feel sad for me."

December 1820

"It's perfectly beautiful, Giovanni. You are extravagant. Thank you, I shall treasure it." Lizzie caressed the soft fox tippet, lined with satin and tasseled with tawny silk. Belzoni had brought it back from

Paris where he had spent the past weeks arranging for the French publication of his opus. They reclined on the bed of his lodgings in Half Moon Street, surrounded by mummy-cases and crates marked "Antiquities."

"I remembered you said London feels cold to you now. At least this will keep your hands warm. Madame Abydass!" The Italian enjoyed her disguise, especially removing every part of it down to the skin.

After the urgent lovemaking, Lizzie attempted to discuss the details of the Egyptian Hall exhibit, but Belzoni was too full of his recent successes to listen.

"Do you know there is a new word for what I am, *cara*? Egyptologist. A scientist of the ancients. A *dottore* of discoveries. I am respected wherever I go. My narrative will be published all over Europe, in Italian and German, too." He sat up to light a cigar. "No one calls me the Patagonian Samson now. No more driving chariots in a circus of horse-dung. No billing below General Jocko."

"And it goes without saying, no more bears."

"I kept a trunk of the Great Belzoni's magic tricks and musical glasses in storage all this time. I sold the lot to a rag-and-bone man yesterday. Except for one article I found inside. A silhouette of you. Would you like it?" Belzoni put down his cigar to take a flimsy bit of paper out of the drawer by the bedside. "Made the day we met *dottore* da Ponte, remember?" He placed the image of her girlish self between Lizzie's naked thighs.

"Oh, I remember, *caro*."

"Those days are long ago, Lisabetta. It would be best to never mention them."

Lizzie put the memento inside her gift from Paris. Giovanni's hand was idly stroking her belly, as she drew the sheet over them both. *Had the circus days been as bad as that? Our past, our hopeful, striving, cherished past...he dismisses. But now, his present is even more...hopeful.*

She sat up. "The Grand Opening of your exhibition is May first. I'm so relieved you returned Giovanni, you have barely four months to prepare. Walls must be painted, the models put in place, chandeliers and seating planned, the advertising begun—so much to accomplish."

"And to think, Papa expected me to work in his barber shop." Belzoni picked up the cigar again to puff deeply. "You know Eggleston has quit, and Dibdin is in debtors' prison."

"I have heard. Dear Mr. Dibdin. It is deeply distressing." Lizzie wished to speak more of their old acquaintances, but the Italian wished only to speak of himself.

"They have fallen by the wayside, while I, the man in the cat skin, am celebrated for my 'pyramidical brains.' Ha! Did I mention the author, Sir Walter Scott, wants to meet me?"

"I understand he is charming." She took his hand. "Listen, *caro*. What do you think of giving a private party for the Royal Society before the official opening? It could make a splendid impression. A small dinner, perhaps an oud-player strumming behind some drapes, then you could lecture...."

"I should unwrap a mummy. That was a fine suggestion." He blew a smoke ring.

"They will be fascinated."

"You could dance."

"You forget, I am socially invisible these days. It will be your moment, *caro*."

"But you must help me, Lisabetta." He looked at her with a lover's certainty, lacing his fingers through her hair.

He still needs me then. For a while longer.

He took a long draw on his cigar, "I shall be the talk of London. Who would have thought it?"

"I would, Giovanni. I am very proud of you."

"Mamma will be proud."

Lizzie swung her legs to the floor and commenced a search for her stockings so Belzoni would not see her face. "*Certo, caro*, very proud. How could she help it?"

ᥱᲛ

January 1821

He felt strong enough to do some business. The bells of Saint Paul's rang through his lodging, scarcely disturbing the inhabitants. They rarely crawled out to face the morning light.

The man scratched at his unkempt mustache and started to button his trousers. Doses of mercury had diminished his symptoms of pox, but did nothing to drive out the blue devils that nested in his brain. These monstrous thoughts fed on his medications, pressing his spirit into darkness and isolation. The mirror that once was a favored friend had become his enemy. How hateful the sight of his body, covered from knees to chest with a scrofulous, crusting rash. His scalp was patched with random baldness, his mangled penis prone to weeping in his hand, disabled and retired completely from the acts of love. His self-loathing was only surpassed by his contempt for those who walked about free and whole. He lived to make the world suffer for his monumentally foul luck. In a haze of mercury-poisoning, with a headache pounding nails into his brain, he slid a pistol into the deep pocket of his dirty gray coat.

Actors traditionally received their pay of a Saturday morning. Leading men lined up with lesser lights, sharing the warm camaraderie evoked by the receipt of cash. Mallory, the seedy character actor who had so shaken Lizzie's memory of her own history, sauntered away from Drury Lane. He headed towards the neat bachelor room where he would deposit his three pounds of salary in a mattress. Oblivious to his surroundings, he muttered the speeches for his next role, a footman in the old comedy *Ways and Means*.

"*And I, Tiptoe, who once stood above all the world, came into a position in which all the world stood on Tiptoe.*'"

Out of nowhere, a sharp-toed boot kicked the back of his right leg, knocking him flat. A gun barrel pressed against his ear as a quick hand emptied his pocket.

"Don't shoot. Don't shoot, sir." Money taken, the boot struck another cracking blow into Mallory's ribs. The shocked man cowered. "Not my face, please, I am an actor."

The criminal in grey took vicious aim, and for good measure, kicked in a dozen of Mallory's yellow teeth.

Chapter Forty-Five

February 1821

"SKIPFORTH, IS it customary to tip?" inquired Charles Dibdin. Now fifty-two, his cheeks sagged as he clutched a leather portfolio of papers to his chest.

"No obligation, sir," replied the gatekeeper of King's Bench Prison. "But, may I say, it makes a gracious gesture, and shows the expectation of more fortuitous times ahead."

Swiftly, the inmate searched deep in his pocket for a satisfactory coin. He flourished a sovereign into Skipforth's out-stretched palm.

"'Twas a memorable experience having you lodge with us, sir. We hope never to see you in this place again. Look to it." The small door within the heavy prison gate swung open upon the beauties of Horsemonger Lane. The freed man passed through into liberty.

Waiting in the street was a fellow with ears like the handles of a sugar bowl. He walked up to the older gentleman who was spilling his papers and peering dazedly around in the sooty freezing air. "Mr. Charles Dibdin, is it, sir?" he asked politely raising a tall hat then retrieving the fallen papers with a scoop of his hand. "A very good day to yer, and this way, if yer please." Linking arms unasked, he maneuvered the composer to a closed carriage where Marco Mantino presided over the horses.

"I say, who are you?"

"Noddy's my name, sir. Now, if you'll just step inside, sir, Madame Abydass is awaitin' yer." Hesitantly, Dibdin mounted the carriage. Noddy shut the door and climbed up onto the seat. Marco made a kissing sound to the horse, which shook its bridle and walked on.

"How do you do?" Dibdin began, quite bewildered but genteel. "I have no memory of our previous meeting, Madam Appy Ass." The lady in the veiled bonnet, holding a fine fox muff, covered her mouth. "Should I infer that you, madam, are responsible for my being awakened this morning with the magistrate's directive to vacate the premises a free man? Free, though I have not paid a penny towards my indebtedness?" Silence. "If you know the name of that good soul responsible, please enlighten me. I am on the cusp of tears."

"It's Madame Ah-bee-dass, not happy ass," a voice rich with consonants answered through the veil.

"Oh, pardon. My hearing is not what it used to be."

"And you are grown thin."

"Madam, please. Who is the one I must thank?"

Slowly, Lizzie pulled off her bonnet. "The name is...Trumpet."

Dibdin's puffy eyelids opened wide. "My God, Elizabeth, it's you. Are you my benefactor?"

"Yes, Charlie. As you were mine. Carlo Tomassi told me you had been locked up for a year. I could scarcely believe it. Long ago, when I needed money so desperately, you gave me my first job. Those wages saved my family, though you never knew it. My first steps upon a stage were thanks to you. Of course, you will forever occupy a great share of my heart. How could I leave you to languish in debtors' prison?"

"Everyone else did." The threadbare showman's once-prosperous round tummy had shrunk to flatness. His ink-stained fingers trembled. "My dearest little Trumpet, such unimagined kindness. And once I behaved so boldly, so thoughtlessly to you. It quite staggers me. You, who have known such difficulties of your own, even to the very ruin of your name. Oh...." Dibdin could not control his tears.

"There, there, Charlie." She looked away to give him privacy, deeply moved herself. "How did they treat you in that dreadful place?"

Dibdin wiped his eyes on a fraying sleeve to gather himself. "Oh, I had the best of it, Trumpet. Skipworth judged me a celebrity and put me in Emma Hamilton's old suite: four moldy walls and a piss-pot." He laughed limply. "A choir of financial miscreants was training under my tutelage. Actors came to see me for new songs. So, my writing earned the occasional shilling or bottle of wine. I made a show of being resigned, as all the forgotten people do in there. But, it was hopeless." He looked outside the carriage at London flying by. "I can scarcely believe I'm free."

Lizzie watched him struggle into the happy present, unable to stop reviewing the dreary past. A hard rain had begun to fall, gurgling in the gutters.

"How did you come to be locked up, Charlie?"

"I had staged one extravaganza too many. All my creditors filed suit against me at once, making 'common cause.' Two hundred pounds owed, and you know the law, I could not set foot out of the place until it was completely paid."

"I well know the law," Lizzie remarked flatly. "Your creditors are satisfied. I hired Mr. Kipper, a solicitor of the smallest reputation to attend to them before your release."

"But, you have not appeared on the stage in years. Where did the money come from? Surely you have not purchased my freedom with your life savings."

"Not quite, Charlie. I have just received an unexpected dividend, and this is how I chose to spend some of it. Henceforth, the renowned tunesmith of England, reunited with his family, may repair to his keyboard and get back to work in the theatre he loves so well."

"I shall write such music for you, Trumpet." He waved the leather portfolio expansively. "A burletta! An opera!" He drew her gloved hand out of the glamorous muff to kiss it with some of his old impetuosity.

"No more songs for me, Charlie. Not a word to anyone about who paid your creditors. You are free, but Elizabeth Trumpet is still an outlaw. You will remember that."

His nod jostled the tears from his eyes. "Then how can I ever thank you?"

"See it another way. I became an actress because of you. Those were the happiest years I've known. Bless you, Charlie, I think they were worth two hundred pounds."

᷂

April 29, 1821

"Lisabetta! His Majesty is in the hall. He and Lord Dampere are admiring the Sekhmet statues," Belzoni hissed elatedly through the curtains of a makeshift stage in Egyptian Hall. His face had a hint of the rising sun in it. Plainly, this night was fulfilling the Italian's greatest dreams.

"Calmly, Giovanni. Keep your head on straight. I will introduce you with the royal presence in mind. We must begin. Calmly now, *caro*, calmly."

Belzoni's pre-opening party for the gentlemen of the Royal Society and taste-makers of London was humming with excitement. The learned men, wearing evening clothes, were enthralled by the exhibits in the outer rooms. The host moved amongst his guests using an exuberance of courteous phrases, only appreciated by those who had traveled in Italy. He addressed everyone as "*dottore.*"

Lizzie's role was to formally introduce Belzoni in an unforgettable manner, yet remain incognito. For this, her last theatrical appearance, she chose to dress as a divine being. Arms bare, a slit sheath gown of sunset tones covered her body to the ankles, stitched like the feathers of a gorgeous bird. Below her breasts, she tied a silk cord in the sacred knot of Isis. Across her shoulders was a jeweled collar of carnelian, matched bracelets of lapis encircled her upper arms and wrists. Her massive headdress shingled down her back, glittering with hundreds of jet beads weighted with gold spangles. The circlet on her forehead supported a metal disk, polished like the sun. She had painted her eyes with long bands of her precious green and black kohl, the dark brows extended like wings. Her full lips were dusted with shimmering, powdered gold.

Behind her stood the re-creation of the Chamber of Beauties, with its open-armed goddess floating on the indigo ceiling of stars. The great men and doctors of science were settling into gilded ballroom chairs. As the gas-lights dimmed, she heard a well-bred crescendo of murmurs. The hidden musicians began drumming and shaking the sistra cymbals, spattering the guests with ancient tones.

Lizzie cued the curtain to open and began a slow sensuous walk from the rear of the chamber towards the seated King of England. She made obeisance, allowing the masculine audience to get a good look at her, then proudly began to dance. Slowly she glided, in serpentine gestures of arms and hips, seducing the imaginations of her watchers. Her moves displayed passion with regal dignity. At the shuddering climax, every man in the room felt he had been made love to. Lizzie bowed to the king once more and stood center stage to speak in a resonant voice with the accent of Egypt.

"*Salaam*, Majesty, anointed by heaven, ruler of the Seven Seas, powerful king of a powerful people, inspiration of artists, gift to the ages. *Salaam*." Placing her right palm on her forehead, Lizzie bowed deeply.

She raised her arms to include the rest of the audience. "*Salaam*, honored subjects of this king, masters of learning, explorers of the world and philosophers of nature. You have planted wisdom in the many gardens of our globe. *Salaam*.

"Welcome to Egypt. We have waited for you these thousands of years. I, Isis, lover of mankind and goddess of life reborn, invite you to behold the long forgotten beauties of my kingdom, sacred to my ancient people. Welcome to the tomb of Pharaoh Seti. I implore you to study my mysteries with the strength of your intellect that my riddles may be solved for the enrichment of all generations. Each treasured fragment of the past has been retrieved from oblivion beneath the sands of time, to ornament the glory of your realm and the wisdom of your scholarship.

"One man alone accomplished this. He searched through my deserts and stony redoubts to open doors thought sealed for eternity. His narrative tells the tale of fearless years under my blazing sun, guided only by his genius and perhaps a whisper from me. He has re-

435

created the sights he beheld, that you, without the dangers of a long journey, may see them, too. This evening he will answer your questions and, for your wonder, open the mummy-wrappings of a noble young man, preserved with all the magic of my sacred rites. Your Highness, distinguished guests, Isis blesses your studies and withdraws to present...Giovanni Battista Belzoni."

A soft rustle of sistrum and drum sounded as Lizzie backed into the shadows, and Giovanni entered dressed in turban and robes. He bowed to the king and drank in the fulsome applause.

The monarch spoke up before the Italian had finished filling his chest with air. "Not many men have a goddess introduce them." Lord Dampere, craning his neck in the second row, laughed aloud. "Tell me, Belzoni," the king asked, "what were your thoughts upon seeing the ruins of Thebes for the first time?"

"Your Highness, it was as if entering a city of giants who, after a great conflict, had all been destroyed, leaving the ruins of their temples the only proof of their existence."

Lizzie observed her old friend's face, glowing with joy.

May 1, 1821

Opening day, nineteen hundred people crushed into Egyptian Hall, queuing down Piccadilly, paying a half-crown each to see the wonders. The cognoscenti of the world mixed with the merely curious. Belzoni instantly became a celebrity. The king invited him to Carlton House for private chats. He was quoted, toasted, and painted in turban and robes. Thomas Hope, designer of Egyptian-style furniture, burned with jealousy and also was painted in turban and robes. Sir John Soane, the architect and collector of all things ancient, frothed at the lips to acquire Belzoni's treasures. Old acquaintances Irby and Mangles braved the crowds to give their congratulations, published a jointly authored account of their adventures in Egypt, and were likewise painted in turban and robes.

Elizabeth Trumpet did not attend the exhibition.

Chapter Forty-Six

June 1821

GEORGINA TRUMPET swung off her borrowed pony to the mounting block at Mantino and Sons Livery. "What a lovely canter, Aunt Lizzie. Can we go out again tomorrow? Please, please?" The pretty seven year old was mastering the art of equitation these summer mornings, turned out in a pale blue riding habit lovingly tailored by Emily.

Her poised aunt looked far less elegant in chamois britches with her hair tucked under a moth-eaten old hat. Disguised as a man, Lizzie always rode out early to avoid notice by a possibly curious neighbor. A story in *The Morning Post*, describing the retirement of Mr. Kenneth Mallory of Drury Lane due to a savage beating, had disquieted her greatly. The ghost of Jack was never assuredly laid to rest. For all her dash and courage, a part of Lizzie still warily watched for his phantom to rise.

"Aunt Lizzie, can we go out again tomorrow?"

"I give you praise today, Gina. You avoided the cow flops in the pasture and guided your pony with soft hands on the reins. Brava!"

"But can we ride tomorrow? Say yes, Aunt Lizzie."

"We shall see, pet," Lizzie answered, preoccupied with rubbing down her mount and noticing the doings down the lane at Duncan

Terrace. "Do you spy that hackney cab outside Longsatin House? Hurry along, Gina. I believe we have a visitor."

The visitor was Sidrack Sloane, still the manager of Adam & James of Savile Row. Of late, his sight and hearing had begun to fail and his perfect posture was settling into the hunched slump of an aged man. Yet he faced the world immaculately dressed, as always his own best advertisement. As Sloane's physical powers diminished, his regard for the people he cherished increased. The generations of Trumpets, with all their talents and trials, had always had a place in his heart. On this morning, spurred by grief, he wished to open that heart.

Georgina made her curtsy to him in the grey salon and was collected by Emily so Lizzie and her caller could be alone.

"I bring tragic news, Elizabeth dear. Roger's bright little wife Susannah is no more. She died giving birth to their third child."

"No."

"My son is quite destroyed, as am I." He lowered himself into William's old chair.

"Oh, Uncle, I am so sorry. God bless her soul." Lizzie closed her eyes to imagine Susannah on Roger's arm, as she remembered them, both exhilarated by love. "And the child?"

"The baby lived, a girl. I would make the journey to Charleston to be with Roger and my grandchildren, but my strength has deserted me. It is all I can do to climb stairs now." He pulled a starched handkerchief from his sleeve to mop tears from his withered cheeks. "From my couch in the rear office, I watch Turkolu do business through a crack in the door. I only get up to greet the older customers who ask for me. Time rushes on, and I feel ancient as Methuselah. I'm quite, quite useless."

"You could never be useless, Uncle, only tired from doing so much for so long. Thank you for bringing me Roger's sad news. I shall write him directly. My grandmother sent a letter a month ago, with a watercolor she painted of the Charleston family. Let me show you."

Sidrack drew on his spectacles as Lizzie took the picture off the mantel then sat on the arm of his chair. They studied the piece of paper that described a different world. Flowering bushes framed a white porch where the family posed. Nana had painted herself seated in a rocking chair just in front of Lizzie's slender grandfather. Roger and Susannah held the hands of two small children. A caged canary watched a snoozing, fat-tailed cat.

"Please tell me who everyone is, Uncle." Lizzie pointed to the children.

"That's Roger's son William, called 'Billy,' and Nancy, his pretty little sister. She inherited her mother's curly red hair. Roger wrote to me if the new baby proved to be a girl, Susannah wanted her called Elizabeth. He obeyed her dying wish. So now you have a namesake."

"Susannah did that for me?" *A woman who hardly knew me...such a kindness.* "I'm deeply honored, and I'll write my thanks to Roger." She took Sidrack's hand. "Tell me more. Tell me everything."

"Roger built his home on King Street, right beside your grandparents' house. He takes his duty to watch over them seriously, as I had hoped. He purchased land outside Charleston, and has many responsibilities besides the shop. He is a good son."

In the painting was another couple, African of countenance, sitting on the porch steps. "The black folk are their slaves. Ceres is the slender turbaned woman in red and her husband is Silenus." Lizzie looked at the regal black man sporting a magnificent hat. "Let me see, the cat is Claudia." He scratched his chin with a small smile. "I don't remember the canary's name but it's something Italian. Sopranino, perhaps?" Sidrack handed the picture back.

Replacing it on the mantel, Lizzie realized frailty had settled on her Uncle. *Like spider webs on a neglected old treasure. The tide of time surges over us all. What treasures have I neglected?*

"There is another matter." Sidrack cleared his throat. "An apology I have owed you, Elizabeth."

She gave a questioning look. "I cannot imagine...."

"This is no small matter to me, dear. I am pained by regrets. When you were a fledgling actress, really just a headstrong girl trying to help her family, I had much to say about it."

"But that was so long ago. No one could have stopped me from pursuing the theatre and, not to say it too plainly, Jack Faversham. I, too, have regrets, Uncle. I was swept away with—"

"Wait, my dear, this is not about your acting at all. Hear me out.

My son Roger cared for you. Smitten with you from the cradle, Elizabeth. A worshipful devotion. Growing up, you were never aware. I could see that much. Not a forward child, my Roger. Poor lad, he was that shy. I doubt you ever noticed him."

Lizzie sat still, remembering, as Sidrack fought a lifetime of reserve to speak aloud of his feelings.

"Of course, I loved my boy, but I didn't believe he had the strength of character to match yours. When you matured into such a spirited girl, I advised Roger to beware of you. I thought he could never please you, and if he tried to, it would end in tears. But, I was wrong to interfere. If I had encouraged Roger to follow his heart, to court you, perhaps your history would have been a happier one. That is my great regret, Elizabeth. I kept you from an honest man who loved you. I did you a wrong, and Roger, too." Sidrack pressed his handkerchief to his watering eyes.

"Uncle, you could never do me a wrong. Where would this family have been without you?" Lizzie embraced him in the chair, patting his thin shoulder. She drew back to examine his words. So, Roger had loved her. *How many cues have I missed in the drama of life?* "Now you speak of it, I had no idea Roger favored me in that way. And I was headstrong. But he married a wonderful woman." She searched for comforting words. "You can be proud of the life he has made. Surely it was all for the best."

"Roger has more to him than I imagined. He will find his way. And so will you, my dear. Thank you for hearing out a sentimental old man." He pocketed the crumpled handkerchief. They both looked at the watercolor, feeling the presence of the past. "How glad the Trombettas would be to see you again, Elizabeth."

Gently, Lizzie helped Sidrack to his feet and, with careful steps, out to his carriage. She waved farewell.

In the oak tree, singing birds delighted in the high tide of life. *Roger Sloane.... How different it all might have been.*

Coronation Day: July 19, 1821

"But you will come inside, Lisabetta. I was invited by the prince himself. I will not have you slip away when we reach the Abbey."

"No, no, *caro*. The risk of being recognized is too great. Newspapers say the doors will be guarded to keep out poor Caroline, the Princess of Wales. Giovanni, I cannot afford to be scrutinized by those protecting the new king from his unhappy wife."

"Then why are you here at all?" the Italian asked petulantly.

"To spend time with you, *caro*. I knew it would take forever to get through the Coronation traffic."

The two former entertainers were overheating in a line of carriages between grandstands full of Londoners. Looking out the coach window, Lizzie mused the whole world seemed gathered to observe the crowning of King George the Fourth.

The transit of Prinny into a consecrated monarch would reflect the Regent's chronically lavish taste, since he planned every extravagant splendor. The twelve-foot-long crimson velvet cloaks, edged in packs of snowy ermine, were his design. They draped over the shoulders of his many brothers and scads of other English dukes. For the immensely long garlands the belles of society would wag into the cathedral, he had selected every rosebud. At the moment of his anointing, Handel's solemn theme "Zadock the Priest" was to pipe over the guests. Only court favorites were to witness this royal rite of passage, and Belzoni would be among them.

Trapped in the standstill traffic, still thousands of feet from the stained glass windows of Westminster Abbey, Lizzie sighed in her "Madame Abydass" costume.

"Ah me. Well, tell me, Giovanni, how have you been passing the time?"

He crossed his arms. "Lisabetta, it is not as I expected, this celebrity life. I'm required to tell the same stories over and over, until I bore myself. I'm very nearly sick of The Young Memnon and talking of moving his big stone head."

"You addressed The Royal Society at Somerset House. That was a great achievement, *caro*, as I remember once the very pinnacle of your dreams."

"Yes, well...then. Now, not so much. Everyone of importance has read my Narrative. I have requests to speak from all over Europe. I am invited to the royal courts in Paris, and Stockholm." He ran a finger around his neck-cloth uncomfortably. "Even the court of the Czar in St. Petersburg!"

"You will go, of course?"

"Of course, but it will be the same."

"Surely you enjoy the medals and esteem? There are no higher circles to enter, Giovanni. This is the life of fame. 'The Great Belzoni' has a distinguished reputation. You wanted your name to be known. Well, it is."

"I am still an entertainment, Lisabetta. People look at what I have done for their amusement, and because they know me, they think to claim me. Society wears me like an ornament. It is exhausting."

Lizzie let him fume. *If anyone on earth should be happily satisfied, it's you, Giovanni. I wonder if Kean grew bored at playing Hamlet? I think...not.* "You are just restless for a change, some sort of challenge."

"I spent an evening at Carlton House last week."

"A happy occasion, I'm sure."

"His Highness is still talking about you...well, that speech of Isis. Ha! As we spoke, he personally refilled my glass."

"Maraschino liqueur, was it?"

"Yes. How did you guess?" Lizzie shrugged and smiled. Their coach rolled ten feet closer to the Abbey. "His Highness suggested I go to Africa, Lisabetta, to explore the uncharted areas and find a route to Timbuktu, as Burckhardt wanted to do."

"Well, that would certainly make a change."

"It was Burkhardt's quest. But I would not rot like Burckhardt, waiting for a caravan to carry him over the desert. I would go in by sea, make my way north by river to the mysterious city."

"You've given this thought then?"

"His Highness thinks I'm the perfect one to go. And truly, *cara*, I'm bored to death with talking about Egypt. I've proved myself to the world. It's time to strike out again, go exploring for the new king." Lizzie sat silent, as he tapped his fingers on the plush carriage seat. "A new adventure in Africa. What do you think, Lisabetta?"

"I think men die in Africa. The slave coast is a dangerous place."

"Danger is exciting, and I am never ill. Serpents, crocodiles—nothing brings Belzoni down."

"Have you never heard this? *'Beware, beware, the Bight of Benin. For few come out, though many go in.'*"

"A poem?"

"A sea chanty, I believe."

"Only that?" He turned to her. "Well, I am going. Will you come with me, *cara*?"

She looked into his handsome confident face. *This is seduction.... I know the plot...passion and hardship. The man takes the bows.*

"You must be tired of hiding from your English law in this dirty city."

"England is home and my family's home. How could I ever be tired of it?"

"This will be a great adventure, Lisabetta," he said earnestly. "I would invite no other person in the world but you."

"Really, *caro*? No men of science, mapmakers or botanists? Just me?" They had finally achieved the Abbey doors where throngs of people crowded around the coach. *Tell him the truth.*

"Lisabetta, you must come with me."

"There are other people in my life who need me."

The Italian reached across the carriage to hold her, crushing the folds of his linen. "If I'm a great man now, you helped to make it so."

"You were always a great man. My help didn't make it so."

"No, Lisabetta, my good luck began when you walked out of the Nile to me on the island of Isis."

"What sweet words, Giovanni. Thank you for them."

"You will come with me then? To see the African stars?"

Lizzie saw those stars in her heart. *They belong to him. I must live for another's dream no more....* "Not this time, *caro*."

"What is left for you in this place?"

The faces of Arthur and Georgina flashed in her mind like lights. *Like stars. The little ones...they need me.* "I have journeys of my own to make."

"Lisabetta! I love you. Is that what you want? I do, I swear it."

No, Giovanni, my gift from Isis...I want my own life. She pressed her mouth to his. "Good bye, *caro.* Thank you for so many things. Godspeed."

Lizzie grabbed the door handle and leaped out into the crowd to disappear from Belzoni's sight forever.

Chapter Forty-Seven

July 20, 1821

"Y OUR PARDON, Sir Richard."

"Can't a man digest his coffee and peruse the morning's news in peace? Has some noble head been cracked in the national jubilation over the coronation?" Sir Richard Ford, dry and thin, snapped his paper testily. "Why are you disturbing my few moments of respite from thuggery and squalor, Markham?" He withdrew into his overbite. "My court opens in a quarter hour. Let the sorting out of mayhem and misery begin then."

In his private office above the court at #4 Bow Street, the Magistrate and Chief of the Bow Street Runners had been reading *The Morning Post* account of how Queen Caroline, attended by her large Italian lover, upon demanding admittance to Westminster Abbey as the rightful Queen Consort of England, had been dragged away screaming from its guarded doors, per the king's orders.

The security detail of Irish pugilists had been less successful in barring the entrance of another known Italian, Giovanni Battista Belzoni. The authenticity of his coronation invitation was in doubt. Displaying the national trait for high histrionics, he had quashed debate by overpowering the skeptics on the cathedral's steps with a display of matchless strength and bulled his way in.

"My Lord, I would not have troubled you," the perspiring Markham insisted, "but this fellow has information about a returned fugitive—a rather famous fugitive, sir."

"Is this informer a blackguard? A rambler, known to you?"

"He's more of a citizen, sir, well spoken, quite unknown to me. Decidedly down at heel, but he seems to be the genuine article, Sir Richard."

Wearily, the magistrate drew his goat-hair wig of powdered curls from the enameled box on his desk. In five minutes by the clock, the "genuine article" was being interviewed in the dark hallway outside Magistrate Ford's private seat of ease.

"The infamous Elizabeth Trumpet has been going about London bold as brass these many months."

Ford took in the sickly pallor and agitation of the emaciated man with rheumy eyes and deferential manner, an unsteady man, obviously reduced by sickness and circumstances.

"The Trumpet creature masquerades in many disguises, but I know her, your lordship." The citizen tapped his forehead with a dirty finger.

"From close acquaintance?"

"Observation, sir. I saw the so-called actress many a time on the great stages in the neighborhood of this very building. I've taken to investigating her whereabouts. I can tell you where she lives and obtains her horse and carriage."

"Why is this case of interest to you, sir? There is no reward posted."

"I saw the hell-bitch stab that poor man on the stage five years ago. A sight of horror. It is my duty to come forward, that justice may be served."

"I recall the victim disappeared, as well as the actress. Did you know him?"

"Me? No, no. I didn't know him at all, your lordship. Poor bastard, he must have died in agony. Take her up and you'll find a thousand other witnesses that can identify the criminal Elizabeth Trumpet."

"And your name?"

The citizen bowed his head in humbleness. "Rykes Bowtree, your lordship."

"Your vigilance appears to have exhausted you, man."

"Though it be my last act on earth, I feel gratified to have done my duty as a faithful subject of King George, a loyal citizen of England, a child of fair Britannia...." He grasped his frayed lapels and cleared his throat.

"Yes, quite, thank you. Markham!" Ford summoned the clerk to his side. "Take down Mr. Bowtree's information and show him out."

When it was done, Sir Richard called Markham back to the door of his court as he prepared to enter and give justice. "That peach of yours is a 'case,' Markham. Poxed, with a grievance against the fair sex because of it, I should say. Plainly barking mad. We can ignore his account of the fencing actress." Ford brushed some flecks of powder off his black robed shoulder. "I don't credit it."

Frederick, Lord Dampere, had not creased the sheets of his bed since participating in the coronation ceremony, an orgy of ostentation, followed by a lavish banquet. Such a memorable day required staying up all night to toast the new reign. He recovered in the soft arms of Octavia Onslow, his full-blown rose, whose familiar affections never failed to comfort. In the morning, she proposed a drive to Islington so Lord Freddy could share the details of George the Fourth's historic bacchanal with the ladies of Longsatin House.

Two hours later, all were playing a good knife and fork over a breakfast of shrimps, oysters, and a quantity of Peer's Proud Ale. Lizzie was the least hilarious, a bit preoccupied, but in general, spirits were high.

Noddy placed a platter of Dutch cheese and fresh-pulled garden radishes on the mahogany table as a rider dismounted in Duncan Terrace, unnoticed by any save energetic Arthur.

"Mother, there's a soldier outside."

"What, darling?"

"Not a soldier," Octavia corrected, peeling a shrimp and glancing out the front window from her chair. "That's a Robin Redbreast, Arthur, of the Bow Street Horse Patrol. They are the police."

Conversation stopped. Lizzie pushed back from the table to run on silent feet out of the room.

"Where's Auntie going, Mother?" Arthur asked, reaching for a taste of Dampere's Ale.

"Put that down, Arthur," Emily snapped. "You and Georgina go upstairs this minute. Scurry now."

"There's just one man. No posse with him," Octavia whispered. An officer in blue coat and scarlet vest was pounding the knocker of the door.

"I'll answer it." Emily buttoned the cuffs of her morning dress.

A very young "Robin" removed his tall black hat, but did not put down his truncheon when Emily opened the door. "Yes?"

"I am Officer Meredith, ma'am, of the Bow Street Patrol. Is there an Elizabeth Trumpet keeping herself here?" He eyed her with the boldness of authority. "And, what is your name, madam?"

"I am Emily Trumpet, widow of Major George Trumpet of the Tenth Hussars. Elizabeth Trumpet was my sister by marriage," Emily answered with dignity. "This is my house, sir."

"It's reported she's been seen coming and going, disguised as various persons."

"That's very vague, Officer Meredith. Various persons are seen coming and going everywhere. Elizabeth has not lived here for years," Emily lied with cool propriety.

"This person has been seen in carriages belonging to the Mantino Livery Stable."

"Then surely you must talk to the Mantinos."

"I've been sent to investigate, you see."

"Doesn't your patrol generally guard the major roads, protecting us from highwaymen and such?" Emily asked, all big blue eyes and innocent gullibility.

"Yes, ma'am." The Robin lowered his truncheon. "I'm off to join the lads working the Great North Road."

"Here, Meredith, you must be thirsty after your ride from London." Octavia slid into the little vestibule, proffering a mug of ale to the Robin. "We were just toasting the new king's health." She touched her drink to his and offered a wide, winning smile.

"Oh, thank you, ma'am. God save him." He drank. "And who would you be?"

Dampere's urbane voice answered. "This lady is Miss Octavia Onslow, my trusted employee at Peer's Brewery of Pimlico." His flushed face loomed over Octavia's shoulder, crowding the ladies in the vestibule. "And, before you ask, I am Frederick, Lord Dampere, of Ten Park Place and the House of Lords."

"Oh yes, my lord. Of course."

"Care for a shrimp, Officer?" Octavia asked brightly.

"I personally assure you Mrs. Trumpet is speaking the God's truth. Are you here with a proper writ or warrant, or did Lord Richard just send you to investigate?" Dampere demanded with moral authority.

"Oh, my, no. I'm not the investigator." The Robin gave a subservient nod to his social superior. "Lord Richard's clerk, Mr. Markham, thought I could have a look-see on my way up the North Road."

"Well, tell him you did, and give my compliments to Sir Richard." Dampere forcefully shut the door.

⚞

Noddy stepped into the lane a few minutes later to water the big piebald horse harnessed to Dampere's caleche. Leather bucket in hand, he looked around for loiterers, but saw no one.

Lizzie was ready to bolt the house, believing a posse of Redbreasts was sure to return. Her friends gathered in consternation around the mahogany table.

"The new Thames River Police that guarded shipping in the Pool of London might have been alerted already," Dampere warned.

"You can't leave town from The Sign of the Angel. With all the travelers, it's the first place the police will be watching," Octavia said sensibly.

"If there's any possible way, I could get to Charleston...." Lizzie felt torn in two as she looked at Emily. "My grandparents are there."

"Whoever has seen you, my dear, they have pierced your disguises." Dampere caught Lizzie's shaking hand. "Nowhere in England will be safe for you anymore. America is a fine suggestion, the best sanctuary. Don't panic, everyone. I think this can be done."

"Do you, Dampie? What must I do?"

"If Lizzie has to flee, this time I'm going, too!" Emily declared. "Instead of a woman alone, wouldn't it be better for her to travel with a family?" Lizzie looked across the table at her brave little sister with relief.

Octavia spoke up. "Emily, you astound me." She touched her friend's shoulder. "If you are to travel with the children, as a family, you could use a man to play the beleaguered father."

Lizzie left them for the kitchen and returned swiftly with Noddy, who was wringing a bit of towel and looking baffled.

"Noddy, I am glad to go off to America, but we do not ask you to leave your home," Emily told him with urgency. "It would make things better, but we do not require it. You are a free man, Noddy, not bound to us in any way."

"My 'ome's the people in it, Miss Emily. I've served Miss Lizzie and the Trumpets all me life. If yer going travelin', I expect you'll need a 'and with Master Arfur. It suits me right enough. What would I do with me'self alone in Islington with your family walkin' the world?" Gratefully, Lizzie set him to finding William's trunk for their journey.

Octavia took the extra set of keys after asking to be responsible for Longsatin House. Dampere would arrange passage on whatever cargo ship might be bound out of England on tomorrow's first tide.

When the case clock struck one, the friends were saying farewells, embracing and clinging, telling each other not to fear. Emily climbed the stairs to inform her children they were bound for an adventure.

Lizzie heard Emily's voice through the bedchamber wall. *Good people are risking so much to protect me.* As she bundled clothes together, her old fury at Jack burned afresh. *Because of that lunatic's jealousy that provoked me to take up a sword in anger, I'm like Jane Shore...outcast forever.* Even in this turmoil she remembered the play's lines.

"One false step entirely damns her fame;
In vain with tears the loss she may deplore,
In vain look back on what she was before;
She sets like stars that fall, to rise no more."

Weak with the shock of her feelings, she dropped on the bed. *Am I never to be done with the ghost of him?*

Jack Faversham was not a ghost yet, but close to it. Curled in the back of a hack at the end of Duncan Terrace, he strained to watch Longsatin House. He'd meant to destroy Lizzie himself, but syphilis had moved through his body with its own scenario of revenge. Instead, Jack had played his last scene, offering her up to Magistrate Ford and the retribution of English law. He watched the Robin depart without her. The law had failed. Sickened with disappointment, he snarled at the jarvey to wake up as Lord Freddy's caleche rushed past them.

After some high words with his loathsome looking customer, the cabby trotted his horse towards London. Jack told him to keep a distance behind the caleche. They waited as Dampere sprinted into a bank on Lombard Street, left in a rush, and drove to the ticket office of Butterfield Shipping, in the shadow of Blackfriars Bridge.

Getting Arthur and Georgina into bed that night required Homeric struggle. By ten o'clock the children were down, spent with upset and excitement.

Lizzie planned to rouse them at two in the morning, when a Peer's Proud Ale delivery wagon would roll up and convey them to the London Docks. She prayed Dampere's connections and Octavia's efficiency could make this happen. Her bravado of the morning had worn thin as night fell. Passing Emily on the stairs, Lizzie begged her to sit for a moment on the wooden steps.

Her hair half fallen from its golden knot of braids, the distracted mother leaned back against the banister. "What is it, Lizzie? Oh, I just remembered, Noddy said Mrs. Mantino is pleased to take over the livestock."

"Listen, Emily dear, you don't have to do this. Are you sure leaving is best for you and the children? I know you love me, but you don't have to sacrifice your home to prove it."

"No. Understand, I'm glad to go. If Arthur grows up in England, with constant reminders of the regiment, he will believe there is nothing better to do with his life than be a soldier. I don't want him pledged to the Tenth Hussars because his father was a hero. I want him to have a long life. I won't see him die for glory, like my darling."

"You've never said a word to me. How long have you felt this way?"

"I thought nothing could be changed, but I tell you now I am happy. These are not the circumstances I would have wished, of course, but I am happy. Optimistic even."

"What of your mother and the Widewells? Can you leave your family so abruptly with no misgivings?"

Emily began to draw the pins from her hair. "I'm afraid the Widewells are more devoted to money than me. Mother could never bestir herself out of Sheffield in all these years to meet her grandchildren. What does that say of her love? The loss is hers. My family has no imagination and no more courage than a pack of mice. But I am no rodent. I married into the famously brave Trumpet clan. Whatever happens, I am Major George Trumpet's widow and Elizabeth Trumpet's sister. We shall make a new start in a new world."

"Oh, Emily. I'm not so lifted with optimism."

"Then I'll say it. This is the best chance for you, too, dear."

Nana and Papi will be there...Roger's family. "Perhaps so."

"Noddy's the one who doesn't know what he's getting into." Emily twisted the released braids of her hair. "He thinks the Carolinas are just an afternoon's sail beyond the cliffs of Dover."

"I must set him straight."

"Don't try, Lizzie. His trust in you goes beyond geography. It would break his heart to learn we could get along without him. Now I must lie down. I just drank a cordial in hopes of sleeping for a few hours." The women rose, Emily taking Lizzie by the shoulders to pass on the powerful confidence she felt. "God will guide us safely to that ship. Believe."

Lizzie walked downstairs, her preparations for departure finished, but too alive with worries to be drowsy. The house in its midnight sleep was dreaming of her, sending up visions of the past. Her tall shadow went pacing through the dim rooms, recollecting, lingering over the scenery of her childhood, making her goodbyes.

In the grey salon, she pulled the bound folio of Hamlet from the books on their shelves. The flyleaf was of Florentine paper, swirled in purple and gold, with "William Trumpet" inked bold and unmistakable across the page. How often her father's hand had touched this. For a moment, his presence was almost real enough to see. *Oh Papa, my first love. I do not forget you.*

Inside the silver bowl that had once been her mother's pride, Lizzie had packed keepsakes to take to America: Aunt Peg's rosary, the miniatures of her parents on their wedding day. She decided to add the folio, too.

Emily had removed the violin and every souvenir from Georgie's little shrine to fold in her bundle of clothes for the voyage. Her brother's useful dagger, her talisman against evil, Lizzie laid out with her traveling clothes. On a ship, a knife was good to keep handy. She looked at the faded spot on the wall where her watercolor of Major Trumpet had hung.

"I'll support my girls in style. If you wish to be the busiest actress in England you can, and never be saddled with Faversham again!" They had drunk to home and beauty. Now her brother was sleeping in his Waterloo grave, and she could never step on an English stage.

Lizzie moved into the kitchen. Stoppered on the kitchen table waited the cordial bottle. Deliberately, she drank three little glassfuls.

"Put those weapons out of my sight. One day you're going to hurt someone, Lizzie." What a sibyl her mother had turned out to be, like a character in myth, weighed down with sadness in love and the sorrow she foresaw. *I'll never have a chance to put lilies on her grave*

again.

"I wish you had come with a kind word tonight, Mama, instead of a warning," Lizzie said aloud. It was an old conversation she had been having one-sidedly for years.

In both hands, she picked up Aunt Peg's salt pig that lived on the kitchen table giving savor all its life. *I would take you, dear old porky thing, but you're too heavy, you see. So instead I've packed Auntie's beads, though we know she had more salt than sanctity in her.* The little tin pig warmed in her hands.

"*And just down the road, too. As good a place as any to learn performin', if you want to. Be bold and willing. Not too willing, mind. Ye'll keep a smile on yer face and yer big yap shut.*"

"*And if I fail to be chosen, no one will ever know?*"

"*You'll be chosen, darlin', if you but try. Or shall I tell Noddy to make a dressmaker sign right now and spare you an encounter with those clowns and dancing dogs?*"

"*Did you see me, Auntie? After the Harlequinade, the clowns told Mr. Dibdin I should be dismissed! But he's keeping me! I'm still in the show!*"

I saw everything, dearie. Sure it was a wonderful debut.

The case clock struck twelve times as the cherished ghosts walked in Lizzie's heart.

Chapter Forty-Eight

July 24, 1821

*T*HE *MERRY Alice* was bound for Baltimore and southern ports of the American coast. Three days out of England, the "family of immigrants" was safe on the sea. Captain Elijah's cargo ship always packed in a few such passengers. The bark that showed all her forty years of hard weather sailed smoothly as seven bells rang out. A brilliant moon frosted the spread canvas sails with silver light.

Below, in an airless cabin berth six-feet long and wide as a coffin, Emily was fast asleep with Georgina squeezed against her. The girls in their top bunk slept fully clothed. In her lower accommodation, Lizzie preferred to rest unencumbered in her shift, under a rough blanket. She slumbered in profound unconsciousness, rocked by the rolling rise and fall of the ship's belly plowing the blue waters.

"Wake up. Wake up, Miss Lizzie, for the love o' God." A man's hand shook her bare shoulder. Slowly, she began to climb out of sleep's deep well.

"Did I miss my entrance? What's the scene?"

"It's Noddy, Miss Lizzie." The faithful face came into focus, its usual expression of dazed bewilderment mixed with panic. "You 'ave to 'elp me. I can't find Arfur anywheres." The boy had been assigned a berth with Noddy in the sailors' cabin, where he suffered miserably in the close quarters. During the second watch, Arthur had escaped. The moment Lizzie grasped that her nephew had disappeared, she rushed topside with Emily following in dismay and Georgina at her heels ready to cry.

"Have you seen a boy, a little boy running loose?" Emily begged the helmsman at the wheel.

"No, I ain't, 'ave I," he said, yawning.

The press of sail made it impossible for the women to get a clear view of the entire ship. Shadows and towers of billowing canvas looked black and white in the moon's glow. The deck was empty except for the sailor on watch, named Keith. He smoked his pipe, his mind taken up with celestial navigation. Franticly, the women ran past the ship's jollyboat, lashed to the deck under a tarpaulin. Beneath that heavy sheeting, a person coiled like a snake in repose, heard their frightened voices, and stirred.

"Look aft, Noddy. No, that way!" Lizzie went forward.

Quick to obey, Noddy raced astern, peering in corners and calling out, "Master Arfur!" He bolted up the aft ladder to the quarterdeck, lost balance, fell on his face, bounced up again and scrambled to the rail, all the while shouting, "Arfur! Arfur!"

Seaman Keith dropped his pipe and started for the muddled passenger dressed in his nightshirt, slip-sliding about on the highest deck, where he did not belong. "You there! Avast! You stupid bugger, get off!"

Noddy jerked round at the command and lost his balance completely.

Emily and Lizzie passed under the foremast. "There's my brother." Georgina pointed to the sky. Arthur was high, high up in the rigging, almost all the way up to the foretop gallant, clutching the ratlines, frozen motionless with fear.

"I'll fetch him." Lizzie dropped the wool blanket she had thrown over her shift and stepped up into the rigging. "Arthur, what a brave boy you are. It's your Auntie, darling," she sang up to the child, who looked back down, terrified.

"I can't get down, Auntie."

"Yes, you can, darling. Look up, it's very helpful." She started climbing into the shrouds. The boy was fifty feet above her.

"Oh, Arthur!"

"Steady, Emily, don't frighten him more. Arthur, your mother wants to know if you can see the man in the moon."

The creature that had stowed away for three days, surviving without food or drink, sustained in his reptilian mind by hope of vengeance, crawled out of the jollyboat to the shadowy deck.

"Man overboard!" Seaman Keith shouted on the empty quarter-deck.

Lizzie stopped her assent. *Noddy. It must be Noddy.* She heard a body hit the water. Keith had jumped in to save the man who was flailing a fathom below the surface.

"Emily, that could be Noddy. You and Georgina go see. The more eyes on the water the better. Arthur is fine. Go this instant!" Mother and daughter hurried aft.

The helmsman let go the wheel to stop *The Merry Alice's* forward motion. The sails flapped loudly as the ship turned into the wind. At that, Captain Elijah roared out of his cabin. Awakened crew and passengers were coming up from below, pushing to the rail. Someone threw a buoy into the sea. Two crewmen struggled to lower the jollyboat down the side. The ship was dead in the water. The crowd on deck peered into the rippling sea for the drowning man.

"Do you see the overboard?"

Lizzie climbed swiftly up the forward rigging with her arms and legs bare. "Auntie is coming to get you, darling," she said in a calming voice, finding her footing on the damp ropes. *Ten feet, twenty, thirty, past the foretop, forty.* "Almost there, sweeting." She was above the yardarm, balancing just inches from Arthur. "What a grand view. No wonder you went skylarking." *Right hand, left hand.* She reached up. "There! Auntie's here. Do you feel my hands on your ankles? I'll place your feet on the ropes, and we'll come down together. Steady now. Don't fear, darling, I've got you."

"No, Trumpet. I've got you."

Lizzie clutched tight to Arthur. *Jack's voice. But Jack is dead.* Her head turned slowly to look down. Emerging through the lubber's hole of the foretop was a man with a nightmare of a face, waving a pistol in his hand: Faversham.

By the stern lantern, Captain Elijah saw a flash of white in the phosphorescent ripples less than a hundred feet from the ship, a man's head breaking the water. "Dead astern!" the captain yelled and gestured to the men at the oars of the jollyboat. The passengers on deck were gabbling with excitement, straining against the rail.

"'Elp!" Noddy screamed with his best effort, kicking wildly, in terror. When Keith swam to his side, Noddy grabbed and flayed so furiously the sailor subdued him with a fist to the jaw. Then he lay in the seaman's arms like a platter of haddock, alive but more senseless than usual.

Jack aimed his pistol at Lizzie's heart.

"I'm going to send you to hell, Trumpet. That's where I've been."

"They said you were dead."

"Worse than dead. But you couldn't kill me. You're not strong enough." His half-blind eyes could see her easily, dark hair silhouetted against the white sail. The ship stood still. "Now in this last act...." He cocked the glistening pistol. "You pay for ruining my life."

"Aunt Lizzie?"

She had taken her right hand off Arthur's shoe to face the nemesis of her life. "No, Jack."

"What pleasure this gives me." His arm stiffened to fire.

"All passengers stand back!" shouted Captain Elijah. His crew strained to hoist aboard the jollyboat, which held Seaman Keith and what looked to be a corpse.

But Emily stayed at the rail, clutching Georgina. "We shall remain, sir. We are his family."

Keith was first out of the little craft. He had regained his wind while flushing some of the Atlantic out of the passenger.

"Drownded?" the helmsman quietly asked, surveying the limp fellow in the sodden nightshirt.

"Not altogether," Keith returned cheerfully. "Rather too lively for 'is own good. I persuaded 'im to take a bit o' rest."

Noddy opened his eyes to see Emily's relieved face. Captain Elijah ordered the helmsman to resume course.

⚓

One hand holding tightly to the shroud, the other pressed against her side, Lizzie knew a bullet fired at her could kill Arthur, too. Quick as thought, she pulled Georgie's dagger from the sheath strapped to her thigh and flipped it straight at Jack's face. The blade spun once and plunged point-first into Faversham's left eye, piercing the blue jelly to drill his brain. The life and hatred drained from his face as Jack died without a sound. Braced by the foretop, he remained standing, gun in hand, staring up at Lizzie. She screamed within, her fingers turning to stone on the ropes. *Sweet Christ, I've done him to death.*

With a great groan from the timbers and a crack of sound as the sails filled with wind, *The Merry Alice* came around. Flung by the lurch of the ship, Jack's body tumbled backwards. In horror, Lizzie watched the actor plunge outward and into the deep.

"Are you still there, Auntie?"

Lizzie had no wit to answer.

"Auntie, where are you?" Arthur cried, panicked.

"I'm here!" Gasping, she pulled her consciousness back from hell to the child. "I'm with you, darling." And so she was, hanging between heaven and the abyss below, where Jack was. Forever. "We can go down now."

"It hurts my neck to look up, Auntie."

"But, you must do it, Arthur." Painfully, she unlocked her grip on the rigging. "You are a brave boy. Your father is proud of you."

"Were you talking to him just now?"

She fought for calmness. "No, darling." They began climbing down and down.

"I thought I heard him, but I can't be sure."

"Don't think about that now, Arthur. Think about where you step." Slowly, steadily down.

"Are we almost there?"

"Almost, darling. I see your mother waiting for you. I see Noddy, too."

"I know what I heard, Auntie."

She stopped moving. "What, my darling?"

"You were talking to the man in the moon."

⤢

Noddy's brush with death raised his animal spirits to a giddy pitch. In the Passengers' Common Cabin, he repeated the story of his rescue—noisily and endlessly—to the curious people gathered at the long teak table where Emily and the children were taking breakfast. Little Arthur slowly stirred his bowl of food, paying no attention to the commotion around him.

"Eat your pease porridge, my darling," Emily urged. "Cook made it especially for us."

Spattering crumbs and munching audibly, Noddy turned to the quiet boy. "Last night is one the fam'ly will remember, eh? I was on me way to Davy Jones's Locker, right 'nough. 'Orrible dark and cold down there. I swallowed 'nough water to float the fleet, I did!" He laughed till he choked. "We was at sixes and sevens findin' you. But all's well now, Arfur." The happy man slurped at his mug of hot tea, sweetened with a splash of grog from Seaman Keith's private reserve. "I'm so sharp set, this ship's biscuit tastes like Christmas cake t'me."

Emily asked him to not talk with his mouth full, hoping to end his lively account before it upset the children. But it was not to be.

"Master Arfur, could you see me when I was the overboard?"

"No. I couldn't. Auntie told me not to look down, so I was watching the moon."

"You're in trouble now for being so wicked naughty." Georgina's big eyes sparkled with delight at her little brother's shame. "Noddy nearly drowned, and Auntie having to climb so high to catch you."

"That's quite enough, Georgina. Be grateful your brother met with no misadventure and Noddy survived." Emily cupped her son's soft pink chin in her hand. "But you must never, never try such a trick again." Striving to be stern, she added, "Do you hear me, Arthur?"

"Yes, Mother." Not to be outdone by Noddy's tale, the child raised his piping voice. "When we were hanging in the sails, Auntie talked to the man in the moon."

Georgina scoffed with an older sister's disdain. "Are you telling us Auntie has left her senses?"

The boy pondered and shrugged. "Don't think so. He answered her."

Emily pushed away her breakfast bowl with exasperation. "Arthur, we have had enough near catastrophe, without you making up a story about it. I cannot abide a story." She looked at her precious child, solemn as an owl. "I venture to say you saw no one. Tell the truth now, did you see the man in the moon?"

"No, Mother. I didn't see him."

"Well, there it is then. Not another word." Emily looked over the heads of her fellow passengers—belching, sneezing and scraping their bowls. Absently, she asked Georgina and the teapot on the table, "And where is your Aunt Lizzie keeping herself?" Neither ventured an answer.

Lizzie had found a place to be alone, perilously mounted on the bowsprit. The wind tore at her unbound hair and soaking wet chemise, but she felt none of it, her mind in the grip of a hundred emotions at once. Shock, sorrow, fear, and relief washed over like the sea spray. *I killed him. And no one is the wiser.* Jack's presence on the ship, their confrontation in the rigging, and his fateful dive into the ocean had been unobserved. She had returned Arthur to his mother with all her acting skills in play. *If the child didn't realize…if the crew and passengers were taken up with Noddy…no witnesses.* Jack was simply gone.

Memories, some ugly, some beautiful, would not set her free. *Did the Jack I loved ever exist? The man with the pistol was mad. He came for me like a rabid dog. A rabid dog must be put down. And yet? And yet? Forgive me, Lord.*

A seabird darted by.

If the sea had been less calm, the moon less bright, I could never have thrown the dagger so true. It was the blessing of God, or luck, or the intercession of angels that Georgie must have sent. Tears welled, and the tearing wind pushed them down her cheeks. She gazed at the foamy lace of blue water below her. *Goodbye, Jack. God rest your troubled soul.*

The ship plunged ahead on a sea grown choppy, as the sun climbed the brightening sky. *The Merry Alice* figurehead of a buxom dame, that so delighted the children, rode along impervious to the trials of the travelers she carried. The ocean kissed the ship's side with a soft hiss, as if to say, "Lizzzzieeee." She was sensitive of it and, mind adrift—listened.

"There, there," she heard the painted *Alice* whisper. "Let go of the night and feel the breaking day. There is a long journey yet ahead."

Gradually aware of the salt on her skin and the seabird crying as it dipped and glided by her side, Lizzie returned to herself. "Glory, what am I doing out here in the wet?" She inched backwards on the bowsprit, clambored onto the prow, and sprang down to the safety of the deck, shivering but calm. *I'm still standing and my family is safe.* Arms raised, she spun around to feel the sun on her body, the wind lofting her drying locks of hair.

A sailor, scraping the deck on hands and knees, looked up, and caught his breath. "Like the picture, damn my eyes. Winged Victory, to the life!"

Chapter Forty-Nine

*T*HE MERRY *Alice* touched land in Baltimore to off-load cargo of precious blue and white porcelain, fired by English hands, but made to look as Chinese as possible. In Norfolk, merchants collected the barrels of heavy silver, elaborate tea sets, candlesticks, punch bowls, and drinking cups they would sell to the prospering citizens. Bolts of calico-patterned cloth, manufactured in English towns from American cotton, returned home to North Carolina, at a good profit for all concerned, except perhaps the poor children who labored at the giant looms in Britain's industrial cities. The empty spaces in the vessel's hold refilled with fat bales of more cotton, exuding clouds of lint that made Emily sneeze. Tons of bright-leaf tobacco, cash crop of the new world, and dried to golden sweetness scented the ship with fragrance.

Slowly the weeks went by, sailing south down a coast of wild country. Circling flocks of birds rose up between the plantation landings and the old colonial towns of white-steepled brick churches. Sultry heat pressed down on strong black men, forever hauling other people's wealth on and off the trading ships. Passengers disembarked at each port, until only the man who nearly drowned and his family were left.

At long last, Captain Elijah roused Lizzie from her impatient pacing of the deck to point to a low green coast and say, "Charleston, ma'am."

⌒∂

In the waving shade of a spreading palmetto, a fine open carriage stood back from the quay. The black driver sat stiff with a sense of occasion, while his slender gentleman passenger, with a mourning band sewn to the sleeve of his linen coat, avidly watched The Merry Alice approach the pier. A tide of citizens, dock workers, stray cats, and barking dogs lined the bank to see the ship come in. With many a "handsomely now," Captain Elijah gave orders as the ship dropped anchor in her usual berth. Three sailors tied their barky up to the landing bollards, and the captain steadied the ship's gang-plank with his own hands.

The gentleman left his shade as a ragamuffin party appeared on deck, shook hands with Elijah, and moved to disembark. The little boy darted ahead like a ball. The ladies and an awkward fellow clutched the weathered rope handrails and a few bundles of belongings, till they set foot on dry land. The gentleman smiled to see the tall woman looking everywhere with an air of repressed anticipation, but the burning sun was in her eyes. He approached her, doffed his wide brimmed hat, and bowed before the family.

"Welcome to Charleston, dear friends. I give you joy of your arrival."

"Roger, it's you!" Lizzie's mouth opened with surprise and her arms reached out with affection. She hugged him with such happy glee that Southern passers-by remarked on the shocking display of feeling before supper. "Here to greet us, what a providence! But how did you know?"

"What ship to meet? Octavia wrote to us when you left London." He said nothing of the murky circumstances of their departure. What mattered was the sight of Lizzie, dashing, tanned, and thin in her faded spencer. He beamed at her. "The Merry Alice makes this run three times a year, but she's a slow sailer. We've been expecting to see

464

Trumpets on the horizon for weeks."

"What joy! Where are my grandparents?"

"Waiting for you at home. They rarely venture out now. Ah, Lizzie, I can scarcely believe this day." He smiled amiably at the rest of the party, eager to make them feel at home, and took Emily's sunburned hand to kiss. "Welcome, Emily dear, I trust the journey was not too exhausting?"

"Memorable, Roger, and my, how good to see you again. Georgina?" The proud mother poked her daughter clinging to her skirts. "Make your bob to Mr. Sloane." The pretty girl curtsied obediently. "Now you, Arthur." The boy made a leg and nearly toppled over.

"You must find your land legs again, Arthur. My son Billy is just your age."

"Yes, sir." He was having a hard time of it standing still.

"It is my hope the boys will be comrades," Roger said to Emily. "Just as his father and I were." She nodded and made a grab for the wiggling Arthur. Roger cocked his eyebrow with a charming smile. "Noddy, I hope you remember me?"

"Oh, yes, Mr. Sloane." He raised his hat. "Call me puddin', but I remember you, right 'nough."

Lizzie gently touched her hand to the black band on Roger's sleeve. "The Trumpets were destroyed to hear of Susannah's death."

"Thank you, Lizzie dear," he whispered. "I sorely miss her." He swallowed and beckoned to the black man who had quitted the carriage to collect the travelers' trunk. "And this is Silenus, the one man in all the world your grandparents could not manage without."

The handsome slave in his forties ceremoniously raised two parasols against the burning light and presented them to the ladies with a gracious smile. "Miz Emily. Miz 'Lizabet, you be needin' these."

"My dears, we must get you all out of the sun." Roger herded them across the cobblestones to the carriage, with Noddy dropping bundles as he waved farewell to Seaman Keith. Carefully, Roger loaded the party and their belongings into the carriage, and sprang up onto the driver's bench. "Home, Silenus."

᪻

Lizzie's heart thundered in her breast. *Twenty-four years since I've seen them.* She looked around as the horse pranced by pastel-colored houses ornamented with wrought iron fences and balustrades. There were more African faces in the streets than she had ever seen. Mosses hung from the trees in smoky wisps. Lush plantings she recognized from her grandmother's watercolors seemed to charge out of a damp earth. She nervously fingered her diamond earrings as the children chattered and pointed at an astonishingly pretty black girl gliding across Church Street, balancing a huge basket full of scarlet geraniums on her head. *I've done the very same.* Lizzie remembered carrying her dancing clothes through an Egyptian bazaar. In the flow of time, the desert days with Giovanni were fading fast away, like a tale she had read that happened to someone else. They clopped past a fine-porticoed church with a triple-storied steeple. *Was that Saint Michael's where Roger saw Susannah singing in the choir?* The carriage made a turn at the sign for King Street. Fine houses. Flowering wisteria vines. Sticky heat like honey oozed down her neck. Pulse racing, she released the buttons of her spencer. A white house, *the one from the painting*. The horse slowed. Stopped. Roger leapt down to open the carriage door, but Lizzie was already out, running through a gate to the people standing on the high porch beyond. Papi, her white-haired grandfather, hand in hand with the partner of his life, beautiful Nana.

"Lisa–cara," Papi called out in a tenor's voice, and she was up the steps, kissing those luminous faces, laughing, holding her precious people in her arms. In the afternoon's glow, they enfolded one another like the petals of a rose, radiant with the giving and returning of love.

᪻

All was serene by eight o'clock that evening. In the grasses of the Sloane garden, Billy allowed Arthur to play with his amazing pet tortoise. The red-headed Nancy Sloane overcame her shyness to climb onto Emily's lap. Georgina made friends with Claudia, the pampered cat, and Lizzie held her four-month-old namesake for a gratifying hour. Sopranino, the canary, threatened to sing all night with excitement, until Roger wound a muffling cover over the cage. Papi and Nana stole away to say their prayers with more than usual gratitude. When the travelers made for their beds in the Trombetta house, they discovered every chamber was blessed with tall windows, a pure luxury in the low-country heat. Noddy was to live over the carriage house and appreciated an absence of chickens in residence.

The evening breeze stirred through the piazza, the Charleston side porch designed for coolness. Lizzie walked out of the close sitting room with one candle in a hurricane chimney to rest in her grandmother's rocker a while. She heard Ceres upstairs, singing a lullaby to the children Emily was soothing into sleep. Papi and Nana—*close to being angels*—yet still clinging to the earth. *Such a welcome! Roger grown into his true maturity and so prodigiously kind.* The sky changed color, into something between blue and darkness. She stretched and breathed in a sweet flower fragrance wafting from the September night.

A bottle of port in one hand and two crystal glasses in the other, Roger walked up to the porch in his white linen shirtsleeves. "I'm returned from kissing Billy and Nancy goodnight. May I sit with you, Lizzie? Or are you too tired for talk?"

"No, it will gladden my heart." She waved for him to take the other rocker. "Who is minding little Elizabeth?"

"Sally-Ibo, the wet nurse I bought when Susannah departed this life." He sank into the matching rocker, put the glasses on a table, and poured out some ruby drops. "You'll meet her tomorrow, a formidable creature, uncommon tall and strong."

Roger passed her a glass, and raised his own. "To the end of your journey, Miss Trumpet."

Lizzie returned his openhearted gaze, seeing only goodness. "And I shall drink to family...mine...and yours." They sipped in silence, cautious of what to say or to feel, after so many years. "Does Ceres prepare such feasts every day? The she-crab soup was delicious, the whole dinner superb. Those benne biscuits!"

"Once, father tried to press the recipe upon you, but you refused."

"What an ignorant girl I was," she sighed. "I've grown up a bit since acting was my all-in-all."

Roger's brows knitted slightly. "I received a letter from father last week."

Oh, no! Has Sidrack unburdened himself to his son as he did to me? Surely not.

"May we discuss the future?" he asked.

Lizzie's stomach lurched. *I could not bear to hurt him, and I cannot throw myself into an alliance*—her hands clenched into fists.

"I have considered of it, and judge Emily's skills will make a fine addition to Adam & James of Charleston. It is unprecedented for a lady to choose such work, but I am ready to take her on, if she wishes employment."

The tailoring—Emily's future, not mine.

"Of course, she will not have to measure the male customers. The rakes of Charleston are even wilder in their habits than the dandies of London. It wouldn't do to expose her to—"

Lizzie laughed out loud with relief. "Wonderful! Perfect! Oh, Roger, that will set the seal on her happiness. I shall tell her tonight. Or would you prefer to?"

"It would please me greatly to tell her tomorrow at dinner. We'll dine at two, as is the Charleston custom. Hominy and shrimp, ham, fried chicken." Lizzie rolled her eyes at the menu. "And we must include a special guest, my business partner and brother-in-law, Owen Lewis."

"Redbeard the pirate! The wild Welshman! You have a pirate for a partner in a tailoring shop?"

He shook his head good-naturedly. "Owen was never a pirate. He still owns the ship called *Thrygg Goch*."

"The devil you say."

"It means 'Red Dragon' in Welsh. But mostly these days he reads law."

"The pirate has become a lawyer?"

"This is America, my dear. Together, we have made some success with ginning and milling."

Trying a wink she hoped looked canny, Lizzie guessed, "You own a tavern for pugilists?"

He barked out a laugh. "No, dear, we are in the cotton business. Your grandfather, like most Americans, saved to buy land and taught me the same. When war with England strangled the cotton trade, I built a textile mill. Over the years it's grown. These new inventions of Eli Whitney and others easily process raw cotton, making it a profitable crop. I invested in that machinery, so now the planters need me for more than waistcoats."

"You look very close to smug, Roger. I was wondering how all the prosperity I see could come from buttons and trousers."

"I have widened my horizons, as your Aunt Peg suggested." Proud satisfaction radiated from his face, plainly delighted at surprising her. "Tomorrow morning, I've ordered Silenus to tour your family all over Charleston in the carriage, so you may know your new home, and venture out on your own as you used to like. Noddy had best go, too, since he will probably escort you when you enter society and begin to 'make calls.'"

"You have high hopes of Noddy." *Roger is so different, poised— he carries himself with an air of assurance.* "Old friend, you've changed, as though you see further now than you did as a lad in London. Does time itself teach us how to live?"

Roger left his chair to stand at the porch railing, reflecting awhile before he answered. "My wife's love made all the difference. Susannah believed in me, and now I've come to believe in myself."

Lizzie moved to his shoulder, struck by his simple candor. She felt the pain of his loss almost like a presence between them. Here was a man who had received love, been changed by love, and appreciated its power. Roger had touched the happiness she had searched for in passion and performance all her life. The candle was nearly burned away.

Roger broke the silence. "The flowers have opened in the dark, do you notice?"

"Yes. A rare fragrance all around us. What is it?"

"Carolina jessamine. A vine that does well here. I planted it myself years ago in honor of your grandparents. It's a golden trumpet flower that only blooms in the evening of the day."

"Beautiful."

"Would you fancy a ride into the country one day? I'll take you out to our enterprise, the mill. My show. Not so wonderful as the Wells or Covent Garden, when you were onstage, but a show, nonetheless."

"Your 'show.'" Touched, she nodded. "Yes, Roger, I should like it, of all things."

Chapter Fifty

Late September 1821

*T*AP, *TAP tap* on the bed-chamber door. "Emily, are you asleep?" *Tap, tap.*

Emily raised her head from the rumpled pillow. "Not any more. Come in, Lizzie." She reached for her wrapper and slid off the bed, the luxurious afternoon nap regretfully concluded.

Her sister-in-law propelled into the room, as if she was still riding a horse. "You should have come with us. Oh, Emily, I am in a daze."

"Take a chair by the window and sit. You look quite blown with the experience, whatever it was."

"Roger showed me the mill, and the gin, the factory on the Cooper River, and...."

"Well, I wanted to place Georgina in school this morning, and it could not wait. So, you must tell me all you saw."

Lizzie fiddled with a palmetto leaf fan she found on the chair, but did not sit. "I saw the future, Emily, and it belongs to men like Roger Sloane. Not born to position or privilege, men different from dear Georgie, who gave his life to defend the old world. But new men, who are changing the way the world works."

"Is it possible?" Emily's blue eyes squinted at her agitated friend.

"This textile mill is a factory with more than a hundred workers.

Not like a shop where every man is known and rated, but where every man is a part of the great machines. Roger holds it all together in his mind and with his will. All the workers are slaves—men, women, and children. You would not believe the racket and chemical stench. I don't know what I imagined, but nothing so big. Ten times bigger than a ropewalk, Emily, and Roger created it."

"When Sidrack came to see you, did he mention Roger's business?"

"No, we spoke of other things." Lizzie stood in the window, fanning her face so quickly the loose hairs above her brow whipped back and forth, remembering the painful intimacy of that conversation. "I doubt even Sidrack realizes what an enterprise Roger is embarked upon."

"Explain yourself."

"Some planters bring their picked cotton to Roger's gin, the first machine he invested in. It cleans the cotton of trash—seeds, stems, what the pickers caught in their hands—then packs it into those terrible great bales we saw on The Merry Alice that made you sneeze. The planters pay for the ginning and send the raw cotton off to England. Well, Roger told me he was too small a fry to own a plantation, and from his tailoring he knew the value of cloth, so he decided to step into the middle and manufacture cotton cloth right here in America."

"Did he borrow...?"

Lizzie rolled on. "He and Owen invested every penny they had into the machines that turn cotton into cloth. He bought slaves to work the machines, taught them, and now they are skilled. They have dwellings there, and he pays each one a wage, a pittance, but he hopes to build in other towns with those same people. Such clattering and banging in the place, Emily, like a tunnel in hell."

"Hell, eh?"

"There's a machine to open the bales with monstrous great teeth." Lizzie demonstrated the actions she described, waving her arms in a dance of industry. "'Picking' and 'scutching' with rollers, 'carding' with 'slivers,' 'combing' into ropes they call 'drawing' and 'roving,' then spinning onto bobbins and 'plying' that into thread." She made a loom of air in the window. "The children are excellent at threading the bobbins and winding the 'pirns.' All to make the cloth for this." She grabbed the bedsheet and waved it like a flag.

"Stop, Lizzie!" Emily laughed and clapped. "That was a ballet."

Lizzie collected the fan again and used it briskly.

"So, dear, I take it you were amazed."

"Indeed. My amazement is in Roger, whose life I thought I knew. Such risk and responsibility he has taken up."

"Well, I've not seen the mechanical wonders you describe, or Roger's powers of organization. But this I have seen—he is thoughtful, attentive, and kind."

"Yes, Emily, he is that."

⌛

September sweltered into October. Discreetly, Emily had begun to tailor for Adam & James. The Lewis family had entertained them and introduced them to the congregation of Saint Michael's Church. Arthur and Georgina had begun school in an academy that reminded Lizzie powerfully of Madam Bonnet's. Noddy had not disturbed the smooth running of the Trombetta household noticeably. Charleston life was charming to Lizzie in many ways—the soft Southern voices, the drooping, sweet flowers of her grandparents' gentle existence. But her place in this new world was not yet clear, and she began to stir under her skin.

"Lord God, it's hot tonight." She dragged a wrinkled handkerchief around her wet neck. "Hotter than Egypt, and I ought to know!"

Emily poured another splash of punch from a tall pitcher into the guests' glasses. Roger, Owen Lewis and the elder Trombettas had spent the past hour at cards in the sitting room. "Have some more lemon juice with mint, it's truly refreshing."

"It's the rum that's refreshing you, Emily." Owen put down his cards to watch her take the Carolina parakeet from its woven sea-grass cage to her finger, pleased at her pleasure in his gift. "Give him a taste of that punch Silenus made, and he'll start talking straight away."

Lizzie sauntered restlessly by the card table to tease Owen. "Speaking in vile couplets from a sailor's vocabulary, I expect."

"Never in life," he protested. "I captured the fellow in the woods just for Emily. He's innocent as Adam before the fall."

"Such a little beauty you are." Emily stroked the bird's rose-colored head. "Look at these turquoise green wings, the soft yellow collar. He'll inspire you to paint again, Lizzie, even if he never talks."

The pigeon-sized bird parted his beak and shrieked, "Bugger all." Roger and Owen stifled their mirth with hisses and snorts.

"Eh? What did he say?" Grandpa Trombetta asked.

"*Buona notte*, I believe. Come to bed, *caro*, the hour grows late." Nana swayed to her feet, helping her frail husband to his. Lizzie took each by the arm and eased them to the staircase.

"I loved singing '*Scacciapensieri*' with you, Lisabetta," Papi wheezed. "What a song! We must have it every evening when we draw the cloth and pass the port. Your *bella voce* is a gift to these ears, *cara*."

"Thank you, Papi, I call that praise from Caesar." Lizzie's hand lovingly pressed the small straight back of her grandmother to support her up the steps. "Remember me in your prayers, Nana."

"We always do." The little lady paused her ascent to look in Lizzie's face a while. "When we meet your father again, and that will be soon, I know, I shall tell him about his girl who became a famous actress." Nana touched her cheek. "You've known a harder life than my William, more glory, more pain. You've been polished down to true beauty. My Lisabetta is like a diamond, unbreakable and shining." Nana kissed her granddaughter on the lips. "Sleep well, *cara*, and God bless you."

Lizzie watched them reach the landing and pass into their chamber. A longing for her father stirred and retreated in her breast. With a quiet sigh, she turned towards her guests and was startled to find Roger standing behind her, in the attitude of a mischievous boy.

"Run and fetch some old quilts, Lizzie. Quick as ever you can, and no noise." She looked in the sitting room. Emily and Owen had disappeared, and likewise the pitcher of punch. "Meet us in the carriage house?" he asked with an impish look.

Why not?

⌘

"What is he humming?" Emily raised her voice. "Silenus, what is that song?" The genteel blonde widow had turned rather tiddley with punch and riding backwards in the carriage. They were far out of town, rolling along near the Ashley River bank, disturbing a few herons night-fishing in the shallows.

"Dat's a jubilee song, Miz Emily. I don't s'pose you folks know 'bout dat one."

"Sing out, Silenus, please," Lizzie asked. "There's no one to hear but the birds and the fishes." She giggled, having also enjoyed a measure of rum and mint libation by this time.

Silenus threw back his head and sang in a rich, deep basso.

"Jubilee stand for freedom,
Jubilee mean forgiveness,
Jubilee is new beginning."

He kept the horse trotting on the dirt byway, almost in step with the song.

"Jubilee for you an' me,
You an' me, you an' me, you an' me."

His voice died in the hot night air.

"That's a freedom song, Silenus" Roger noted.

"It is, Mars' Roger, it is," Silenus whispered from the driver's bench.

"Stop the horse in those trees yonder, and wait for us, Silenus, if you please." Roger and Owen helped the ladies out of the parked carriage with their quilts and a picnic basket. They proceeded round a bend and through some trees, the females stumbling in the brush but intrepid. "We can just see by the moonlight, but are secluded enough not to be scandalized." A bull frog in the reeds agreed. "Who's for a swim in the river?" Roger was already unbuttoning his cuffs.

"No peeking, no poking?" Lizzie laughed, thrilled at the prospect and more than ready to make a run for the water's edge.

"On my honor," Roger vowed. "Owen's, too." He led the way,

spreading the quilts, undressing behind a bush, tip-toe quiet, then whooping like a lad when he and his piratical partner dived in. "Come in, Lizzie, the water is so cooooool."

Emily required a bit of coaxing, yet finally entered the wetness as naked as her sister-in-law had become. They splashed like children in the dark, Roger and Lizzie swimming while Emily sat in the stream, washed up to her chin and laughing at Owen making antic splashes and outlandish-sounding remarks in Welsh, many yards away.

In the moonlight, Lizzie could see Roger's athletic male body, and the sprouting tumescence that preceded it by several inches.

"Georgie would have loved this," he called out to her. "Remember when we swam in the New River in Islington?"

"Stuff, Roger. I swam. You fell in. Don't deny it."

He dived underwater, heading towards her with dangerous intent, but Lizzie made for the bank, laughing and pulling Emily out, too.

Dried and clothed again, they sat on the quilts to share wine from the basket Owen had contributed. As the moon set, he began to sing the freedom song and Lizzie joined in.

"Jubilee means forgiveness,
Jubilee stands for freedom,
Jubilee is new beginnings.
Jubilee for you and me,
You and me, you and me, you and me."

"Let us drink to new beginnings," Owen suggested. The swim had left drops on his red curls that sparkled in a halo around his happy face.

Emily lifted her glass. "First, to George Mario Trumpet."

Roger and Lizzie closed their eyes, both whispering, "God rest him."

"To forgiveness," Lizzie offered, explaining nothing and remembering a "wedding" in the moonlight.

"And to my sweet Susannah, may she never be forgotten," Roger said. They all drank deeply. The breeze moved high through the trees.

"I believe the heat has broken," Owen mused.

ᘒ

The return to Charleston was subdued. Owen said goodbye in the carriage house and bounded down King Street with a light step, still humming "Jubilee."

"Good night, pirate," Emily called into the night, before disappearing to hang up the damp quilts. Looking bedraggled, smelling of the river, Lizzie and Roger crept onto the piazza.

"Thank you for the delicious swim, Roger. Did you peek?"

"Not I."

"I did." They both laughed low. She brushed a lock of floppy hair from his eyes. "You've been my friend all my life, Roger. For a long time, that was a blessing I scarcely knew I had. But now I treasure it." *There, I said it out loud.* Roger looked into her face with unguarded hope. She inhaled the perfume of the night-blooming flowers—and his hair. She took a step closer. "Would it be a scandal if just this once you kissed me goodnight?"

His arms wound around her with a force that grew, as his lips touched cheek, brow, the closed lids of her eyes, and finally the warm, waiting mouth with a kiss that honored the woman she was. Lizzie relaxed against his body, pressing her heart into the unknown. Breathlessly, they drew apart, searching each other's faces for the affirmation of new passion. It was there, the spark, the giddy, soul-lifting closeness that needed no words. Just as Lizzie was ready to abandon all her years of self-control, he slipped out of her clutching arms to gaze into her eyes.

"Goodnight, my friend, my darling friend. Sleep well. Until tomorrow." And he stepped back to disappear through the trumpet vines.

"Tomorrow," Lizzie whispered to herself.

On bare feet, she went upstairs to her chamber, ready to throw herself on the four-poster bed. She shut the calico curtains against the approaching sunrise, pulled off her dress and shift. When she sat at the dressing table to brush her tangled hair, still tasting Roger's kiss on her lips, she noticed a packet of letters leaning against the mirror.

Ceres delivered the afternoon mail rather late. A thick missive from Octavia, what looked like invitations with Charleston addresses, and an envelope stamped with the visage of Benjamin Franklin, addressed in a slap dash hand. *Odd.* She opened that letter first.

> *Darling Girl,*
> *What matchless news. Octavia Onslow writes that you have set sail for America. We shall once again be on the same continent! My experience of this country has been on the whole positive. I do not speak of the roads or rustics, but the reception—the happy reception—my music has received. Philadelphia is not an outpost in a hollowing wilderness. Timothy and I have yet to be set upon by naked Indian braves, though that might be a thrilling encounter. I am a true impresario here, with a fledgling opera company. We are not bankrupt either. Quite the opposite. Timothy is becoming known as the star he was born to be. I am respected by the audiences of the Walnut Street Theatre as well, staging comedies and making my own mark with dramatic readings. This is happiness.*
> *The thing of it is, Lizzie, I dream of putting you on the stage again. Timothy needs a soprano voice equal to his gifts and the talent here is somewhat lacking. If you join us, there will be roles to sing and parts to play. Do not consider yourself retired, a player with no access to the apron. An artist such as you must never retire. Mrs. Siddons, who always played her cards so close to preserve a reputation, has made three more farewell appearances since the year '12. Obviously, she regretted departing the boards.*
> *Trumpet, you are yet in the high summer of life! Confess all. Do you not long for the camaraderie of the profession, the high spirits of* performers, *the inspiration fired by creative company?*
> *The remuneration is a reflection of the box office, and your share will be worthy. I swear it. The season begins in late November with* The Marriage of Figaro. *Our favorite. I*

trust you have kept "Dove Sono" in your trunk? You could return to your family's Italian name. The Americans expect all musicians to be Italian. Pure bosh, but you see where my thoughts fly. Da Ponte himself has turned up in Pennsylvania, selling groceries and dreaming of new libretti. What a pageant life is. Have I tempted you, darling girl?

When you have settled the family and given your grandparents all the kisses they can hold, consider what this could mean to you, and to me. Do the proper thing. Come be the prima donna *of the Tomassi Opera. I am with child to hear from you again.*

Your servant, and most loving,
Carlo

~ABOUT THE AUTHORS~

BILL HAYES has been a singer/actor his entire adult life, performing in all forms of entertainment—hundreds of recordings, topped by Best-Record-of-1955 'The Ballad of Davy Crockett;' over a hundred plays and musicals, including Broadway (*Me and Juliet, Brigadoon*), and a national tour (*ByeBye Birdie*); films (*Stop! You're Killing Me, The Cardinal*); literally thousands of hours of television (*Your Show of Shows, Days of our Lives*, and a surprising list of variety, dramatic, game, and talk shows); concerts and cafes (solo, also with Florence Henderson, Ann Blyth, Gogi Grant and wife Susan).

For four years, Hayes was spokesman for Oldsmobile. He has earned Bachelor of Arts, Master of Music, and Doctor of Education degrees, written songs, and—with Susan—published a successful memoir called *Like Sands Through the Hourglass*. His five children produced twelve grands and eighteen great-grands.

He still goes to tap-class.

SUSAN SEAFORTH HAYES began acting at age four with the New York Metropolitan Opera in *Madam Butterfly* and has been performing ever since. Born in California to an actress mother, she attended Los Angeles City College focusing on history. Cast as "Julie" in NBC's long running *Days of our Lives*, Susan received four Emmy nominations for best actress in daytime and married the man of her dreams, co-star Bill Hayes. Their romance produced the best-selling autobiography *Like Sands Through the Hourglass* and forty years of theatrical adventures together.

Hayes has addressed the House Judiciary Committee, served on the board of the Screen Actors Guild, been a docent of Western History, and traveled the globe as a cruise ship lecturer. She lives in Studio City, continues to play "Julie," attends the opera, and always keeps a good book handy.

Also Available from Decadent Publishing and Bono Books

The Wayward Child by Rita Lowther

The Wayward Child is the true story of an Australian family, set in the WWII years and beyond. You will instantly warm to Rita, the wayward child, and her older sibling Joan. These two children share the common bond of a pitiful existence, played out with a rough diamond father who clearly wanted sons instead of daughters. Their ladylike, demure mother was instrumental in the keeping of matrimonial harmony, with her sweet genteel nature, but lacked the fortitude to oppose any unfitting decisions that served to make their lives more difficult in times of tremendous hardship. With a strong-willed paternal Grandmother, whose love and loyalty to her only son knew no bounds, this story will keep the reader entranced from start to finish. The WWII era in Australia is a sadly neglected piece of history in the literary world.

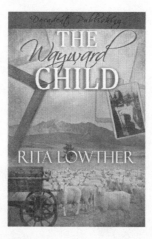

Pillars in Time

Determination is Cadence Hamilton's middle name. She sets her sights on a lofty goal in a man's profession: to be the most sought after architect on the West Coast. When she hears of the chance to draft the renovation of a 14th Century Scottish castle, she jumps at her dream job...never expecting to be whisked away to the century itself.

Nicholas Kincaid, sole heir to Dunmaben castle, is in a horrible predicament: marry or forfeit his lands. But the woman who visits his dreams keeps him from falling into wedded bliss. With the clock ticking, he follows duty to marry to avoid losing his beloved home and will do whatever it takes to ensure the security and safety for all, both in and outside of his walls. Except the woman, who beholds secrets he seeks, becomes his distraction....

Neither Nicholas nor Cadence anticipates the threats close to home, or the lives that will be lost in the process. As their relationship is tested and unknown enemies revealed, will their love conquer all? Even the boundary of time?

Diamond Heart

After catching her no good cheat'n rat bastard ex-fiancé in bed with her best friend, Rowan Belmont leaves the mills and factories of the Midwest to move nearer her sister in San Francisco. After being robbed in Kansas City, she loses the money to complete her journey and she tries to pawn her engagement ring, only to find out that it's fake. Alone, broke, and on the edge of giving up, Rowan hopes for a miracle.

Marcel Champlain can't get the beautiful woman he met at the Kansas City hotel out of his mind. When she turns up at his family's jewelry store he knows that God has brought them together. He makes Rowan a job offer: Go with him to Freewill, Wyoming to open a new jewelry store and pose as his wife.

With only three months to convince Rowan that she should become his wife in truth, Marcel intends to show Rowan that no other man on earth will ever love her as much as he does. Their time together may be cut short by when it seems like fate will take Marcel from Rowan all too soon and leave her once again alone in the world.

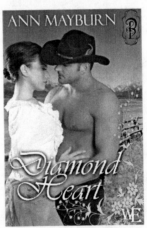

www.decadentpublishing.com
www.bonobookstore.com

CPSIA information can be obtained at www.ICGtesting.com
Printed in the USA
LVOW092155260612

287820LV00001B/40/P